THE REBOOT

CLODAGH MURPHY

Balally Books

THE REBOOT
CLODAGH MURPHY

ISBN: 9781916265684

Published by Balally Books

Cover design by Books Covered

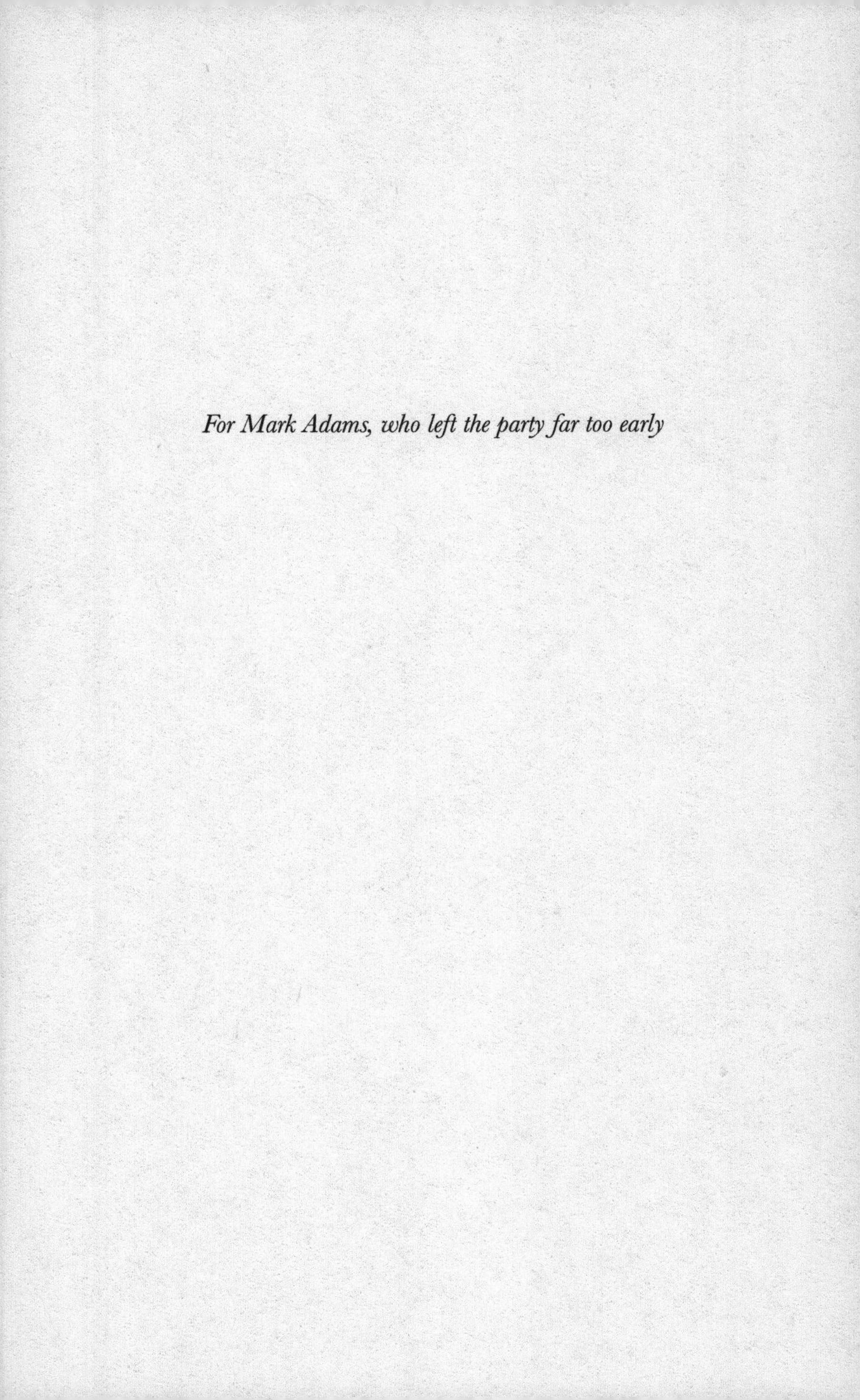

For Mark Adams, who left the party far too early

1

Perched on the edge of a squashy yellow sofa in the reception area of Citizens of the Wild, Ella tried to relax and look like she could belong here. But she'd felt dowdy, out of place and behind the times the moment she'd walked through the glass doors of the warehouse-like Temple Bar building. She'd been greeted by a pretty young black girl who'd introduced herself as Kerry and waved Ella to a seat, before disappearing up a spiral staircase at one side of the room.

Left alone in the vast empty space, Ella took in her surroundings as she tried to steady her nerves. Exposed pipework painted in primary colours stood out against bare brick walls, and oversized bean bags dotted around among neon-bright soft furnishings made it feel more like a soft play centre than the offices of a start-up techwear company. The walls were adorned with framed photographs of good-looking people snowboarding down mountains and hanging onto sheer cliff-faces by their fingernails, which did nothing to put her at ease. On the coffee table in front of her there was a pile of magazines dedicated to various dangerous-looking outdoor activities.

'Ella?'

She looked up at Kerry, crossing the floor towards her with a friendly smile. 'They're ready to see you now. Follow me.'

Too late to run now, she thought, as she followed Kerry towards the staircase. Kerry was wearing a wide-legged scarlet jumpsuit that set off her glowing dark skin, a pair of chunky trainers, and lots of statement jewellery that clinked and jangled as she walked. Ella immediately regretted the Marks & Spencer suit she'd bought at the local charity shop, which had seemed like such a brilliant find at the time.

At the top of the stairs, Kerry led her through a bright-red door across the landing, and Ella had the fleeting thought that she might need to invest in sunglasses if she got the job here. They walked into a small lounge area with a pair of sofas facing each other across a low coffee table. Two young guys stood as they entered, one tall, angular and greyhound-lean with sharp, pointed features and wire-rimmed glasses, the other broad and stocky with a shock of white-blonde hair and an open, friendly face.

Ella made a conscious effort to smile and maintain eye contact as Kerry introduced them, keeping her handshake firm. Jake was cool, arty and beautiful – pale-skinned and dark-haired, with soulful brown eyes, hollow cheeks and a full, pouty mouth. Dylan was a boyishly handsome boy next door, exuding an air of energy and outdoorsy good health that she supposed spoke to their brand.

They were both dressed casually, but with obvious intent – the kind of look that Ella admired, but could never pull off. Her casual look had a 'whatever was on top of the linen basket' vibe, whereas they looked ready for a trendy menswear photoshoot in skinny chinos and sharp jackets, topped off with thoughtful accessories. She suspected the devil was in the detail, and she tended to forget little touches like the tiny gold cross dangling from one of Jake's ears or the silver and black leather bracelets wrapped around Dylan's wrist.

It's your first interview, she told herself as Kerry left the room and she took a seat on the couch opposite Jake and Dylan. *You don't have to get the job. Just look on it as practice.*

'Would you like a coffee? Or tea?' Dylan waved to a drinks station in the corner.

'No, thanks.' She was gasping for a coffee, but she was twitchy enough already. She'd barely slept last night.

It started off okay. Jake and Dylan were ostentatiously relaxed and friendly, clearly intent on keeping it casual and putting her at ease.

'So, Ella,' Jake said, after some preliminary chat about the weather. 'Do you know anything about what we do here?'

'Yes!' She pounced on the question eagerly, glad that she'd done her homework, and all the time she'd spent researching the company online hadn't been in vain. 'I know you started up just over a year ago with a crowdfunder for the Heatsmart jacket, and you exceeded your initial campaign target by over two hundred per cent. You achieved profitability in your first year and have increased revenue in the first quarter of this year by almost fifty per cent.'

'Wow! Impressive!' Dylan grinned.

'It really is. Most companies don't make a profit at all in their first year, so—'

'I meant your knowledge of the company. But we do sound the shizz when you put it like that.'

'She knows more about our financials than you do,' Jake said to Dylan. 'You're fired, mate.'

'If we can afford to lose anyone around here, it's you.' Dylan turned to Ella. 'He's all style and no substance.'

'Seriously, bro, get your coat.' Jake clapped Dylan on the shoulder. 'It's been great working with you, but we always knew this day would come.'

Ella smiled politely, hoping this exchange would end soon and they'd get on with the interview. She appreciated they were trying to make her comfortable, including her in their little private jokes and banter. But somehow their chumminess just had the opposite effect, knocking her off balance and only adding to her tension. She'd prepared for a formal grilling about her skills and experience, not a cosy chat with a couple of guys who seemed more interested in charming her than finding out anything about her qualifications or employment history.

'Save yourself!' Dylan stage-whispered to Ella, shielding his mouth with his hand. 'There's no loyalty in this company.'

'You said it yourself,' Jake said to Dylan. 'I'm the whole reason our stuff looks so good. Sure, our jackets are technically superior to everything else out there—'

Ella nodded, grateful once again for her research. 'Lightest, most advanced heat-sensitive technology, longest battery life…'

'And made from mostly recycled materials, don't forget,' Dylan added.

'The Heatsmart is state of the art,' Jake said. 'But it's not just about functionality. Our jackets have become desirable fashion items in their own right.'

Ella wondered did people really care what they looked like when they were abseiling down a cliff face or spelunking around a dark cave. She wasn't likely to ever find out. 'And you're branching out now into urban tech-wear,' she said to show she knew her stuff.

Jake nodded. 'It's a big emerging market, and we're perfectly placed to be at the forefront of that. We're developing our range at the moment, and we're putting as much focus on design as functionality. There'll be no compromise on either, no sacrificing comfort for style, or vice versa.'

'We'll have our first collection ready to show at London Fashion Week next year,' Dylan told her.

'That's very exciting!'

'So, Ella. Enough about us.' Jake picked up her CV from the coffee table and Ella felt herself tense as his eyes skimmed over it. It was thin – skimpy even. But that was okay, wasn't it? All the advice she'd read said to keep it short and snappy. Nobody cared about your school grades or part-time college jobs by the time you were thirty. These days it was all about your gig economy experience – the zero-hour contracts and innovative side-hustles you'd cobbled together – and she'd had plenty of those over the last few years, albeit sporadically. She'd resisted the urge to pad her CV out with irrelevant skills and achievements that would only draw attention to her lack of solid hands-on work experience.

A slight frown of concentration drew Jake's perfectly sculpted eyebrows together as he scanned over the CV. He turned the page over quickly, checking there was nothing on the other side. But no. That was it.

'You graduated with a first from Trinity. Impressive.' He leaned back against the sofa and gave her a relaxed smile.

'You're certainly the most qualified candidate we've seen,' Dylan said.

She knew the reality, though. She may have the

highest academic qualifications, but she couldn't imagine they'd had any applicant with a sketchier employment history.

'You took a couple of years out after college.' Jake's eyes flicked over the page again. 'And you've done a lot of freelance gigs. You've always worked remotely?'

She nodded. 'Yes.'

'Were you travelling?' Dylan asked. 'Doing the whole digital nomad thing?'

Oh, the irony! She'd been whatever the opposite of a digital nomad was – a digital stick-in-the-mud? But he was offering her an out, and for a moment she was tempted to accept it. She could just say yes. They didn't need to know all the gory details, did they? But she didn't want to start off on the back foot if she did somehow end up working here. Besides, she had nothing to be ashamed of. Why should she hide it?

'No.' She cleared her throat and smoothed her unwrinkled skirt. 'I was meant to be starting a PhD, but I got sick and had to drop out of college.'

Jake raised his eyebrows, waiting for more.

Remember what Mum said – picture him in his pants. Unfortunately, that didn't make him any less intimidating, because when she pictured Jake in his pants, he looked like an underwear model, all washboard abs and ripped muscles. She could see him posing in designer boxers on one of those arty black and white posters, cuddling a baby to his perfectly sculpted pecs. Yeah, that wasn't helpful at all.

'I had M.E.,' she said.

Dylan's eyebrows shot up, and then he frowned. He was trying to figure out which one that was, she could tell, his eyes wary as they flicked to her. Then he half-turned to Jake. 'M.E.? Is that…?'

'Chronic Fatigue Syndrome,' she said, putting him out of his misery.

'Ah, right,' Dylan said, relief softening his features. 'Didn't your aunt have that?' he murmured to Jake.

Jake grinned. 'Nah, my aunt was just a slacker.'

Ella clenched her fists, trying to remain calm.

'Terrible pothead,' Jake said to her as if by way of apology.

'But you're okay now?' Dylan asked.

Jake was fidgeting with her CV, his leg jiggling rapidly under the table. She hoped for his sake he wasn't a poker player.

She nodded. 'It's taken a long time, but I've made a full recovery.' She wrapped an arm around the back of her chair and surreptitiously knocked on the wood. She always felt she was tempting fate saying that. 'I've been very lucky.'

'Because this is a full-time position,' Jake said. 'It's a pretty dynamic environment and the hours can be long at times. It's a small team, and we need everyone to pull their weight and give it a hundred and ten per cent.'

A hundred and ten per cent – had he actually said that? 'Well, I'm sure you know that's mathematically impossible, but I understand the commitment.' Gah! Cut the snark, Ella – that's not the way to endear yourself to people.

'Are you sure you can cope with the crazy?' Dylan asked with a grin.

God, could she? She didn't mind hard work, and she was looking forward to having a focus and some routine to her life – not to mention earning proper money. But could she handle this pair's double act day in, day out? She'd only been in their company for five minutes and she was already exhausted.

'Well, no one could accuse *you* of being a slacker,' Jake

said. 'You've certainly kept yourself busy. All these online courses … is there anything you can't do?'

'I tried to upskill as much as I could whenever I was able.' She'd done every online course she could get her hands on that would allow her to make some money working from home.

'You certainly have a lot of useful experience,' he said, his eyes once more trained on her CV. 'Book-keeping, SEO, digital marketing, data entry, virtual assistant … you sound like you'd be a useful person to have around.'

Ella was grateful that Jake saw her rag-bag of freelance jobs in a positive light.

'We're pretty sorted on the tech and production side, but admin and marketing … not so much.'

'We're definitely floundering in the book-keeping department,' Dylan said with a rueful smile. 'It'd be great if you could help us out with that. Our accountant hates us.'

'We could really use someone like you who could muck in and do a bit of everything.'

'But we won't ask you to take our shirts to the cleaners,' Dylan said with a grin.

'No, that's his job.' Jake jerked his head towards his partner, who laughed.

'So you've always worked from home?' Dylan asked. 'On your own?'

'Yes, but I'm excited about being part of a team.' Holy shit! Where had that come from? Was their chirpy gung-ho vibe rubbing off on her already?

'Great!' Dylan rubbed his hands. Mercifully, he didn't seem to think she'd made herself sound like a complete dick. 'Well…' He turned to Jake. 'Let's do the interview questions.'

Ella tried to hide her surprise that the interview apparently hadn't already been going on for some time. Everything up to now must have been some sort of preliminary round, and she was tempted to say how psyched she was that she'd made it through to the interview proper, but she bit her tongue.

'Okay, you're miniaturised and put in a blender,' Jake said. 'What do you do?'

'Um … sorry?' She frowned, confused. 'I'm … here for the admin position?'

Dylan grinned. 'Yeah, we ask all job applicants these questions. We like everyone who works here to be able to think outside the box. It's an innovative business, you know?'

'We try to promote a culture of creativity and resourcefulness throughout the company,' Jake said. 'From the bottom to the top; top to bottom.' He sketched the structure in the air with his hands.

'Right.' She wondered would they ask the tea lady these questions. But then they wouldn't have a tea lady, would they? They'd probably have a barista inventing his own blends to the accompaniment of smooth jazz.

'So … stuck in a blender?' Jake prompted, raising his eyebrows.

Oh god. 'Okay.' She smiled, trying to look like she thought this was fun. She wanted to come across as a good sport and a team player, bouncing off their energy and giving back as good as she got. It so wasn't her. 'I'd … call Amnesty International.' That was good, right? Thinking on her feet, kind of funny, socially aware …

Jake and Dylan turned to each other and had a silent consultation via the medium of raised eyebrows.

'You don't have a phone,' Jake rapped back.

'Then … I guess I'd die in the belly of some sports nut as part of his superfood smoothie. I'd be the first martyr of clean eating and the patron saint of Wellness.' She was quite impressed with herself for coming up with something remotely witty but they looked disappointed.

'Okay, favourite sandwich,' Dylan said, pointing a finger at her like he was aiming a gun.

'Egg mayonnaise.' Shit! Why had she said that? The most boring, least edgy sandwich on the planet. She hadn't even thought to inject it with a hint of irony. Jake looked frankly shocked, while Dylan smiled at her pityingly and said 'Hey, you can't argue with the classics.'

'Totally,' Jake said, rallying. 'Egg mayo's got a bad rep thanks to stinky school lunches and kids' parties, but it's stood the test of time. It just needs a rebrand.'

'If you were a dog, what breed would you be?' Dylan asked.

'Corgi!' It was the first one that came into her head.

'Because?'

'Um … at least I'd have a shot at living in Buckingham Palace.'

Dylan giggled gratifyingly.

'You have to sing with one of us at karaoke. What duet would you pick?'

'"Don't Go Breaking My Heart".'

'Yes!' Dylan punched the air. 'You're with me.'

'That's his song,' Jake said. 'If you'd said "I Got You Babe", you'd be with me.'

'What if I'd said neither?'

'Then it could go either way.'

'Wait,' Dylan said, 'are you Elton or Kiki?'

'Kiki.' Theoretically. She'd never done karaoke in her life, and didn't intend for that to change.

'Excellent. If you'd said Elton, I'd have to fight you for it.'

'He does a mean Elton, in fairness. Uncanny, really.'

'Are you Sonny or Cher?' Ella asked Jake.

'Cher. Always Cher.'

There followed a rapid-fire round of increasingly daft questions – favourite colour Smarties, five celebrities you'd invite to a dinner party (dead or alive), what emoji do you use most often (Ella said eye-roll, which was true, but immediately regretted choosing something so negative), favourite pizza toppings, muffin flavour, cocktail, coffee order, last thing she watched on TV (the actual last thing was a documentary on dogging, so Ella swapped in the second-last thing, a rewatch of the 'Open Mic' episode of *Schitt's Creek*), who would you root for in a fight between Spiderman and Batman…

'Wouldn't they be on the same side?'

'Good point,' Jake said, nodding thoughtfully. 'Let's scrub that one,' he said to Dylan.

'Okay, final question,' Dylan said, and Ella sagged with relief that this ridiculous ordeal was almost over. Her energy levels were actually pretty good at the moment, but this interview was wearing her out. She needed a lie down. 'A penguin walks in here wearing a sombrero.' He nodded to the door. 'Why is he here and what does he say?'

'Um … I guess…' Oh, who was she kidding? She should save her energy and go home. There was only one question these two wanted the answer to: are you cool enough to work here? And the answer was… 'No.'

Dylan frowned and looked to Jake.

Jake shrugged. 'I don't get it.'

'That's not the penguin saying no, that's me saying no. Sorry, but this isn't going to work.' She waved a hand between them. 'I'm obviously not what you're looking for.' She smiled to show there were no hard feelings as she lifted her bag onto her shoulder. 'We might as well call it a day and not waste any more of each other's time.'

They both stared at her dumbfounded as she stood and held out her hand, and Ella felt a little gleam of triumph that she'd silenced them at last. 'It was lovely meeting you,' she said graciously.

They both shook hands with her, looking bemused.

'It's been fun,' Dylan said. 'Great to meet you.'

'Thanks for coming in. We'll be in touch by the end of the week,' Jake was saying as she turned to go.

'Really there's no need,' she called over her shoulder. 'But thank you for your time.'

'Ella!' They both called after her as she made her way to the door, her heart pounding in her ears. 'Wait!'

She didn't turn around, ignoring their shouts as she reached for the door handle, determined to make a dignified exit. She was proud of herself for taking control of the situation and ending the interview on her own terms.

'Hang on, that's not—'

She pulled the door closed behind her – and found herself plunged into total darkness. Oh no! As her eyes adjusted to the gloom, she realised she had walked into a store cupboard.

2

'How did it go, honey?' her mother called as Ella closed the front door behind her.

She fought against the irritation that bubbled up inside her. But jeez, couldn't she at least have a minute to take her coat off first?

'Really badly,' she replied, unwinding her scarf as she walked down the hall.

'Oh no.' Her mother and her Aunt Nora turned to her as she stood in the doorway to the kitchen. All her annoyance melted away, and she couldn't help smiling. They were sitting at the table, a bottle of red wine open between them. They were keeping vigil, she realised with a pang of tenderness. She felt bad now that she'd delayed coming home straight after the interview. But she'd felt in need of some time alone to decompress, so she'd walked through town and had a look around the shops, then treated herself to an early evening movie at the cinema. She'd always enjoyed going to the movies on her own, and loved being able to indulge in such simple pleasures once again.

'Have a glass and tell us all about it,' Nora said, lifting the bottle.

Ella nodded and took a glass from the cupboard. She shrugged out of her coat and sat down between them.

'Have you eaten?' her mother asked. 'There's some lasagne in the fridge, if you want it.'

'Thanks, but I had a hot dog at the cinema. I'm not hungry.'

'So, tell us about the interview.' Nora poured a glass of red and slid it across the table to her.

Ella did what she always did when sharing something painful or humiliating. She turned it into a joke. She was fully aware that she used humour as a defence mechanism, to deflect mockery and hide her hurt. Did that self-awareness make it okay that she was turning her life into a comedy routine? It was probably only a matter of time before she started doing bits about her period.

But true to form, she was funny and self-deprecating as she recreated her dismal attempts to field Jake and Dylan's bizarre questions, and her mother and Nora were an appreciative audience, laughing in all the right places.

'We never got asked things like that in our day, did we, Ruth?' Nora said, turning to her sister.

'No, we just got asked if we were planning to have children.'

'That's illegal!' Ella said.

'Oh, I've had worse.' Nora topped up her glass. 'I was once asked if I'd be willing to dress sexy and flirt with customers to get them to spend more. It was for a job in a car showroom.'

'That's outrageous!' Ella shrieked. 'I hope you told them to shove it.'

'Of course I did.'

'You worked in a car showroom.' Ruth narrowed her eyes at her sister.

'Well … I said they could shove it unless they upped my commission.'

Ella tried to look disapproving, but couldn't help smiling.

'I made a fortune at that place. The blokes I worked with were furious! They were on fifteen per cent, and I was on twenty-five. Ritzy place it was too – Mercedes and BMWs and that, so there was good money to be made.'

'Well, it *is* a bit unfair, I suppose,' Ruth said.

Nora shrugged. 'They could have worn low-cut tops and short skirts if they'd wanted to. Though much good it would have done them. None of them had my assets.'

'So when will you hear about the job?' Ella's mother asked her.

'Oh, I don't need to wait to hear. I know I didn't get it.'

'Come on now,' Nora said. 'You never know. Think positive.'

Ella shook her head. 'No, I definitely didn't get it. I walked out.'

She watched their faces carefully, and there was just a second where she caught a flicker of disappointment, worry and confusion. It was gone in an instant, but she still felt she had to explain herself, to make them see that she hadn't recklessly thrown away an opportunity to earn some decent money and get back on her feet. 'I knew it wasn't going to work out. They wouldn't have hired me anyway, so I called an end to it before they did.'

'Good for you!' Nora said staunchly.

'Absolutely!' Ruth agreed. 'You don't need those silly boys with their idiotic questions.'

'So you just walked out?' Nora was looking at her

admiringly, which made Ella feel very proud of herself, because her aunt was pretty sassy.

'Yep. I thanked them for their time, said it wasn't going to work, and walked out … straight into the stationery cupboard.'

There I go again, Ella thought, as they collapsed in laughter. But she could hardly complain about being the butt of the joke when she was the one telling it.

'Yeah, it did kind of take the shine off my grand exit.' Jake and Dylan (or Tweedledum and Tweedledee as she'd started to think of them) had been very nice about it, playing down their amusement as they rescued her from the cupboard and ushered her out. Dylan had even walked her through Reception to the main door. But she had no doubt they'd collapsed in giggles as soon as she was gone. They'd probably spent the rest of the day laughing about it – probably regaling the rest of the staff with it too. Oh well, at least she'd never see either of them again.

'Speaking of inappropriate questions,' Nora said, 'the other day I got asked if I like it up the bum.'

'*What*! Now, that is definitely illegal.'

'Not on dating apps it's not. Anything goes there. Still, I must admit I was a bit shocked. I mean, a complete stranger just coming straight out with it like that – as if he was asking me if I like Thai food or something!' She sighed. 'Times have changed. There were no bums when we were young, were there?' She appealed to Ruth.

'I'm pretty sure there were always bums.'

'Yes, but they weren't … out there. At least, I certainly never came across them. They're a whole thing now. Bums! I'm telling you, it's a different world.'

Ella spluttered a laugh and almost choked on a mouthful of wine.

'I mean, it used to be you'd warm up to stuff like that,

get to know each other first. Now people just put it out there on their dating profile – I enjoy long walks on the beach, Coldplay and giving anal.'

'Well … two out of three's not bad?' Ruth said.

'Yeah, but Coldplay is a deal-breaker.'

Ella laughed. Maybe she wasn't the only one who tried to make light of her disappointment by laughing it off. Poor Nora. 'Men!' She rolled her eyes and topped up their glasses, draining the bottle.

'You'll have to deal with it when you start dating again,' Nora said to her. 'Best to be prepared.'

'Well, I'm glad I cashed in my chips before bums became a thing. Will I open another?' Ruth asked, already standing.

'Yeah, it's definitely a two-bottle night,' Nora said.

'I'm not in any hurry to start dating,' Ella said. 'I'm just concentrating on finding a job for now. One thing at a time.'

'Very wise.' Her mother placed another bottle on the table.

'It's lovely to see you getting back on your feet.' Her aunt put a hand over Ella's and gave it a squeeze. 'And don't worry, I'm sure something else will turn up soon.'

'Yeah. For you too,' Ella said and they smiled at each other sympathetically. 'Oh, I got something for you!' She leaned down to root in the satchel at her feet and produced a thick travel brochure, placing it on the table between her mother and aunt.

'Ooh, lovely!' Nora smiled, pulling it towards her. 'A nice bit of armchair travelling.'

'Where will we go next?' Ruth moved her chair closer to Nora's, looking over her shoulder as she flicked through the pages.

'It's about time you did some travelling for real,' Ella said. You know, where you go to an actual airport—'

'With actual luggage that almost gives you a hernia getting it off the carousel,' Ruth joined in dreamily. 'Surly security staff patting you down and making you take your shoes off.'

'Eating terrible airplane food,' Nora said wistfully.

'Getting bitten by mosquitoes and ripped off by dodgy taxi drivers.' Ruth sighed.

'Delhi belly and sunburn, and drunken trysts with awful foreign pick-up artists.'

'The scary toilets!'

'The enormous creepy-crawlies!'

'You make it sound so appealing.' Ella laughed

'Oh, but then there's setting off at dawn along dusty roads with that special early-morning smell in the air.'

'The sunsets!'

'The sunrises!'

'Warm seas. Empty deserts. Chaotic markets.'

'The smells, the sounds … the food!

'Oh god, the food,' Ruth sighed.

'So do it!' Ella said. 'Now that I'm back on my feet, there's no need for you to be stuck here any longer. You can finally go on that big trip you've always talked about.'

Her mother looked at her doubtfully. 'I don't know. It's a bit soon, isn't it? I know you're getting better, but I wouldn't like to leave you on your own just yet.'

'Maybe next year,' Nora chimed in.

Ella's heart sank. They'd already put it off for years, thanks to her, and she hated it. She didn't know how to say it, but they weren't getting any younger, and she knew all too well that you couldn't count on the future. Things changed, plans fell apart. There was no knowing where they'd all be next year, what would be possible for them.

'I'd be fine here on my own,' she protested, but she knew it was futile. There'd be no persuading them.

'What if you have a flare-up?' her mother said.

'I could manage. Anyway, you'd only be gone for a few months. I haven't had a relapse in ages. What are the chances I'd have one just when you happened to be away?'

'I know you can cope, but it's not just that. I don't like to think of you rattling around here on your own when you're just finding your feet.'

'I'd be fine, Mum. You have to cut the cord sometime. I'm ready.'

'Well, *you* may be, but I don't think Nora and I are just yet.'

'No,' Nora agreed. 'We wouldn't enjoy ourselves anyway if we were worrying about how you were getting on all the time.'

'We'll do it next year, when you're more settled.'

'And in the meantime, we'll have loads of time to organise it all – sure, planning a trip is half the fun!' Nora said cheerfully.

'Exactly. And besides, I need all the time I can get to work on my squatting game.'

'Good point!' Nora said. 'We're very out of practice, and squat toilets are challenging at our age. We'll start doing the Shred again tomorrow.'

Ella knew there was no point in arguing. She'd try again in a couple of months. Maybe once she'd got a job, it'd be easier to convince them she could manage on her own. Damn, she shouldn't have been so quick to walk out on Tweedledum and Tweedledee.

She was a little tipsy by the time she went to bed, leaving her mother and Nora still at the kitchen table, poring over the travel brochure, and reminiscing about previous adventures. Even though her energy levels had improved greatly, she still didn't have their stamina.

Tucked up in bed with her iPad, she logged onto Facebook and wrote a quick update about her disastrous job interview. She was touched by the sympathetic comments and emojis that flooded in, many of her online friends saying they'd been thinking of her and waiting to hear how it had gone. It cheered her up that she had so many lovely friends in cyberspace, even as she longed for a closer kind of connection.

She chatted with a couple of her groups on WhatsApp, while simultaneously scrolling through Facebook, Twitter and Instagram, catching up with her extended tribe. She was grateful to live in a time when so many people shared their lives online. She didn't know how she'd have coped in the last ten years without the internet friends who'd let her into their lives, allowing her to be part of a world beyond the confines of her room.

But grateful as she was for the community at her fingertips, sometimes it didn't seem enough to tether her to the world, and she felt cut adrift, overwhelmed by her isolation and loneliness, and submerged in its depths where no one else could see her. She knew how lucky she was to have her mother and Nora, and she would be eternally thankful for all the comfort and company they'd rallied round to provide when she'd become ill. She'd have been lost without them. But there was another, deeper layer of loneliness that was always there, and she longed for a different kind of closeness – not just a romantic relationship, but friends her own age, people on the same path as her who she could share the journey with.

The trouble was, for the last ten years she hadn't been on any path. She'd been going nowhere, while her contemporaries had gone ahead without her until eventually they'd disappeared out of sight. Sometimes she felt like she was so far behind now, she'd never catch up – as if she was lost in a forest so deep that no one would ever find her and she'd be alone for ever, always just making the best of things and trying to jolly herself along and convince herself she was happy.

It wasn't just her life that had been curtailed by her illness – it was her mother's and Nora's too. Nora had always been a big part of the family, her mother's best friend as well as her sister, and a second mother to Ella. She'd lived in New York for a while, and Malta, and as a child Ella had always looked forward to her visits when she'd sweep into their lives briefly, bringing with her an air of glamour and romance. She'd never married, but had had lots of boyfriends and several proposals. Her longest relationship had been with a professional gambler, who Ella remembered vaguely as a tall, sleek man with a deep mahogany tan, who seemed more like a character from a James Bond movie than someone who could exist in real life. He and Nora had travelled the world together, living the high life from Monte Carlo to Macau, and Ella loved listening to Nora's stories of life in other countries, and poring over her photographs of ritzy parties, beautiful clothes and fabulous houses.

When that relationship ended, Nora had finally come home to settle in Ireland. Shortly afterwards, Ella's father died suddenly of a heart attack and Nora moved in with her and her mother, the three of them becoming a tight unit.

Ruth and Nora both loved travelling, and in the long summer holidays, they'd taken Ella on trips to Morocco or Jordan while her school friends played on Mediterranean beaches. The last trip the three of them had taken together was the year before Ella left school, when they'd hired an RV and driven across the southern States of America.

The following year, while her classmates headed off on gap-year trips across South-East Asia and Australia, and her mother and Nora went on a cruise down the Nile, Ella had gone to a Spanish resort with Julie and enjoyed the novelty of her first package holiday, soaking up the sun by day and the bar life by night. She lay on crowded beaches reading fat novels and sleeping off hangovers. Ruth retired early from teaching the year Ella graduated, and she and Nora planned to do the big trip across Asia they'd always dreamed of. Then Ella fell sick, and all their plans were shelved.

Her phone rang, shaking her out of her reverie. It was her friend Hazel, who'd responded to her Facebook post with a sad-face emoji and an offer to call if she wanted a chat – which Ella very much did.

'Sorry the interview was a bust,' she said when Ella answered.

'It's fine. It wouldn't have been right for me anyway.' She told Hazel all about Tweedledum and Tweedledee.

'Gosh! Sounds like you dodged a bullet there all right.'

'Yeah. Something else happened afterwards, though, that kind of … blindsided me.' She was glad Hazel was up for a chat. It was something she hadn't told her mother and aunt – not that they'd judge. She knew she *could* tell them. But she didn't want to.

'I was walking around town after the interview, and I saw Matthew. I passed him in the street.'

'Matthew? You mean … Matthew Redmond?'

'Yeah. And I automatically went to say hi … but then I stopped myself. Because I thought nah, he wouldn't remember me. So I said nothing, just walked right by him.'

'Okay…' Hazel sounded confused, like she was waiting for the punchline.

'I mean, that's fucked up, isn't it? We were together.'

'For like five minutes, in first year.'

'It was almost a month.'

'Still…'

'A pretty intense month.'

'You're not still hung up on him, surely?'

'No! God. I wasn't "hung up on him" even then.'

'So why are you so shook up about seeing him again?'

'It wasn't seeing him. It's nothing to do with him. It's the fact that I could have that thought about someone I've had sex with!' It had stopped her in her tracks, literally. She'd passed him and then caught that thought going through her head and did a double-take. She literally stood still in the street for a moment, shocked at herself. 'I just casually thought he wouldn't remember me.'

'He probably wouldn't – it was a long time ago. But so what?'

'So what? He's seen me naked. He's been *inside* me, for fuck's sake! That's seriously disturbing!'

'It's just modern life, isn't it?'

'Is it?' Ella sighed. Had she fallen that much out of step? She felt fed up and left behind, out of practice at sleeping with strangers and thinking outside the box. 'I guess I have a lot of catching up to do.'

3

Roly fizzed with impatience as he stood in line at the convenience store. He tried to quell the urge to fidget that itched beneath his skin. It wouldn't make the queue move any faster, and he'd only draw attention to himself, ticcing and twitching because he had to queue to pay for a pint of milk and a packet of biscuits like a regular person. If he just kept his cool, acted casual and bored, no one would notice him. He had the hood of his sweatshirt pulled up, his eyes trained on the ground, careful not to look around and risk catching someone's eye.

There were only – he counted – three people ahead of him now. It was a quiet Monday afternoon. He felt safe going out at this time of day, when most people would be at work – people who had proper nine to five jobs with water coolers and annual leave and all that. Still, there were always more people out and about than you'd expect. It surprised him every time – housewives and stay-at-home mums, he supposed; students; the unemployed; pensioners.

He stifled a howl as the old lady who was now being served fumbled in her bag for her purse when all her purchases had been rung up. What was that about? Had it only just occurred to her that she'd have to pay? Finally, she moved on and struggled out through the doors with her shopping trolley. It was almost bigger than herself, but he resisted the impulse to leave the queue and go over to help her with it. She might recognise him. Grannies loved him for some reason.

Roly glanced at the cashier – a young Asian bloke, bored arseless by the look of him. He wasn't even making eye contact with customers as he served them. Clearly not one of those cheery types who thought they were making the world a better place with small talk – that was good. Roly didn't want to engage with anyone, and it looked like he'd get away with it.

He didn't mind going to the meetings – he looked forward to them, in fact. It was the journeys there and back that he found daunting – having to go out on the streets and risk being recognised. The thought of being looked at with pity or derision made his insides shrivel up. There was no danger of that at his meetings. Everyone knew who he was, of course, despite the 'anonymous' tag. But they didn't care. At NA they were all in the same boat, and no one looked down on anyone else. They'd all fucked up royally and lost everything they'd had, whatever that happened to be. He may have had further to fall than some, but when you fell all the way down it didn't really matter where you'd started. You landed in the same place.

When it was finally his turn, the cashier didn't even look at him, keeping his eyes trained on the register throughout the whole transaction. Roly felt irrationally pissed off, and deliberately tried to make eye contact as he took his change.

'Miserable day,' he said, nodding to the door.

'Hmm,' the cashier hummed vaguely in response,

glancing at Roly for a nanosecond. Nothing. Not even that vague flash of recognition when you know someone is familiar, but you can't quite place them. Huh! Maybe he really was anonymous now.

Out on the street, he tested the theory. He pulled his hood down as he made his way to his nan's house, eyeballing passers-by as he went, almost daring them to see him. He tried to look open and approachable, like he'd welcome someone asking for a selfie or an autograph. But it didn't make any difference. He didn't need to hide anymore, because apparently he was invisible. People looked through him – or worse, looked right at him and saw nothing but some chubby loser in sweats with a bag of biscuits and nothing better to do in the middle of the afternoon than eat himself into a diabetic coma. It seemed his notoriety had finally worn off. He didn't like it as much as he'd thought he would.

He could probably strip naked right here in the street and still not even make the sidebar of shame, because who'd care about some nobody flashing his bits and howling at the moon. There'd be no opportunistic photos or banner headlines – Roly Punch papped leaving his Narcs Anonymous meeting; the former boy band hottie gone to seed, an arrow helpfully pointing to his flabby belly as if you couldn't spot it for yourself. Roly Poly! Punch Drunk! His name had been a tabloid editor's wet dream and the asinine headlines had practically written themselves. The last time he'd seen himself in any kind of news story, it was one of those social media clickbait articles – 'you won't believe how shit these former celebs look now' or some such crap, with a picture of him looking like his nan in bad drag to draw people in. He suspected it was photoshopped. There was no denying he'd had some bad days, but he refused to believe he'd ever looked quite *that* grotesque.

Well, fuck it! Maybe this was the wake-up call he needed. He'd turn over a new leaf, get his life back on track – for real this time. When he got home, he'd throw out all the crap in his cupboards and go for a run. He hesitated as he passed a bin. Maybe he should start right now, and chuck the biscuits out. If he brought them home, he'd just sit on the sofa and scoff the lot while he played FIFA. But then he thought what his nan would say, and he couldn't do it. Because, after all, there were people starving in the world. You couldn't just throw away food like it was nothing. It was disrespectful. He'd bring them to his nan's and they could have them together – that way, even if they ate the lot between them, he'd still be halving his calories.

'How was your meeting?' his nan asked when they were sitting at the table in her cosy little kitchen, a pot of tea and plate of biscuits between them. Christine Punch's ex-council house in the Liberties was tiny, but it was warm, cheerful and homey, and it was where he had always felt safest and happiest. Whenever the meditation teacher in rehab told him to 'go to his happy place' this was where he went.

'It was good. Tinky Winky fell off the wagon at the weekend, though. Went on a bender.' He picked up a chocolate digestive and bit into it. He'd start the diet tomorrow.

'Oh no! And he'd been doing so well.'

'Yeah, he was gutted. I felt really bad for him.'

'And how about Laa-Laa? How's she doing?'

'Great.' He nodded. 'She spoke to her daughter at the weekend. It looks like they're going to patch things up.'

'Oh, that's good news.' His nan smiled, reaching for a biscuit. She loved hearing about his NA group, and followed their stories like her favourite soap opera. He knew it was all supposed to be confidential and he shouldn't tell anyone what happened at the meetings. But he'd named them all after children's TV characters to preserve their anonymity, so he didn't see any harm in it. She had no idea who they really were, and even if she had, it wasn't as if she was going to hunt them down.

'How's your mum? I haven't seen her all week.'

'She's good. She has a new boyfriend.'

Christine rolled her eyes. 'Honestly, I don't know why she keeps putting herself through it. I wouldn't mind if it made her happy, but she really knows how to pick them.'

'Maybe this one'll be different,' he said hopefully. It was true his mum had awful luck with men. He didn't know why because she was lovely – kind and good-humoured, and really pretty. She looked after herself – dressed well and wore make-up and all that – and she still looked good, even though she was almost fifty. She deserved someone nice who'd see how great she was and treat her well. But her boyfriends never stuck around for long. She seemed to have an unerring knack for attracting absolute fuckwits. But she remained ever optimistic, so he tried to be too. He'd feel disloyal if he admitted to sharing his nan's scepticism.

'Well, I suppose stranger things have happened.' Christine sighed. 'Though I can't really imagine what. Where did she meet this one?'

'Online – some dating website, as far as I know.'

'Well, I suppose that's a step up from a phone app, at least.'

Roly didn't think it was really, but he said nothing. He

wouldn't give her any more ammunition for criticising his mum.

'What's he like?'

Roly shrugged. 'Don't know. I haven't met him yet. Neither has she, actually – not in real life.'

Christine tutted exasperatedly. 'I don't know what Loretta thinks she needs a man for anyway. It's not how she was raised.'

That was the trouble with his nan – she didn't get it, because apart from Roly and his grandfather, she thought men were basically a waste of space. She had various mugs and posters around the place saying as much in different ways. 'A woman needs a man like a fish needs a bicycle' was printed on the T-shirt she was wearing right now. She'd been a major hippie and feminist in her day, always going on marches about women's rights and torching her underwear. He'd seen the photographs of the protest rallies and bra bonfires.

'But she never had the sense she was born with when it came to the fellas,' Christine continued. 'Starting with that father of yours.'

'Yeah, she's a sucker for romance,' Roly said with a grin.

'There was precious little romance involved with that gobshite.' His nan had no illusions about Roly's father, a Premier League footballer who'd got her daughter knocked up at eighteen and promptly abandoned her. His mother, on the other hand, had long held out hope that he'd come to his senses and settle down to playing happy families with her and Roly. Instead, after his football career was brought to an abrupt end following a leg injury, he'd moved first to Australia and then to Singapore, before finally settling in Thailand, leaving a trail of abandoned women, children and debt in his wake.

Thankfully, his mum had eventually realised he was never coming back and moved on. But Roly couldn't help feeling his nan was right and she'd be better off giving up on men altogether. He hated seeing her so sad and disappointed all the time when the latest wanker let her down and screwed her over. He felt guilty too, because being lumbered with a baby at eighteen had seriously curtailed her love life, and he knew he'd been responsible for scaring off more than one of her boyfriends. So he tried to keep out of her way and be encouraging about her new relationships, even as he didn't hold out much hope of them making her happy.

'Speak of the Devil,' his nan said as the front door opened, and Roly heard his mother's quick step in the hall.

'Roly, you're here!' She breezed in and hugged him from behind, enveloping him in a cloud of warm perfume as she kissed his cheek. 'Been to your meeting, love?'

'Yeah.' He smiled at her as she shrugged out of her coat. She got a mug from the cupboard and helped herself to tea, as at home in this house as if it were her own. It was where she'd grown up, and where Roly had spent the first five years of his life, before she'd got them their own place.

'You look good, Mum,' Roly said as she sat beside him.

'Thanks.' Her cheeks were pink, her eyes bright, and she looked happier than he'd seen her in a while. She'd seemed so dragged down lately, little cracks showing beneath the well-tended surface, but there was a definite glow about her today.

'You do,' Christine said. 'That's a gorgeous scarf.'

'It is, isn't it?' Loretta smiled as she took the brightly coloured scarf from around her neck and handed it over to Christine for inspection.

'Gucci, no less!' His nan's eyebrows raised almost accusingly as she stroked the silky material. 'Very nice.'

'My boyfriend gave it to me.' Loretta beamed with pride and pleasure.

Roly pretended not to notice his nan trying to catch his eye. He didn't want to collude in her disapproval and pessimism. He was glad to see his mum so happy, and he wanted to believe that maybe this time she'd found a decent bloke who'd treat her well.

'How did your meeting with the solicitors go yesterday?' his mum asked, and his heart sank. At least his nan hadn't bombarded him with questions about that the minute he came through the door. 'Any news?'

'No. There isn't going to be any news – nothing good anyway. The money's gone. That's not going to change.'

'All of it?'

'Yep. I'm broke. Bankrupt, basically.'

'But … there must be something you can do.'

'Like what? Marty's dead, so I can't take him to court. Even if I could, I doubt I'd get any of it back. He'd already pissed it all away, apparently.'

His mother sighed. 'Poor Marty!'

Of course – how could he have forgotten she'd dated Marty briefly? He should have known then that he'd turn out to be a scumbag. That was her type.

'Poor Marty indeed!' Christine scoffed. 'After what he did to Roly!'

'Well … I'm sure he didn't mean to. He probably just got into difficulties and thought he'd be able to fix it before anyone found out. You know how these things happen. He couldn't have known he was going to die suddenly.'

God bless his mum, she always gave people the benefit of the doubt. No matter how many men let her down, it never seemed to dent her core belief that most people were basically decent and were just doing their best. It was equal parts infuriating and endearing. She always made allowances – even for his slimeball of an accountant, who it turned out had been robbing him blind for years.

It was some comfort to Roly that he wasn't the only one. Marty's sudden death from a brain aneurysm a month ago had come as a shock, but it was nothing compared to the bombshell of discovering he'd been embezzling from his rich and famous clients for years. Roly had thought he was a friend, and he was still reeling from the betrayal. Marty had been almost like a father to him – which should have been his first clue, he thought bitterly.

'Death was the easy way out. He should be rotting in jail.' His nan took a harsher view than his mum. 'But you must have some money left?' she asked Roly. 'It can't be all gone.'

'It is, apart from whatever's in my bank account.' He knew he shouldn't have put all his eggs in one basket, but he'd handed over control of all his money to Marty. He'd been his financial adviser and personal banker, with carte blanche to make investments on his behalf. Whenever Roly needed money, he just went to Marty for it.

He'd been an unusually flamboyant and profligate character for an accountant, making the most of the entrée to the celebrity lifestyle that his high-profile clients gave him. He'd enjoyed having VIP access at events, and loved rubbing shoulders with the rich and famous at their swish parties. His generosity had been legendary, and he'd lavished his friends with extravagant gifts. He'd once given Roly a guitar that had belonged to John Lennon. It had cost him a fortune at auction – someone else's fortune, as it turned out.

'What will you do now?' his mum asked. 'What about your agent? Could he get you something?'

'Dave was the one who introduced me to Marty. He's got his own problems.'

'Well, at least you have your house. You could always let it out and move in with me.'

That would really play havoc with her love life! He didn't want to do anything to stymie her new romance, if there was any chance she might finally be having some luck in that department. It was still tempting, though. His money problems were preying on his mind a lot lately and he was finding it hard to go to sleep, his mind whirring with worries and schemes. He'd wake up in the middle of the night sometimes in a cold sweat, sick with panic about how he was going to dig himself out of the hole he was in.

'I don't think that's a good idea,' he said to his mum. 'It'd put a bit of a dampener on your love life.'

'That'd be no bad thing,' Christine muttered under her breath.

'Well, we could sell my house,' his mum said.

'Mum! I'm not turfing you out of your house.'

'I could easily downsize – get a little one-bed apartment. I don't need all that room just for me.'

'But it's your home – you love that place, and you've done so much work to it. I'm not selling your house, Mum.' It had been the proudest day of his life when he'd bought her that house. She'd worked so hard to give him a good life growing up – to get their own place and send him to a good school. It hadn't been easy for her as a young single mother, and he knew she'd made a lot of sacrifices. But she'd always been cheerful and content, and never made him feel like a burden or as if she hankered after any other kind of life than the one they had. He'd been so happy to be able to do something for her in return when he started making real money with Oh Boy!

He remembered the day she'd got the keys and the three of them had gone up there with a bottle of champagne. His mum had been teary and emotional as she went from room to room, saying over and over that she couldn't believe it was hers, and that Roly had done this for her. She kept thanking him, and telling him how proud she was of him. His nan had said 'He's a credit to you,' which was a lot from her and made his mum cry all over again. He'd been barely twenty, a multimillionaire. It had felt like all her hard work and sacrifices had paid off at last, and all she'd invested in him – of time, of money, of faith – was finally being rewarded.

It would kill him if she had to sell that house. It was the one good thing he'd done with his money and he wasn't going to let that be wiped out by his stupidity along with everything else.

'Well, *I* can't offer to downsize,' his nan said, looking around the tiny kitchen. She'd refused his offer to buy her somewhere fancier. She'd lived in this house all her married life, and she'd grown up in the neighbourhood. She had no interest in moving, but she had let Roly buy her a new kitchen and pay for some renovations.

'But no one has to worry about being on the street,' she continued. 'There'll always be room for you here, you know that – both of you.'

'Thanks, Mum.' Loretta smiled. His nan could be a tough old boot, but she had a heart of pure marshmallow, especially when it came to family. She'd never 'see anyone stuck' as she'd put it.

'We did it before, and we can do it again.'

'Roly's grown a bit since then,' Loretta said drily.

Christine shrugged. 'It'd be a squeeze, but we'll work it out.'

'Anyway, I'm sure it won't come to that,' Roly said. 'I still have enough in the bank to live on for a while.' He tried to sound like he wasn't worried, but it scared him how quickly it dwindled when there was nothing coming in –

and no Bank of Marty now to top it up when stocks got low. He'd got used to having a cushion – a very big cushion – and it was frightening knowing it wasn't there anymore.

'You could always get a lodger,' his mum said. 'You have the spare bedroom.'

'Maybe.' He drummed his fingers on the table, considering the idea. It could be the ideal solution, as long as he didn't end up sharing the place with some weirdo. It would give him some income while he got back on his feet. He had no mortgage to pay, so he didn't need much. He'd have to look up what rents were like when he got home.

'Well, I'm sure something will turn up.' His mum squeezed his hand.

That was her all over – just hope for the best and somehow things will miraculously 'work out' or 'turn up'.

'Don't worry,' she said more forcefully, putting her hand on his arm and looking him square in the eye. 'We'll manage, okay?'

He nodded, feeling soothed. 'Okay.' His lovely mum – she was all pillowy softness on the surface with her pale-blonde hair, big blue eyes and soft breathy voice. It was easy to underestimate her. But underneath her fluffy exterior there was a core of pure steel that was all the more effective for being unexpected. There was no one better to fight your corner, and she'd always been able to fix things for him. Whether he was worried about his homework or having trouble with some guy at school, he could rely on her to sort it out and make everything all right again.

'Okay?' she said again.

'Yeah, I'll be fine.'

When he got back to his house, he pulled out his laptop and ate half the packet of biscuits he'd forgotten to give to his nan while he looked up property sites. He began to feel more optimistic when he saw what rents you could charge for a bedroom in a house share. For the first time since Marty died, he felt like he could breathe. He was even a little bit excited at the prospect of having a steady income. Even the thought of having a roommate was kind of appealing. He'd have to vet them, of course, but he could get someone really cool, someone who'd be a friend rather than just a lodger, someone he could hang out with. He treated himself to a bowl of ice-cream in front of the TV to celebrate. It felt like the start of a new chapter. He could really turn things around.

That night he slept soundly, and the next morning he got up and stood in front of the full-length mirror, taking in the flabbiness of his belly, the pallor of his skin, the dark bags under his eyes. Then he went downstairs and went through the kitchen, throwing out frozen pizzas, a bin-load of sliced white bread, family size bars of chocolate and what was left of the biscuits he'd bought yesterday. He didn't even feel guilty about it. Because yes, there were people starving in the world; but he wasn't one of them.

4

'NICE GAFF.' Roly looked around as Charlie led him down a timber-floored hallway into the vast living space of his penthouse apartment. So this was what you could afford when you went the distance in Oh Boy! – when you didn't fuck it up and throw it all away.

'It's mad, isn't it?' Charlie chuckled. 'I can't believe you've never been here before.'

Roly could believe it. He'd been surprised when Charlie had called him out of the blue and invited him over. He hadn't seen any of the band in ages – even Charlie, the one he'd been closest to. After they'd spoken, he'd done some quick calculations, and he reckoned it had been almost a year since they'd been in touch, and then it had only been on WhatsApp.

The last time they'd seen each other in person, Charlie was living in London and about to embark on his first solo tour. Roly had gone over for the opening night at the Roundhouse in Camden. He really hadn't wanted to go. It was too humiliating to be back in that world as an outsider, like some hanger-on with his nose pressed against the window, with all those industry pricks looking down on him and feeling sorry for him.

But Charlie had been so nervous about playing his first solo gig and had begged Roly for his support, anxious to have some friendly faces in the crowd. So out of loyalty to his friend, he'd swallowed his pride and made the effort to show up. At least he knew Liam, Zack and Alex couldn't make it, so he wouldn't have to face any of them. They were all too busy with their own careers, which while it was a relief, made him feel like even more of a loser for being available. He was the only one with nothing better to do.

The gig went well, and Charlie had invited him to hang out backstage afterwards. They'd barely spoken, though. After a quick hello and a selfie for his Instagram, Charlie was too busy schmoozing more important people than Roly to do more than wave to him from across the room occasionally. Roly got it – it was Charlie's night and everyone wanted a piece of him. It was like being the bride at a wedding – everyone was just there for you, but you couldn't possibly give that level of attention back to each one of them. But no matter how much he rationalised it, it still pissed him off that he'd been left feeling like a chump for doing his mate a favour.

Charlie had texted since and there'd been lots of talk of getting together when he was next in Dublin and having a proper catch-up, just the two of them. But it never happened. Charlie had been back in Dublin several times, visiting family and friends, but he never seemed able to make time for Roly – not until he had another album to launch or gig to promote. To add insult to injury, Roly had seen him on Twitter trying to persuade Liam or Alex to come to Dublin to meet him the last time he was home. After that, Roly had ignored Charlie's pleas to attend his gigs or post about his latest album on social media, making vague promises to 'try to make it' that were as phony and meaningless as Charlie's 'catch up next time'.

They'd drifted further and further apart, until now Roly only saw Charlie the same way he did the other guys from the band, when he was hate-scrolling through their Instagram or Twitter feeds. It sucked that even mild-mannered, easy-going Charlie, the peace-keeper of the group and the most sweet-natured of them all, had turned out to be a user. Roly resented him for making him feel so spiteful and bitter. He didn't like being that person, and he hated that he cared. But he'd thought Charlie was a mate, and the rejection hurt. It just did.

Charlie waved him to a large sectional sofa, but Roly was drawn to the floor-to-ceiling windows. Sliding doors led to a terrace overlooking the curved glass structure of the Aviva Stadium, its blue light glowing into the night. It was strange to think they'd lit that place up once – him, Charlie and the rest of them – filling it with so much energy and love. He struggled to feel it, but he was so detached from that life now, it was like it had all happened to someone else.

'Drink?' Charlie asked from the kitchen area. 'I mean, I've got Coke or Sprite,' he added quickly.

'Coke, please. Diet if you have it?'

He nodded and opened a big American-style fridge.

'But you have whatever you want,' Roly added as Charlie pulled out two bottles of Coke. 'I'm cool with it.'

'Nah, I don't drink much these days anyway,' Charlie said, as Roly turned back to the view. 'I might have a beer later.'

He joined Roly at the window and handed him a bottle. 'Well, cheers!' He crashed his bottle against Roly's and took a long slug. 'It's hard to believe we were on stage there, isn't it?' He nodded to the Aviva.

'I was thinking the same thing. It seems like another life.'

'It *was* another life.' They were both silent for a moment, lost in their own thoughts. 'Listen to us,' Charlie said then with a laugh. 'We sound like old men.'

Roly smiled.

'Chilli will be ready in about ten minutes,' Charlie said, nodding towards the kitchen as Roly followed him to the sofa. A bowl of tortilla chips and a tray of dips were laid out on the low glass coffee table in front of it.

'You cooked?'

Charlie grinned. 'Yeah, I'm a bit of a domestic goddess these days. I made that too,' he said as Roly scooped up guacamole on a tortilla chip.

'It's really good.'

'I've even started making my own bread.'

'Bread? Seriously? You know you can buy that in the shops now?'

Charlie shrugged. 'It's something to do. I was kind of at a loss after the band finished.' He shifted awkwardly. 'You know what it's like.'

'You had your solo career, though.'

'So did you.'

'Hardly the same thing,' he said wryly. Charlie's couple of solo albums hadn't exactly set the world on fire, but they hadn't bombed as comprehensively as Roly's. 'You didn't get shat on from a height and laughed out of town.'

'Maybe not, but it took me a long time to get my act together. Too long, really. I kind of screwed that up.'

'Your first album did well, didn't it?'

'Not as well as it should have done. When Oh Boy! finished everyone was telling me I had to move quickly, get something out as soon as possible, not let the grass grow under my feet. They were right. If I'd done it straight away, I'd have been flying. Look at Zack.'

'Yeah.' Zack had got his solo career off the ground with almost indecent haste after the band split up. He was the least-talented member of the group musically, but he really excelled at showing off and his self-promotion was second to none. His debut solo album had gone straight to number one and the supporting tour was a sell-out. 'You don't want to be like him, though, do you? His stuff is shite.'

'Ah, it's not that bad,' Charlie said with typical grace. 'Fair play to him. He did what I should have been doing. But I just couldn't get on with it. Getting over the band was tough. I kind of lost the plot there for a while.'

'In what way?'

'Drinking, doing too much drugs, partying too hard. It was a strange time. It took me a while to pull myself together. It was like I was paralysed. I couldn't shift myself to do anything. I felt kind of … lost. Was it like that for you?'

'Well, no. It was a bit different for me. I mean, I got kicked out. And I went straight from the band into rehab, so it's not like I was left to my own devices.'

'Yeah. You were lucky.'

'Seriously?' Roly screwed up his face. That was such bullshit!

'Sorry, I didn't mean…' He shrugged. 'I don't know. I didn't know what to do with myself. One minute I was in the band, and I was being told where to go and what to do every second of the day – what to say, how to dress, even who I should be going out with. And then the next thing, I was on my own, and there was just … nothing. I could do whatever I wanted, but I had no idea what that was. I hadn't even had to think about it in years. So I just sort of

… drifted.' He sighed. 'At least in rehab you had a structure. You knew what you were doing.'

'Yeah. Group therapy.' He rolled his eyes.

Charlie laughed. 'Post-group therapy. That's what we all needed.'

'Even Zack?'

'Yeah, probably not Zack.'

Roly felt a surge of warmth and sympathy towards Charlie. They'd first bonded over slagging off Zack.

'Did you hear him on the radio the other day?'

'Aw shit, I missed it.'

Charlie smiled. 'He said that Liam had predicted when we split up that Zack would be the most successful of us all – and Zack says "and he wasn't wrong"!'

'Yeah, modesty was never his strong point, was it?'

'Once he started believing his own publicity, there was no stopping him!'

Roly laughed.

'Sometimes I envied you, you know,' Charlie said quietly.

'*Me*?'

'Yeah. That you got out when you did – when it was still a laugh, you know? Before it all got so serious and all the bitching and in-fighting started. You had the best of it, and then you got out, got your life back.'

'You think that's what happened?'

Charlie turned to look him square in the eye. 'Honestly? I envied the shit out of you. It was like you had the best of both worlds – you got to be in Oh Boy! when it was all new and exciting and … *fun*. And then you got to not be in it and go back to having a normal life.'

'Yeah, it must have been a nightmare travelling the world, making tons of money, going to all those parties, girls throwing themselves at you everywhere you went…' It came out more bitterly than he intended. He got where Charlie was coming from, so why did he have to sound so angry? It was pathetic.

Charlie smiled. 'I'm not saying it was all bad. It had its moments.'

'And rehab isn't exactly normal life.'

'No, I'm sure. I just mean we all had to go through it at some stage – Oh Boy! being over. And it was always going to be an adjustment. At least you got to do it before things went sour.' He drained his Coke and stood. 'Anyway, the chilli should be done. Let's eat.'

'So, do you see much of the guys now?' Roly asked. They'd moved to the kitchen/diner and sat on high stools at a marble-topped counter.

'No. I used to see Liam a good bit, but not for ages now. We're still in touch pretty regularly, though. The others, not so much … well, until recently.'

Roly raised his eyebrows.

'That's kind of what I wanted to talk to you about. Zack rang the other day. He's going to be in Dublin in the next couple of months. We're meeting up … all of us.'

'What? Everyone?'

'Yeah.' Charlie looked down at his bowl, concentrating on crunching a handful of tortilla chips into his chilli, then adding a dollop of sour cream, a sprinkling of cheese and a spoonful of guacamole. 'I thought he might have rung you,' he said finally.

'Uh … no. Why would Zack ring *me*?'

'I just thought…' He broke off and sighed, stirring his chilli thoughtfully. Leaning back in his chair, he put down his fork and eyeballed Roly. 'The thing is, he's talking about a reunion.'

'A reunion? What kind of reunion?' But Roly already knew he wasn't talking about a get-together for a few drinks and a trip down memory lane.

'You know – the group getting back together. Making an album, doing a tour – a comeback, basically.' He picked up his fork and resumed eating.

'Oh.' Roly swallowed and reached for his Coke. Suddenly his throat felt very dry. 'And … did Zack want you to talk to me about it?'

Charlie threw him a wary look. 'No. He actually said not to mention it if I was talking to you. I thought maybe he wanted to tell you himself – you know, extend an olive branch sort of thing.'

Roly gave a bitter laugh. 'No. I've heard zip about this. I doubt I'll be getting any olive branches from him.'

'Well, I thought I should give you a heads-up either way.'

Roly nodded. 'Thanks. I appreciate it.' He felt bad for thinking ill of Charlie in the past. He'd had his own problems to deal with, but he was basically sound. 'So when is this happening?'

'Nothing's been decided yet. It's just an idea at this stage; we haven't thrashed out any of the details. It may not even happen. He was just throwing it out there, seeing how we all felt, if we were up for it.'

'And are you?'

'Hell, yeah!' Charlie grinned, his eyes wide with enthusiasm. So much for envying Roly for getting out when he did.

'You'd go back to all that?'

'In a heartbeat.'

'What about your solo career?'

Charlie shrugged. 'It's dead in the water. My heart

wasn't in it anyway. I loved being in the group. It wasn't the same doing it all on your own.'

'Well, there's no point in doing something you're not enjoying if you don't have to. It's not as if you need the money.'

'Yeah, exactly.'

It wasn't fair – Roly *did* need the money. Of all of them, he was the one who had the most to gain from an Oh Boy! comeback. But it didn't look like he'd be part of it.

'Maybe Zack will call you yet. It'd be a laugh if all five of us were back together. It was never the same after you left.'

'What about the rest of you?' Roly hated asking, but he couldn't afford to be proud. This was the lifeline he needed, and he had to at least try to grasp it. 'Can't *you* ask me? It's as much your group as Zack's.' It was true on paper, but Zack had somehow become the de facto leader by dint of shouting the loudest and being the biggest success.

'I know. I said we should sound you out about it.'

'And he said no?'

'He said we'd discuss it when we meet up, but his thinking was that it should just be the four of us. He said that's what the fans would want.'

'Bullshit!'

'That's what I said – well, not in so many words. But I said fans would totally want to see you. I mean, you were probably the most popular one.'

'And what did he say to that?'

'He, uh…' Charlie's eyes slid away and he looked sheepish. 'He said that was a long time ago, and you left the group so early, everyone has forgotten by now that you were ever in it.'

'Wanker!' He'd always known Zack was a total shitbag, but this was low even for him.

'He's just jealous,' Charlie said with a shrug. 'You know he was always a bit envious of us.'

He and Charlie had been the most musically gifted members of the group, the only song-writers among the five of them and the only ones who could play instruments. They'd been the ones everyone expected to make it big on their own. Zack had resented their song-writing credits and musical ability. He'd always been more of a showman, good at dance routines and goofing about in interviews, but with no substantial talent. Even his voice needed a lot of production to sound halfway decent. Yet against all the odds, he was the one whose solo career had gone supernova.

'I'm surprised he even wants to go back to sharing a stage with anyone else. And do you seriously want to be working with him again? To be stuck in studios and on tour buses with him and his ego?'

Charlie shrugged. 'I liked being part of a group. I still miss it.'

'I thought you were glad to be out of all that.'

'It'd be different now, though, wouldn't it? We're older … wiser, hopefully.'

'Hmm.' Roly wasn't so sure about the wiser part. Growing up inside Oh Boy! wasn't the same as growing up in the real world. They'd been exposed to a lot of stuff, of course, that most kids their age never got to experience. They'd travelled the world, meeting presidents and prime ministers, soaking up different cultures and partying with rock legends and movie stars. There'd been cocaine and Kristal, and exotic food that his mum and nan had never even heard of. But they'd been shielded from a lot of stuff too. He'd only realised once he'd been kicked out how cocooned he'd been in ways, how ill equipped he was to function in normal life. It had been too much too fast, and at the same time too little, too late.

'Anyway,' Charlie said, 'I thought you had a right to know, so you won't be blindsided if you see it on social media or something.'

'Thanks. I appreciate it.'

'And maybe Zack will still call you.'

'I don't see that happening. What about Vince? Will he be involved?'

'Of course.' Charlie rolled his eyes. 'As if we could make a move without our puppet-master.'

'Well, I guess that's me out, then.' Vince, the man who'd made and managed them, was a ruthless music mogul, who'd never forgiven Roly for fucking up.

'Would you even want to do it?' Charlie asked.

'Yes, I would.'

'Really?'

'Like you say, it'd be different now. I'm not going to go off the rails again at this stage. And it'd be fun, all of us back together. I mean we had a laugh, didn't we?'

'You're only remembering the good parts – how it was at the start.'

'Maybe. But even so, worst-case scenario, it's just a job, and there are a lot harder ways of making money. Any job has good and bad parts. Besides, I could really do with the money.'

'Yeah, I heard what happened with Marty.' Charlie threw him a sympathetic look. 'That sucks.'

'It really does.' But maybe his mum had been right about something turning up. An Oh Boy! reunion might be the miracle he needed. He just had to do whatever it took to make sure he was part of it – even if it meant sucking up to Zack.

5

When he got home that night, Roly flopped on the sofa and took out his phone to check out Twitter and Instagram – just a quick look, he told himself. He'd mostly managed to stay away from social media lately. He knew no good ever came of it. But every so often he couldn't resist and went back to scrolling through his feed, looking for mentions of him or the band, checking to see if anyone was talking about him and what they were saying. He also had a bad habit of hate-stalking Zack, even though everything the twat posted only enraged him. He jumped on every trending hashtag and espoused every topical cause going. He was a self-styled hero of feminism one week, a staunch critic of racism in the music industry the next, an ally to the dispossessed and disadvantaged. He was always pontificating sanctimoniously about one thing or another, though his 'activism' seemed to mainly consist in wearing T-shirts printed with various trite slogans. Roly doubted the dickhead could even spell 'feminism'.

When he started typing 'Oh Boy' into the search bar on Twitter, it immediately autofilled with a list of hashtags

– alongside the usual and unsurprising #Ohboy, there was #Ohboyreunion. There was nothing particularly significant about the fact that that was trending. The fans had been speculating about one practically from the moment the band broke up, constantly sending their baseless longings out into the ether, and every so often a rumour would surface that seemed to have more substance to it. Fans would pick up on something one of the band had tweeted or said in an interview, and they'd be off, reading meaning into every glance or soundbite, weaving together a story from a random collection of social media posts and interview comments, forensically examining every statement and photograph for evidence to back up their theory.

That seemed to be what was happening now, and he spent the next couple of hours following the thread of the story. The fans were avidly piecing together clues, working themselves up into a fever about it. It all seemed to have been sparked by a casual throwaway remark of Zack's on some chat show about 'all the lads' having been in touch again recently. Yeah, not *all* the lads, Zack. But the band members themselves seemed to be at it now too, dropping coy hints on their Instas and Twitter, posting cryptic messages to each other on their public platforms. He was tempted to post a few bitter subtweets aimed at them, and to make some cryptic posts of his own.

At least the fans hadn't forgotten him. There was plenty of chatter about whether he'd rejoin the band for any potential comeback, lots of them fervently wishing and hoping for his return and saying it wouldn't be the same without him. He was touched by how often his name came up, showered with heart emojis and kisses. God, he loved his fans – well, maybe not the ones who'd written fan fiction about him and Zack getting it on (eww!), which Zack had insisted on reading out sometimes when they were all stoned. It was excruciating. Not even the drugs could dull the toe-curling horror of the images that story had planted in his brain.

Eventually he managed to tear himself away from his obsessive scrolling, tossing his phone on the couch in disgust. But then he turned on the TV and started looking through YouTube. It had been years since he'd gone down this particular rabbit hole. It made him melancholy and nostalgic, but, once he started, he couldn't seem to tear himself away, watching old music videos, interviews, snippets of live performances…

It had been years since he'd seen the video for their first single 'Cool Like You'. Objectively, he knew it was corny and clichéd, the five of them horsing around on the beach, dancing in the waves. But he had no detachment from it now. Watching it wasn't like remembering; it was as if he was there, living it again. He could feel the sting of the icy water on his legs, taste the salty ozone of the air, and his heart raced once more with the heady mixture of nerves and excitement that they were actually doing this – they were making a video for their single. It had been so much *fun* – five young guys, just goofing off. It had been hard work too, but, at the same time, it had seemed laughable to call it work when they were having such a fucking blast.

There was Zack, lying down on the sand, letting the waves wash over him. Prick! He always had to go one better than the rest of them, push things further, incessantly pulling focus and hogging the limelight. But he was just a kid, Roly thought, feeling a strange wave of tenderness towards him – just a skinny young kid like the rest of them, five teenagers who'd lucked out and couldn't believe that this was their life. They looked like utter gobshites, and it was so beautiful he wanted to cry.

Even though it made him ache with longing and loss, he couldn't tear his eyes away, and he watched video after video – live shows, interviews, TV appearances, awards ceremonies. The songs were mostly crap, the melodies so simple and catchy that they were irritating by the second listen, and the choreography was embarrassing. They looked like twats doing the ridiculous dance routines, or clutching their hearts as they powered through schmaltzy ballads, their faces contorted into earnest pantomimes of devotion and heartache that they'd never actually experienced. Yet somehow the energy was beautiful, and it touched him as he watched and watched, wallowing in the nostalgia, tears rolling down his face.

His eyes started to droop over footage of a concert at the Aviva. It had been a brilliant gig, a triumphant homecoming at the end of a hugely successful European tour, and they were all on a high. But there was a nauseating lurch in the pit of his stomach as other memories crept in. It was just before Christmas, so he'd been staying in Dublin for a few days, and he'd met up with Ella the following night. It was the first time in ages they'd been out together, just the two of them. She'd worn a sparkly silver dress, and those thick black tights she was so fond of. She'd looked amazing, and he'd been a total prick to her.

He'd been at the height of his asshat phase. He'd taken her to some pretentious bar on the quays, and spent all night snorting coke in the loos and boasting about the band to her. It was all a bit hazy, but he knew he'd been off his head, all pumped up on chemically induced arrogance and free-floating spite. He'd been full of his own importance, showing off about his money and fame, trying to impress her with what a big deal he was.

She was in Trinity and she was seeing some guy, he recalled. She'd seemed really excited about it all. But he'd hardly listened when she tried to tell him about it. He couldn't even remember what she was studying. Philosophy, maybe? As he thought about it now, he realised he'd felt resentful of her that night. He couldn't for the life of him fathom why, because he'd been on top of the world then – he was in the biggest boy band on the planet, rolling in cash, travelling the world, living in five-star hotels … Everything he could wish for was on offer. The world was one giant buffet of money, sex and drugs, all his for the taking. His life was amazing.

But he hadn't felt it, he realised now. He'd had this incredible life, but it didn't touch him. He'd felt remote from it, jaded, empty and joyless. It was like fireworks were going off all around him, but he couldn't catch a spark. Whereas Ella … she'd positively glowed when she spoke about her studies, her new boyfriend, her part-time job in some crummy cafe … He saw now that he'd envied her. Because he'd had it all, but she was the one who was happy. She was enjoying her life, and he wasn't. So he'd tried to shit all over it and make her feel small. He couldn't recall exactly what he'd said, but he was sure it would have been mean, belittling and thoroughly nasty, because that was him, back then. It was no wonder she'd given up on him and cut him out of her life.

He'd never really understood why they'd kept in touch since school in the first place – just that sometimes he felt the need to talk to her and only she would do. They'd only seen each other a handful of times over the years, and their friendship had always seemed tenuous at best – not built to last. So it hadn't been a surprise when they'd finally drifted apart. It had seemed inevitable, just a matter of time, and he knew it was his fault when it finally ended.

That night was the last time he'd seen her. He had a vague recollection of inviting her to the concert at Croke

Park the night that everything fell apart. But as far as he could remember, she'd made some excuse and didn't come. He was glad now that even if she remembered him at his most obnoxious, at least she hadn't seen him at his absolute lowest, most abjectly pathetic. Then again, she probably had – the whole world had seen that. He cringed at the thought of her looking at that photograph, the image that had gone viral and brought his whole world crashing down.

He hadn't thought about Ella in a long time. He wondered what she was doing now. Last he'd heard she'd been about to start her PhD. She was probably a professor or something by now. He'd considered calling her sometimes in the intervening years, apologising for how he'd been that night. In group they'd talked about going back to people you'd hurt in the past and apologising for the pain you'd caused them. He'd mostly thought about his mum and nan, of course, and he'd done all his apologising to them at first. Then he'd gone on to Charlie, Alex and Liam. He'd even tried with Zack, but it hadn't gone down well. And occasionally, Ella had nudged at the edges of his mind and he'd wondered if he should call her too. He didn't flatter himself that he was a big part of her life and that his apology would mean anything to her. She'd probably long forgotten that night by now, and she'd find it odd that it still preyed on his mind. But he hated that he'd been such a shit to her the last time they'd met when she'd never been anything but kind and caring with him, and it bothered him that she didn't know how sorry he was.

He'd never had the nerve to call her in the end. It seemed too weird to apologise to her after so long – too little, way too late. But he still regretted it and it niggled at his conscience whenever he thought of her. Maybe he should still do it, he thought, as his eyes drifted closed. On the TV, Oh Boy! strode onto the stage of the Aviva, waving to a crowd of screaming fans as they took their home town by storm.

The next morning he woke up exhausted and bleary-eyed, but with a new sense of purpose. He had a goal now. He'd spent last night steeped in nostalgia, longing for a past that was out of reach. But now it was all happening again, and maybe he could have a second chance. He could get that life back, but this time he'd do it right. He wouldn't waste one second of it, and he'd enjoy the hell out of every moment.

He knew he had some fences to mend. He had Charlie on side, and he still spoke to Liam occasionally. He'd never openly fallen out with any of them, not even Zack, but there was still a lot of resentment bubbling beneath the surface – and you didn't have to dig too far down either. It wouldn't be easy, but he could get it all back – everything he'd loved, everything that had been great about his life then. Including Ella, he thought, suddenly overwhelmed by that old urge to talk to her and only her. He'd definitely call her this time. Maybe…

6

Ella was just finishing transcribing a podcast for a client when her phone rang. The caller ID showed a number she didn't recognise, but she answered tentatively, hoping it might be an enquiry about her virtual assistant services. She could do with some new business.

'Hello, Ella?'

'Yes?'

'Hi! This is Dylan from Citizens of the Wild. How are you doing?'

'Oh, hi! I'm fine, thanks.' She was surprised to hear from him. It was almost a month since her disastrous interview, and she certainly wasn't expecting them to call to tell her they weren't hiring her.

'So, the thing is, we were wondering if you're still looking for a job. You've probably found something by now, but just on the off-chance…'

'No, I'm still looking,' she said quickly, intrigued.

'Okay, great! So are we. We did take someone else on, but they didn't work out.'

So maybe asking people what they'd do if they got

stuck in a blender hadn't been such a great way of assessing interviewees after all. Who knew?

'So, if you'd be interested, we'd love for you to join the team.'

'Oh! You mean…'

'We're offering you the job – if you'd consider us, that is,' he added with a little laugh. 'So, would it … interest you at all?' he asked after a pause when she was too stunned to speak.

'Yes! It does. I'm very interested. Thanks. I'd love to join the team.' Gah! She was babbling.

'Great! That's brilliant. Do you have any questions?'

'I don't think so.' She knew she should have questions, but it eluded her what they were.

'Okay, well—'

'Oh! What's the salary? And the hours? And when would you want me to start?'

Dylan chuckled. 'If you'd stayed to the end of the interview, we'd have gone into all that.'

'Right. Sorry.'

'Look, why don't you come in for a chat and we'll go over everything.'

'When you say a chat…'

'Don't worry. There'll be no more wacky hypotheticals. We were impressed with you.'

'You were?'

'Well, up to the point where you told us to shove it and walked into the stationery cupboard.'

'Ha ha.' She didn't suppose they'd ever let her forget that. Still it would be a small price to pay if it meant she could start earning decent money and get some proper work experience. Her mind was already whirring with the possible implications. She could start paying her mum back, save up for a deposit on a flat, think about moving out… Maybe she could even persuade her mum and Nora to go on their big trip. She'd have colleagues, she could make new friends, so they wouldn't have to worry about her being lonely…

'You rejected us, remember, not the other way around,' Dylan was saying.

'You would have hired me?'

'Yeah, we would. We're not as daft as we seem, you know.'

'Well, that's a relief.'

'Plus Nicola – the girl we hired – didn't have a note in her head, and insisted on being Elton. So that wasn't going to work.'

Ella laughed and wondered what she was letting herself in for.

'It's nice to see you back,' Jake said to her the following afternoon, when she returned to Citizens of the Wild. Jake and Dylan were waiting for her in the reception area, hovering by Kerry's desk when she arrived.

'We thought you'd given us the thumbs down,' Dylan said.

'Sorry. I just thought I wasn't going to fit in here.' She looked around as a young guy with a messenger bag slung across his body skate-boarded through the door, waving to them as he whizzed past. 'I mean, I'm still not sure…'

'Don't mind him,' Dylan said.

'Besides, no one has to "fit in",' Jake said. 'There are no moulds. Just be yourself.'

'Right.' Ella nodded. Kerry caught her eye and gave her a little conspiratorial smile.

'I'm guessing there's no dress code, then,' Ella said, nodding after skater-boy.

'No, it's very casual. Well, apart from Kerry.' Dylan nodded to her, smiling. 'But she's a fashion graduate. Casual isn't in her wheelhouse.'

'Just wear whatever makes you comfortable.' Jake's eyes flicked over Ella's dated M&S suit, which she'd dug out again.

'This isn't it, by the way,' she said. She was relieved she wouldn't have to waste money buying clothes she didn't like, and could fall back on her beloved jeans and sweat-shirt combo.

'That's cool.' Dylan shrugged. 'Just wear whatever you normally would – apart from dress-up Fridays.'

'Oh?' Her heart sank. It looked like she'd have to hang onto this bloody suit after all. Still, at least it was the reverse of most companies, where formal business wear was the order of the day and dressing down was a weekly novelty.

'Don't look so worried,' Dylan said. 'It's only once a month. It's fun.'

Even better! Not her idea of fun, but once a month would be bearable. 'What on earth do *you* do for dress-up Fridays?' she said to Kerry. 'I mean … where have you left to go?'

Kerry grinned at her, looking pleased.

'Yeah, she puts us all to shame,' Dylan said. 'One month she came as Wanda Maximoff – you know, the Scarlet Witch? Suddenly everyone decided they needed to work down here for the day. There were fights over the beanbags.' He shook his head. 'It was chaos.'

'We had to have a word with her, didn't we?' Jake was looking at Dylan, but side-eyeing Kerry, his lips twitching in a smile.

Dylan nodded solemnly. 'I don't want to have to go through that again.'

'So try not to look *too* spectacular, is what we're saying.'

'Oh, I'm sure I can manage that.'

'They just don't want you stealing their thunder,' Kerry said to her.

'Oh, they don't need to worry about that.' She turned to Dylan. 'So when you say dress-up, you mean … fancy dress?'

'Yeah, fancy dress, cosplay … whatever you want to call it. You'll get the hang of it.'

Yikes! Would she?

'But it's not compulsory. There's no pressure to join in if you're not comfortable with it,' Jake told her hastily, perhaps worried that she was getting ready to bolt again.

'Well, come up and we'll show you around and introduce you to everyone.'

Ella followed them upstairs to the main open-plan workspace, on the opposite side of the landing to the room where she'd been interviewed. It was a small team – a couple of designers, Sarah and Mark, huddled together on a bright-green sofa, engineers Catherine and Dan, hunched over a laptop on a coffee table, and the 'back office' guys Philip and Gordon, who took care of tech, marketing and everything else.

'Where would I sit?' Ella asked, looking around. There were a few unoccupied desks dotted around, but everyone seemed to be sitting on the sofas or bean bags. Maybe they were on a coffee break?

'Wherever you like.' Dylan waved an arm around to encompass the whole area.

'We don't have designated work spaces,' Jake explained. 'It's very informal. You just work wherever you feel comfortable.'

'Go with the flow.'

'So … people move around?'

'Yeah. Wherever the mood takes you on the day.'

Ella had been kind of looking forward to having a desk of her own – a place where she could head straight for every morning. She'd already visualised herself personalising it with some photos and stuff, filling the drawers with her own bits and pieces.

Maybe her disappointment showed, because Jake said 'But you can sit in the same place every day, if you like.'

'Okay. I might do that.'

'We just want you to be happy here,' Dylan said.

'Happy staff, happy gaff.'

Ella smiled. They seemed so eager to please.

As well as the ubiquitous bean bags, there were a couple of pods – great for focusing if you wanted to work on your own, according to Jake – some low sofas grouped around coffee tables for informal meetings or getting together with colleagues to thrash out ideas, and a few regular desks dotted around the floor. Ella's eyes were drawn to one tucked into a corner in front of a window. She decided she'd make for that on her first day. It would be nice to know where she was going. There were regular tea and coffee stations set up around the space – 'Just help yourself whenever you want,' Jake said – but there was also a dedicated break room.

It was clearly Jake and Dylan's pride and joy, and they beamed with delight as they led her inside, like excited kids showing off their project.

'Oh!' Ella gasped as she stepped inside. She was aware of Jake and Dylan watching her reaction closely. 'Wow, this is … really nice,' she said, looking around, taking it all in. There were some gaming tables with consoles, shelves lined with books and comics, and some cosy-looking armchairs. But the main focus was a climbing wall that covered one side of the room.

There was a guy halfway up in a complicated-looking harness, wearing a helmet and kneepads. He turned and waved as they came in, and Ella recognised skater-boy. She wondered if he ever did any work. He'd only just come in – surely it was taking the piss to be on a break already?

'Good job, Dara!' Jake called to him. Dara gave him a thumbs-up in response. 'This is Ella – she's going to be joining us.'

'Hi, Ella!' Dara gave her a friendly wave, and she waved back.

'Dara's our intern,' Dylan told her.

'We don't have any formal breaks,' Jake said. 'You can come in here any time you want and play a game, have a go on the wall or whatever, or just chill.' Ella wandered over to have a closer look at the shelves, and was pleased to see that as well as video games there was a substantial collection of board games.

'Have you ever done any climbing?' Dylan asked her.

She gave him a sceptical look. 'No. I mean, until recently I was barely even doing any walking.'

'Right. Sorry.'

'It's fine.'

'Well, if you'd like to have a go, feel free to use the wall any time. You'll always find someone around to help you if you need it, show you the equipment and so on.'

'I doubt that'll be happening. I've never been the sporty type.'

'Well, it's there if you ever change your mind,' Dylan said casually, but she could see he was deflated. Dylan's default expression was less 'resting bitch' and more 'excitable puppy', and it didn't hide disappointment well. He always on the verge of a grin, as if he was constantly poised on the brink of a roller coaster or about to hear some juicy gossip. Right now he looked like a very dejected puppy who'd failed to please with the wonderful offering he'd dropped at her feet. Even Jake, who exuded an air of profound gnomish calm, looked a bit hurt. Ella felt bad.

'But I love board games!' she said, pointing to the shelves.

'Really?' Dylan cheered up immediately, and she was rewarded with a toothy grin. 'We've got loads.'

'So I see.' She inspected the boxes, genuinely pleased there was such a wide variety of games – all the old favourites, plus some more obscure ones. Maybe she wouldn't be such a total misfit here after all.

'All the classics, and a lot more besides,' Jake said proudly. 'Whatever your pleasure, you'll always find someone to geek out with.'

'Kerry is our resident Scrabble champion.'

'And there's a Dungeons and Dragons club if that's your thing.'

Beside the shelves there was a notice board with a sign-up sheet for a hike up to the Hell Fire Club on Saturday.

'You're welcome to come along, if you like,' Jake said, nodding to the board. 'You can just go at your own pace – no pressure.'

'Thanks, but I don't think I'd be up for that just yet.' It wasn't just the hiking. The thought of doing group activities with a bunch of people she didn't know was daunting. She was so out of practice.

'We do something most weekends,' Dylan said – a hike or canoeing, sometimes a swim in the summer or a game of rounders. Feel free to suggest anything.'

'And there's karaoke on Fridays, of course,' Jake said.

'Kiki Dee, don't forget,' Dylan said with a grin. 'Don't let me down.'

Oh god, karaoke! How could she forget?

'Before you go, let me give you one of our jackets,' Jake

said as they led her back to the main space. He opened a cupboard and pulled out a big cellophane-wrapped packet.

'It might be a bit big,' he said as he handed it to her, 'but try it out anyway, and see what you think.'

'We don't have many left because we're working on the Heatsmart Neo at the moment, and we're expecting to get the prototypes in any day now.'

'But give that one a wear and let us know if you have any feedback.'

'Thanks. I will.' Ella was surprised how light the jacket was as she took it from him. But then she remembered from her research that that was one of its big advantages over previous state-of-the-art heated jackets.

They walked her back to reception, making the inevitable jokes about wanting to avoid her ending up in a cupboard.

'Right. We'll see you Monday then,' Jake said at the door. 'Any other questions?'

'Um ... just one.'

'Shoot.'

'A penguin walks through that door wearing a sombrero. What does he say and why is he here?'

Dylan threw his head back with a shout of laughter.

'Touché,' Jake said, smiling. 'Welcome to the team, Ella. I think you'll fit in here just fine.'

7

THE FOLLOWING Friday Ella breathed a sigh of relief as she closed the hall door behind her and was greeted with the delicious aroma of herby tomato sauce and melting cheese. Her mother had promised her homemade pizza to celebrate her first full week of work, and Ella had been looking forward to it all day.

'Tired?' her mother asked, turning from the oven as Ella flopped into a chair at the kitchen table.

Ella nodded. 'Knackered.' But it was a good kind of tired. Working a full week had been exhausting and she'd conked out every night almost as soon as they'd finished dinner. It wasn't just that she wasn't used to going out of the house and working full days, it was the level of social interaction too. She'd found it a strain, though not as much as she'd expected. Her first week at Citizens (as everyone casually referred to it) had been surprisingly enjoyable, and she'd been pleased with how well she'd coped.

She liked having a clear demarcation between her work and home life, and it felt good to have made it through the week and earned that 'Friday feeling'.

'Smells amazing!' she said to her mother. 'Anything you want me to do?'

Ruth shook her head. 'It's almost ready. You could set the table.'

Ella stood and opened the cutlery drawer.

'It's just the two of us,' her mother told her. 'Nora's out on a date.'

'Oh, good for her!'

Ruth sighed. 'Hopefully.'

'You don't sound very optimistic.'

'I just don't know why she puts herself through it when her heart's not in it. You should have seen her this evening – you'd think she was going to the gallows. She even said she'd much rather stay in and have dinner with us. I kept telling her she could do that if she wanted to. No one's forcing her to go out on dates. But off she trudged – a martyr to the cause.'

Ella laughed. 'Well, I can't believe she chose a man over your homemade pizza. But maybe this one will surprise her and she'll have a good time.'

'Maybe,' her mother said doubtfully.

'Mmm,' Ella closed her eyes and groaned as she bit into her first slice of pizza. 'This is so good. Better than a man any day.'

Ruth smiled. 'It is pretty amazing, if I say so myself.'

As they ate, Ella talked about her first week at work. It had been fun, and much more interesting than what she'd expected when she'd applied for what sounded like a routine admin position. She'd been surprised at the amount of freedom she'd been given to use her initiative, especially in her first week. She also liked that she was allowed to do a bit of everything to see what was the best fit for her skills and interests, and didn't just get stuck with the most boring jobs that no one else wanted to do. Philip had given her all the passwords for their various social media advertising accounts, and she'd worked with him on some campaigns. Yesterday they'd given her access to their accounts, which turned out to be in a bit of a mess. Their book-keeping was sketchy to non-existent, so she'd spent the day getting stuck into that, doing some forensic tracing of invoices and receipts, and trying to sort it all out. On Monday she planned to set up a new record-keeping system to keep everything on track in the future.

She hadn't expected to be given so much responsibility, and she loved that she was left to her own devices to get on with things. She could decide what needed doing and then go ahead and do it without asking anyone's permission. She may not have much office experience, but she knew that wasn't how things worked at most companies. It may be unconventional and a bit chaotic at Citizens, but she thought it was going to suit her very well.

Everyone had been very friendly and helpful too. Jake and Dylan checked in regularly to make sure she was finding her way around and knew she could ask if she needed help with anything. But they didn't hover, and she never felt they were looking over her shoulder. Kerry had been almost motherly, taking Ella under her wing, despite being almost ten years younger.

'So you reckon Tweedledum and Tweedledee are keepers?' her mother concluded.

'Yeah.' Ella nodded, smiling. 'It's not the sort of place I ever saw myself working. But I think I may have landed on my feet there.'

. . .

She was still exhausted, so she went to her room straight after dinner and crashed out on her bed, catching up on social media. She was scrolling through Instagram when she noticed she had a new message request. She opened it, prepared to delete the usual dodgy greeting from some random dude chancing his arm. Sure enough, it was an account she didn't recognise, with an anonymous string of letters and numbers for a handle and a cartoon character avatar. The character looked vaguely familiar, but she couldn't place it – someone from Pokémon maybe? Then she opened the message and gasped.

Hi Ella, It's me, Roly! Roly Punch, remember? Sketcher of ox-bow lakes? French conversationalist extraordinaire? Sorry for the bait and switch. You were probably expecting a message from Charmander, so hope you're not too disappointed. Anyway, how are you? I was wondering if you'd like to meet up. I'd love to see you. It's been so long. I promise not to be a knob this time, but cool if you'd rather not. R x

Roly Punch! That was a name she hadn't heard in a very long time; a person she hadn't thought about much if she could avoid it. She smiled, the thought of him bringing up warm, fond feelings, though still tinged with guilt even at this distance of years.

The few times he'd come to her attention in the last few years, it was usually some mean article in the paper about his solo career floundering or a grossly unflattering photo snapped by paparazzi when he was out and about. The story was always about how much weight he'd put on, how bad his solo album had been, how well Oh Boy! had done without him. She felt so sad for him, for all he'd lost — and she hated knowing she'd played a part in his downfall.

Still, she told herself it could have been so much worse. He'd lost money, fame, friends, his career. But he was still alive. He hadn't lost his life. And she consoled herself that maybe she'd had a hand in that too.

She sank back against the pillows, rereading his message. What would it be like to see him again? They'd had a strange, episodic friendship over the years, and every time she saw him, she thought it would be the last. But he'd pop up in her life again when she least expected it, and they'd take up where they left off.

She remembered the first time he'd spoken to her during morning break in their final term of school, the summer sun streaming in through the windows of the classroom. She'd had her head buried in a book, and he'd asked her what she was reading. It felt like an anointing because if Roly showed an interest in you, other people started to sit up and take notice. He was the most popular student in their year – even with the teachers, which really pissed off some of the nerdy kids who were cleverer than him and way more eager to please. They didn't get why Roly was so liked – because he was funny and friendly and kind, but most of all because he was genuinely interested in other people.

Ella had never been one of his inner circle, but he wasn't elitist, and eventually he befriended pretty much everyone. Unfortunately for Ella, there were a lot of people to get around, and her turn didn't come until the last term of their final year, so she didn't benefit from it for long. She sometimes wondered what might have happened if the consecration had happened earlier. How might her life have been different? If they'd been closer, maybe she'd have gone on the Leaving Cert holiday to Magaluf with his crowd instead of interrailing across Europe with Julie. If she hadn't been in Italy at the precise time she was, maybe she would have avoided that opportunistic virus that had put her life in a choke-hold for the past ten years.

As it was, school finished a few weeks later and they all went their separate ways. She thought she'd seen the last of Roly. Then somehow they'd ended up together after the Debs. She'd spent the official last hours of her school days sitting across from Roly Punch at a little table in a greasy spoon cafe, eating breakfast the morning after the dance.

It wasn't a story she could tell anyone now. No one would appreciate what it meant, or understand how strange and wonderful it was. They'd assume it was noteworthy because Roly had become a member of the biggest boy band of their generation – because he was Roly Punch from Oh Boy! They wouldn't get that it was because he was lovely, friendly Roly, the most popular boy in school, the one all the girls wanted to be with and all the boys wanted to be around. And because she was who she was, and they weren't a pair, and he was out of her league. And yet, despite all that, she was the one who got to spend those last moments of their schooldays with him. She was still ridiculously pleased by that.

CLOSING TIME

AFTER LEAVING the hotel at two am, a gang of them had gone to an after-party at an apartment owned by somebody's boyfriend. The Debs was their last hurrah, the severing of the very last connection they all had, and the atmosphere had been equal measures of maudlin and exuberant. They were high on life and cocaine, drunk on cheap alcohol and the endless possibilities that seemed to stretch out before them. The Debs happened in September, so they'd already taken their first tentative steps into their new lives. But until tonight there was still this one last tie linking them together, a rite of passage marked, as tradition dictated, by a bland dinner in a nondescript city centre hotel, and dancing until the small hours in a glorious blur of silk, sweat and sobbing.

As dawn broke, Ella found herself slumped on a sofa in front of a big window overlooking the glittering water of Grand Canal Dock. On the floor at her feet, a couple lay passed out on top of each other, while beside her, a guy was asleep on his back, snoring loudly. A girl she vaguely recognised was slumped in an armchair, drooling onto her lilac silk dress as she dozed. The room was littered with empty bottles and half-drained glasses. She'd nodded off, and most people seemed to have left while she'd been asleep.

She felt drunk and woozy, too tired to move. She just wanted to curl up on the sofa and sleep, but she knew she'd regret it later, so she heaved herself up with a groan, her head spinning as she stood. She wasn't so out of it that she didn't worry about the guy sleeping on his back beside her, and with an enormous effort, she managed to manoeuvre him onto his side. She checked the other sleeping bodies, but none of them seemed in danger of choking on their vomit. She grabbed her bag from beside the sofa and pulled out her phone to call a taxi. Her heart sank as she saw it was out of charge.

Damn! If only she hadn't spent half the night posting crap about the Debs on social media, wasting battery life on all those photos that she already knew would only be fit to delete. Still, she could always walk home. It might do her good, help stave off the hangover she could already feel building behind her eyes. But even as she thought it, she moved around the room searching for a socket to plug in her phone.

'We're the last men standing.' She was crouched down, plugging her mobile into a socket behind a side-table when she heard the voice behind her.

She straightened up and turned around. Roly Punch stood there, looking sleepy, dishevelled and very much the worse for wear, but still magazine-ad gorgeous. In his beautifully tailored tux, bow tie hanging loose around his neck, his snowy white shirt crumpled and his messy hair artfully tousled, he could have been the poster boy for a designer men's cologne. Debauchery by Calvin Klein.

'Where's Sarah?'

He shrugged, his beautiful mouth twitching in a crooked smile. 'I lost track of her somewhere along the way. Last I saw she was shifting Mr Hogan.'

'The maths teacher?' Ella gasped.

'Yeah, that Mr Hogan.'

'Wow!'

'She's been after him all year and this was her last chance to get with him, so fair play to her. Though I'm surprised she still went for it after witnessing his dad-dancing tonight.'

'You don't seem very cut up about it.'

'We weren't really serious. And it's all coming to an end anyway, isn't it? She just got in first. I don't mind. Makes it easier for her.'

'Easier for you too.'

He smiled. 'Yeah. Where's your … friend?' He gave a little smirk.

Ella and Julie had pulled the classic nerdy-girl move of going to the Debs together, without dates.

'She left earlier.' Ella wasn't sure why she hadn't gone with her, what had made her stay on. Had she been hoping to establish some lasting connection at the eleventh hour? Or was she just clinging on to this world for as long as she could, reluctant to let go of the last thing separating her from fully-fledged adulthood?

'So…' Roly ran a hand through his hair. 'Are you getting a taxi?'

'Yeah. I just have to wait for some charge on my phone.' She pointed to it.

'We could get one together?' He pulled his mobile from his pocket and looked at her questioningly.

'Thanks, that'd be great.' She bent to unplug her phone.

'Want to go and get some breakfast?' he asked her when she stood back up.

'I doubt there's anywhere open yet.' She looked to the window where grey clouds hung low over the water, the sky shot through with rays of pale light.

'I know a place near here.'

'In that case, yes. I'm starving.'

She grabbed her coat and they let themselves out of the apartment.

'You've got something on the back of your dress,' Roly said as she walked down the stairs ahead of him.

She twisted around to look. There was a dirty black stain right on her bum. 'Ah, a casualty of "Rock the Boat",' she said, smiling ruefully as she brushed at it. Julie had wanted to stand apart from it all, literally looking down on their fellow classmates as they got down and dirty on the dance floor. But Ella had thought, *Fuck that!* Once she'd decided to go to the Debs, she'd committed one hundred per cent to the experience, and she wanted to do it all.

'Come on,' she'd said to Julie, 'We've come to the Debs, so let's *be at the fucking Debs!*' So she'd joined the squealing throng rushing to drop to the floor as the iconic song began, throwing herself into the corny dance routine wholeheartedly, while Julie remained resolutely on the sidelines, a sardonic twist to her lips as she watched.

Commuters were starting to make their way to work, and Ella and Roly got curious looks and indulgent smiles from passers-by as they walked along by the canal. Ella thought what a romantic figure they must cut in their crumpled morning-after finery. Everyone would assume they were a couple who'd partied the night away together. The idea pleased her more than it should.

Roly led the way to a greasy spoon and they dissected

the Debs over vast fried breakfasts and copious mugs of coffee.

'So, good night?' Roly asked.

She shrugged. 'Schmeh.'

'Schmeh?' He laughed. 'So eloquent. I can see why you got top marks in English.'

'How about you?'

'Brilliant night,' he said happily. 'Deadly.'

'Seriously?'

'Had a good feed, got rat-arsed, swore undying love to some randomers I'll never see again ... what more could you ask?'

'Good feed?' She gave him a sceptical look.

'What, watery veg soup and chicken à la sawdust didn't do it for you? You must be one of those food snobs I've heard about.'

'You didn't mention the dessert. What even was that?'

'Custardy ... thing.'

'Yeah, I got the custard bit. But as for the rest—'

'Yeah, I've no idea what they were aiming for there.'

Ella laughed. 'I'm surprised you came back for the Debs, to be honest.' Roly had moved to London straight after school to play some gigs with Oh Boy!

'Wouldn't have missed it for the world.'

'Are you home for long?'

He shook his head. 'I'm going back to London tomorrow. We're starting recording our first album next week.'

'That's exciting!'

'Yeah, it is. Are you not eating that sausage?' He pointed a knife at her plate.

'No, I'm stuffed. It's all yours.'

He leaned over and pronged it with his fork. So what's next for you?'

'College. I'm starting at Trinity next week.'

'I suppose you got amazing results in the Leaving?'

'I did pretty well.' She'd achieved the highest possible marks, but she decided not to mention that. 'I got the points I needed for my first choice at uni anyway.'

'Congratulations!'

'Thanks.'

'And what is it you'll be studying?'

'PPES. It's a multidisciplinary course – Philosophy, Political Science, Economics and Sociology.'

'Gosh, that sounds like … a lot.'

'Did you…' She felt it was only polite to ask him about his results in return, but what if he'd done really badly? She didn't want to embarrass him. 'Did you … get what you wanted?'

'Yeah. I passed, which is all I needed to do. I'm not planning to go to uni or anything. I only stayed on for the Leaving because my mum made me, so I'd have options – you know, in case my pop career goes tits up.'

'That's sensible.'

'Yeah, so if you ever need someone to sketch you an ox-bow lake, I'm your man,' he said, pointing his fork at himself.

Ella laughed. 'I believe people who can sketch ox-bow lakes will be in big demand in the future. And you could branch out into other things – volcanoes, for instance.'

'My volcanoes are top notch! And I know an interlocking spur when I see one. So whatever happens with the band, I'm sorted.' He leaned back, grinning. 'Win, lose or draw.'

It would always be win for the likes of Roly, she thought. She was glad. Happy for him.

'Do you still feel drunk?'

She shook her head to test it. It didn't hurt. 'No. I think breakfast took care of that. Do you?'

'No. Just tired.'

'Yeah.' She yawned. 'Me too.'

'I guess we should go.'

She nodded. I'll get this if you get the taxi.'

'You don't have a corsage,' Roly said when they were in the taxi, his eyes flicking to her wrist.

'Drawback of going with a girlfriend,' she said with a crooked smile.

'Aww. Have mine.' He took the flower from his buttonhole and held it out to her.

'Thanks.' She took it from him and smiled, looking down at it in her hands, touched by the sweetness of the gesture.

They fell silent, both lost in their own thoughts.

'It's exciting, isn't it?' Roly said, when they were near her house. 'Going out into the big, bad world?' He widened his eyes.

'Yeah.'

'But a bit scary too.'

'Yeah, it is.' It was what she was feeling, but she was glad he'd had the guts to say it out loud.

'Ah, you have nothing to worry about, my brainiac friend,' he said, putting an arm around her shoulder and pulling her into a hug. He pressed a kiss to her forehead. 'You'll be fine.'

The taxi pulled up outside her house, and that was it. That was her moment with Roly Punch. 'Thanks for the lift,' she said, turning to him as she unfastened her seat belt.

'Thank you for breakfast.'

Suddenly emboldened, she leaned over and kissed his

cheek. 'Well, good luck with everything. Have a great … life.'

'Thanks. You too.'

'Bye, Roly.' She opened the door.

'See you!' he said as she got out.

See you. It was just something people said. She knew she wouldn't see him again. She stood on the pavement as the taxi pulled away, and watched as it carried him out of her life. When it got to the corner, she waved, but Roly was looking ahead and didn't see. The taxi disappeared out of sight, and she turned and went into the house.

8

Roly spotted Ella the moment he walked into the coffee shop. She looked up as the bell over the door tinkled, and waved him over. He kept his head down as he made a beeline for her, his eyes swivelling right and left, automatically scanning the place. It was a habit, a hangover from the days when he was super-famous, though back then he was secretly hoping to get noticed. He'd loved being recognised in public, and had lapped up the attention. Being famous for crashing and burning was a different matter. But there were only a handful of customers, and no one paid any attention to him as he made his way to Ella's table.

There was an awkward moment when she stood just as he bent to kiss her, and their faces crashed together clumsily.

'Sorry,' she said as they laughed and hugged. 'I'm out of practice at this whole being a person in the world thing.'

He took a seat opposite her. 'Sorry, am I late?' She had a coffee in front of her, already half empty.

'No, I was early.'

The waitress came over and barely glanced at him as she took their order, and Roly felt an irrational surge of irritation. Didn't she know who he was? Didn't anyone remember? How long had it been since he'd been approached by a stranger in the street? A few times lately he'd even had 'before my time' said to him when he mentioned Oh Boy! It was probably only a matter of time until he'd be getting 'my mum used to love you'.

'Wow, this is weird.' He still couldn't believe he was sitting here across from Ella after all these years. She hadn't changed much. Her dark hair was still cut short, and she had the same big, clear eyes that could see right through you. She'd put on a bit of weight, though, same as him. Her face was plumper, more rounded, the bones of her jaw softer and less defined. He felt bad for finding that cheering. But Ella had always been so clever, so in control of her shit, that he'd felt like an also-ran next to her. He'd been nervous about meeting her today, in the shape he was in. This seemed to even things out a bit between them, and it was a relief.

'Weird?' She smirked.

'I mean, it's amazing to see you. It's been...'

'Almost ten years.' She took a sip of coffee. 'I worked it out after we messaged.'

'Wow, that long?'

She nodded. 'It was a real surprise to hear from you. I thought I'd seen the last of you.'

'Hoped, you mean?' Roly quirked an eyebrow, giving her a crooked smile. He'd been such a dick to her the last time they'd met. The shame of it broke over him like a wave.

'No.' She frowned. 'Why would you say that?'

They were interrupted by the waitress returning with a frothy cappuccino for Roly, and another Americano for

Ella. Roly smiled – in all things she was still so much more grown-up than him.

'It was Christmas, right?' he said after the waitress had gone. 'At that pretentious bar on the Quays. I can't remember what it was called…'

'Fifth & Liquor?'

'Oh yeah!' He laughed. 'You were wearing a silver dress. I had a terrible beard and wore the apparel of a hobo who'd fallen on hard times.'

'Apparel!' She laughed. 'Where do you get this stuff?'

'It's a real word. Look it up.'

She frowned, looking confused. 'That wasn't the last time we saw each other, though.'

'It wasn't?'

'There was that party at Marty's, remember? Just before…'

His stomach plummeted. 'Before the American tour.' Did he remember? How could he forget? That party … the American tour he hadn't gone on. 'You were there?' He didn't recall her having been. But then, a lot of that night was a blank. 'Did I see you?'

'You don't remember?'

'Sorry. I was pretty out of it that night.' That was an understatement.

'We … I said hi, but we didn't really talk.'

'That was the night…' He shook his head. He didn't want to dwell on that. 'Anyway, how have you been?'

She shrugged. 'Not great. I wasn't well for a long time.'

He listened as she filled him in on her illness, how she'd spent most of the last ten years at home living in a kind of limbo, all her plans for college and career shelved, her dreams put on hold. It sounded horribly familiar.

'So you've been out of action pretty much as long as I have,' he said. 'But you're better now?' She looked well, but he detected a lingering weariness in her pale face, tell-tale dark smudges under her eyes.

'I'm getting there. I've been gradually improving over the last couple of years. It's been a slow process, but I'm getting my energy back, and I'm able to do more. I just started a new job last week.'

'Good for you! I suppose you're a professor or something by now?'

'Hardly.' She raised the steaming mug to her mouth and blew on it before taking a sip. 'You don't make professor stuck at home in bed. I didn't even get to start my PhD in the end.'

'Sorry.' He gave her a sympathetic smile. 'That sucks.'

'Yeah, it does.'

'Are you still living with your mum?'

'Yeah. I was on benefits, and doing bits and pieces of freelance work when I could. But I racked up a lot of debt, so I can't afford rent at the moment.' She shrugged. 'It's fine, though. We get on really well and she's been great about getting lumbered with a grown-ass daughter still at home.'

'I'm sure she doesn't mind.'

'No, but *I* mind. She never makes me feel like I'm a burden or anything. But I hate that she's missed out on so much because of me. She and my Aunt Nora—'

'She's the one with the pen? Of *la plume de ma tante* fame?'

'Yes! The very one.' She laughed. 'Anyway, she and Mum always planned to go on this big trip when Mum retired. But then I was sick, and even now that I'm better, they're still putting it off because they don't want to leave me on my own. It's not just the physical stuff. They worry about me … being lonely, I guess.'

Roly nodded understandingly. It did sound like she'd been pretty isolated.

'And I would be.' He was taken aback by her honesty in admitting it. He was lonely too sometimes, but he felt he had to hide it like a shameful secret.

'So what's your new job?'

'I'm doing general office admin and marketing in a techwear company. It's just a stop-gap, but it pays the bills and it gets me out of the house.'

'Techwear? Is that, like, anoraks and stuff?'

'Kind of – functional clothing for people who do extreme sports. But cool anoraks, not what your dad would wear for a day down the allotment.'

'Do you like it?'

'Yeah, I do. It's surprisingly interesting. I'm enjoying it much more than I thought I would.' She smiled. 'I thought I'd blown the interview. It was like one of those daft Facebook quizzes – you know, if you were an animal, what would you be kind of thing?'

'Chimpanzee!' Roly said, pointing at her.

'Gee, thanks.' She laughed. 'Hairy and annoying?'

'No, but they're one of the smartest animals on the planet, aren't they? Do me!'

'Hmmm.' She narrowed her eyes. 'I guess you'd be … a dolphin.'

'Chatty and good at swimming? Nose like a bottle?'

She shook her head. 'Because they're friendly and people feel good being around them.'

'Awww.' Roly couldn't help grinning. He realised he felt happier than he'd been in a long time, just sitting here having coffee with Ella. He'd forgotten how much he liked her, how easily they'd always fallen into sync with each other, even after long gaps apart. 'I'm sorry I lost touch,' he said tentatively.

She shrugged. 'It was as much my fault as yours.' She looked uncomfortable, and he got the impression she really believed that and wasn't just saying it to be nice and let him off the hook. 'Anyway,' she continued, 'I kind of dropped off the radar with most people when I was sick.'

'That's crap.'

'It was kind of inevitable. I don't blame anyone. My friends were all travelling, getting married, starting their careers … taking the world by storm,' she said, nodding to him. 'And I was stuck at home in my bedroom, watching TV. They had their own lives to lead, and I just couldn't keep up.'

'So you got left behind.' He knew what that felt like.

'We had nothing in common anymore. Even when I did see them, we had very little to talk about. They had news. I never had any news.' She looked down at her mug broodingly. 'But it didn't all suck,' she said, brightening. 'I mean, I got to watch a lot of Netflix. And I was on top of every Twitter ruck going.'

Roly laughed, but he could sense the sadness behind her bravado, the effort she made not to wallow in self-pity, and he felt guilty all over again for being one of the friends who'd left her behind.

'Hazel, my best friend from college, stuck around, though. We're still friends.'

'Still – it sounds lonely.'

'It was. Thank goodness for the internet.'

'Hah!' He gave a harsh laugh. 'I can't say the same thing. Anyway, you're up and about now. And I'm not taking the world by storm anymore, so…'

'No more excuses?'

'Right. Let's not lose touch again.'

'Deal.' She smiled. 'I could use a friend.'

'Me too,' he said simply, and it felt good being able to admit it.

'So, what have you been up to?'

'Oh, you know – broke, unemployed … spent most of the last few years stuck at home eating biscuits and feeling sorry for myself. So yeah – riding high.'

'Oh, sorry. You're not really broke, though, surely?'

'I wish! But I really am.'

'Oh?' She frowned. 'How come? Surely being in Oh Boy! should have set you up for the rest of your life?'

'That's what I thought until a couple of weeks ago. But it turned out my accountant was ripping me off. All my money's gone.'

'Your accountant? You mean Marty?'

'Yeah.' He'd forgotten she knew Marty. But it stood to reason. He'd always been around. He'd been like family … so Roly had thought. Of course she'd have met him.

'Shit! Can't you sue him? Try to get it back?'

He shook his head. 'No. He died, and he blew it all before he shuffled off this mortal whatsit. So … that's that.'

'Oh, I'm sorry. That's horrible.' She reached out and put a hand over his, and he felt a rush of affection and gratitude. He realised he'd been bracing himself for a different reaction, half expecting her to get on her high horse and tell him off for not realising how privileged he was to have that kind of money to lose. He was used to any bad luck that came his way being met with schadenfreude and barely concealed glee, so her sympathy took him by surprise. He knew he didn't deserve it. He'd lucked into a fortune and lost it all again through his own stupidity. He had no one but himself to blame. But that just made Ella's genuine sympathy all the more comforting. He was glad he'd decided to look her up again. Even though they'd seen so little of each other over the years, she was a real friend, someone he could count on to be on his side. It was weird, but he immediately felt close to her every time he saw her.

'Yeah, it's shit.'

'I can't believe Marty of all people was stealing from you. That's awful.'

'Yeah, that's kind of the worst thing. I thought he was a friend, you know? I really trusted him.'

She nodded. 'I know. I mean, I can't say I was his biggest fan, but—'

'Yeah, I know I was a chump to trust him with my money.' Of course Ella would have known. She'd have seen right through Marty with those big clear eyes. 'But it wasn't just me. He ripped off loads of people.'

'That's not what I meant. You had every reason to trust him. You hear about that sort of thing happening all the time – stars being swindled by managers and agents. I'm not saying I'd have been suspicious of him or anything. I didn't like him very much, but I thought he was on your side … at least when it came to your finances.'

'What else?' He frowned. 'I mean, he was an accountant. It's not as if he was involved in the artistic stuff – if you want to call it that,' he added with a self-deprecating laugh, feeling arsey for talking about Oh Boy! in those terms. 'He had nothing to do with decisions about the music or the shows.'

'No, but … your welfare. I didn't feel he took care of you like he should have done.'

Roly sighed and concentrated on rubbing a circle on the wood of the table with his thumb. 'Maybe he tried. But you know, I wasn't very open to getting help at that stage.'

'I guess.' She bit her lip, looking troubled.

'Anyway, it wasn't his job to look after me. I was a grown-up. I should have been able to take care of myself.

Ella looked like she wanted to argue, but said nothing.

Roly looked around the cafe. It had been filling up as they'd talked. Glancing at the clock on the wall, he saw it was almost one. He'd arranged to meet Ella for coffee at eleven so that if it was awkward, he could cut and run quickly. But he hadn't even noticed the time passing, and it was as if it was only yesterday they'd last spoken to each other. Now he didn't want it to end. He felt like he always had when he was saying goodbye to her, just wanting to prolong the brief snatches of time they had together.

'Another?' he asked, pointing at her mug.

'I'd better not. If I drink any more coffee, I'll get the jitters.'

'Do you want to get some lunch?'

'Yes, I'm starving!'

'My treat,' he said quickly, remembering what she'd said about being skint.

'Thanks, but I'm sure I can afford a sandwich … if you can. I mean, it sounds like we're both kind of in the same boat money-wise.'

'Oh, yeah.' He kept forgetting he was poor now. That would take some getting used to. No more playing the big shot for him – not that springing for lunch was being a big shot. Or maybe it was now? That was a depressing thought.

'We could stay here, or … there's a great pizza place across the road. Best in Dublin for my money – and they've had a *lot* of my money. It's takeaway only, but I live near here, so we could go back to my place?' He felt reckless asking her back to his, considering how he'd left the place – the dirty mugs strewn around, the takeaway cartons, the piles of plates and papers that littered every surface. He'd decided to meet Ella here because he'd rather risk sitting somewhere public with her than spend hours trying to make the house presentable. But now he thought: Fuck it! Ella wouldn't care.

Her face lit up. 'That'd be brilliant!'

'Just to warn you, though, it's a bit of a shithole.'

She shrugged. 'I'll take my chances.'

9

It was a mild March day and the street was busy with Saturday shoppers as they stepped out into the sunshine. They bought huge pizza slices from the takeaway counter across the road and walked back to Roly's house in nearby Portobello. Delicious smells of hot dough and herby tomato sauce wafted up from the warm cardboard boxes they carried, and Ella couldn't stop smiling. It had been so long since she'd spent a freewheeling weekend morning with a friend, drifting from coffee to lunch to wherever the mood took them. It was the ordinary, everyday life that had been out of her reach all those years, and she was fizzing with excitement to be part of it again … which was pathetic. No, fuck it. It *was* exciting, and she wasn't going to let herself feel ashamed about that. She was allowed to enjoy it.

It was a short walk to Roly's house in a quiet street of terraced red-brick houses.

'It doesn't look like a shithole,' Ella said, looking around as Roly fumbled in his pocket for his key, while balancing the pizza box in his other hand. There was a small pebbled garden to one side, and a prettily tiled path led to the navy-blue door.

'It's not a shithole in itself. It's more what I've done with the place.'

'Oh.' She smiled. 'Slob?'

'Yeah. You've been warned.' He pushed open the door and nodded to her to go ahead of him.

'Oh, I see what you mean.' She followed Roly into a large airy living room with a Victorian cast-iron fireplace and large sash bay windows. Ella looked around, admiring the high ceilings and original features. It was a beautiful room, but every surface was buried under piles of clutter, and the floor was littered with takeaway boxes and empty bottles. There were used plates and mugs mouldering on the coffee table and random items of clothing strewn across the furniture. It could be mistaken for the aftermath of a wild weekend, but Ella recognised the signs of depression and inertia in the mess. She'd let her room get like this sometimes when she was going through a particularly low phase and even throwing a pizza box in the trash was too much effort.

'I did warn you.'

She shrugged. 'It's lovely. It just needs some tidying up. I love these old Victorian houses.'

'Well, have a seat.' He waved her to the pale-blue sofa facing the window. Only one side was clear – obviously where Roly usually sat – and she folded herself onto it.

He cleared a space on the coffee table for the pizza boxes. 'Drink? he asked, rubbing his hands. 'Tea? Fizzy water? I don't have anything stronger, I'm afraid.'

'That's fine. Drinking in the middle of the day doesn't agree with me anyway.'

'I'd offer you a Coke or something, but I kind of threw out all my food yesterday.'

'Oh. That was a bold move.'

'Yeah, I want to lose this.' He patted his belly. 'So I'm turning over a new leaf – after this, obviously.' He nodded to the pizza.

'Yeah, me too. I've put on so much weight since I've been ill. I'll have fizzy water, please.'

When he went to get the drinks, Ella got up and explored the room. Everything about the place interested her. It had been so long since she'd been let into someone else's home like this … it was like getting a peek into someone's life. She studied the shelves, looking at Roly's things as if they might give her some insight into who he was now – the abstract painting above the fireplace, the blue and white kilim rug in front of the sofa, the rows of games and DVDs. It was weird to think of Roly as someone who owned rugs and lamps. She couldn't imagine him buying them, picking out sofa cushions, choosing window blinds, deciding what shade to stain the polished wooden floorboards and what colour to paint the walls. It seemed so grown-up, and made him feel more distant from her now, someone she no longer knew.

He came back with drinks and napkins, then cleared a space on the sofa and sat beside her.

'I can't believe you're here,' Roly said as they ate. It's really great to see you.'

'You too.' She smiled at him – her periodic Huckleberry friend. She'd missed him, she thought, with a sudden rush of longing, as if she wasn't right here with him. Maybe she was pining for all the years she'd lost with him. She took a sip of water. 'It's been such a long time…'

He gave a sad smile. 'Yeah, well, I wouldn't blame you if you never wanted to see me again after how I was the last time we met.'

She frowned. He was still talking about that night

before Christmas in Fifth & Liquor, and thought she'd been the one to let their friendship fizzle out. There was some truth in it in a way. He'd always been the one to initiate their meet-ups, and it had taken her by surprise every time he'd got in touch again. But she could have reached out to him if she'd wanted to. If she was honest with herself, she'd been relieved when she hadn't heard from him again after that night at Marty's. She couldn't have been around him after that, couldn't have continued to be his friend, without telling him what she'd done – and she didn't see herself ever having the courage to do that. Even if she had, it would likely have been the end of their friendship anyway. So it was easier not to see him again and content herself with the fact that she'd done the right thing – letting him go had been a necessary part of that.

'It was nothing to do with you or how you were that night. I think we both just drifted apart. I mean, I never heard from you either. You were busy with the band, and then rehab … I got sick.'

'You mean you would have forgiven me? For how I was that time?'

'Of course. There's nothing to forgive. I knew it wasn't really you.' But would *he* have forgiven *her*? She didn't dare ask. 'You were off your head.'

'I wish I'd called you afterwards … apologised. I almost did a couple of times, but I lost my nerve.'

'Anyway, I *did* see you again after that night at Fifth & Liquor. I told you I was at that party in Marty's house, after the concert in Croke Park.'

'Oh, yeah.' He frowned. 'I forgot.'

She wished she hadn't mentioned it. Something happened to his face when he was reminded of that night that she didn't like, and she felt a stab of guilt. It had all fallen apart for him after that party. Because she'd thrown him under the bus … or pushed him out of its path. Sometimes she still wasn't sure which.

In fact, the very last time she'd seen Roly, he hadn't been obnoxious at all – just sad and pathetic. Her mind shied away as it always did from the image of him hunched in a corner of Marty's guest bathroom chopping out lines, a half-empty bottle of vodka beside him. He'd looked so lost – gaunt, pale and dead-eyed, staring at her unseeingly when she came into the room. She'd been so scared and sad for him. When she forced her mind back to that night, she knew she'd done the right thing. He'd been drowning and she'd thrown him a life-belt. Anyone who loved him would have done the same.

'Do you still see any of the guys from the band?'

'Yeah, I see Charlie occasionally since he's moved back to Dublin. The rest of us sort of drifted apart. The band was all we had in common, really. Once that was gone…' He shrugged.

'But you were so close. You'd been through such intense experiences together.'

'I know – like people who survived the Titanic or something. There were things we could only really talk about with each other – things only the five of us understood. We were the only ones who knew what it was like being in Oh Boy! I thought we'd be friends for ever.'

'Do you miss it? The band?'

'Only every other minute of the day.'

She gave him a sympathetic smile. 'Yeah, I know what that's like.'

'But I plan to get it back – all of it.'

'Well, you've made a good start.'

He frowned, confused. 'You think?' he asked sardonically.

'You did rehab. You've got clean and sober.'

He gave a dismissive shrug. 'Oh, that.'

'That's a big deal, Roly. You should give yourself credit.'

'I suppose. But in case you haven't noticed, I'm not exactly living my best life, am I?'

'What does your best life look like, then?'

'Pretty much what it was when we met that night at Fifth & Liquor – only without the drugs, obviously. And the dickish attitude.'

'Take away the drugs and the dickishness, and what's left?'

He laughed. 'Just money, fame, success. Plus I was really fit when I was in the band.'

'No you weren't. You were just skinny.'

'Skinny, then. And I was with Pippa. We were all loved up. How about you? What's your best life?'

'Same, actually.'

'You were in love with Pippa too?'

She laughed. 'No, but how things were when we met that night – I was at Trinity, I was in love…' Just talking about it, she could feel the excitement of it again, smell the earthy tang of the air, feel the warm surprise of Andrew's lips on hers, see the fog of their breath mingling in the chill autumn air, the memories all wrapped up in the golds and rusts of fallen leaves. 'I'd just moved in with my boyfriend.'

'Oh yeah, I remember you telling me about him.'

'Really?' He'd hardly listened to her that night. She'd be surprised if he remembered a word she'd said.

'What was his name again?'

'Andrew.'

He nodded as if he'd heard it before, but she could tell it was new to him. 'What was he? A philosopher or something?'

'Yeah.' Maybe he'd listened more than she gave him

credit for. 'He was on the same course as me, but he went on to specialise in Philosophy. He's a lecturer now in Trinity.'

'So you keep in touch?'

She shook her head. 'No, I just … heard on the grapevine.'

'Stalked him on Instagram, you mean?'

'No! I'll have you know I've done no such thing.'

Roly smiled. 'He doesn't do Instagram, does he?'

'No,' she admitted sheepishly. 'Facebook, though … that's a different matter.'

Roly looked at her thoughtfully. 'You look really happy when you talk about him. Your face sort of … lights up.'

She sighed. 'It was the happiest time of my life. But it wasn't just about him. Everything was so new and exciting … college, discovering new ideas, making friends, falling in love. It felt like the world was opening up for me, like my life was really beginning.' She remembered the day it started, when she'd seen Andrew on his way to the library, and he'd stopped and waited for her to catch up so he could talk to her. She could still feel the breathless sting of frosty air and the fluttering in her stomach. The whole world had seemed box fresh and hers for the taking.

'So you split up?'

She nodded. 'After I got sick. He tried for a while – he wasn't an asshole. But it was too much, in the end, my illness. Everything was about me, my issues, and it wasn't fair to him. We were young. He had a life to live and, unlike me, he could live it. So we broke up.'

'Sounds like an asshole to me.'

'He really wasn't.' Selfish, maybe, but who wasn't? She'd worked hard at not resenting him and she didn't want to start now. 'What about Pippa?'

'Yeah, Pippa was an asshole.'

Ella laughed. She'd only met Roly's girlfriend once, but she hadn't taken to her.

'But so was I, so I guess we were well matched.'

'So how come you split up?'

Roly shrugged. 'I went into rehab. We drifted apart.'

'Oh.'

'And she went onto *Celebrity Cell Block* and shagged Adam Leader.'

'Ah. That'd do it all right.' The Leaders were an Irish family pop rock band, and Adam was the frontman.

'Every time. Can't blame her really. Adam still had it all going on.'

Ella's initial dislike of Pippa was solidifying by the second.

'Do you plan to go back to college, now that you're better?'

'Hopefully … eventually. But it'll have to wait. I need to pay off my debts and save up a bit first.'

Roly sighed. 'Yeah, me too – as it turns out.' He raked a hand through his hair. 'I mean, I'm not in debt – I don't think.' He frowned and blanched as if the thought had just occurred to him. 'But I've been worried about money for the first time in my life. It's made me realise what it must have been like for Mum all those years.'

Ella only vaguely remembered Roly's mum from the odd school concert or sports day. But she knew she was a single mother and she'd raised Roly alone.

'At least you've got this place.'

'Yeah, but maybe not for much longer. I might have to sell.'

'Oh, that would be awful. Isn't there anything else you could do?'

'My mum suggested getting a lodger. I'm considering it. But it'd be kind of humiliating, you know – being me.'

'The great Roly Punch reduced to house-sharing!'

'Shut up!' He laughed. 'You know what I mean. I'd probably get some knob who thought he was cooler than me just by virtue of never having been in Oh Boy! Or a crazed fan who'd follow me around all the time taking sneaky photos and plastering stuff about me all over social media.'

'Yeah, those are probably the options all right.'

'I may not have a choice. But I really don't fancy living with a stranger.'

'I know what you mean.' She knew that even when she could afford to move out of her mum's, she wouldn't be able to rent on her own. But she couldn't face the idea of house-sharing, and was secretly relieved she didn't have to yet. She didn't have the energy for making herself appealing to potential housemates.

'Are you planning to move out of your mum's?'

'Not for a while yet. Rents are crazy.'

'But you'd like to?'

'If I could afford it, yeah.'

'How would you feel about moving in with me?'

Ella laughed. 'This is so sudden! Do you usually ask girls to move in with you after one coffee and a pizza slice?'

He grinned. 'You have to move fast when you've fallen behind like we have. I mean, I should be on my second marriage by now.'

'That's true. We're way behind.'

'I'd have to charge you rent—'

'Of course. I wouldn't expect to live anywhere for free.'

'But I could give you mate rates.'

'I wouldn't want to take advantage, though. You could get someone who'd pay proper rent.'

'I'd rather not take my chances with a stranger. Seriously, you'd be doing me a favour. I don't need much coming in – just enough to stave off the panic attacks until I figure something else out.'

'Well, I *could* promise not to follow you around fangirling over you.'

'Does that mean you're considering it?'

'I don't know…' She was touched by the offer, but did he really mean it? And would it be a good idea? She looked around the living room, trying to envision herself living here.

'I'd clean the place up,' he said quickly. 'And there's plenty of space.'

It could be the perfect solution. She could move out, and her mum and Nora could go on their trip without worrying about her being alone. A slow smile spread across her face. 'Roly, is this a genuine offer? Because I have to warn you, I'm tempted to take you up on it.'

'Of course it's genuine. It'd be great, the two of us living together. We're kind of both on the same page – trying to get back on our feet, get fit. We could do it together.'

Ella was starting to get excited about the idea. She loved a project, and she was already envisioning Kanban boards and goal-setting sessions. 'It would be good to have an accountability partner. We could do our own personal boot camp.'

He nodded. 'We can cook healthy food and work out together. We could start running!'

'Or not. Suddenly I'm less tempted.'

He grinned. 'Okay, we don't have to go running. Why don't I show you around, and you can have a think about it?'

• • •

Ella loved the house, and was already picturing herself having coffee in the little terrace garden – 'it's a total sun trap in summer,' Roly told her – or snuggled up in the big armchair in front of a real fire on a cold winter day.

It was only when Roly was showing her the bathroom and they were both standing in the small space that she began to have doubts. They hardly knew each other really. Would it be awkward sharing a bathroom? It seemed scarily intimate.

'And this would be your room,' he said finally, leading her into a large airy room with a double bed and lots of wardrobe and drawer space. Like the rest of the house, it was crammed with junk, the bed buried under a jumble of clothes. 'Obviously I'd clear it out. And there's an en suite through there.' He pointed to a door, and Ella immediately felt better about the whole thing as she stepped through into a small bathroom. This might be doable after all.

'So, what do you think?' Roly asked as they walked back downstairs.

Ella grinned. 'I think you've got yourself a lodger.'

THESE ARE DAYS

Ella had been surprised and, though she'd barely admit it to herself, hugely flattered, when Roly stayed in touch with her after they'd left school and he'd moved to London with the band. He messaged her occasionally with updates about his exciting new life when Oh Boy! were recording their first album and they'd all moved into a vast warehouse apartment in Shoreditch paid for by the record company. She sometimes wished she had something more interesting to tell him in return. She'd started college and she was enjoying her studies and the new friends she was making. But her life largely went on much the same, and compared to Roly's it seemed dull and uneventful. He was busy touring the world, playing giant stadiums and appearing on TV, while she was writing essays, studying for exams and working part-time as a waitress in a small cafe to supplement her grant.

As time went on and the band became bigger, his communications became increasingly sporadic. It was sad, but inevitable, she thought, that they'd eventually drop off completely. Their lives were so different, they had nothing in common now — and they'd had little enough to begin with. It still sometimes puzzled her how they'd become friends in the first place. But always just as she gave up and decided she'd heard the last from him, a message would appear out of the blue. She suspected she mostly heard from him when he was a bit down or homesick, or when he'd fallen out with one of the guys in the band.

Then last week, almost a year after he'd left, Oh Boy! were coming to Dublin on their first tour, and he offered to put Ella on the guest list. She didn't want to hurt his feelings by saying no, even though Oh Boy! really weren't her kind of thing. She didn't know if she'd see Roly afterwards or if he just wanted to show off. But she talked Julie into going with her, and the two of them sat in the 3Arena amongst a crowd of hysterical, squealing teenyboppers and their parents.

'We should have brought a kid with us,' Julie hissed at her, making an ostentatious display of not enjoying herself. A memory of the Debs flashed through Ella's mind; Julie standing on the sidelines, a supercilious smile on her face.

She regretted bringing Julie tonight. Why couldn't she just let go and enjoy it for what it was, in all its insane, ridiculous glory? She thought it was funny that they looked so out of place among the sweaty, over-stimulated children, and it was fun seeing Roly up on stage doing his thing, bumping and grinding his way through the preposterous dance routines. The whole thing was cheesy and over the top, but it was kind of wonderful in its way, and it was nice to see all the kids so into it, screaming their heads off and sobbing with joy and emotional overwhelm.

So the music wasn't her and Julie's kind of thing, but the show was fun, and she could see how it could be kind of cathartic if you just let go and went with it. She'd never experienced anything like it before. The venue was a boiling mass of emotion, the kids swept along on a huge swell of love, longing and hero worship, like a Mexican wave of emotion rippling through the crowd.

The band had real charisma, and their performance was smooth and polished. The songs weren't awful, just bland and nauseatingly repetitive, so you were sick of them by the time the second chorus came around, and were almost grateful for the ear-splitting screams threatening to drown them out. But they were undeniably catchy, and as the teenyboppers sang along at the tops of their voices, waving phones above their heads, Ella found herself itching to join in – to just let herself go and ball out the songs while she waved her arms in the air and sobbed unreservedly for no particular reason.

To her surprise, when they'd turned up at the door, the woman doing the guest list had handed her a backstage pass before waving them inside. She was relieved when Julie announced she was going home as the lights came up and the crowd streamed towards the exits. She'd been pointedly looking at her watch and heaving loud sighs throughout the encore.

'You don't want to come backstage?' Ella silently prayed she'd say no.

Julie smiled crookedly. 'No, thanks. I need to go home and have a long, hot shower to scrub myself clean after that.'

Oh, fuck off, Ella thought. Why was she still friends with Julie? 'Well, I'd better just go and say hi to Roly. Thank him for the tickets.'

She didn't really expect to see Roly, assuming he'd be too busy with industry people and adoring fans to have time for her. When she showed her pass and was led backstage, he was standing to one side with the rest of the band, surrounded by a group of people. When she managed to catch his eye, she waved and mouthed 'thanks', lifting her lanyard, and thought that would be that. But Roly's face lit up and he gave her an ear-splitting grin, motioning for her to stay where she was. Seconds later, he broke away from the group and came over to her.

'Hi. I just wanted to say thanks for the tickets.'

'No problem. You came on your own?'

'No, Julie came with me, but she had to get home. She's got an early exam tomorrow.'

'I'm hurt,' Roly said, clutching his heart. 'She didn't want to come back and get me to sign her boobs?'

'Maybe next time.'

'So, what did you think? Cheesy, right?'

Ella smiled, relaxing. She'd forgotten he was good at sending himself up, not taking himself too seriously — or maybe she'd assumed he'd have lost it, started believing his own publicity. 'Yeah, cheesy as fuck,' she said, 'but in a good way.'

After he'd taken her around and introduced her to the guys from Oh Boy!, they all drank champagne in a tiny, cramped dressing room. There were industry people milling around, and fans coming and going, giving security the slip and somehow making their way inside to ask for autographs or selfies before being hauled away by security guards. Ella found herself wondering where their parents were. Some of them were alarmingly young to be hanging around with a bunch of horny teenagers in this overwrought environment.

She thought she'd slip away when Roly eventually lost her in the crowd. But to her surprise, he kept her by his side the entire time, taking her with him as he worked the room and introducing her to everyone, but mostly just sitting beside her, chatting quietly and watching from the sidelines as the others schmoozed.

Eventually, the crowd dispersed and she ended up going to a small exclusive club in Temple Bar for the after-party. They sat next to each other in deep leather club chairs, drinking and talking while their eyes drooped. Roly seemed reluctant to let her go. It was after two in the morning when she said she had to go home and was going to get a cab.

'Come back to my hotel.' Roly wiggled his eyebrows suggestively.

She laughed and shook her head.

'Come on, I'm joking. No funny stuff.'

She wasn't sure if she should feel insulted. 'How come you're not staying at your mum's?' she asked him.

'She has a new boyfriend. I don't want to cramp her style. I'll see her tomorrow.'

So she went back to his hotel with him and they spent the night together, lying side by side on the vast double bed, chatting desultorily and drifting in and out of sleep. It was strange, but years later, the memory of that night would still fill Ella with warm, fuzzy feelings and seem like one of the most intimate nights of her life.

The next morning, her phone alarm went off at seven, and she jerked awake with a jolt. Shit! At least they'd slept in their clothes, so she didn't have to waste time getting dressed.

'Hey,' Roly sat up, rubbing his eyes groggily, watching her in bemusement as she pulled on her boots. 'What's going on? You're leaving? Stay for breakfast.'

'I can't. I have to get home and change. I have a lecture at nine.'

'Oh! I forgot you're still a student.' He gave her a mocking grin.

'Yeah.' She went and sat on the bed. 'But thank you for a wonderful time.' She leaned forward and gave him a peck on the cheek. 'And wait until I tell everyone where I spent the night. What do you reckon the tabloids would pay for my story – local teen's night in hotel room with teenybopper idol Roly Punch?'

'Hey! They're not all teenyboppers, you know.'

'I know, I'm just teasing. Some of the parents were really into it.'

He laughed, cuffing her on the cheek. 'At least stay for breakfast. We could get room service.'

She shook her head. 'I'd love to. But I can't go into a lecture like this.'

His eyes flicked over her. 'Why not? You look great. It'd do wonders for your street cred.'

'Hmm. I do have some to make up after going to an Oh Boy! concert. What if I was *seen*?'

'Shut up! Can't you say you're sick or something?'

She was tempted. But she shouldn't skip a lecture just to spend a couple of hours more with someone who was barely part of her life. 'Sorry. Can't.'

'I'm sure you could miss one day and still be top of the class, Brainiac.'

'I really can't. But it was great to see you, Roly. And the band. It's really impressive.'

'Seriously?'

'Seriously.' She stood. 'Well, I'd better be off. See you in ten years maybe?'

'Sooner than that. I'll call you.'

'No you won't.' She couldn't figure out why he'd invited her tonight, why he'd wanted to see her. But this time she knew it was really goodbye.

10

ELLA'S MOTHER wasn't convinced when she announced she was going to move in with Roly. 'So now there's nothing stopping you going on your trip!'

'I don't know…' Her mother looked to Nora. The three of them were sitting at the kitchen table after dinner.

'I won't be on my own, so you don't have to worry about me. It does mean I won't be able to pay you back as quickly, but—'

'Don't worry about that. I've told you you don't have to pay me back.' She held up a hand as Ella began to protest. 'But if you insist, at least take your time. You've waited long enough to get back on your feet. If you really want to move out, don't let that stop you.'

'Thanks, Mum.'

'But Nora and I are perfectly happy to put off travelling a little longer.'

'We are,' Nora chipped in.

'Don't feel there's any rush for you to move out.'

'It's not just about you, though – honestly. I really want

to do this. It's like you said – my life has been on hold for long enough. I want to get on with things, now that I can.'

'Moving in with a boy, though…'

'It *is* a bit drastic,' Nora said.

'It's not like that. Roly's a friend.'

'Is he? You haven't seen him in years, have you? Not since you got sick.'

'No, but … he's had problems of his own. He was in rehab for a while. But he's okay now,' she added quickly, seeing the flicker of concern in her mother's face. 'He's totally clean and sober.'

'Still…'

'Don't rush into anything on our account,' Nora said. 'We've put our trip off this long, we can wait another year.'

'But there's no need to. Please don't. I don't want to hold you back any more than you want to hold me back. I really want to move in with Roly, whether you go away or not.'

Nora chewed her lip, a little smile tugging at the corners of her mouth. 'What do you think?' she asked Ruth, and Ella saw the twinkle of excitement in her eyes.

Ella turned to her mother. 'If you don't want to go, that's fine. But don't use me as an excuse.'

'I happened to be looking at the website last night,' Nora said, 'and there are a couple of places available on the next departure of that South-East Asia trip we fancied.'

Ruth bit her lip, but Ella saw the dreaminess in her eyes, and could tell she was relenting.

'There you go,' Ella said, grinning. 'It was meant to be!'

. . .

The following Saturday, Ella stood surrounded by packing boxes in her new bedroom at Roly's house questioning her choices. Until now, she'd been too preoccupied with organising the practicalities of the move to think much beyond this moment. There'd been so much to do, and she'd spent the week packing her things, arranging transport and sorting out admin. Then today, she'd been busy directing operations, overseeing the delivery guys when they got to Roly's house, showing them where to put everything. But now it was all done. The movers had just left, and she suddenly felt adrift.

She could hear Roly moving around downstairs, and it struck her anew how little time she'd spent with him over the years. They'd been out of touch for so long, she hardly knew him anymore. Maybe her mother was right and she should have thought this through more. She sank down on the bed, looking around at the boxes, not sure where to start.

'Do you need a hand with unpacking or anything?' She looked up. Roly was hovering in the doorway, hands dug into his pockets, and Ella realised he felt as awkward as she did. Strangely, that made her feel more at ease.

'Thanks, but I need to do it myself really.'

He nodded. 'I'll leave you to it, then. Oh, I got you keys cut.' He took a set of keys from his pocket and handed it to her. 'I have to go out for a while,' he said. 'So I'll leave you to get settled in. Help yourself to anything in the kitchen.'

She nodded. 'Thanks.'

She suspected Roly was just going out to give her some space, and while she didn't want to chase him out of his own home, she was grateful for the breathing room.

She spent the rest of the morning unpacking. She'd

had breakfast early, and by midday she started to get hungry. But she ignored the rumbling of her stomach and pressed on until she'd finished putting all her clothes away. Then she decided to take a break and went down to the kitchen to find something to eat.

The cupboards, however, were bare – and so was the fridge, apart from half a packet of butter and a couple of cans of some sort of luridly coloured 'sports drink'. Groaning with frustration, she flicked the switch on the kettle. At least there were tea bags – and a high-end coffee machine, she noted with satisfaction. Then she noticed a bread bin on the worktop that she'd overlooked before. But that was another disappointment when she opened it to find nothing but a box of very dry-looking energy bars. Was this what Roly had meant when he said she could help herself to 'anything in the kitchen'?

Well, they'd have to do since she couldn't be arsed going to the shops. The kettle was just coming to the boil when she heard the door opening and Roly striding down the hall.

'I got some food,' he said, hoisting aloft two shopping bags.

'Oh, phew! I'd resigned myself to having one of these cardboard bars of sadness,' she said, waving the energy bar she'd been about to open.

'Oh yeah. I started buying healthy food, but that was as far as I got.'

'Okay, just FYI – these things aren't healthy.'

He frowned, dropping his bags on the counter. 'Yeah they are. Look, it says so right there.' He leaned over and pointed to the word emblazoned on the wrapper. 'Plus it's low fat, high in fibre and has twenty per cent of your daily requirement of protein.' He pointed to the nutrition information. 'Oh, and it's gluten-free too.'

'Are you gluten intolerant?'

'No, but … that's still good, right?'

'Not really. Let's see what else it's got.' She turned it over and read 'Fructose, glucose, corn syrup – so that's sugar, sugar and sugar – guar gum, a bunch of E numbers. I don't even know what half these things are, but they sound gross.' She tossed it back in the box. 'I'd say one of those has about a thousand per cent of your daily sugar requirement.'

'Really? What's the daily requirement of sugar?'

'Zero.'

'Oh.'

'Just don't believe everything you read.'

'Right. Well anyway, there's stuff for lunch if you're hungry.' He began unpacking the bags onto the counter. 'I mean it's probably not the healthiest, but…'

'At least it's real food. And yes please, I'm starving.'

Roly unloaded cooked chicken, coleslaw and crusty sourdough bread, and they ate together at the kitchen table.

'Are you finding everything okay?' Roly asked her.

'Yes. The place looks great, by the way,' she said, casting her eyes around the room. The house had been spruced up a lot since she'd last been here.

'Yeah, I had a cleaner in.'

'This bread is so good,' Ella sighed.

'I went to the Bretzel. You know it?'

Ella nodded.

'It's great being so near it. Won't help with the weight loss, though, will it?'

She shrugged. 'I think we should let ourselves off the hook for the weekend. Start the new leaf on Monday?'

'Sounds good to me. God, I'm going to miss bread.'

'Me too.' It was going to be a special kind of torture

living so near to one of the best bakeries in Dublin and trying to resist the lure of their shelves.

Ella decided now would be a good time to establish exactly what kind of arrangement this was. When she'd accepted Roly's offer, she'd been thinking of it like a house share, but the reality was she was Roly's tenant. For some reason that had only dawned on her this morning, and it just added to her discomfort. Now they were here eating food Roly had bought, and she didn't know if she should offer to pay half or if he'd be insulted by that. She didn't want every single thing to bring up this kind of anxiety. She needed the lines to be clearly drawn so they both knew where they stood, and it would be best to sort it out on day one.

'We should make some rules about how we're going to do this.'

'Do what?'

'This co-habiting thing.' She waved a hand between them.

'Oh. Okay. Like … what sort of rules?'

'You tell me.' She shrugged. 'I mean you're the landlord.'

He reared back in his seat. 'No, I'm not! That's a horrible thing to say.'

Ella laughed, taken aback by his reaction. 'Um … it's just a fact. What's horrible about it?'

'First, we're friends. And, second, landlords are mean, greedy bastards who destroy society. It's an awful thing to call someone.'

'They're not *all* like that. Mean, greedy bastards don't give mate rates for a start. Or buy their tenants lunch. Thanks, by the way.' She'd decided he'd definitely take offence if she offered to pay him now.

'There you go, calling me a landlord again.'

'Well, I'm paying you rent to live in your house. It's pretty much the definition.'

'Shit!' He hung his head. 'So this is what I've come to. My mum would be so ashamed. She didn't raise me to be a landlord.'

'Well, you are. You're just going to have to come to terms with it and try to be one of the good ones.' She took a gulp of tea. 'So – it's your house, your rules.'

'So … you want me to give you a curfew and stuff like that? Ban boys in your room after dark?'

'Hey, I said you're my landlord, not my dad.'

Roly frowned, shifting uncomfortably. 'I know you're paying me rent, but I'd rather treat this as friends house-sharing. If that's okay with you? I mean, I don't want to be … in charge.'

She smiled, relieved. 'That's fine with me. I just want to know where we stand.'

'Good. The first house rule is no talking about house rules.'

'We should still establish some basic terms.'

'Like what?'

'Well, groceries, for instance,' she said, nodding at the food on the table. 'Who buys what, that sort of thing.'

'Let's not do that thing where we put our names on the yoghurt and, like, have our own shelf in the fridge.'

'Hard agree. No "hands off my cheese" signs.' She had no wish to relive that particular aspect of student life. Been there, done that, didn't enjoy it the first time round.

'Or a cleaning rota. I don't want to have a cleaning rota – at least not one that has my name on it.'

'You have a cleaner, right?'

He nodded. 'Anita. She's really good. I guess I have to cut back on stuff like that now, though.'

'I think in the interest of domestic harmony, we should

keep on the cleaner and split the cost between us.' Ella had no desire to waste her precious reserves of energy scrubbing the bathroom. 'Anyway, I don't want to put Anita out of a job.'

Roly smiled. 'Good, because I'd hate to let her go. She's really nice.'

'We can do a budget later, and organise a kitty for household expenses,' she said, getting up from the table.

'Leave that,' Roly said as she began gathering up plates and mugs. 'I'll clear up.'

'I'll just put these in the dishwasher.'

'I said leave it,' Roly growled in a menacing tone. 'As your landlord, I command you.'

Ella laughed. 'Okay. I'll get back to my unpacking then. See you later.'

'Oh, I was going to make spag bol for dinner. That okay with you? Unless you have plans?'

'No plans,' she said. 'That'd be great. And after dinner, we could do some planning for our project.'

'We have a project?'

'You know, getting back to our best lives – Operation Reboot.' She thought it would help them both relax into this new living situation if they had something to focus on. It would certainly help her.

'Is that what we're calling it?'

'Have you got a better name?'

'Nope.'

'Okay. We can make our goals, and plan strategies for achieving them. I'll show you how to make a Kanban board.'

'Sounds kinky.' He grinned.

She laughed, all her lingering awkwardness dissipating. 'Believe me, it's not. But it'll be fun.'

She felt more relaxed as she headed back to her room. This was going to be fine.

11

'MMM, SMELLS GREAT.' Ella sniffed the garlic-scented air as she went into the kitchen that evening.

Roly turned from the hob. 'Perfect timing. It's just ready.'

'You don't drain the pasta,' she noted approvingly, looking over his shoulder as he dragged pasta from the pot straight into the Bolognese sauce.

'Hey, I'm not a savage. My mum taught me to treat pasta with respect. Pasta, women and my elders. But mostly pasta.'

'You're a credit to her. Anything I can do?'

'You could just grab the garlic bread from the oven.'

'There's garlic bread too?' Ella beamed.

'Yeah, I thought we should go all out for our final binge.'

'I like your thinking.'

She took the garlic bread out of the oven and followed Roly to the table, which was set for two. She was surprised to see an open bottle of wine standing in the centre.

'Dig in,' Roly said as he put the steaming bowl of pasta

on the table and sat beside her. 'The wine's for you, obviously. You drink red, right?'

'Yes. Thanks. But you really shouldn't have.' She felt awkward. Obviously Roly's addiction problems were no secret, but it still somehow felt like an invasion of his privacy that she knew this about him.

He shrugged. 'No biggie. I'm trying to be one of the good guys, remember?' He picked up the bottle and poured her a glass.

'Well, it's really nice of you. But I'm fine with not drinking.'

'It doesn't bother me, if that's what you're worried about. I'm okay with people drinking around me.'

'Are you sure? I'd hate to make you uncomfortable.'

'Totally. What makes me feel awkward as fuck is when people tiptoe around me like I'm some kind of loose cannon who's going to fall off the wagon at the mere mention of alcohol.'

'Okay, noted. No tiptoeing.' Ella had to admit, she was really glad she could have wine if this meal was going to be her last big blow-out for a while. She took a sip. It was a deep, rich shiraz at a perfect temperature. 'This is lovely. Thank you.'

'You're welcome.'

'But just so you know, I'll be cutting down on alcohol anyway if I'm trying to lose weight,' she said, winding spaghetti onto her fork. 'Nothing to do with you, I promise.'

He nodded. 'Okay.'

'This is delicious. You can cook, then.'

'Yeah – basic stuff anyway. I used to be in charge of dinner sometimes when Mum was working and I'd get home before her.'

'Is she a good cook?'

'Yeah, but baking's really her thing. She makes amazing cakes. She even tried to do it as a business once, but it was too hard to make money.'

'What does she do?'

'She's a medical secretary – works for an orthopaedic surgeon. She only does a couple of days a week now. How about yours?'

'She was a teacher. She doesn't work now, though. She retired early.' It struck her how strange it was to be sitting here chatting with Roly about their families and backgrounds. They'd known each other for years, but their time together had always been fleeting, and it took place in bars, hotel rooms and restaurants, backstage at stadiums, at parties in other people's houses ... never anywhere that constituted home for either of them. This felt different, domestic. It was nice.

'Okay, ready to do some planning?' They'd cleared the table after dinner and Ella had produced a couple of A4 pads and pens.

He smiled at her, shaking his head. 'You're such a nerd.' He pulled a notepad in front of him and picked up a pen. 'Okay, what are we doing exactly?'

'First we have to set our goals. Then we can make an action plan for working towards them. So think about what your best life looks like and write down everything you want to achieve, big or small.'

'Okay.' Roly leaned forward and began writing.

Ella picked up her pen and tapped it against the table as she thought. She glanced over at what Roly was writing.

'Hey, no cogging!' He leaned forward, curling an arm around his sheet of paper, as if they were back in school and she was trying to copy his test.

'Sorry.' She turned her attention back to her own notepad.

'Done!' Roly said seconds later.

'Already?'

'Yeah.' He grinned, sitting back and slid his pad across to her.

Roly's list was concise. It just had five goals:

Get fit

Lose weight

Famous

Rich

Pippa

'Pippa? Seriously?'

'What?'

'I just didn't think you'd want her back, that's all.' She'd spoken without thinking, not masking her surprise, and she blushed when she realised how blunt she sounded.

'Why wouldn't I?'

'Well, you said she was an asshole.'

He shrugged. 'The heart wants what it wants.'

'And your heart wants an asshole.'

Roly laughed. 'I guess it does.'

'These goals are all a bit vague. You need to be more specific. Like, what does "get fit" mean? How much weight do you want to lose? Set definite targets.'

'Okay. What have you got, smarty-pants?' He glanced across at her page, which was blank.

'I was still thinking.'

'You can copy me if you want. I won't tell. I mean, we both basically want the same things, don't we?'

'Broadly, I suppose. I don't want to be rich though, just solvent. And I definitely don't want to be famous.'

'But you want to get your career back on track, right? Go back to college, do your PhD, become a hot shot professor?'

'Yeah … not in the short term, though. At the moment I'm focusing more on my financial goals – getting out of debt and building up some savings.'

'Well, we both want to get fit and lose weight.'

'Yeah.' Besides that she wanted to overhaul her whole image – buy new clothes, do something different with her hair, maybe invest in some make-up. It was very superficial, but it would be nice to focus a little on trivial things. It was a luxury she hadn't been able to afford in a long time. Besides, it was all straightforward, easily achievable stuff, so she could tick off some smaller goals while she built up to the big ones.

'Which brings us to this.' He tapped the last item on his list.

'Yeah, I definitely don't want to get with Pippa.'

'What about sex, though?' He wiggled his eyebrows, grinning.

She shrugged. 'I don't think I have the energy for dating right now on top of everything else.'

'Come on! You can't give up on sex at your age!'

'I'm not. But it's not top of my priorities at the moment either. I'm taking it all slowly – baby steps. Besides, I've kind of got used to celibacy at this stage.'

'Well, that's just tragic. All the more reason to get back in the game. The longer you leave it, the harder it'll be – as the bishop said to the actress,' he added with a snigger. 'Besides, what's the point in getting all fit if no one's going to see you naked?'

'I'm doing it for myself,' Ella said primly.

'How about your ex?'

'Andrew?'

'Yeah. If you went out with him, it wouldn't be like dating someone new. What's he doing now? Is he with anyone?'

'Not as far as I know. He was, but they split up a few months ago. He doesn't update his Facebook a lot, though, so I don't know for sure.'

'No harm in finding out. You did say it was the happiest time of your life when you were with him.'

'But that was ages ago. We've moved on. Well,' she said with a little laugh, 'he's moved on. I more stayed put.'

'Still, you should look him up at least – see if you still like him.'

'What if he is with someone and just hasn't put it on Facebook yet?'

Roly shrugged. 'What have you got to lose? Just keep it casual, meet up as friends and see where it goes.'

Ella sipped her wine. Maybe he was right. It would be less of a slog than trying to meet someone new. The thought of putting herself through all the hassle and stress of dating filled her with horror. Then again, maybe it wouldn't be the best idea to get back with her ex just because it was less bother. 'I'll think about it.'

'Anyway,' she said, 'once we have our main goals refined, we need to plan actionable steps we can take for achieving them. So fitness, for example – what are we going to do to lose weight and get fit?'

'Diet and exercise.'

'Right, but how much exercise, and what sort? What kind of diet?'

'Well … we could join a gym, and go on one of those diets where you replace meals with drinks?'

Ella shook her head. 'We can't afford that. We need to bootstrap this if we want to achieve our financial goals.

Those fad diets aren't good for you anyway. We could go running. That doesn't cost anything.'

'I thought you were anti-running.'

'I wouldn't mind trying it, if we start off slow. We could do Couch to 5K?'

Roly pulled a face. 'Isn't that, like, for old ladies?'

'No.' Ella frowned.

'I'm pretty sure my nan does it.'

'Well, just because your nan does it, doesn't mean it's *only* for old ladies. All sorts of people do it. And it's free, so we might as well give it a go.'

He nodded. 'Okay.'

'And we could do workouts at home. My mum has some DVDs we can borrow.'

'DVDs? So we'd be working out … here? Together?'

'What's wrong with that? Afraid I won't respect you after I've seen you leaping around the living room in Lycra?'

'Dream on! I am *not* wearing Lycra.'

Ella grinned. 'Well, I'll do them anyway. You don't have to join in. I know she's got Davina McCall and The Shred—'

'The Shred? My mum definitely does that.'

'Maybe she'd like to join us?' Ella said with a smirk, and Roly shuddered. 'There are lots of free workouts online too. Is Joe Wicks man enough for you?'

'My mum loves him.'

'He's got some good recipes too.'

Roly groaned. 'Oh god, are we going to have to cook all the time?'

'It won't be so bad. We can take turns. And we could do intermittent fasting. That's meant to be really good for you, and it'd save calories, time *and* money.'

'The triple whammy.'

'Speaking of money, are you signing on?'

'What do you mean?'

'Signing on – you know, for benefit.'

'You mean like … the dole?

'Social welfare.'

'No. I doubt I qualify for that.'

'I'm pretty sure you would. You should apply for Jobseeker's.'

'Jobseeker's?' He screwed up his face. 'That definitely doesn't sound like something I'd qualify for.'

'Why not?'

'Well, I mean, the clue is in the name. It's for people who are, you know … seeking a job.'

'And you're not?'

He shrugged. 'There's not much demand for my skill set. But if you know of any boy bands that are recruiting…'

'Oh, come on, I'm sure there are lots of other things you could do.'

'Like what?'

'You could be a waiter, work in a shop…'

'Who'd hire me? I don't have any experience and I'm not qualified for anything. I've never had a normal job in my life.'

'Well, maybe it's time you got one. But in the meantime, you should apply for benefit. You're entitled to it – you paid tax after all.'

'I did that all right.' He frowned. 'But I'm not sure it was the right kind.'

'Well, no harm in applying anyway. It's insurance – you've paid into it in case of a rainy day, and now that rainy day has come, you have a right to claim it. I mean, you pay house insurance, right?'

'Yeah…'

'And if there was a fire, you'd expect them to pay out.'

'Well … not if I'd burned the place down myself.'

'It's not like you committed arson! Maybe you didn't take care of some dodgy wiring, or you left a faulty appliance plugged in overnight. But you didn't deliberately torch the place. It was an accident.'

'Even if it was really my fault?'

'Yes. You'd still be entitled to claim on your insurance. Same with benefits.'

'Still … I don't want to be one of those welfare cheats like you read about in the papers.'

Ella rolled her eyes. 'Do you always think in such stereotypes? People on benefits aren't all lazy scroungers who just can't be arsed getting a job. You shouldn't believe everything you read in the papers – you of all people should know that. It's not cheating if you're genuinely struggling and you legitimately qualify for it. That's what it's for.'

'Am I struggling, though?'

'Do you have any other income apart from my rent?'

'No.'

'It's hardly a living, is it? Have you really never considered doing something else?'

He shrugged. 'I did get offered a couple of reality shows. But I didn't want to eat spiders or spend the summer banged up in prison with a bunch of superannuated soap stars.'

'Really?' Ella smiled, perking up. 'You got offered *Celebrity Cell Block*?'

'Yeah. But I turned it down. I mean, I may be washed up, but I don't want to make a career of it. Anyway, I'm too young for the has-been circuit.'

'Would have been interesting, though.'

'Humiliating is what it would have been.'

'Well, maybe you should consider training to do something else? You know, in case your solo career doesn't take off in the way you hope.' She was trying to be diplomatic. 'Our goals need to be realistic and achievable. Even if you really work at it, you can't rely on the fame thing happening – and, even if it does, it won't happen overnight. You should set some more short-term goals in the meantime.'

Roly gave her a careful look. 'Okay, I'm going to tell you something. But you have to swear you won't tell anyone.'

'Okay.'

'I'm serious. This is big, okay? If it got out…'

'Roly I won't tell anyone, I promise.'

'Okay.' He took a deep breath. 'I saw Charlie the other day. It's all very hush-hush, and nothing's definite yet, but … they're talking about a reunion.'

'An Oh Boy! reunion?'

'Yeah.'

'Wow, that *is* big. And they want you to do it with them?' Her heart lightened, not just for him but, shamefully, for herself. Maybe the damage she'd done wasn't irrevocable. She beamed. 'Oh, Roly, that's brilliant!' She moved to hug him, but he pulled back, shaking his head.

'No. Charlie gave me a heads-up, but I'm not even supposed to know about it.'

'Oh.' Her smile faded. Roly was trying to hide it, but she could see how hurt he was. Fuckers! 'Well, screw them. You don't need Oh Boy! anyway. I hope their comeback is a massive failure.'

'Well, I don't. I mean to be part of it, and I want it to be a huge success.'

'You're sure that's what you want?'

'Yeah, of course. That's what this is all about, isn't it? Getting back to my best life.'

'Yes, but … it doesn't have to be exactly what your life looked like back then. I mean, Oh Boy! always had a shelf life anyway, didn't it?'

'What do you mean?'

'It was a boy band – haven't you kind of grown out of that?'

'Lots of boy bands make comebacks when they're older. The fans have always wanted a reunion. They'd love to see us back together again – all five of us.'

'I'm sure they would. But what about you? Aren't you interested in doing your own thing anymore?'

'Eh … no. Been there, still have the bruises.'

'You really want to go back to singing those throwaway pop songs? Doing those cheesy dance routines? Having little girls screaming at you and perving over your arse?'

'Our fans are all grown up now. It'd be twenty-somethings perving over my arse.' He grinned, wiggling his eyebrows suggestively. 'You're just a musical snob.'

'I'm not! I just thought you might want to … evolve. Do something different. You really want to be in a band called Oh Boy! at your age?'

'Yes. I really do.' He sounded annoyed now. She should back off, be more supportive. She was just a little shocked that this was what he wanted. But he was right – it was his life, his goals, and she wasn't going to be responsible for taking his dreams away from him a second time. Maybe she could even atone if she helped him get back what he'd lost.

'I just wanted you to think it through and be sure these goals are what you really want – not just what you think you *should* want, or what you wanted ten years ago. I mean, you were only in Oh Boy! for three years. Maybe you have a slightly rose-tinted memory of what it was like.'

'You sound like Charlie. He said I was lucky I got out when I did, before it all got too serious and wasn't fun anymore.'

'That is such bullshit!' Ella said, her hackles rising. Some of her old college friends had done the same to her – people who had the career she'd wanted trying to tell her she was better off out of it, because it turned out the meetings were boring or the in-fighting was relentless or the hours were longer than they'd hoped. 'Be careful what you wish for,' they'd say ruefully as they complained about difficult students and rigid bureaucracy. Hazel had never pulled that crap on her. She didn't pretend that she found academic life a bed of roses – she'd had her share of disappointments and frustrations, and she was honest and upfront about them. But she also never tried to convince Ella she'd had a lucky escape.

Roly smiled. 'Yeah, that's what I said.'

'Sometimes things are just shit, and you're allowed to think they're shit. You don't have to find some silver lining in everything. Beside, just because that was his experience, doesn't mean it'd be yours too.'

'Yeah, I'd rather find out for myself.'

'I presume Charlie's up for the reunion?'

'Of course.' He rolled his eyes.

'Okay, sorry.' She held her hands up. 'If that's what you want, then go for it.' She really wanted it for him now. Fuck Charlie and the rest of them!

'It may not even happen. There are no firm plans yet or anything. But I want to be ready if it does.'

'So how are you going to go about getting back with the band?'

'I'm going to work on some new stuff. Record a few

songs and send them to Charlie, maybe even release a few tracks. Plus I'll get back in shape, of course.' He patted his belly. 'You need to be fit for those cheesy dance routines.'

'And in the meantime, you should sign on for Jobseeker's Allowance.'

Roly sighed. 'Okay, I'll make you a deal,' he said eventually. 'I'll sign on if you call Andrew.'

Ella chewed her lip, considering. It *would* be interesting to see Andrew again. And she really wanted Roly to sign on… 'Okay. Deal.'

'Yes!' Roly high-fived her.

'What about Pippa? What are you going to do to get her back?'

'All the other stuff on this list, basically – get fit, be famous, have money…'

Ella raised her eyebrows, but said nothing. She didn't want to seem judgey. But she was totally judgey.

'Pippa wasn't so bad, you know,' Roly said, as if he felt the disapproving vibes coming off her. 'I know you never liked her, but—'

'I only met her once. I didn't know her. But I didn't like her for *you*,' she said defensively. 'I thought you could do better.'

'Me?' He gave a hoot of laughter. 'I was totally punching with her.'

'No you weren't. That's ridiculous.'

'Come on. I'm not an idiot. There's no way she'd have been with me if I was just some Joe Bloggs.'

'And you're okay with that?'

'Why shouldn't I be? She was an underwear model,' he said, as if that explained everything.

Ella rolled her eyes. 'Of course, the pinnacle of human achievement – getting paid to stand around pouting in your pants.'

'Hey! She didn't just stand around in her pants. She walked for Ariana's Boudoir, I'll have you know.'

'I don't even know what that sentence means.'

'Yeah, you do.'

'Okay, yeah, I do. It means she can walk as well as standing still. So versatile!'

'You're so judgmental! It's not very feminist of you, shaming a woman for her career choices.'

Ella sighed. 'You're right.' Why was she being a bitch?

'Everyone wants the best, don't they? And when you're rich and famous, you can get it.'

'That's a seriously depressing view of human relations.' She yawned. Glancing at her watch, she was surprised to see it was almost midnight – way past her bedtime. 'Well, I think that's enough life planning for now. I'm going to hit the sack.'

Roly looked up at her as she stood. 'I'm going to my nan's for dinner tomorrow with my mum. We have dinner together most Sundays. You're welcome to come if you want?'

'Thanks, but I'm going out with my mum and aunt. They're going away on Wednesday, so it's sort of a farewell celebration.'

'Cool.' He nodded. 'So we'll both have one last big blow-out tomorrow and start this new regime on Monday.'

12

Over the next couple of weeks, Ella and Roly settled into a routine. They started running together on alternate mornings, and Ella was surprised to discover she enjoyed it. She didn't put any pressure on herself to keep up with Roly, just going at her own pace and focusing on building up her stamina. She was pleased with the progress she was making. She could feel herself getting stronger and fitter each day. They shared the cooking between them and ate together in the evenings, taking turns to try out new low-carb recipes and experimenting with intermittent fasting and time-restricted eating. Roly had applied for benefits, as promised, and was going through the screening process while spending his days writing songs. He had committed to working on his music for at least four hours each day with the aim of finishing a new song every week.

On non-running days, Roly tended to get up later and exercise after Ella had gone to work. So she was surprised to hear him up and about early one Friday morning as she ate her breakfast, still in her dressing-gown.

'What are you doing up so early?' she asked when he shuffled into the kitchen.

'I've got that social welfare inspector coming this morning,' he said, his voice still thick with sleep.

'I thought he wasn't coming until twelve?'

'He's not. But I need to get ready.' He yawned, rubbing his hair, further tousling his bed head. 'I want to make the right impression. I have to decide what to wear and sort this place out.'

Ella thought it was sweet how anxious Roly was about the welfare inspector's visit.

'So I wanted to catch you before you went to work, to get your opinion.' He stood in front of her, and held his arms out wide. 'What do you think?'

'Of?'

'My outfit.'

'Oh! Would you call it an outfit? I thought you just got out of bed.'

He looked down at himself, plucking at the grubby grey joggers he was wearing. His feet were bare and his off-white T-shirt looked two sizes too small and had a hole under one arm.

Ella put down her spoon and gave him her full attention. 'This is what you're planning to wear when the inspector comes?'

He shrugged. 'It was the best I could come up with.'

'Seriously? I mean, what look are we going for here?'

'Poor, obviously.'

'If you mean poor as in weak effort, you've nailed it.' She looked him up and down. 'What shoes are you planning to wear?'

'No shoes.'

'Roly, even poor people have shoes.'

'Yeah, but not ones like mine. All my shoes are really

nice. I mean, they're not going to give money to someone with Air Max 90s, are they?'

'Yes, they are. Man cannot live on Air Max 90s alone.'

'But I won't look like I'm in need of money. I mean, it's bad enough that I have this house…'

'People still qualify for benefits, even if they own shoes and have somewhere to live.'

'Okay.' He nodded, but he looked dubious.

'You don't have to be completely destitute and homeless,' she said, trying to drive the point home. 'And you definitely don't have to dress up as some … Dickensian orphan.' She waved a hand at him. 'Were you planning to smear some coal dust on your face too?'

'Um … no. But I thought I might skip a shower.' He raked a hand through his dishevelled hair. 'You know … look a bit grungy.'

'How much do you think shampoo costs?'

'Well, my Abercrombie shower gel is pretty expensive…'

'Roly, have a shower and just wear what you normally would. And put on some shoes.'

He sighed. 'I have a pair of Vans that I might get away with. If the dude doesn't know his footwear…' he mumbled as he headed back towards his bedroom.

Ella finished her breakfast, and went to her room to get dressed. It was her first dress-up Friday, and she needed to work on her own outfit. As she came back downstairs, Roly was emerging from the living room carrying his Playstation.

'I'm going to stash this under my bed,' he said, heading for the stairs.

'What? Why?'

'I thought I should hide some of my stuff. I've put my

iPad down the side of the sofa. He'll never look there, will he?'

She couldn't help laughing. 'He's not going to be searching the place, Roly. Just put everything back. And if you're planning on tearing down curtains…'

'I'm not! But I should probably get rid of some of the artwork. That painting over the fireplace cost me fourteen grand.' He jerked his head back towards the living room.

'Leave it,' she said sternly.

'Oh, what about food? There's smoked salmon in the fridge.'

'He's not going to inspect the fridge.' Ella glanced at her watch. 'Look, I've got to go or I'll be late. Just calm down and leave everything as it is. It'll be fine.'

Ella glanced at the time on her computer screen. Two minutes to go until she could knock off for her eleven o'clock coffee break. Of course, there was nothing stopping her going right now – as everyone kept reminding her, there were no rigid rules at Citizens, no fixed times for having lunch or taking breaks. But she liked having some order in her life, and she had enough upheaval to deal with at the moment, what with her mother and Nora going away and adapting to her new living situation with Roly. So she'd imposed her own structure on her working day. She took a break away from her desk every morning at eleven and sat in one of the pods reading a book or chatted with whoever was in the break room if she was feeling sociable. In the afternoons, she varied her routine in keeping with the spirit of Citizens. She didn't want to be a spoilsport, so she took her break at different times with studied breeziness or just had coffee at her desk and worked through.

It wasn't officially *her* desk, of course, because the staff of Citizens of the Wild roamed free like wildebeest in the vast Serengeti of their open plan office space, hot-desking wherever took their fancy before moving on to another location, lest staying in the one place too long stifled their creativity. But Ella had sat at this desk every day since she'd started. She liked feeling she had a place here that she could make her own.

'Ella!' She looked up to see Jake striding towards her. He was wearing a pink wig and a skin-tight catsuit, the chest padded out with fake boobs. Dress-up Fridays were going to take some getting used to.

'How are you?' He perched on the edge of her desk.

'Good, thanks.'

'We just want to have a little chat – Dylan and I. Is that okay?'

'Yes, of course.' She blinked up at him, bewildered. Was she in trouble for some reason? Had she done something wrong?

'So, Ella, you've been here a month now,' Jake said, hands clasped together. 'How's it going? Happy?'

'Yes. Very happy.'

'If you have any problems or concerns, you know you can always talk to me or Dylan.'

She nodded. 'Thanks. But I don't have any issues. Everything's great.' Was this some kind of employee review, she wondered. She'd forgotten she was on a six-week probation period. It was all too easy to forget that Jake and Dylan were her bosses, but maybe they weren't happy with her and they'd decided to let her go at the end of it. Or perhaps they'd give her a pep talk and tell her she had two weeks left to pull her socks up if she wanted to be made permanent.

She didn't imagine they had any complaints about her

work. But it could be that they'd decided she didn't fit in here – that she was too dull and set in her ways and was ruining the casual, easy-going vibe they strived for.

'You like this desk?' Jake ran a hand along its surface. 'You sit here every day.'

'Yeah.' Shit, they'd noticed. She should have made more of an effort to work in different spaces. Maybe they didn't like that she'd taken this desk out of rotation for everyone else. 'But I can move around if that's a problem.'

'No, not at all. Whatever makes you comfortable.'

'I just like having a base, knowing where my stuff is.'

'Sure, sure.' Jake nodded. 'Excellent costume, by the way.'

'Um … thanks.' She'd dreaded her first dress-up Friday, but she'd made an effort to show willing and join in. Unfortunately, the best her meagre wardrobe could stretch to was a cut-rate Harry Potter with a grey jumper and an off-brand maroon tie and scarf that only roughly approximated the Hogwarts' school colours. She already had the short dark hair, and she'd dug out an old academic gown of her mother's and bought a cheap pair of off-the-shelf reading glasses. 'You look amazing!'

'Thanks. Brite Bomber,' he pointed to his chest, which was adorned with a unicorn motif. 'You know, from Fortnite?'

She shook her head. 'I never played it.'

'Did you tell her?' Dylan's voice came from behind her.

'No, I was waiting for you, mate.'

Oh God, they were going to let her go, weren't they? They'd come to tell her it wasn't working out. Ella turned around. Dylan was coming towards her carrying a small round tray. He was dressed as Cher from *Clueless*, in a yellow-check mini-skirt suit, white thigh-highs and a long, blonde wig. He looked spectacular, and he was grinning from ear to ear. Jake hopped off the desk and stood beside him.

'Congratulations, Ella!' Dylan said. 'You're our Employee of the Month.'

'Oh!'

'Just a little token of our appreciation.' Jake took a mug of coffee from the tray and placed it on her desk alongside a large muffin adorned with a fizzing sparkler.

'Gosh, seriously?' Well, this was weird. She'd barely been here four weeks and she was employee of the month already? But they probably did this for everyone, she reasoned – they were so eager to make their staff feel valued. Still, it was sweet. 'Thanks.' She took a sip of coffee as the sparkler fizzed out.

'Skinny caffè mocha, right?' Dylan said, beaming.

'Right.' And the muffin, she noticed, was blueberry – her favourite. Then Dylan presented her with the last thing on the tray, a little bowl of Smarties.

'Brown ones only,' he said, putting them on the desk in front of her.

'Oh! Thank you.' Ella was ridiculously touched. It seemed those inane interview questions hadn't been so pointless after all. They'd been listening, paying attention to her answers because they really wanted to know. It dawned on her now that it wasn't an accident that they always had egg mayonnaise sandwiches at team meetings, and a good supply of her favourite oat biscuits in the break room.

'Congratulations!' Jake said, beaming at her. 'You deserve it. You've done an amazing job organising our accounts. This is the first month since we started that I haven't had our accountant shouting at me about the state of our books.'

'And Gordon was really impressed with the work you

did on our Facebook ad campaigns. He said you really know what you're doing and they're performing brilliantly – better than he and Philip have ever managed.'

Ella smiled. She'd been really happy with her work on those campaigns and was pleased that she'd been able to make a substantial contribution. She'd run pay-per-click ad campaigns for some of her virtual assistant clients, so she did know what she was doing, whereas Gordon and Philip were techies who'd ended up handling the company's marketing by default, and it wasn't their forte. They knew how to use the data, but they weren't so good when it came to the creative side of advertising and their copywriting skills left a lot of room for improvement.

'So that's an area you could pursue more, if it interests you. Or you could take over the accounts. Anyway, that's a discussion we can have down the line when you've settled in and decided what you'd like to focus on. We'll leave you to enjoy your break.'

'Where did all the other Smarties go?' she asked, peering into the bowl.

Dylan pointed to his stomach with a wry smile.

'He's been scoffing boxes of Smarties all week.'

'Well, you were no help!'

'I have to watch my figure.' Jake ran his hands down his sides, squeezed into the slinky catsuit. 'I'm cosplaying Deadpool this weekend.'

'You also get this.' Dylan produced a tiny gold cup from the shoulder bag slung across his body and presented it to her. The base was engraved 'Employee of the Month'. 'You only get to keep it for the month, though – unless you win it again next month.'

'Something to aim for,' Jake said with a wink. 'Well, enjoy your cake.'

'Thanks, I will.'

'Proper drinks tonight,' Dylan said pointing to her. 'You're coming to the pub, right?'

'Oh, well…' So far she'd avoided Friday night drinks with her colleagues. She didn't want to push her luck and over-stretch herself, so she'd been taking it easy at weekends.

'As Employee of the Month, you're the guest of honour.'

'It's just, I was supposed to be spending the evening with my, um … the guy I live with.'

Dylan brightened. 'Well, bring him! We'd love to meet him.'

'Okay, I'll ask him. But I'm not sure…' She chewed her lip. 'If he came, could you ask everyone not to post anything about it on social media?'

Dylan frowned, confused. 'Sure.'

'I know that sounds wanky. It's just he's kind of—'

'Shy?' Jake said.

'Famous … sort of. I mean, he used to be.'

'Really?' Dylan's eyes widened excitedly. 'Who is he?'

'Um…' Oh god, cringe. They were going to be seriously unimpressed and this would seal her uncool rep completely. 'He used to be in Oh Boy! Roly—'

'Roly Punch!' Dylan gasped, his face lighting up. 'Oh my god, your boyfriend is Roly Punch?'

'Oh, no! He's not my boyfriend. We just live together. We're housemates … friends.'

'This is amazing!' Jake seemed just as excited about it as Dylan. These two would never cease to surprise her.

'Definitely bring him,' Dylan said. 'It'd be so cool to meet him.'

'Really?'

'Of course. I loved Oh Boy!'

He and Jake then went into a spontaneous rendition of 'Cool Like You', with surprisingly impressive harmonies.

Ella laughed. 'Okay, I'll bring him. If he wants to come.' She wasn't sure how Roly would feel about it. He seemed to have a very ambivalent attitude to his fame, on the one hand not wanting to be recognised, while at the same time getting pissed off when he wasn't.

'Brilliant! No photos, we promise,' Jake said. 'We'll be cool.'

'Right, I'm off to start my diet,' Dylan said, 'or I'll never fit into my favourite Cher suit again.'

Ella felt quite emotional as she drank her coffee and ate her cupcake. Dylan and Jake might act like eejits, but there was a lot more to them than met the eye, and she was getting really fond of them. Citizens of the Wild was shaping up to be a great place to work.

'Congratulations on Employee of the Month!' Kerry said to her later as she passed through the reception area.

'Oh yeah. Thanks!' Ella laughed to show she wasn't taking it seriously and knew it didn't mean anything.

'Really, well done. I was here almost a year before they gave it to me.'

'Oh!'

'Although apart from the month Steve came up with the Eaziglide zipper, I've won it every month since.' Kerry grinned smugly. 'Until now.'

'Oh. Sorry.'

'It's cool.'

'I don't feel I've done anything to earn it. I think they just gave it to me as a bit of encouragement because I'm new – to make me feel like I'm pulling my weight as part of the team.'

Kerry nodded. 'Yeah, they're very keen on building in rewards to keep everyone motivated. Maybe you did earn it, I don't know. But to be honest, they'd probably have given it to you anyway.'

'Oh!' Ella had suspected as much, but she'd have thought Kerry would at least go along with the charade out of politeness.

Kerry laughed at Ella's obvious dismay. 'Sorry – no offence. I'm not being mean. I'm glad they gave it to you. I just think they're worried you're going to leave and they're a bit desperate to make you stay.'

'Really? Ella frowned.

'Yeah, you're the best admin person we've ever had here – and they know you're well over-qualified for the job. Dylan and Jake are great to work for, but they're not so good at attracting the right people when it comes to the business side of things. It's the same with investors and bankers – they have a hard time getting people to take them seriously sometimes.'

'I wonder why,' Ella said under her breath as Jake strode past in his Fortnite outfit.

Kerry laughed. 'They're really good at what they do, but they like to have a laugh at the same time. Nothing wrong with that, is there?'

'No. Nothing at all. How did you end up here anyway? I mean, Jake said you studied fashion—'

'Yeah. I knew Jake from college. I helped them with their crowdfunder, and then they asked if I'd come and work for them when they started this place. It's not easy to get a break in fashion design, to put it mildly. So here I am. It was supposed to be for just a few months,' she said with a wry smile.

'Wow!'

'Yeah, they kind of suck you in. Get out now while you

still can!' She laughed.

'You're really happy here, aren't you?'

Kerry nodded. 'I love it. It's the best job I've ever had. The most fun, definitely. They're great employers – decent pay, sick leave and all that, obviously – but they also make you feel part of it, you know? Like you have a stake in the business, and it's something you can be proud of. You feel appreciated, and they notice if you go the extra mile. You don't get many jobs where you can say that.'

'Careful, you sound like you're trying to convince me to stay.'

'I am. I don't care if I never win Employee of the Month again. Honestly, you should have seen the one they hired before you. Some old school friend of Dylan's. Totally clueless.' Kerry rolled her eyes. 'And not in a cute Cher kind of way either.'

Predictably, Roly was a big hit with Jake and Dylan. They cornered him and Ella as soon as they arrived at the pub and monopolised them for most of the evening, bombarding Roly with questions and generally geeking out over him. They kept him supplied with a steady stream of exotic mocktails as they plied him for stories about his time in Oh Boy!, making no attempts to tone down their enthusiasm or hide how impressed they were by his stardom. They weren't acting cool at all, and she loved them for it.

Roly had taken a little persuading to come along with her tonight, but he was in his element now, enjoying the attention and adulation. She could tell he liked Jake and Dylan, and the three of them gelled instantly. Ella felt like a proud matchmaker.

'So, how do you two know each other?' Dylan was

looking at her and Roly like they were the most fascinating creatures on the planet, his eyes glittering excitedly.

'We were at school together,' Ella said.

'You're such a dark horse,' Jake said. 'You've been with us a month now, and you never mentioned you live with Roly Punch.'

'What was this one like at school?' Dylan asked Roly, nodding to her.

'Same as now, really. Brainy, over-achiever, teacher's pet...'

Ella swatted him playfully. 'Shut up!'

Roly laughed, fending her off. 'Come on! Only you could come home from work with a fucking trophy!'

Jake and Dylan watched, laughing.

'Kind of fierce,' Roly continued, 'as you can see. Very cool.'

'Okay, that's a lie. I was never cool.'

'Yeah, you were. You were so ... self-contained, I guess.'

'Unfriendly, you mean?'

'No,' he frowned. 'You weren't unfriendly. Just ... not needy, like most of us were. Not desperate to be liked by everyone. You were just like "this is who I am, take it or leave it", sort of thing.'

Ella's smile faltered as their eyes met and she could tell he meant it.

Jake nodded. 'I can see that.'

'That's exactly how you were at the interview with us,' Dylan agreed.

'Until I walked into the stationery cupboard.'

He laughed. 'Yeah, that wasn't cool at all. It was funny, though.'

'Gosh, cool...' She tested out the concept, trying to

relate it to herself. 'I wish I'd known that's how people saw me,' she said to Roly.

Ella had expected the night to be a drain, but the time flew by, and she was surprised how much she was enjoying herself. She'd had her excuses ready, but she'd had no desire to cut out early, and, before she knew it, they were calling last orders.

Dylan looked at his watch. 'Well, at this point in the night, we'd usually go to our favourite karaoke bar—'

'*You* were going to do karaoke?' Roly grinned at Ella, eyebrows raised.

She shrugged.

'She was,' Jake said. 'Dylan's already bagsed her for a duet.'

'Okay, that I have to see.'

'Seriously? You'd come to karaoke with us?' Dylan grinned excitedly.

Roly drained his glass and nodded. 'Let's go.'

'But unfortunately, they're too intimidated to perform in front of you,' Ella said, nodding to her bosses. 'Right?' She was glad of the excuse to leave now and avoid karaoke.

Jake shrugged. 'We'll get over it. Come on.'

If someone had told Ella a month ago that she'd enjoy a night of karaoke, she wouldn't have believed them. But she was having a whale of a time. She'd had enough vodkas to let go of her inhibitions, and didn't even make a token protest when Dylan pulled her up to duet with him on 'Don't Go Breaking My Heart' – though she was glad they'd hired a private room, so she didn't have to perform in front of total strangers. Kerry sang 'I Got You Babe' with Jake, and Dara turned out to have a powerful voice that seemed to come out of nowhere in his narrow, wiry frame. Sarah, Mark, Catherine and Dan teamed up to do a hilarious version of 'Bohemian Rhapsody'. But, mostly, everyone wanted to have a go singing with Roly, and he was happy to oblige.

Now Jake, Dylan, Roly, Gordon and Philip were performing Oh Boy!'s first single 'Cool Like You', totally hamming it up with exaggerated dance moves and facial expressions. Ella laughed as they pointed to members of their 'audience', clutching their hearts and gazing into their eyes as if they were singing just to them. 'Wish I was cool like you,' they sang and Roly pointed at her. Their eyes met, and it felt like he was singing just to her.

13

Ella was jittery with nerves as she walked into the coffee shop. But fair was fair. Roly had applied for Jobseeker's Allowance, so now she had to uphold her end of the bargain and go through with this.

Andrew was already there, smiling up at the waitress who stood by his table, charming her no doubt. He was such an incorrigible flirt. For a moment, she was tempted to turn and run. She'd thought it would be easier to suggest meeting for a coffee in the afternoon; it would feel less like she was asking him on a date. But now she wanted a darkened bar with alcohol to soften the jagged edges of her nerves.

Then Andrew looked up and saw her, his mouth widening in a smile, and the moment passed. When she reached his table, he stood and kissed her cheek, then called the waitress back to take her order. By the time their coffee arrived, her anxiety had melted away. It was just Andrew.

'You look really well,' he said.

'Thanks. I am.'

He was as handsome as ever, the smattering of freckles across his broad nose and high cheekbones still giving him a boyish air. She studied his face wonderingly. He seemed almost a stranger now, yet she used to kiss that wide mouth, those full, pouty lips. His thick dark hair was cut shorter now; his curls didn't flop over his forehead in the way she used to love. She could still feel its softness brushing against her fingers.

'It's great to see you again, Ella. I was glad to hear from you.'

'You didn't think it was weird, me contacting you out of the blue like that?'

'No, not at all. It was a surprise – a nice one. I've often thought about you – considered calling you. But I wasn't sure how welcome that would be, so I could never get up the nerve.'

She smiled, startled by the admission.

'So, what are you up to now? Tell me everything.'

She told him about her job at Citizens of the Wild, their dress-up Fridays and karaoke nights, the climbing wall in the break room…

'Sounds like your worst nightmare.'

'I know, but I'm actually really enjoying working there, and the people are so nice. It pays well too.'

'What do you do there?'

She shrugged. 'A bit of everything – general admin, some book-keeping. I work on marketing a lot, running ad campaigns and managing the company's social media accounts. It's interesting.'

'So you've sold your soul to Mammon,' he said with a smile.

For fuck's sake! 'No, I haven't. There's no pact with the Devil involved. It's just a regular office job with regular people that allows me to pay rent and stop living on benefits.' He'd always done this, she remembered now. When they were students, he'd made a virtue of being broke, not only scrounging money off her, but trying to shame her for having it to give in the first place. For some reason he thought being skint automatically gave him the moral high ground, even if it meant leeching off someone else's hard work – just as long as he wasn't the one 'selling out'. It had always pissed her off.

'Being sick has given me a different perspective. It's made me more appreciative of—'

'The superficial things in life?'

Oh, grow up! Instead of rising to his bait, she said 'Yeah, maybe it has. Because the superficial things in life can be pretty great – being able to buy some new clothes or to go out for a meal, not having that constant nagging worry about how you're going to pay your bills or buy your next cup of coffee.'

He wouldn't know about that, because being broke was just a posture for Andrew. It was something he played at. He had no idea what it was really like to live with that constant background hum of anxiety that intermittently escalated into full-on panic, like intervals on a relentless treadmill. He'd probably never experienced the dizzying feeling when you logged into your bank account and held your breath as you checked the balance. 'Being high-minded and above all that is a luxury some of us can't afford.'

Maybe Andrew had done all the growing up he wanted to do. It occurred to her that he'd pursued an academic career partly because he couldn't let go of the student life he loved. He'd wanted to stay in college so he could carry on as he always had, being nobly skint and flirting with undergraduates.

'Sorry. I'm not having a go. I'd just hate to see you waste that first-class mind of yours.'

'I'm not. I do intend to go back and do my PhD eventually.' She was being unfair. She knew working in academia wasn't about an unwillingness to grow up. After all, it was what she had wanted for herself. If things had been different, she'd be in the same place he was now. Andrew had always been her biggest supporter, spurring her on to achieve more, encouraging her to keep her eyes on the prize and not let herself get side-tracked from her goals. He'd pushed her to fulfil her potential, and she'd felt like a better version of herself when she was with him.

'But it'll be a while before I can afford to do that.'

'Well, just don't get too used to the money or you might find it hard to go back to being a student.'

'It's not just about the money, though. I want to do something less intense for a while, to ease myself back into work.'

He nodded. 'That makes sense.' He took a gulp of coffee.

'Really? You're not going to give me grief about it? Even when I took a summer job at Top Shop, you gave me a load of shit about acting in bad faith and being a "slave to the man".'

'I was a young idiot, in love with Sartre and the sound of my own voice.'

She smiled, surprised at the self-mockery. Maybe she was wrong, thinking he hadn't grown up at all. He didn't use to have that kind of self-awareness.

'Honestly, sometimes I've fantasised about doing that myself – just getting some mindless clerical job for a while and taking a break from all the pressure.'

'So, what about you? What have you been up to?'

'Still pounding the hallowed halls of academia. I have

a temporary lecturing post and I'm doing a lot of research at the moment on theories of punishment and social control in relation to social media. I'm presenting a paper on it at a symposium next month.'

'Well done. It sounds like you're achieving everything you were aiming for.'

'Oh, and my doctoral thesis was the basis of a chapter in a book co-authored by Cyril Leavy. It was published last year.'

Cyril Leavy had been Andrew's thesis supervisor. 'Congratulations! I didn't know.'

'Well, it wasn't exactly a bestseller.' There was that self-deprecation again. It was new and she liked it. 'I'm really glad we're doing this. I wanted to call you so many times. But I always chickened out.'

She frowned. 'Why?'

He shrugged. 'I felt shitty about the way things ended.' He glanced away. 'I should have talked to you, instead of … disappearing, basically.'

There'd been no drama in their break-up. Andrew hadn't shagged her best friend or dumped her for someone else or even ghosted her. He'd just quietly slid out of her life, so gradually she couldn't even say exactly when it had ended.

'It must have been confusing for you. I mean, it's not as if we'd been having problems in the relationship.'

'Hadn't we?' She could hardly remember now, but she seemed to recall arguments. 'Anyway, it wasn't that hard to figure out. It was my illness, wasn't it?'

He grimaced.

'I'm not accusing you of anything,' she said quickly. 'I mean, I get it. It was kind of impossible to be in a relationship with me then.'

'That makes me sound like such a dick.'

'No! It's understandable. We were young. It was a lot for a twenty-something to be lumbered with. Believe me, if *I* could have run away from it, I would have.'

He sighed. 'I guess I just didn't like always being the asshole, you know?'

She frowned, puzzled.

'I mean, you were sick. You couldn't help it, and you were dealing with this huge, life-changing thing. My problems seemed – *were* – ridiculous in comparison. If I'd had a bad day or, I don't know, got a terrible haircut—'

Ella laughed. 'Oh my god, that time you got the mullet!'

He grinned. 'Okay, that *was* a ridiculous problem. But I never felt like I could talk about my bad day because you'd always had a worse one. You'd had a whole year of them. I couldn't complain about a bad meal in a restaurant or a horrible train journey because you couldn't even go to a restaurant or get on a train. It was like there was no room for *my* feelings – no space for me to be a bit down or disappointed.'

'I get it. You didn't feel entitled to your feelings.'

'This is going to sound like such a cliché, but it wasn't you. I didn't like who *I* was in our relationship.'

'You were tiptoeing around me the whole time. It sounds like it was *all* about me.'

'Because it had to be all about you, I understood that. What you were dealing with was … all-consuming.'

That was true. It had eaten away at her entire life, swallowed everything down whole, including her relationship with him.

'I guess I was just too immature to deal with it,' he said with a shrug.

'You didn't have to. It wasn't that I was any more mature or brave or anything. I just didn't have any choice.'

'Still, I felt so guilty for abandoning you when you most needed someone. I wish I'd handled it better, been there for you. I wouldn't blame you if you hate me.'

'I don't hate you.' She smiled. If she was honest, she'd been more relieved than anything when he'd dumped her because making an effort for him had been exhausting and it meant she could finally give up. They'd stopped going out because it took too much out of her, and she'd conserved all her energy for the nights they'd spend together. She'd tried to be a good girlfriend – engaged, sympathetic, interesting, sexy – but as her illness progressed, it became more and more of a strain, and one she couldn't afford. Sex had become a chore that she avoided as much as possible and got through increasingly rarely in an attempt to preserve the relationship, her nerves jangling with the strain of trying to enjoy it when really she just wanted it to be over so she could sleep. When they broke up, any sadness she'd felt had been far outweighed by the bliss of being able to surrender to vegging out in front of the TV.

'Don't beat yourself up about it,' she told him now. 'You were young, you're supposed to be immature.'

He looked at her wonderingly. 'You're amazing.'

'Really? Based on what?'

'Sorry?'

'What's so amazing about me? Be specific.'

He laughed. 'I'd forgotten how exacting you can be.'

She shrugged. 'I don't like those vague meaningless compliments. How did you reach this conclusion? Show your work.'

'No, I like that you don't let me get away with lazy thinking – keeps me on my toes.'

'So tell me – what's so amazing about me?'

'Well, this for a start – your intellectual rigour, the way you don't just take a compliment lying down.'

She laughed. 'I'm glad you like that because, believe me, it's not a popular attribute.'

'You're also kind and wise and forgiving of human frailty, and I like that underneath your tough, snarky exterior you have an incredibly good heart. You have no time for sloppy sentimentality, but you're upfront and honest about your feelings. You're the most authentic person I've ever met.'

'Wow! I do sound kind of amazing.'

'And I like that when a guy gives you a compliment, your response is to challenge it and interrogate his reasoning.'

'Yeah, I could have just said thanks.'

'But then you wouldn't be you.'

'So I haven't debunked your proposition that I'm amazing?'

'No, you've rather confirmed it. This is exactly what I love about you.'

Love. Not *loved*. She was taken aback by his casual use of the present tense. 'So where are you living now?' she asked.

'I have an apartment in Stoneybatter.'

'Do you … live alone?'

'Yeah, I do.'

'So, are you seeing anyone?'

'No.' A slow smile crept across his face. 'I'm not.' He reached across the table and took her hand, and she felt a spark of something she hadn't had in a long time.

Could this really happen, she wondered. Could they pick up where they left off?

'How about you?'

'Hm?'

'You mentioned paying rent. So you're not still living with your mother?'

'No. I'm actually living with Roly Punch.' She raised her eyebrows in a can-you-believe-it expression.

'Oh!' He jerked back, releasing her hand.

'Oh no, not like that!' She grabbed his hand. 'We're not shacking up or anything. We're just … housemates.'

'How did that happen?'

'Long story.'

He gave her a slow smile. 'I've got plenty of time. Another coffee?'

14

Hi, honey, I'm home!'

Roly looked up as Ella came into the living room. He was sitting on the sofa with his guitar, an A4 pad and pen on the table in front of him. 'Hi. How was your day?'

'Good. You're still writing?' She nodded to the pad.

Yeah.'

'Well, don't let me interrupt. I'll get started on dinner.'

'Do you mind? I'm kind of in the zone.'

'No worries.'

When she'd slung her coat in the bedroom, she went to the kitchen and emptied her shopping bag. She was making fajitas and had bought the ingredients for guacamole on the way home. As she chopped coriander, squeezed limes and pounded avocados and garlic, the sounds of softly strummed guitar and Roly's sweet, husky voice drifted into the kitchen in intermittent bursts, as he repeated chords and snatches of melody. She'd never heard him sing like this before, solo and acoustic, and she was surprised by the deep, rich tone of his voice. She was annoyed when she started cooking and he was drowned out by the sizzle of peppers and onions in the pan and the roar of the extractor fan.

When she'd finished cooking, she popped back into the living room. 'Are you ready for dinner?' she asked. 'It can wait if not.' She didn't want to interrupt his creative flow.

'Yeah, I'm done. What are we having?' He sniffed the air. 'Smells great.'

'Fajitas. I just have to microwave the tortillas.'

'Are we allowed tortillas?'

'Just one each?'

'Great.' He licked his lips. 'But do you want to hear this song first?'

'You've finished already? That was quick.'

He shrugged. 'It's been going around in my head all week, so it was mostly already there. It just needed some tweaking.'

'I'd love to hear it, if that's okay.' She sat beside him on the sofa and he began playing. Even though she knew he'd been used to playing giant stadiums, she was still surprised how unselfconscious he was about singing to her like this, especially something he'd written himself. It felt so intimate and personal. She admired his confidence. More than that, there was something very appealing about it – sexy, even.

And the song was a revelation. She'd expected something simple and generic with a bouncy chorus and silly rhymes, but it was slow and gentle, with a lovely stripped-back melody and poetic, insightful lyrics. It was utterly unlike the insipid bubblegum pop of Oh Boy! She clapped when he finished.

'So, what do you think?'

'Wow! It's gorgeous, Roly. I love it.'

'You don't have to say that, just because I'm your landlord.'

'I'm not! I mean it. It's really, really good.'

He beamed. 'Thanks. I'm pretty happy with it myself.'

'You should be. It's amazing!'

'You don't have to sound so surprised.'

'I'm not! It's just ... very different to what I expected.'

'Yeah, well, it's pretty raw at the moment, obviously. But I'm sure a good producer could do something with it.'

'Do something?'

'You know – give it a bit of oomph. Polish it up.'

'I think it's got plenty of oomph as it is. Not that I'm an expert,' she added quickly, not wanting to sound like she was telling him his job. It was ridiculous since he'd been in a band, but she'd never thought of Roly as a musician until they'd started living together. 'When did you start playing guitar?'

He gave her an indignant look. 'I always played guitar. Well, since I was about eight.'

'Really? How come you never played it in Oh Boy!?'

He shrugged. 'There wasn't much call for it. And I needed my hands for dancing.'

'Ah yes, the dancing!' She grinned.

'Anyway, I'm just using the guitar for writing. When I get into a studio, there'll be proper musicians. I'll have a whole band with me.'

'*You're* a proper musician. You're really talented.'

'Thanks. But I'm not planning to become some singer/songwriter type.'

'Wouldn't you like to be? It could be good to do something different – surprise people. And you'd have complete creative control.'

'Maybe.' He put the guitar down and leaned it against the sofa. 'Anyway, let's have those fajitas. I'm starving!'

. . .

It was nice to see Roly so happy. He chattered enthusiastically and ate with the gusto of someone who'd earned dinner. Ella could relate. Unwinding after a good day's work was so much more enjoyable and satisfying than the smooth slide from day to evening, from sofa to table to bed that she'd got used to.

'How did it go signing on today?' she asked casually. It was his first day collecting Jobseeker's Allowance, and Ella knew he was nervous about it. She'd been anxious all day that he'd be too worried about being seen and bottle out. But she didn't want to sound like she was checking up on him.

'It was amazing! I just queued up, signed my name and they handed over the cash, just like that! I even got back pay to the day I was approved for benefit.' He reached into his pocket and pulled out a wad of notes to show her. 'I couldn't believe it was so easy.'

'Well, what were you expecting to happen?'

'I dunno.' He shrugged. 'More of an interrogation, I suppose.'

'Someone shining a big light in your eyes?'

He nodded. 'Being exposed as a fraud in front of the whole post office.'

'Ending up in the sidebar of shame in tomorrow's papers.'

'Exactly! But there was none of that. I didn't even get any dirty looks. The woman who gave me my money barely glanced at my social security card, got me to sign the electronic thingy and then started counting out the cash. She even smiled and told me to have a good day.'

'So she didn't make you feel like a criminal for collecting social welfare? That was nice of her.'

'Yeah, it was. I was still half expecting someone to stop me before I made it to the door. But there was nothing.'

'No hand on your shoulder, no "stop right there"?'

'No being hauled away by the guards.' He shook his head. 'I totally got away with it.'

Ella laughed. 'You were collecting benefit, Roly, not staging a hold-up.'

'Still, I can't believe they just hand out free cash like that for doing nothing! I kind of get why people who work are so pissed off about it.'

'How many times do I have to tell you? It's not free. It's your own money – you're entitled to get some of it back when you need it. That's how social insurance works.'

'Well, anyway, it's a big relief. Thanks for making me do it.'

'You're welcome. And you mightn't have to do it much longer. That cafe around the corner are hiring. I passed it on my way home and there's a sign in the window.'

He was spooning guacamole and salsa onto his plate and didn't even look up, which immediately irked her.

'You know, that one with the funny name?'

'Insider Out?'

'Yes, that's the one! They're looking for a waiter. You should apply.'

That got his attention. He looked up at her, eyebrows raised. Then he smirked. 'Yeah, right,' he said with a little laugh and returned to assembling his fajita. He thought she was joking.

'I'm serious.'

He raised his eyes to her again. 'Me? Work in the local greasy spoon?'

'Yes, you. Why not?'

'I can't be some … waiter.'

'Of course you can. It's not that difficult. I used to work in a cafe when I was in college.'

He looked irritated now. 'You know what I mean. I can't get a normal job, like a…'

'Normal person? What, you think you're too special?'

'No, but … well, yeah, in a way. I mean, it's humiliating. And there's the whole fame thing.'

'You're worried you'll be swamped by hordes of ravening fans?'

'I could be. And what if the press got wind of it?'

She shrugged. 'So what if they do? There's no shame in doing an honest day's work for an honest day's pay.' She wiped her hands on her napkin.

'But it wouldn't leave me much time for writing, and it's going really well at the moment.'

'You really should make some effort to find a job while you're getting Jobseeker's.'

'It doesn't seem to be an issue.'

'Maybe not yet, but eventually they'll want to see that you're genuinely making an effort to find work.'

'I'm working on my music. Doesn't that count?'

'Not really, when you're not making money from it.'

'Well, hopefully I will be before too long. Anyway, you're the one who kept telling me I should sign on for benefits, and now you're saying I should get a job? I thought the whole point was that I wouldn't have to worry about money and it'd free me up to focus on song-writing.'

She could have pointed out that he'd had years of not worrying about money when he'd spent his time playing video games and watching TV, but he'd been in a slump and she knew what that was like. 'Yeah, you're right.' She didn't want to be a nag, and he *was* working really hard on his writing. 'It's only your first month on Jobseeker's. I'm sure it'll be a while before they start hassling you about finding work.'

'And hopefully I'll be back with Oh Boy! before they do.'

'Are you doing anything on Friday?' Roly asked her later as they cleared up after dinner.

'No, I've nothing planned.'

'I have some tickets for a gig at the Olympia, if you'd like to come? It's a band my agent manages: Rainmaker. They're good.'

'I've never heard of them, but yes please!' Ella loved live music, and it was ages since she'd been to a gig.

'Great! You could bring Andrew.'

'Oh. So … you have three tickets?'

Roly shook his head. 'Four. I'm asking Pippa.'

'Oh, great.' Shit! She'd thought it would just be her and Roly. But she'd already said yes, so it'd look weird if she suddenly changed her mind now that she knew Pippa was involved. She really didn't relish the thought of spending Friday night with her.

But maybe she was being unfair. She'd only met her once, after all. Besides, Roly liked her, so she couldn't really be that bad … could she? Nice people didn't fall in love with horrible ones, did they? Then again, even he'd said she was an asshole.

'Are you in touch with Pippa again, then?'

'Not yet, but I'm about to be. It's the one area of my goals board where I haven't ticked anything off.'

'So what's your first step?'

'I'm going to start flirting with her on Instagram.'

'Just like that? Doesn't she have a boyfriend?'

'No. They've just split up. So I have to strike fast, before someone else gets in there.'

'So you start chatting to her on Instagram? Why not just call her?'

'That's the easiest way in. Her Instagram is basically one big thirst trap, so all I have to do is start liking all her photos, commenting on how hot she looks, bringing the flame emojis…'

'Ah yes, the way to a girl's heart.'

Roly laughed. 'It's the way to Pippa's heart, believe me. Then I slide into her DMs and ask her out.'

'So it'd be like a double date?'

He shrugged. 'Or just four cool people going out together. We don't have to label it, do we? It'll be easier if we keep it casual, don't you think?'

'So it's a stealth double date?' she asked with a sly smile.

'Yeah. They need never know.'

'Okay, I'll ask Andrew.' It *would* be easier than asking him out on a proper date, and being in a group would take the pressure off. 'But if he says no, you can find yourself another wingman. I'm not third-wheeling it with you and Pippa.'

15

ANDREW, of course, didn't say no. Ella had never known him to turn down a freebie, and that clearly hadn't changed. They all arranged to meet up on Friday for pre-gig drinks in the bar of the Olympia.

Ella checked out Pippa's Instagram in preparation. She wanted to get some idea of what she was in for, figuring forewarned was forearmed. What she saw did nothing to allay her misgivings or make her any more enthusiastic about hanging out with Pippa for an evening. As she'd expected, there were lots of selfies; Pippa posing in front of mirrors and describing her outfits or the make-up she was wearing to her gazillion followers. She was obviously making money as an influencer too, and there were videos of her sampling and demonstrating various beauty products. She'd also recently collaborated with an upmarket leisurewear brand to design her own range of clothes. Ella had to admit her stuff looked really nice, but then anything would look good on Pippa. She was intimidatingly beautiful – a big, brash Amazonian with wide blue eyes, voluminous hair and a booming foghorn voice that would carry across several football pitches and was tailor made for the shouty gameshow she used to present.

She came across as bright, friendly and fun, relentlessly upbeat with a dazzling smile that never quit. She sent herself up a lot, conveying an image of someone relatable and down to earth despite her obvious advantages, who didn't take herself too seriously. But all Ella saw was an incessant appeal for approbation and admiration, and she thought it must be exhausting to be constantly chasing external validation from thousands of strangers.

She wondered was it driven by insecurity or vanity, but even the posts where Pippa was allegedly showing how shit she looked without make-up, unfiltered, with a break-out of spots or having a bad hair day were just obvious humble-brags and an invitation for her friends and followers to jump in and reassure her that she was stunning no matter what and praise her bravery in 'keeping it real'.

Andrew was already in the Olympia bar when Roly and Ella arrived, sitting at a table near the door. He stood and greeted Ella with a kiss on the cheek, and she introduced him and Roly.

'I'll get the drinks,' Roly said. 'What'll you have?'

'I'm fine, thanks,' Andrew said, nodding to the tall glass in front of him.

'A glass of red wine, please.' Ella sat beside Andrew while Roly went to the bar. He looked good in a pale-pink shirt and black chinos. He liked clothes, and he'd always dressed well.

'What are you drinking?' She nodded to the glass of clear liquid on the table. 'Gin and tonic?'

He shook his head. 'Just water.'

'Oh.' She was surprised he wasn't having a proper

drink when it wasn't a school night. She hoped it wasn't because he was playing the impoverished student.

'Pippa's running a bit late,' Roly said as he returned with the drinks. 'She was held up at work, but she should be here soon.'

'This is such a great venue for concerts,' Andrew said as Roly sat on the banquette opposite them. 'It's a while since I've been here.'

'My mum brought me to the panto here a few times,' Roly said. 'But I think I've only seen a band here once.'

'Really? We used to come here a lot, didn't we?' Andrew said to Ella.

'Yeah, we did.' Her mind flooded with memories of nights spent streaming from bar to student party to midnight gig at the Olympia; spilling out onto the streets in the early hours of the morning and eating cheap burgers from food trucks; the taste of red wine on Andrew's greasy lips, the warmth of his arms around her as she shivered in the cold air of dawn…

She felt Roly watching them closely, and he gave her a surreptitious wink when Andrew wasn't looking.

'Hello, hello, hello!' Pippa breezed in in a cloud of perfume and flopped onto the banquette beside Roly with a gusty sigh. 'Sorry I'm late, guys. You wouldn't believe the day I've had. Night. Mare!'

She was one of those people, Ella realised, who behaved as if you already knew each other the first time you met.

'Anyway, hello!' She addressed this final greeting to Ella and Andrew, and Roly took the opportunity to introduce them.

'You remember Ella? You've met her before.'

'Only briefly, and it was aeons ago,' Ella said as they

shook hands. She wanted to make it clear she didn't expect Pippa to remember her.

'Oh yeah!' Pippa beamed. 'Your schoolfriend? Aww, that's so sweet, you're still chums. Anyway, I need a drink.'

'I'll get it,' Andrew said, standing. Ella was pleased he was offering. 'Anyone else want another?'

Ella and Roly both said they were fine.

'I'll have the biggest glass of white known to man,' Pippa said. 'A New Zealand Sauvignon Blanc, if they have it. And ask them to make sure it's really cold. Thanks, Andy.'

Ella waited for Andrew to correct her, but he said nothing.

'Ella and I actually live together now,' Roly said as Andrew went to the bar.

'Oh, *really*?'

'Just in a housemates kind of way,' Ella said.

'So, is Andy your boyfriend?'

'Andrew, no. We used to go out. Years ago.'

Andrew returned and placed a large glass of wine in front of Pippa.

'Thanks, Andy. You're an angel.' She picked it up and took several long gulps. 'God, that's delicious.' She set it down again. 'Okay, scooch up everyone! Selfie time!' She picked up her phone and shifted along on the banquette. 'Come on, Andy.' She patted the empty space beside her with a jangle of bracelets. 'If it's not on Insta, it didn't happen, right?'

Andrew hated selfies, and strongly disapproved of social media and the whole culture of narcissism around it. Ella expected him to flat out refuse, or at least to be a curmudgeon about it, griping and groaning and making sure everyone felt his displeasure. But no, there he was scooching, without so much as a murmur or protest. In fact, he was cosying up to Pippa with almost indecent haste, leaning into the shot with his face against hers.

Ella bowed to the inevitable and perched on the banquette beside Roly while Pippa held her phone aloft and told them to smile. She took several shots in rapid succession, then spent some time tapping on her phone, choosing the best one, applying filters and texting captions and hashtags. 'I've tagged you,' she said to Roly. 'Will I tag you guys?' she asked, looking at Ella and Andrew.

'I don't have an Instagram account,' Andrew told her. Was Ella imagining it, or did she detect a note of regret in his voice? He could probably earn a lot of cool lecturer points if his students saw him at a gig, snuggled up to a glamorous model and influencer.

'You can tag me,' Ella said and gave Pippa her handle.

'There, done!' Pippa tossed her phone on the table and picked up her drink. 'Now that's out of the way, we can relax.' She took another long slug of wine. 'So, what do you do, Andy?'

'I'm a Philosophy lecturer at Trinity.'

'Wow, get you!'

Andrew smiled smugly.

'The closest I ever got to university was a "hot for teacher" photoshoot for Ariana's Boudoir.'

Andrew's eyes were bugging out.

'Yeah.' She laughed. 'I was the slutty student, trying to seduce the professor.' She undid the top buttons of her shirt, exposing a purple lace bra, then she leaned forward, pressing her boobs together and stuck a finger in her mouth, making sultry come-hither eyes at Andrew.

'Gosh!' Andrew reddened.

'Yeah, it was mad stuff.'

Effective, though, Ella reckoned. Andrew looked about ready to buy a bra or anything else Pippa was selling.

'Pity I didn't know you at the time,' she said, sitting back and buttoning up her shirt. 'It would have been nice to have a real hot professor instead of some thick model who thought a pair of glasses and a frown made him look intelligent.'

'So you're a model, Pippa?' Andrew asked.

Ella had to suppress a laugh at Pippa's expression. She obviously wasn't used to not being recognised and she looked affronted for a moment, stunned into silence. But she recovered quickly. 'Yes, but I don't do much modelling now, except for my own line. I've done some TV—'

'Anything I'd have seen?'

Unlikely, Ella thought, given Andrew's attitude to trashy TV.

'I did *Celebrity Cell Block*, *I'm A Celebrity* and *Stranded*, and I used to present *Shout It Out* – you know, the game show?'

Andrew shook his head. 'I never saw it.'

'Anyway, these days my main focus is clothes designing and influencer marketing. How about you?' she asked, turning to Ella. 'What do you do?'

'I work at a techwear company. I'm just doing general admin and marketing.'

Unusually, Andrew didn't jump in and make excuses for her lowly job. She waited for him to say that she was actually an academic and was just on hiatus, slumming it in the world of business until she could get back to her PhD. But it didn't happen.

'Good for you. God, I'm hopeless at organising anything. I have a ton of apps and planners, and I still don't know what I'm supposed to be doing half the time. What's the name of the company?'

'Citizens of the Wild.'

'I've heard of them,' Pippa said. 'Their stuff is brilliant.'

Ella nodded. 'They're going to London Fashion Week next year with their urban range.'

'Maybe I'll see you there.'

Once again she waited for Andrew to say she'd no longer be working there by then, but he didn't.

'You haven't asked me what I do,' Roly said.

'I know what you do,' she said, elbowing him playfully. 'Sod all!'

He shook his head. 'Guess again.'

'Why, what are you doing?'

'I'm signing on. I'm a Jobseeker.'

'Seriously?' Pippa asked, wide-eyed. 'Scumbag!' She laughed.

'Actually, it doesn't make me a scumbag at all. Ask Ella.'

'Well, lose that flab and I could get you some modelling work,' she said, her eyes flicking over him.

'Yeah, I'm working on it.'

Ella was cross on Roly's behalf. He *was* working on it – really hard. He'd already lost half a stone and was gaining noticeable muscle definition.

'I did this fantastic meal-replacement diet before I went into the jungle. I'll send you a link.'

'Thanks, but we're doing it the old-fashioned way,' Roly said, looking to Ella.

'Oh, you're both trying to lose weight? That's great because they have a two for the price of one offer on a subscription this month. And they're clients of mine, so I can give you a discount code.' She picked up her phone and thumbed through it.

Ella looked to Roly to turn down the offer, but he just shrugged at her. 'Thanks,' she said to Pippa, 'but I don't like the idea of those kinds of diets. We'd rather lose weight the natural way.'

'Oh, don't worry about that,' Pippa said, looking up from her phone. 'This stuff is all a hundred per cent natural and organic.' She tapped away at her phone. 'There,' she said, putting it down. 'I've sent you the link.'

'Great. Thanks.' Ella smiled weakly.

'Well, look at us,' Pippa said, 'being all grown up and mature, having a civilised night out with our exes. You know these two are living together now, Andy?' She nodded at Ella and Roly.

'Yes, I've heard.'

'Maybe we should play them at their own game.' She gave Andrew a flirtatious smile. 'What do you say? Should we shack up, give them a run for their money? Sauce for the goose and all that.'

What the hell was she playing at? Thankfully Andrew was saved from having to answer by an announcement that the show was about to begin. They quickly finished their drinks and joined the crowd surging towards the doors.

'Where to now?' Pippa asked later as they poured out onto Dame Street after the gig.

'It's a bit late,' Ella said, glancing at her watch. She'd enjoyed the concert, but she was ready to go home.

'Come on,' Pippa said. 'It's only half eleven. The night is young!'

'What do you want to do?' Ella looked to Andrew, hoping he'd be ready to call it a night. She couldn't very well abandon him with Roly and Pippa.

'We're out now. Let's make a night of it. Unless you don't want to?'

'No, you're right.' She swallowed her disappointment. He was obviously keen to go on somewhere, and she didn't want to be a wet blanket.

So they followed as Pippa led the way to a private club, a short walk from the theatre. She flashed a card and two burly bouncers on the door waved them all through. They descended a narrow staircase into a cavernous basement filled with whirling violet light.

'It's like the third circle of hell,' Ella hissed to Andrew, but he couldn't hear her over the thumping bass and merely shrugged, looking around with interest as Pippa led them to a set of purple velvet sofas grouped around a low glass table.

Even in her student days, Ella had never been a big fan of clubs, and this looked like her basic nightmare. But it would only be for an hour or two. How bad could it be?

What felt like five hours later, Ella glanced at her watch to find only forty minutes had passed. She took a big gulp of vodka and tried to relax, but her nerves were jangling. She was overwhelmed with exhaustion, her energy draining from her as if it was being suctioned from her body by a giant pump. The music pounded aggressively in her ears and vibrated in her chest, and she felt like she was being pummelled by it. It was almost painful, and she didn't think she could stand it another minute.

'You okay?' Roly asked, frowning at her in concern.

'Yeah, I'm fine. I'm just … I'm really tired.' She looked at Andrew. He and Pippa were huddled together on the opposite sofa, shouting in each other's ears. From the few snatches she'd heard, they seemed to be talking about his social media research.

'I'm going to go home,' she shouted across at him, breaking into their conversation. She felt a bit bad for dragging him away when he seemed to be enjoying himself, but she'd only come in the first place for his sake, so fair was fair. She'd stuck it out as long as she could. 'I'm pooped.'

'Aww,' Pippa gave her a pitying look, pouting exaggeratedly. 'Poor you. We're only getting started, aren't we?' she appealed to Roly.

He didn't answer her, looking up at Ella as she stood.

'Are you coming?' she asked Andrew.

'You don't have to go too, do you, Andy?' Pippa asked.

'I think I'll just stay for a while,' Andrew said to Ella.

'That's what I like to hear,' Pippa said, touching his leg. He looked like he was going to pass out with excitement.

'You don't mind, do you?' Andrew asked, looking up at her.

'No, of course not.' She shrugged into her coat. 'Enjoy the rest of the night.'

'You look lonely over there now, Roly. Come and sit here and we'll all snuggle up together.' Pippa patted the sofa on her other side.

Roly didn't budge. 'Really? You're staying?' he asked Andrew, the hint of a challenge in his voice.

'If you guys don't mind having a third wheel?'

For fuck's sake, Andrew, read the room! Surely any tone-deaf idiot could see that Roly wanted to be alone with Pippa.

'Of course we don't,' Pippa said, sucking her mojito through a straw and batting her eyelashes at him.

Ella seethed as Andrew lapped up her flattery. Shallow git! This wasn't his scene at all, but he was pathetically dazzled by Pippa's attention. So much for all his high-minded intellectual pretensions!

'Don't worry, we'll take care of him,' Pippa said to her. 'You go home and enjoy your early night.'

Ella fumed. It was almost one. She'd stayed out way

past the point of exhaustion already, and Pippa still got to treat her like a granny. It wasn't fair.

'Well, goodnight, then. You're sure you don't want to come with me?' she asked Andrew, making one last-ditch attempt to get him out of their hair. 'We could share a cab.'

'No, I'm happy here.'

'That's great!' Roly said. 'Because I'm a bit knackered too.' He drained his drink. 'So I'll head off with Ella and you two can stay here and enjoy yourselves.'

'What?' Pippa looked insultingly put out at the prospect of being left with Andrew, but he didn't seem to notice, still looking very pleased with himself.

Ella felt an ignoble thrill of triumph.

'Maybe we should call it a night too,' Pippa said to Andrew. 'It *is* getting late—'

'No, you guys stay. Don't let us spoil your fun,' Roly said as he stood and joined Ella. 'I'll talk to you tomorrow, yeah?' he said to Pippa.

'You don't have to do this, you know,' Ella hissed at Roly as they walked to the door.

She was enjoying her moment of victory, the look on Pippa's face and the feeling that she was sticking it to her. But it was only fair to let him off the hook.

'Do what?' he asked her.

'I'm fine going home on my own. You don't have to leave just because I am.'

'I know.'

'You're not really tired, are you?' she asked as they walked outside.

He shrugged. 'Maybe not tired exactly. But I'd had enough.' He walked to the edge of the pavement and flagged down a taxi. 'I was feeling a bit fed up, to be honest.'

They got in and Ella sagged with relief against the seat as they pulled away, feeling the irritation and discomfort seep away.

'Maybe that's not your scene anymore.'

'I guess I'm just out of practice,' he said. 'I have to build up to all-nighters.'

'Pippa was looking well.'

'Yeah.'

'Sorry I couldn't peel Andrew off her.'

'Not your fault. She was kind of getting on my tits, anyway,' he admitted. 'Maybe I am tired?'

'Maybe.' She still wasn't convinced he hadn't left with her just to be nice. She smiled and rested her head on his shoulder as they zipped through the traffic. 'I thought you wanted us to leave the two of you alone.'

'No. What gave you that impression?'

'You seemed pissed off.'

'I just thought Andrew should have left with you, that's all.'

'Cuppa?' Roly asked when they got in. 'Or are you going straight to bed?'

'No, a cup of tea would be good.' She felt better already now that she was away from the noise. She took off her coat and tossed it on a chair, then kicked off her shoes and flopped onto the sofa with a heartfelt sigh.

Roly put two mugs of tea on the coffee table and sat down beside her.

'So … will you be seeing Andrew again?'

She picked up her tea, curling both hands around the mug. 'I don't know. Definitely not if he gets lucky with Pippa tonight.'

'In his dreams!' Roly huffed a laugh.

'Well, maybe we shouldn't have left them alone together,' she said, annoyed.

'As if he'd have any chance with her,' he said.

'I don't see why not. She seemed pretty into him from where I was sitting.'

'She was just flirting with him to get at me. Trying to make me jealous.'

'Oh, of course. It's all about you. I should have realised.'

'I'm not saying that.'

'What are you saying, then?'

'Just … I know Pippa, okay? She wouldn't look twice at a guy like Andrew.'

'You think he's out of her league, don't you?'

'Well, yeah. It's obvious, isn't it?'

'Not to me.' She sipped her tea, trying to shake off the irritation that was bubbling up inside her.

'Don't get me wrong. I'm not dissing Andrew – he's a good-looking guy. But Pippa'd have been out of my league too, if I hadn't been in Oh Boy! I told you before, she wouldn't have been with me if I was some nobody.'

'I can't believe that doesn't bother you.'

'Why should it?'

'Because … it's so shallow. If she was just with you because you were rich and famous—'

Roly shrugged. 'It's just human nature, isn't it – animal instinct. Survival of the fittest. You can't blame her. Everyone wants to be with the most successful person they can get – like the alpha gorilla or the head lion or whatnot.'

'Where do you get this stuff?'

'Pippa's a big fan of the Discovery Channel. I saw a lot of those nature programmes when I was with her. She could tell you anything you want to know about the life cycle of the humpback whale or the mating habits of orang-utans. But it makes sense, doesn't it? The female wants a mate who can provide for the family.'

'You think Pippa wanted to have kids with you?'

He smiled. 'No, but you're drawn to it at a subconscious level – to the leader of the pack, the dude with the biggest balls or the best hunting skills or whatever.'

'I think humans have evolved a bit past all that.'

Roly shook his head. 'It's just what's seen as desirable has changed, because we've progressed. Guys can afford to chase after models now; whereas in olden times, we'd have had to look for someone with wide, child-bearing hips who could win a fight with a bear. But it's the same basic instinct.'

Ella laughed. 'And I'm free to date a dweeb like Andrew instead of some muscle-bound caveman?'

'Exactly! Though I think you can do better.'

Ella smiled, secretly pleased. 'What do you suppose the two of them are talking about right now?'

'The sex life of the dung beetle? Fourth wave feminism?'

'How do you know about fourth wave feminism?'

'Why, is it supposed to be a secret?'

Ella laughed. 'By now they've probably moved on from the Ariana's Boudoir spring/summer collection and are discussing the finer points of existentialism.'

'And existentialism is…?'

'You know, the idea that existence precedes essence.'

'Of course.' Roly nodded sagely.

'Because there's no God.'

'Goes without saying.'

'So there's no such thing as human nature.'

Roly reared back, eyebrows raised. 'Who says?'

'Jean-Paul Sartre, among others.'

'Does he indeed? Bloody cheek! And who's he when he's at home?'

'Boyfriend of Simone de Beauvoir.'

'Poor cow. He sounds like a right barrel of laughs. Well, Pippa won't be having that.'

'The idea that there's no such thing as human nature?'

'Yeah. I told you she loves the Discovery Channel; David Attenborough and all that.'

'So?'

'Well, she'd probably say what makes us so special? If hippos and wombats and stuff can have a nature, why can't we?'

'Good point, Pippa.' Ella drained her mug.

'We're all just mammals when it comes down to it, aren't we, Andy?' He mimicked Pippa's voice and fluttered his eyelashes coquettishly.

Ella laughed. 'And Andrew will say he never thought of it like that, and forget all about Sartre because he's drooling so hard.'

'Do you miss all that?'

'What?'

'Discussing philosophy and stuff.'

'Not really.'

'I mean, I'll give it a go if you want.'

She shook her head. 'It's all just going around in circles really – discussing theories and abstract concepts. It doesn't make anything happen. Nothing gets created or changed. I'd rather talk about real life.'

Andrew had never tired of those earnest undergraduate discussions, the enervating afternoons spent sitting around dissecting the ideas of Kant, Nietzsche or Adorno. She'd found it stimulating up to a point, after which it made her twitch with longing to go outside and feel the cold, sharp air on her skin; to run until her lungs were bursting and her heart pounding with energy and life; to swim and swim in an ice-cold sea.

'You don't think they're getting off with each other right now, do you?' Roly asked.

'No,' Ella said, trying to imbue the word with more conviction than she felt.

'One thing leads to another…'

'Yeah. Maybe she'll flash him again.'

'Sorry about that.'

Ella shrugged. 'Not your fault.'

'You could flash me, if you like.' He raised an eyebrow, grinning. 'Get your revenge.'

Ella giggled. 'Nice try. How is that getting my revenge?'

'Like Pippa said, sauce for the goose…'

Their eyes met, and Ella's breath caught. Roly's gaze dropped to her lips and for a moment she thought he was going to kiss her. Suddenly all she could think of was his beautiful mouth, how warm and soft it looked and how much she wanted to kiss it.

'Are you still in love with her?' She was surprised to hear herself saying that. She hadn't planned it. It had just come out.

'What?' Roly seemed as taken aback by the question as she was.

'You sound … fond when you talk about her.'

He frowned, a slow smile curling the corners of his mouth. 'I dunno. I guess I still have … feelings for her.'

'Feelings in your pants?'

He rolled his eyes. 'Shut up! Why do you have to bring everything down to sex?'

She shrugged. 'Human nature, innit?' She fluttered her eyelashes, and Roly collapsed in laughter.

'What about Andrew?'

'What about him?'

'Are you still in love with him?'

She considered. It was a question she'd been asking herself a lot lately. 'I don't know. I think I could be … in time. Sometimes I wonder if I already am. But then I don't know if I'm just remembering how I used to feel or if it's actually how I feel now.' She frowned. 'It's complicated.'

Made even more confusing by the fact that she'd wanted Roly to kiss her just now. Shit! Was she starting to fancy him? She supposed she always had a bit, but it wasn't something she'd nurtured. She'd never expected anything to happen between them, for a whole variety of reasons, so she hadn't given it life, let it breathe. She'd put it out of her mind and got on with being friends. But that had been easy when she'd hardly seen him. He hadn't been a real presence in her life, just an occasional visitor. Now they were together every day, it wouldn't be so easy to ignore.

16

THE FIRST SATURDAY in May dawned bright and sunny, the first dry, warm day after two weeks of blustery rain. It was as if nature had produced summer to schedule. Monday was a Bank Holiday, and Ella had decided to use the long weekend to rest and recharge. So instead of joining Roly for an early morning run, she had a lie-in, luxuriating in her freshly laundered bedclothes. They'd agreed to relax their diet and allow themselves some treats, and Roly went by the Bretzel on his way home, returning with a bag of freshly baked bagels and croissants. While he went for a shower, Ella dusted off the mosaic bistro table and chairs on the terrace, and they had breakfast in the garden.

'This is heaven,' Ella sighed happily as she smeared apricot jam on warm, flaky croissant, the aroma of rich black coffee mingling in the air with the scent of flowers and warm earth. She closed her eyes, savouring her first bite of delicious buttery pastry. One of the nice things about dieting, she'd discovered, was that you enjoyed treats all the more when you had them.

'The garden's lovely,' she said, opening her eyes and

looking around. 'Do you do it yourself?' There were a couple of raised beds with flowers coming into bud, and several large colourful pots planted with lush trees and shrubs.

'No,' Roly said, smiling. 'I haven't a clue. I hired a gardener.'

He yawned and stretched, his T-shirt riding up to give a tantalising glimpse of stomach, which Ella couldn't help noticing was attractively toned and approaching the much sought-after flatness. He'd installed a pull-up bar above his bedroom door, and did free weights most days now on top of his cardio workouts. It was really paying off.

'Any plans for the weekend?' he asked.

'No, nothing. Unless you count not going anywhere and not seeing anyone as a plan.'

'Apart from dinner tomorrow,' he said quickly.

'Yes, don't worry. I'm not going to bale on that.' Every week Roly told Ella she was invited to Sunday dinner at his nan's, and she'd finally accepted the offer. When she'd moved in, she hadn't expected her life to become so enmeshed with Roly's. It just seemed to happen naturally, inevitably, their lives gradually merging together more and more. He'd been out with her workmates, and now she was going to have dinner with his family. She liked it, but she wasn't sure it was a good idea in the long run. She felt she should cultivate more friends of her own, a social circle that didn't include Roly. Sunday was traditionally family time, and should be the perfect opportunity for them to diverge and do their own thing, spend it with their own people. But her people were gone, and, she had to admit, she was glad to have Roly's family step in to fill the vacuum.

'I hope this weather keeps up.' She turned her face to the sun. 'I just want to chill out with a book and take it easy.' She'd considered meeting up with someone over the weekend, but Hazel was going to Paris with her boyfriend, and Andrew was visiting his brother in London. She'd found herself perfectly content that neither of them were available. Her life had been busy the past few weeks, and she wasn't used to that level of activity. She was looking forward to some down time with nowhere particular to be and no pressure to be social.

'How about you?' she asked Roly.

'I'm meeting a few of the lads this evening for drinks. You're welcome to come if you want?' He rattled off the names of some of the guys he used to hang out with at school. It amazed her that he seemed to still be in touch with everyone from back then.

'Thanks, but I'm looking forward to a quiet night in.'

'On Monday I'm playing golf with Jack.'

'Jack?' He'd said the name as if it was someone she should know.

'You know – Jack Golden?'

'Really? You still see him?'

'Of course. He's my best mate. Don't you see anyone from school anymore?'

'No.' She and Julie still sent each other Christmas cards, but that was it. Even the messages scribbled inside those had dwindled over the years, from letters catching up on each other's news, to a well-intentioned promise to meet up in the New Year that never came to pass, to just a signature scrawled under the printed greeting.

'I don't see so much of him now, of course, since he's had a baby.'

'Jack has a baby?'

'Yeah.' Roly's mouth widened in a fond smile. 'Zoe. She's really cute.'

'Wow! I can't imagine that – Jack with a baby.' In her

head he was still a teenage boy, frozen in time in his last year of school, forever poised on the brink of adulthood.

'I know. Weird, isn't it? Everyone's all grown up.'

'Except us,' she said with a wry smile.

'Yeah. We're like...' He snapped his fingers. 'Who was it who fell asleep for like a hundred years and then woke up?'

'Sleeping Beauty?'

'No ... it was a bloke.'

'Um ... Dracula? Edward Cullen?'

'I think we did him in school...' He frowned, thinking. 'Rip van Winkle!' he shouted with relief.

'Rip van Winkle? What subject would we have done him in?'

'I don't know ... history?'

'History?' She burst out laughing. 'A guy who fell asleep for a hundred years?'

'Well ... Science, then? Biology? We learned about that bloke who burst into flames out of the blue.'

She nodded. 'Spontaneous combustion.'

'Was that in History? Something to do with the industrial revolution? Oh! Did it give him the idea for the combustion engine, and he went on to invent it?'

'Hardly, when he was dead.'

'Oh yeah.'

'Anyway, that was Dickens. We did it in English class.'

'Dickens spontaneously combusted? I never knew that!'

Ella could hardly speak, she was laughing so hard. 'No,' she said, brushing tears from her eyes. 'It was a character in a Dickens novel. *Bleak House*.'

'Who's Rip van Winkel, then?'

She shrugged. 'I don't know. I think it's probably a fairy-tale.' She picked up her phone and Googled it. 'It's a short story, apparently. He got drunk and fell asleep – but it was only for twenty years. We definitely didn't "do him in school".'

Roly frowned. 'So how do I know him?'

'I have no idea.'

'Huh! Me neither. Is there a picture?' He nodded to her phone.

'Just a drawing.' She held the phone out to him, showing him the screen.

'He reminds me of someone my mum used to go out with. Same beard. He was a drunk layabout too.'

'When we were in school, you said Mr Casaubon from *Middlemarch* reminded you of your mum's boyfriend.'

'That was a different one. She's gone out with a long line of tossers.' Roly's smile faded and he looked sad. 'But she's met someone recently who seems decent,' he said, cheering up.

'That's good.'

'Yeah, it's great.' He smiled. 'She seems really happy.' He nodded to the plate. 'Do you want the last sesame seed bagel?'

'No,' Ella said, even though she did. 'You have it.'

'Split it?' he asked, reaching for it.

'Yes please!' Ella smiled.

'After all,' he said, cutting it down the middle, 'a carb shared is a carb halved.'

'Will your mum's new boyfriend be there?' Ella asked the following evening as they made their way to his nan's for dinner. She lived in the Liberties, within walking distance of Roly's house, and it was a pleasant stroll on a warm, sunny evening.

'No. He's working abroad at the moment – somewhere

in the Middle East. I can't remember where exactly. She hasn't met him in real life yet.'

'They met online, then?'

'Yeah, some dating site.'

'What's the story with your dad?'

He gave a harsh laugh. 'Your guess is as good as mine.'

'Sorry,' she said hastily. 'I didn't mean to be nosy.'

'Nah, it's fine.'

'Is he … still around?' Roly's father had never really been in the picture as long as she'd known him, and she couldn't remember Roly ever mentioning him. She knew he'd been a Premier League footballer who'd played briefly for Liverpool and had what promised to be a dazzling career cut short by a horrific leg injury. She had no idea where or when she'd heard that. It was just one of those stories that seemed to be common knowledge.

'He's still alive, if that's what you mean.'

'Do you ever see him?'

'No. He fucked off when my mum found out she was pregnant. He lives in Thailand now. Has a wife and two kids, apparently.' His voice had taken on a hard edge.

'So you've never met him?'

'Yeah, I did – once, after the band took off.' He gave a bitter laugh. 'He came to a gig in Manchester. I was over the moon.' He shook his head. 'I was such an idiot. I used to have these stupid fantasies when I was a kid about becoming a famous footballer like him, and then he'd turn up at one of my matches – when I was scoring the winning goal in the World Cup or something – and he'd be absolutely blown away by my awesome skills. So when he turned up that night I thought it was all coming true. Here I was, this big famous pop star. I thought he'd be all proud of me and shit.'

'I'm sure he was.'

'Nah. Turned out he just wanted money. He was hard up. His football career was over and he was drinking – a lot; he had a gambling problem.' He drew a deep, ragged breath. 'I said he should stay and watch the show, and we could go out for dinner afterwards – my treat. I gave him a backstage pass and everything … playing the big man.' He rolled his eyes self-deprecatingly. 'But he wasn't interested in watching me "prancing around onstage, making a prat of myself". He just wanted the money, and he acted like I was making him work for it – like watching the concert would be such a chore. Which, okay, I suppose he had a point.'

'No he didn't! Your shows were brilliant!'

He eyed her sceptically. 'I seem to remember you calling us "cheesy as fuck".'

'Shut up,' she mumbled, relieved when he laughed.

'Anyway, I just gave him the cash and he buggered off. That was the first and last I saw of him.'

Ella was sorry she'd brought it up. She felt a bit ashamed that she'd never realised so much hurt and vulnerability lurked beneath the surface of Roly's self-confidence.

'Well, you're better off without him.'

'Yeah, that's what my mum says. Good riddance.'

Roly's nan lived in a row of narrow two-storey houses in one of Dublin's oldest neighbourhoods, close to the Guinness brewery. The smell of roasting barley hung in the air.

'These used to be all council houses,' Roly told her as they turned into the street, 'but most of the families have bought them out by now.'

'And your nan owns hers?'

'Yeah, they bought it out years ago – her and my grandfather.'

'Your grandfather's dead, right?'

'Yeah, he died when Mum was only five.' He smiled. 'The men in this family check out early one way or another.'

Roly let them into the house with his own key. 'Hi, Nan,' he called loudly as he ushered Ella inside. The door opened directly into a bright living room, with an open-tread wooden staircase to one side. She followed Roly through to a tiny galley kitchen. It was modern and cheerful, with tongue and groove units painted sage green. Sun streamed in through an open window, and colourful crockery jostled for space on the dresser and work surfaces with piles of newspapers and magazines.

'Hello, love.' A short, stocky woman with cropped dark hair turned from the stove, wiping her hands on her apron, and gave Roly a hug.

'Nan, this is Ella.'

'Christine,' she said, holding out her hand to Ella. 'I've not met you before, have I?' she asked as they shook hands.

'No, you haven't. Nice to meet you.' The term 'nan' had conjured an image in Ella's mind of a frail, twinkly-eyed old lady that was nothing like the sturdy, buxom woman standing before her in jeans and an oversized T-shirt. Her eyes were lively and bright, her cheeks ruddy, and her smile jolly and vivacious, carving deep grooves around her eyes and mouth.

'Loretta will be here shortly, and then we'll eat,' she said, turning back to the stove. There was a sizzle of fat as she bent to open the oven door, the delicious smell of roast chicken filling the air as she lifted out a perfectly bronzed bird. When she'd covered it in foil and left it to rest, she took off her apron and tossed it on the worktop.

'Ella, what will you have to drink?' she asked. The little kitchen was hot and steamy, and she was flushed and a little out of breath from her exertions, her face glistening with sweat. 'There's red wine open, and there's a bottle of white in the fridge. Or would you rather something else? Gin? Vodka?'

'Wine would be lovely, thanks. Red, please.'

'It's on the table,' she said to Roly. 'I'll just finish up in here and I'll be with you in a minute.'

The living room was bright and cosy, furnished with an eclectic mix of old and modern pieces, with just the right amount of clutter to feel homely but not overwhelming. But mostly it was a shrine to Roly. Ella looked around in awe at the framed tour posters, magazine covers and publicity photos that lined the walls, alongside the usual childhood pictures that crowded the sideboard and mantelpiece.

'Nan's my number-one fan,' Roly said with a grin as he poured her a glass of wine.

'No kidding!'

When she said she needed the loo and Roly directed her upstairs, she passed a gallery of Oh Boy! photos lining the staircase – on stage at concerts, holding up gongs at awards ceremonies, lined up on colourful sofas in TV studios. Even as she sat on the loo, she found herself eyeballing a photo of the band, waving and grinning as they looked out over a packed auditorium of cheering fans.

Roly's mum had arrived when she went back to the living room, and Roly introduced them. Loretta was a very pretty woman and looked young for her age, despite the tell-tale lines around her mouth and soft blue eyes. She could hardly have been more different to her mother. Where Christine had the unkempt look of someone who wasn't much bothered about her appearance, Loretta was well put together, her clothes stylish and tastefully accessorised, her face subtly made up. She had the kind of effortless style that Ella admired and envied.

'You were in Roly's class at school?' she asked as they shook hands. 'I don't remember you.'

'We weren't really friends back then.'

'Yeah, we only got to know each other in the final term,' Roly said.

'Well, it's lovely to meet you, Ella.'

While Loretta and Christine disappeared into the kitchen to do the last-minute things like making gravy and carving the meat, Ella picked up her glass of wine from the table and walked over to the sideboard, studying the photos of Roly.

'I was a cute baby, wasn't I?' he said, looking over her shoulder.

'All babies are cute,' Ella said, picking up a framed photo of him as a toddler in a yellow babygro. But then another photo, pushed to the back, caught her eye – an iconic image that Ella recognised at once. 'Oh, is that—' She picked it up and studied it, though she'd seen it many times before. It was 1971 and a group of women were marching down the platform of Connolly Train Station behind a large Irish Women's Liberation Movement banner.

'The Contraceptive Train,' Christine said, coming into the room behind her and glancing across at the photo in Ella's hand. 'That was a great day.'

'You were there?' Ella turned to her. She and Loretta were setting dishes on the table.

'I sure was.' She grinned, coming over to stand beside Ella. 'You can just see the side of my face there.' She pointed at a woman towards the back of the group with a mop of curly hair, her face half turned from the camera, one arm punching the air.

'Oh god, don't get Nan started on her glory days in the Women's Lib movement,' Roly said.

'No, I'd love to hear about it,' Ella told Christine.

'Mum was quite the activist in her day,' Loretta said with a smile as they all sat around the table. 'She used to hijack my school art projects and get me to paint placards. She was always marching about something or other.'

'What do you mean, in my day?' Christine said indignantly. 'I'm still fighting the good fight.'

'True.' Loretta smiled fondly at her. 'You can't keep a bolshie woman down.'

'I should say not.'

As they helped themselves to chicken, stuffing, vegetables, and the most perfect crunchy roast potatoes Ella had ever seen, Christine told Ella more about the trip on The Contraceptive Train. It was an infamous event in the history of Irish feminism, when a group of women had taken the train to Belfast to buy contraceptives, which were illegal in Ireland at the time. When they returned to Dublin with their purchases, they faced up to the customs officials who confronted them, defiantly refusing to hand over their contraband – mainly condoms and spermicidal jelly as they'd failed in their mission to buy the contraceptive pill.

'It never occurred to us that you'd need a prescription for it,' Christine said now, laughing. 'So instead we bought loads of aspirin, took them out of their packets and pretended they were the pill. We relied on the customs officers not knowing the difference. And, sure enough, they didn't.'

Ella was familiar with the story, but she'd never met

someone who'd actually been there before; never heard a first-hand account.

'I'll never forget walking down that platform when we got back to Dublin,' Christine said, 'all of us afraid we were going to be arrested. And then suddenly we heard all this chanting – people outside in the station shouting, 'Let them through, let them through!' and we knew they were on our side.' Christine's eyes shone as she reminisced. 'It was glorious! One of the best days of my life.'

'It makes me so angry how women were treated in this country,' Ella said. She'd been listening, rapt.

Christine nodded. 'We really were second-class citizens. And what happened to single mothers back then was barbaric.'

'It was so cruel,' Loretta said sadly. 'It's scary to think what could have happened if Mum and Dad hadn't supported me when I got pregnant with Roly. It's not even that long ago, but it was a very different time.'

'It was the same with widows and deserted wives – if you didn't have a man, you were nobody. We were fortunate that Jim – that's Roly's grandfather – worked in Guinness's. They looked after their employees and their families, including their widows and orphans.'

No wonder she still liked to live in the shelter of the brewery, Ella thought.

'Anyway, enough about the bad old days,' Christine said brightly.

'Yes, let's talk about something more cheerful,' Loretta said. 'We don't want to scare poor Ella off.'

'Oh no, I'm really interested,' Ella said, smiling at Christine.

'I knew you two would hit it off,' Roly said. 'Ella's a bit of a feminist too,' he told his nan.

'What do you mean, "a bit of a feminist"?' she gasped.

'You make it sound like it's something I dabble in at weekends.'

'Okay, okay.' He grinned, holding up his hands. 'You're an all-round full-time bra-burning feminist, like Nan. Well, maybe without the bra-burning bit because I doubt you've ever done that. Did you know that's not just an expression?' he asked her, wide-eyed. 'People actually did that.'

'Yes, I know,' she said with a laugh.

'Well, these two are sick of hearing about my rebel days. But if you're really interested, you should come to my knitting group, Ella. It's a few of my friends from back then. They've got some stories!'

'I can't knit,' she said regretfully.

'Oh, that doesn't matter. We'd teach you. If you'd like to learn, that is.'

'I'd love to!'

'And we don't *always* knit,' she said, shooting her daughter a sly smile. 'Sometimes we paint placards and make banners.'

Ella was glad she'd caved in and finally accepted the invitation to dinner with Roly's family. The food was delicious and the conversation flowed easily. They talked about the miracle of good weather coinciding with a bank holiday, and what they were watching on TV – they were all fans of the *Great British Bake Off* and *Queer Eye*.

'I'm always telling Mum she should go on *Bake Off*,' Roly said.

'You should,' Christine told her daughter.

'I'm not sure I could cope with the cameras.'

'I'd love to have a makeover from the Fab Four,' Ella said. 'Well … maybe not Karamo so much. He'd probably make me do the climbing wall at work to confront my fear or something.'

'Mum's brilliant at doing makeovers,' Roly said.

'Not that I think you need it,' Loretta said to Ella. 'You look lovely. But if you'd like any advice about clothes or make-up, I'd be happy to help.'

'Thanks. That's really kind, and I might take you up on it. I've kind of lost my mojo.'

'Roly told us you'd been sick.'

Whenever she talked about her M.E., Ella braced herself for a whole range of responses – casual dismissal, benign ignorance, outright hostility, well-meaning suggestions about doing yoga or trying herbs. To her relief they were sympathetic, but matter of fact about it.

'My friend Maureen's daughter has that,' Loretta said. 'It's an awful thing.'

'The worst of it is the doctors!' Christine said. 'It was ages before she got one to take her seriously. A lot of them treated her like she was just malingering.' She pursed her lips, shaking her head. 'But you're all right now?' she asked Ella.

'Yes, thank you. I'm one of the lucky ones.'

'That's great. And you've plenty of time to go back to your studies and pick up where you left off.'

Ella smiled, reassured that for once someone didn't make her feel like time was running out.

'Nan went to college when she was in her sixties and got a degree,' Roly told her proudly.

'Well done! That's really impressive.'

'I'd have loved to go to uni when I was younger, but we didn't have the money. But there are advantages to being a mature student. I had a marvellous time.'

'What did you study?'

'History and Political Science. So you see, it's never too late.'

'That's very nice to hear.'

'Roly tells me you two are working out together and you've started running,' Loretta said.

'You did The Shred, didn't you, Nan?' Roly asked, throwing Ella an amused look.

'I used to, but it's been a while. My knees wouldn't be up to it these days. I get down all right, but getting up again is a challenge.'

'I thought I might take up running,' Loretta said. 'I need to get in shape.'

'You're already in great shape,' Christine told her. 'I hope this isn't about that new boyfriend of yours. That's not how you were raised.'

Loretta smiled. 'Don't diet-shame me, Mum,' she said teasingly. 'I just want to lose a few pounds, tone up a bit. It's my body, my choice – *that's* how I was raised.'

'Touché!' Christine laughed, holding her hands up.

'Actually, Ella,' Loretta said, 'I have an offer for a new Pilates class that's starting next week – two for the price of one. You're welcome to join me, if you'd like?'

'Thanks, I'd love to. I'm not very disciplined at keeping up with stuff like that on my own, so a class would be brilliant.'

'Great!'

'So, when are we going to meet this man of yours?' Christine asked Loretta.

'Oh, not for a while yet.' She sighed. 'He was supposed to be moving here at the end of this month, but then his daughter got sick and he's had to put it off. But I have a photo.' She dug in the bag at her feet and pulled out her phone. She thumbed through it, then held it out to them, showing them a photo of a handsome, tanned man with cropped silver hair and white, even teeth, his arm around a dark-haired teenage girl. Their faces were pressed together as they beamed for the camera.

'Very handsome,' Christine said, taking the phone and scrutinising the picture.

'That's his daughter,' Loretta said. 'He's a widower – lost his wife to cancer a couple of years ago.'

'That's sad,' Ella said. 'Where's he from?'

'America – Minnesota originally. But he's in the military, so he travels around the world a lot.'

There was something about the story that gave Ella an uneasy feeling, but she couldn't put her finger on it. Then Christine produced a peach pie for dessert, and she put it out of her mind as everyone groaned that they were too full, but would make room anyway. It looked too good to resist.

'All bets are off for the weekend anyway,' Roly said, accepting a slice of pie from Christine.

'You know where we are now, Ella,' Christine said as they were leaving. 'Call in any time. The door's always open. Don't feel you have to wait to come with Roly.'

'Thank you.'

'I'll text you about the knitting group.'

'And I'll pick you up for Pilates on Wednesday,' Loretta said, waving them off.

'I had a really good time,' Ella said to Roly as they walked home. 'Thanks for bringing me.'

'You're welcome.'

'I love your nan.'

'I knew you would.'

'And your mum too, of course,' she added hastily.

'I hope they weren't crowding you too much.'

'No, not at all. Do you think your nan meant it about me calling over?'

'Totally. She's not the type to say it if she didn't really want you around.'

'That's what I thought.' Ella smiled.

'She liked you. But don't feel you have to join her coven if you don't want to – or go to Pilates with Mum.' He rolled his eyes.

'Why do you say it like that? She just wants to get fit, same as us. There's nothing wrong with that.'

'I know, but … I just wish she wasn't doing it because she wants to look good naked for some dude off the internet.'

That reminded Ella of what Loretta had told them about her boyfriend, and her niggling feeling returned.

'But whatever makes her happy.' He shrugged.

'That's the spirit.'

I'll just try not to think about her motives.'

'Attaboy!' Ella clapped him on the shoulder. 'I'm sure you can do it.'

17

'Roly Punch?'

Jesus, keep your voice down. Roly cringed as a tall, angular woman with lank hair stepped out of her office and beckoned him inside. Thankfully no one paid any attention, and it was a relief to get away from the prying eyes of all the other deadbeats waiting around in the stale afternoon air of the social welfare office, waiting their turn with some bored civil servant behind a Plexiglas screen while a TV blinked silently in the corner.

It had turned out Ella was right, and he'd been summoned for a meeting with his case worker to discuss his employment prospects.

'See, I told you!' he'd said to Ella when he'd shown her the letter. 'I've got a *case worker*, like some … young offender!'

'You're too old to be a young offender.'

'Very funny.'

He'd already had to attend an information meeting about training courses and back-to-work schemes, and now he was going to have to explain himself to this woman who was ushering him into her office. Still, he supposed it was a small price to pay for getting his cash every week.

'Hello, I'm Geraldine.' She shook his hand, then waved him to a seat on the other side of her desk.

He reckoned Geraldine was around the same age as him. It was strange how much people's lives diverged once you grew up, he thought. When you were kids, everyone did pretty much the same stuff – going to school, playing with your friends, doing homework. Then you became adults, and some people became pop stars and went on world tours while others ended up in places like this, sitting at a desk in a dingy government office under fizzing fluorescent strip lighting day in, day out. It was sad how some people's lives turned out.

'So, how are you getting on?'

'Fine, thanks, Geraldine. How are you?'

She seemed taken aback by the pleasantry. Most of her customers mustn't be as polite and friendly as he was.

'I'm grand, thanks, Roly. But I meant the job search. How's that going?' She tapped a manila folder in front of her. He saw his name written on it in Sharpie.

'Oh, the Jobseeker's? That's working out great!' He gave her a reassuring smile. 'I've been going to the post office every week and they hand over the cash, no problem. They're really nice about it, in fact. I've had no trouble from them at all.'

'Right.' Geraldine looked confused. 'Well, I'm glad you're getting your payments. But I meant your actual job search. How are you getting on with that? Any interviews?'

'Oh, um … no. No interviews as such.' Shit! So she thought he was actually looking for work. He'd thought the 'actively seeking employment' thing was just a wink-wink box-ticking exercise. So he'd been right all along. He was a welfare cheat. Thanks a bunch, Ella.

'No leads at all?'

'Well … I was offered *Celebrity Cell Block* this year.' He felt had to give her something.

'And you didn't take it?'

No, Geraldine, he thought. Because here I am before you, while those twats are on the telly in the waiting room, eating slop in the prison canteen and sneaking into each other's bunks. 'Um, no … the timing didn't suit. And my agent said it wasn't the right move for me.'

Geraldine cleared her throat and opened her file. 'Okay. So you're still looking then.'

'Um … yeah.'

'What sort of thing are you looking for?'

'Well, I mean, something in the entertainment line. I've been writing some songs…'

'Okay.' Geraldine nodded encouragingly. 'What about cruise ships, have you considered that? They're often looking for entertainers, aren't they?'

Cruise ships! Jesus! What did Geraldine think he was? 'Yeah, I guess … I hadn't really thought of that.'

'Or maybe you could sing at weddings, something like that?' Geraldine gave him a bright smile.

'Yeah, I don't know if that's really my style.'

'You need to be creative, think outside the box. Let's have a ponder.' She slid an A4 pad in front of her and picked up a pen.

Oh god, he'd thought this was just going to be a quick chat that he could bluff his way through, but Geraldine was actually going to brainstorm his 'career' with him.

'You went to the information meeting about our training and employment services?'

'Yeah, I did.' He'd been the oldest one there. He'd kept his head down as he'd sat watching the presentation with a bunch of pimply jobless youths, in a sweat the whole time that someone would recognise him, take a furtive photo and post it on social media.

'So you know the purpose of today is for us to come up with a plan to progress you back into work.'

'Yeah.' He'd nodded off a couple of times as the presenter had droned on about work experience placements and training courses, but he'd got the gist. 'I mean, I wouldn't exactly say "back to work" since I wasn't really in work in the first place.'

'Well, maybe this is an opportunity to try something new,' Geraldine said briskly. 'There are lots of training courses available to you.' She handed over a pamphlet. 'Have a look through that and let me know if there's anything that interests you, and I'll arrange to get you registered.'

'Okay, thanks.'

'And the council are recruiting right now, so that's a possibility.'

'The council? They hire singers?'

'Oh no.' Geraldine laughed. 'Clerical workers. I could get you an application?'

'Um … sure.' He nodded, wanting to appear willing. But he had no intention of letting Geraldine steer him into a job like hers, stuck in a place like this. 'Though I doubt I have the qualifications for something like that.'

'You did the Leaving Cert, yes?'

'Yeah, I did.'

'Well, that's all you need for an entry-level job.'

'Oh! That's…great.' Shit! Was this the 'something to fall back on' that his mother had set him up for? 'I mean, I'd need something more flexible, though, in case something better turns up.'

'Like what?'

He shrugged. 'Well, if I was offered *Strictly*, for instance.'

She smiled. 'Your friend Zack did that a while back, didn't he? He was really good.'

'Yeah, brilliant.' He'd made it to the final, but at least he'd fallen short of winning.

'Maybe you'd be better off getting a job and doing music in your spare time? I'm sure lots of artists like yourself have day jobs to pay the bills. In fact, one of our senior officers here is an author! She's had two books published.'

'Good for her.'

'And Kevin in Accounts plays in a folk band at weekends. They're really good. They played a few songs at our Christmas party last year. I could ask him to have a chat with you, if you'd like? Nothing official, but I'm sure he'd be happy to give you some tips. He might even have some useful contacts for you.'

'Um … thanks. Maybe later down the line? If I'm…' What was a polite word for 'desperate'? 'I mean, when I've … exhausted other avenues. Tried to make it on my own, you know.' Did she seriously think he should be taking showbiz tips from Kevin in Accounts? It didn't sound like his singing career was the roaring success Geraldine seemed to imagine it was.

'Oh, funerals!' she suddenly exclaimed, her face lighting up.

'What?'

'People are always looking for someone to sing at funerals, aren't they? That could be perfect for you.'

'Right,' he nodded thoughtfully as if he was seriously considering this. 'Well, it's certainly something to think about.' Geraldine was so obviously delighted with her ideas, and he didn't want to be mean.

'How would you get that?' She tapped her pen against

her teeth while she thought. 'You could contact churches, I suppose? No, funeral directors! Yes, that's it! When we were burying my mother, the funeral directors booked the singer for us. They were marvellous – took care of everything. They have lists of singers – we even had a choice!'

Roly peered over and saw she was writing 'funeral singer' on her pad, right under 'cruise ship entertainer' and 'clerical officer'.

'Okay, great start. We're making headway here, Roly. You should contact some funeral directors, get on their books. Do you know "Abide With Me"? "Be Still My Soul?"'

'Um … no.'

'Well, I'm sure you'd learn in no time. I don't know if they have auditions or how it works, but maybe you should start practising a few hymns, just in case.'

'Sure.'

'What else, what else?' She tapped her pen excitedly against her pad as she mused. 'Oh! Bring him home! What about that?'

'Um … is that … a taxi service?'

Geraldine laughed. 'No, the song.' She sang a few bars in a high, shaky voice. It sounded like when the stray cats had sex on the garden wall, only creepier. 'We had that at my uncle's funeral. It was lovely.'

Roly nodded. 'Very … spooky.'

'But taxi could be an idea for you? Or some sort of delivery? Pizzas, flowers, flat-pack furniture … there's all sorts needs delivering. Do you drive?'

'No.' He grimaced regretfully, hoping he didn't look as relieved as he felt.

'Oh. Well, you could be one of those ones that scoot around on bikes? Cycle courier? Or takeaway delivery – you know with the little box on the back carrier? Some kind of shift work like that might suit you. It would give you lots of free time for writing your songs. You could deliver pizzas by night, and have the days free to work on your music.'

'Good idea.' He couldn't see himself working as a delivery boy, but maybe some kind of casual work wouldn't be so bad. It seemed his days of collecting free cash were numbered, so he'd have to come up with *something* to keep Geraldine off his back until the Oh Boy! reunion got off the ground.

'Great! Just let me print you out an application form for the clerical officer job.' She tapped at her computer, and the printer noisily chugged out some pages. She stapled them together and handed him the form. 'Don't look so downhearted,' she said, giving him a bright smile. 'We'll find you something. You won't be unemployed for long on my watch.'

'Thanks, Geraldine. You've been very helpful.' He stood, clutching the application form. 'It's been a real eye-opener.'

'Not at all, Roly. That's what I'm here for. Let me know how you get on. And if there's anything else you need, don't hesitate to give me a call.' She took a business card from her desk and handed it to him.

'Thanks. I will.'

As soon as he got outside, he tore up the application form and threw it in the nearest bin. No way was he going to spend his days in some dusty office, wilting under a fluorescent sky. He already felt like he couldn't breathe, just thinking about it.

Normal life was bullshit, he thought as he stomped home. He'd had no idea the amount of crap he'd side-stepped by running away with the band when he left school.

'Okay, that's it! I have to get a job,' he said to Ella as he shut the front door behind him.

'What happened?' She looked up from the worktop, where she was chopping onions.

'Geraldine – my *case worker* – is already measuring me up for a desk in the council. She wants me to apply for … I'm not even sure what. Some kind of secretarial work, I think?'

'Oh god!' Ella laughed.

'Either that or she'll have me entertaining on a cruise ship, or teaming up with undertakers and doing the entertainment at funerals. So I'll go down to that cafe in the morning, see if they're still looking for staff.'

'Wow, I'm impressed! Geraldine's made a genuine jobseeker of you just like that.' She snapped her fingers.

18

'So, WHAT CAN I GET YOU?' Roly felt self-conscious as he approached the two young women sitting at a table in the window. He had no problem serving customers, and he found chatting to them easy. But he was aware of Ray watching him the whole time from behind the counter and judging his performance. Roly had only been at Insider Out a week, and was still in training.

'Oh my god! Roly Punch!' The blonde woman squealed. 'It's really you!'

'Yep.' Roly smiled, pen poised over his little notepad, ready to take their order. 'It's me!'

'You were right!' the blonde said, grabbing her friend's hand across the table.

'Told you.'

'She told me you work here, but I didn't believe it.' The blonde turned her attention back to Roly. She was cute – big blue eyes, long poker-straight hair, nice boobs. Her dark-haired friend was attractive too, in a more offbeat kind of way.

In reply, he smiled and held out his hands as if to say

'behold, my official notepad and pen, my Insider Out uniform'. It wasn't actually a uniform, just black jeans and a white T-shirt that Ray, the owner, required all the staff to wear.

'Wow! This is amazing!' The blonde giggled, fanning her hand in front of her face rapidly. 'We were such Oh Boy! fans.'

The brunette nodded. 'We were always trying to meet you back in the day.'

'And now here you are, serving us coffee! It's surreal.'

'We used to spend all our money following you guys around.'

'Or we'd just hang around outside your house – sometimes for days at a time.'

'Your mum was really nice to us. She even brought us out lemonade and packets of crisps one time.'

'You probably don't remember me,' the blonde said, 'but I managed to sneak backstage a couple of times and meet you all, and I hung out in your hotel room in Manchester once.' She gave him a flirtatious smile. 'I was a major groupie.'

Roly smiled at her, while at the same time trying to guess her age. Was she implying they'd hooked up? 'We didn't...?' He left the question hanging, almost afraid of the answer.

'Oh no,' she laughed lightly. 'I was more of a Zack girl.'

'Right.' Of course. They were all bloody Zack girls. 'Well, I'd love to stay chatting to you girls, but my boss is watching.' He threw his eyes behind him, where he knew Ray would be standing behind the counter. 'So, what'll you have?'

. . .

'What were you talking to that pair about?' Ray asked, nodding to the two women as Roly joined him behind the counter.

'They were Oh Boy! fans.'

'Oh, were they?' Ray nodded, looking intensely interested. He had the air of a Bond villain cooking up some elaborate plan for world domination. It was a look Roly had already come to know and dread. 'Chatting you up, were they?'

'Um ... yeah. Reminiscing about the old days.'

'Okay, good work. Good work.' Roly could practically see the cogs turning. 'What did they order?' he asked, then held out a hand, like a lollipop lady stopping the traffic. 'Don't tell me, don't tell me. Two cappuccinos, right? Extra foam.'

'Er ... no. Just a couple of Americanos.'

'Americanos,' Ray nodded knowingly as if that would have been his next guess.

Roly liked Ray. He was a squat, chubby man with thinning dark hair and slightly crooked teeth that looked too small for his face. Roly had described him to Ella as middle-aged after his interview, but had since been shocked to discover Ray was only a couple of years older than him. Maybe the cafe business had taken a lot out of him.

Roly began making the coffees, and Ray leaned against the worktop beside him, arms folded. 'When you bring those over, ask them if they want a muffin or...' He shifted his gaze to the two women, narrowing his eyes. 'A brownie. Yeah, they look like brownie people.' Ray liked to think he was an astute judge of character – insofar as character consisted in what sort of drinks or snacks people would order. He was almost invariably wrong.

Roly liked working at the cafe, but he hated this part of the job – what Ray called 'upselling' – which meant trying to get people to order stuff they didn't really want. He especially hated doing it to Oh Boy! fans because they'd order anything he suggested, and then he felt guilty that they were spending money on stuff they didn't want just to please him.

'If you want to succeed in business, Roly…' Ray often gave him little pep talks and business tips as they worked, and Roly pretended to be interested and grateful. He didn't have the heart to tell Ray that he had zero desire to succeed in business. The little neighbourhood cafe was Ray's pride and joy, and he'd been good to Roly, taking him on with no experience or qualifications, and sending him on a one-day barista course, so that now he could make fancy coffees and he had an actual transferable skill to put on a CV. He even had a certificate. So if Ray fancied himself as his mentor, he thought it was only fair to play along and act the part of the eager pupil.

'If you want to succeed in business,' Ray said to him that evening, continuing the lesson as they cleaned up, 'it's all about the bottom line.'

'Right.' Roly nodded as he wiped down the coffee machine.

'You see it all the time in America. They're great at it. You buy a pair of shoes, they ask would you like some socks with that. In McDonalds, "would you like to supersize that" – same principle. So if someone orders a tall, ask them if they'd prefer a grande. Emphasise the value – it's only ten percent more for seventy-five per cent extra.'

'Is it?' Roly frowned, trying to work out the maths in his head.

'It's close enough. They're not going to start doing the calculations on a napkin.'

'Okay.' Roly had no intention of trying to sell someone bigger coffees with dodgy maths.

'If they don't order something to eat, suggest something. Sell the benefits.'

'The benefits? Of, like, a brownie?'

'Yeah.'

'And ... what are they?'

'It's the feel-good factor, isn't it? Serotonin and dopamine and all that. Use your imagination. We've also got the gluten-free muffins, don't forget, so there are the health benefits there too. Flapjacks – full of fibre, very important for our older demographic.'

'Huh?'

'Constipation, Roly. Old ladies are obsessed with it.'

'Oh, right.' Was he going to have to start talking to old ladies about poo? At the same time as he was trying to sell them cakes?

When they'd finished cleaning and closing up, Ray made tea for them both in the back room. He liked to sit down with Roly for tea and a chat after the cafe was closed. He called it a debrief, and he went over the day's business while working his way through the remaining baked goods that had reached their sell-by date and couldn't be put out in the glass display case for another day.

'Tuck in there, Roly,' he said, grinning as he put a plate of assorted flapjacks, brownies and Danish pastries on the table. 'Everything must go.'

'Thanks.' Roly didn't want to be rude when Ray was trying to be nice, and if he said he was on a diet, it could make Ray feel self-conscious about his own weight. It might even sound like he was fat-shaming him. So he took a flapjack, figuring it was probably the least fattening option - and maybe all the fibre would make him poo the calories off again.

'Okay, I've got an idea,' Ray said, taking a Danish pastry from the plate. 'Those two you served earlier – the Oh Boy! fans?'

'Yeah?'

'It's got me thinking. They just came in for a coffee and they ended up staying for lunch, buying sandwiches, cakes, the lot. So good work, Roly!'

'Uh … thanks.'

'It's made me realise that we haven't been maxing out on the potential of having you here. And I've come up with an idea!'

'Great.' Roly dreaded Ray's ideas.

'We should spread the word about you working here – get it out on social media, you know. Maybe even go viral,' he said dreamily.

'Oh!'

'So, are you okay with that?'

'Um … yeah, sure.' He was so far from okay with it, but he didn't feel he could say no to Ray.

'Great!' Ray rubbed his hands. 'I'll tweet about it tonight to kick us off.'

Roly relaxed. He'd seen Ray's Twitter. He hardly ever tweeted and he had less than a hundred followers, many of whom, Roly suspected, were inactive accounts or bots. 'Good idea.'

'And then I want you to retweet it, so all your fans see it.'

'Oh.' This wasn't so good. In fact, it was very bad. Roly rarely went on Twitter anymore, but he still had something like thirty-five million followers – and he didn't want a single one of them to know that he was working as a waiter at Insider Out. What would they think? What would the other guys think? They'd have a right laugh about it. Not only was he working in a cafe, he'd look like he was really proud of it. Shit!

'I don't really tweet anymore, Ray,' he said. At least that was true.

'Well, I'm sure you still have plenty of people who'd see it if you did. And what about Insta? Do you Insta?'

'Um … yeah.' Unfortunately, he did 'Insta'. 'Mostly Stories, though.'

'Good, good.' Ray nodded. 'Well, Insta's even better. We could brighten the place up a bit, make it more photogenic. I think you're onto something here, Roly.' He grinned.

'Well, it wasn't my idea…' Roly didn't want to take the credit for his own downfall.

'No, but you're taking my idea and running with it. Using your initiative. Insta Stories…' He rubbed his chin thoughtfully. 'I like it.'

Roly tried not to panic. Maybe he could post something in the middle of the night when not many people would see it, and find a way to make it disappear quickly. Or maybe there was some way he could make a post so that only Ray would see it? He'd have to look into it when he got home.

'I suppose you'd want to make the place a bit more Instagrammable first,' he said, looking around, hoping to stall for time. 'I mean, it's very nice, but…'

'I hear what you're saying, Roly. Some fairy lights? Lick of paint maybe? New tables and chairs?'

'You don't need to go that far.' Roly couldn't let Ray shell out for painting and decorating because he didn't want his new career to go viral.

Ray slapped the table suddenly. 'Sure, what am I thinking? We don't need any of that stuff. We have our most Instagrammable asset right here in front of me.'

'What? Where?'

'You.' Ray pointed to him. 'If people started coming in and taking selfies with you … that's major bragging rights. It could blow up big time.' He reached out and took a brownie from the pile. 'Now we're motoring. We need to come up with some snappy hashtags. Let's brainstorm it. More tea?'

19

'Ella! Phillip, everyone!' Dylan called excitedly as he and Kerry swept across the office floor, Dara and Jake following behind carrying a couple of large boxes.

'Come on! They're here!' Jake called.

Everyone dropped whatever they were doing and followed in their wake, hurrying towards the meeting room. No one had to ask what 'they' were. They'd been impatiently awaiting the first consignment of Heatsmart Neo jackets for days.

Ella followed the excited procession. In the meeting room, Jake and Dylan were already slicing open boxes. Everyone stood around the large table watching as they pulled out plastic-wrapped packages. Jake quickly opened a couple and slid the jackets across opposite sides of the table for everyone to pass around. Then he, Dylan and the designers huddled together as they opened a couple more, beaming as they pored over the details, murmuring delightedly to each other as they checked out zips and seams.

Ella was shocked to find tears springing to her eyes. She

knew how hard they'd worked for this, the months spent agonising over every detail, coping with factory delays, testing failures and production problems. Now it was finally here, and she felt so proud and happy for them.

Kerry slid a jacket along the table to her, and she picked it up, running her eyes over it. She knew every detail so well already – she'd seen numerous drawings and photos on her computer screen. But now it was a real tangible thing that she could hold in her hands. She couldn't quite fathom it, as she turned it over, putting her hands in the pockets, pulling the zipper up and down, running her fingers over the COTW label. It was perfect. She was surprised how emotional she felt about it. But she'd had a part in this, and she felt a shared sense of pride and ownership as she passed it along to the next person.

'Okay, everyone, that's a wrap! I think we can sign off on this one.' Jake pulled the top off a marker, then lay one of the jackets open on the table and signed his name on the lining with a flourish. He handed the marker to Dylan who did the same before passing the jacket along to one of the designers.

Jake and Kerry were busying themselves taking bottles of champagne out of the fridge and organising glasses. Ella was surprised when Gordon, beside her, passed her the signed jacket along with the fabric marker.

'Oh!' She took it from him uncertainly. She saw that everyone along the table so far had signed it, including Gordon. But surely they didn't mean for *her* to sign it?

'Ella?'

She looked up to see Jake watching her.

'Problem?' He frowned.

'No, I just … I don't think I'm supposed to be doing this?' She waved the marker.

'Everyone around this table did this,' he said, nodding to the jacket. 'We all sign.'

'It'll go into a display case in reception,' Gordon told her.

'Oh, okay.' It would be there like a trophy or a work of art, and her name would be on it, a lasting reminder that she'd been part of this. She bent and wrote her name.

Jake and Dylan popped the corks on bottles of champagne, and Kerry helped pour glasses and pass them around.

'Well done, all of you!' Jake and Dylan raised their glasses when everyone had champagne. Then Jake went around the table and toasted each one of them individually by name, and when he got to the last person and finished 'We did it!' everyone cheered and clapped, and she wasn't the only one wiping tears from her eyes surreptitiously.

They finished work early after the champagne celebration. Ella decided to use the extra time to make a special dinner. She was on a high and wanted to share the moment with Roly. On the way home she splurged on fresh salmon, tiny new potatoes with papery skins, and bundles of fresh herbs. She'd make salsa verde, and they could have a treat dinner without feeling they were completely blowing their diet.

When she got home, she set the table with candles and some flowers she picked from the garden and put in small glasses. She was in the kitchen, listening to music as she chopped herbs when she heard Roly come in.

'Are you having someone over?' he asked, appearing in the doorway. 'Looks fancy.' He nodded at the table.

She smiled. 'No, I'm just making dinner for us. I'm celebrating. The new jackets came in today at work, and we had champagne, so I was feeling a bit giddy. I thought we could have a treat.'

'Oh.' His face fell. 'I can't.' He grimaced apologetically. 'Sorry. If I'd known … I'm going over to Phoenix's. We've been working on some songs.'

'*Phoenix*? You mean – *The*, Phoenix?'

'No. Phoenix O'Reilly from school.' He smiled, rolling his eyes. 'Yes, *the* Phoenix.'

'You know him?' Phoenix was the lead singer of Walking Wounded, one of the biggest rock bands in the world.

'Yeah, he's a mate.' He frowned. 'Haven't I told you?'

'No. I'm sure I'd remember if you'd told me that.'

'Well, he is. He helped me a lot when I came out of rehab. Anyway, we've been working on some stuff together, and he wants me to sing with him when they play here on their next tour.'

'Wow! You mean … on stage? With Walking Wounded?'

'Yeah. At the Aviva, in September. I'll just be doing this one song with them, as a surprise guest kind of thing.'

'That's fantastic!'

He nodded, his whole face lighting up. 'I know.'

'What song?'

'That's the best part – it's this new song we're working on together.'

'Oh wow, that's huge!'

'Yeah. Sorry about dinner, though.'

'It's fine, no biggie.' She painted on a smile, trying to hide her disappointment. But now they had even more to celebrate and she wished he was staying. 'I shouldn't have assumed…'

'It's a pity. It looks great.'

'Well, I haven't cooked anything yet. We could put it off until tomorrow?'

'You've gone to all this trouble. Why don't you invite someone over? You could ask Andrew.'

'Yeah, maybe I'll do that.'

'Anyway, I've got to go. I just came home first to pick this up.' He lifted his guitar, which was leaning against the wall by the door. 'Sorry! See you later.' And then he was gone again, bounding out the door, guitar in hand.

Ella sat down at the kitchen table, not sure what to do. Maybe she *should* ask Andrew if he could come over – or Hazel. Or she could just enjoy a quiet night in by herself. There was no reason to feel so deflated. What was she doing anyway, cooking dinner for Roly like some 1950s wifey waiting for her husband to come home from work. They weren't a couple. Roly didn't have to answer to her, or keep her informed of his plans, and she shouldn't assume they'd spend all their evenings together. They were just friends, housemates.

She'd fallen into a routine with him, and had got into a bad habit of fitting her life around him. She should make an effort to spend more time with other people, nurture other friendships, make a life separate from Roly. Then she wouldn't end up feeling like such a sad sack when Roly had somewhere else to be, other people to see.

After all, they were supposed to be getting their lives back on track. He was out there getting on with it, and she should do the same. Yes! She slapped the table decisively and stood, grabbing her phone from the worktop. She'd open a bottle of wine and ask Andrew over. It was short notice, and he may not be able to come anyway, but at least she could feel she'd tried.

. . .

'Sorry about the short notice,' she said later as she opened the door to Andrew. 'I'm glad you were able to make it.'

'Lucky for you I have a pretty dull social life at the moment. I'm practically a nun!'

Ella laughed as she took his jacket. 'Well, come in, Sister.' She led him down the hall to the kitchen.

'Nice place,' he said, looking around. 'I love these old period houses. If this is where selling your soul gets you, I might be tempted.' He laughed, trying to pass it off as a joke, but it did nothing to hide the bitterness of his words.

'I couldn't normally afford to rent here on my salary. But Roly's giving me mate rates, so I lucked out.'

'He owns it?'

'Yeah.'

'And it's just the two of you here?'

She heard the implied criticism and tried not to let it rile her. 'Yep, just us.' What did he think? That they should be sharing with a family of refugees? That Roly should be taking in students?

'Must be nice to have so much space.'

'Yeah, it's lovely,' she said disingenuously. For god's sake! It wasn't as if the house was flash or anything. Granted, it was a lot more than most people their age could afford, but it was actually a pretty modest house for a world-famous pop star. She was beginning to regret inviting Andrew over instead of chilling out by herself for the night with a quiet dinner and a book.

'Well, sit down.' She waved to the table. He took a seat, and Ella lifted the bottle of wine from the cooler to pour him a glass. She'd already downed one herself while she waited for him to arrive.

'Oh, not for me, thanks,' Andrew said, holding up a hand to stop her.

'Oh? Really?' He'd always been fond of white wine in

the past, but it had been a long time. 'Would you prefer red? We're having salmon.'

'No, no wine for me at all. I'm fine with water.' He nodded at the bottle of sparkling water on the table. 'I'm eight months sober today,' he announced with a proud smile.

'Oh!' Ella sank onto a chair opposite him. Wow, it really had been a long time. She'd had no idea.

'Don't look so shocked!' He gave a little laugh.

'No, that's … great. Well done! I'm just surprised, that's all. I didn't know, or I wouldn't have…' She waved at the bottle.

'It's fine. You didn't know. Though didn't you notice I wasn't drinking the other night?'

She thought back. Now that he mentioned it, she did remember he'd only drunk water in the bar at the Olympia. But she'd suspected he was just being parsimonious. 'I didn't think anything of it,' she said. 'There's nothing unusual about not drinking for one night. And you never had a problem before…'

'Didn't I? I'm not so sure.'

'*Really*?' She cast her mind back, combing through her memories – the boozy student parties they'd been at together, the nights they'd spent in the campus bar, their holiday in Greece where they'd sipped ouzo outside little tavernas – trying to find something she hadn't seen at the time. But she came up blank. He'd overdone it sometimes, same as the rest of them. But it hadn't been a problem. He used to love drinking. He'd even been a bit of a knob about wine. She'd thought he'd appreciate the New Zealand sauvignon blanc she'd opened tonight. One of her former clients had sent it to her as a farewell gift, and she'd been saving it for a special occasion when she'd have someone to share it with.

'I don't remember you having any issues with alcohol when we were together.'

'Don't you? I seem to recall a lot of mornings waking up in a cold sweat about what I'd done the night before. Not to mention the lectures I skipped the next day or the study hours I wasted because I stayed in bed late, sleeping it off.'

'You had hangovers, and The Fear – that doesn't make you an alcoholic. It's called being a student.'

'I'm not a student anymore. Anyway, who said anything about being an alcoholic?'

'Um… you did.'

He smiled, shaking his head, seeming amused at her confusion. 'I said I was eight months sober, not that I have a substance abuse disorder. It's interesting that you automatically jump to that conclusion.'

'It's a reasonable assumption when you throw around phrases like "eight months sober".'

'People are so black and white about it – you either have total alcohol dependency or you're a "normal" drinker. But it's a spectrum, isn't it? Like most things.'

She shrugged. 'I suppose.'

'I don't have an addiction. I can even still enjoy the very occasional glass of wine now and then—'

'Oh!'

'But I came to realise that I had an unhealthy relationship with alcohol. It was adversely affecting my life – my work, my relationships. So you could say I had a drink problem.'

'I suppose you could.' If you really want to have one, she thought, angry on behalf of Roly and all the other real alcoholics who'd rather not. Because she could see this was just another pose for him, like being broke.

'One day I took a long, hard look at myself and I didn't like what I saw.'

Ella could understand that. She was taking a long, hard look at him right now, and not liking what she saw very much. Had he always been this pompous and sanctimonious? Maybe drink had affected *her* relationships too, and she'd seen him through rosé-tinted glasses.

'So when you say you're sober, you just mean you're cutting down a bit on drink?'

'No, it's more than that. I identify as sober, but that might mean not drinking ninety-nine days out of a hundred. I'm more mindful about it. It doesn't have to be all or nothing.'

'Good to know. In that case, you won't mind if I…' She picked up the bottle and poured herself a large glass. He used to love wine. He was probably gagging for a glass right now, but then he'd have to give up the chance to be smug. What a dilemma for him!

'I'd rather you didn't,' he said.

I bet you would, she thought, taking a swig. She had a feeling it was going to be a long night, and was regretting not opting for an evening of indulgent solitude. She might as well have. She was going to be drinking alone anyway.

'Don't worry,' she said disingenuously. 'I'm on the don't-have-one end of the drink problem spectrum, so it's fine.' He looked put out as she took another sip, and she hated how much that pleased her.

'I thought you'd want to be supportive of my sobriety. Doesn't it occur to you that it might be triggering for me?'

Triggering! 'I don't see how. Roly doesn't have any problem with me drinking around him, and he's a real alcoholic.' Gah, why was she being such a bitch?

'Are you sure about that?'

'Yep. He's got a pin from AA and everything.'

Andrew didn't laugh, just gave her a patient, patronising smile. 'I mean, are you sure he doesn't have a problem with being around alcohol? Maybe he's just too nice to say anything?'

Unlike you, she thought, taking a big gulp of wine.

'I mean, it must make it more difficult for him.'

She shook her head. 'No, I believe him. I think it was hard for him at first, when he came out of rehab, but he's learned to cope.'

'But why should he have to cope?'

'Because this is the world he lives in, and he wants to be a part of it. People drink. He can't control what everyone else does, and he doesn't want to. He doesn't expect other people to change to accommodate him.'

'But you're his friend. Wouldn't it be the kind thing to do, to consider his feelings?'

'I am. Honestly, Roly would hate it if I felt I couldn't have a drink in my own home if I wanted one.'

He sipped his water and looked at her thoughtfully. 'You know, I'm finding your discomfort with my sobriety quite telling.'

'Meaning?'

'Maybe you don't like the fact that I'm not your partner in crime any longer.'

'What?' She reared back, indignant. 'I haven't seen you in forever. You haven't been my "partner in crime" for a long time – not that I think having a glass of wine is a crime, by the way.'

'Why so defensive? Could it be you feel threatened by my sobriety because it's something you need to address in yourself?'

Ella frowned, as if giving this serious thought. 'Nah,' she said then. 'I just don't see any point in denying yourself the pleasure if you don't have to. If you have a drink problem, I'm glad you've got it under control. I really am.' She reached for the bottle and topped up her glass. 'Lucky for me I don't, so I can still enjoy this delicious Sauvignon Blanc.'

'You're evil,' Andrew grinned teasingly, as if she was really tempting him. But she knew no wine, no matter how delicious, would ever taste as good to him as being smug felt. 'But nothing tastes as good as being sober feels,' he said, confirming her suspicions.

Had he always been this joyless, she wondered, this earnest? She used to like herself around him; liked the person she was with him. Now he just seemed to bring out the worst in her.

She stood. 'Well, I'll get the salmon in the oven. We're having it with new potatoes, salsa verde and roasted asparagus. Hope that's okay?' It suddenly occurred to her that it might not be. He used to eat fish, but maybe that had changed too. She waited for him to tell her he was a vegetarian now, bracing herself for the onslaught of self-righteousness. She knew he'd be unbearable about it if he was.

'Sounds delicious!' He licked his lips, and she felt irrationally irritated. She didn't want a fight, she reminded herself.

'I was making it for Roly,' she told him, still feeling a childish need to oppose him. 'You just lucked out.'

She gave herself a talking to as she drained the potatoes and plated the salmon and asparagus. She'd invited Andrew over. She'd wanted company, and here he was. He'd done nothing wrong, so why was she behaving so churlishly towards him? So he'd changed. Or she had. That didn't mean they couldn't have a perfectly nice time together. It might be interesting getting to know this new Andrew. And even if it wasn't, if he'd become someone she didn't like and she never wanted to see him again, she could at least be civil and friendly for a few hours. She brought the food to the table, determined to cheer up and try to make it a pleasant evening for both of them. How hard could it be?

'So how's work?' Andrew asked as he cut into his fish.

'It's great. I really love it!' She considered telling him about the new jackets coming in today, the reason she'd planned a celebratory dinner, but thought better of it.

'Really?' He looked dubious. 'Well, I suppose it's a good way to ease yourself back into things, while you look for something more permanent.'

'It is permanent.'

'Yes, but I meant something more in your field.'

'What field? I don't have a "field", Andrew. I'm really lucky Jake and Dylan took me on. And there are lots of ways I can progress there too.'

'But it's not what you want, is it?'

She shrugged. 'It may not be what I'd envisaged for myself before, but things change. People change. It's true I never saw myself working in business, but I'm finding it really interesting.

'You *have* changed. What do you like so much about it?'

'I like that we're putting something real and tangible into the world, not just tossing ideas around.' She thought about those drowsy afternoons in tutors' studies discussing political theory, the endless circular debates around cafeteria tables. 'I like that it's quantifiable, that you can measure results in numbers and percentages. I enjoy working on marketing campaigns because I can see exactly the improvements I've made. It's satisfying.' She smiled.

She'd never analysed and articulated it for herself before. 'How about you?'

'I'm still just tossing ideas around.' He smiled. 'Slaving away at the coalface of academia, griping about internal politics … the usual. I may not be able to see the effects of my teaching in hard figures, but I hope I'm having some positive influence on young minds.'

'What about your social life? You said you're not seeing anyone?'

'No, not at the moment.' He met her gaze across the table and shot her one of his intimate looks. They used to make her go weak at the knees. 'I was in a relationship for the last couple of years, but we broke up a few months ago. Alice is a historian, specialising in Medieval History. She's English, and she moved back there. She's lecturing at Oxford now.'

Trust Andrew to lead with his girlfriend's academic credentials! She was just asking about his love life, not looking to book her for a lecture series. But he'd always done the same with her whenever he was introducing her to someone, as if she was defined by her degrees and qualifications. He was such an intellectual snob.

'Is that why you split up? Because she wanted to move back to England?'

'Not entirely. Her getting offered the job at Oxford was the catalyst, but we could have made it work, if we'd really been committed to each other.'

'But you weren't?'

'Not enough, in the end. What about you?'

'I haven't had the time – or, most importantly, the energy – for a relationship. There hasn't been anyone since you. But my social life is picking up.'

'Oh?'

'Yeah, I'm really liking living with Roly, and I go out

with the crowd from work most Fridays for drinks, and karaoke.'

'Karaoke!' He gave a hoot of laughter. 'Oh god, poor you!'

'It's fun! I enjoy it.'

'Seriously?' He gave her a pitying look. 'I feel like I hardly know you.'

Yeah, she thought. Same.

'And I can't imagine you and Roly have much in common. I mean, he seems like a nice guy, but what do you find to talk about?'

'Plenty,' she said with a shrug. 'TV, music, films, our families, the news of the day … you know, what everyone talks about.'

'Well, I suppose it can't all be sitting around discussing Heidegger,' he said with a supercilious smile.

Thank goodness!

'Did you see that documentary about Rothko on TV the other night?'

'No, I missed that.'

'It was brilliant! You know I don't watch much TV, but every so often there's something worthwhile that makes me glad I didn't get rid of it.'

'I think it was probably on at the same time as *Celebrity Masterchef*.'

'Good lord, is that what you're reduced to?'

'It's good, I like it. And it's interesting because Alex Sutton is in it – you know, from Oh Boy! He's doing really well. Last week he made this amazing chocolate soufflé that reduced John Torode to tears.'

'Who?' Andrew screwed up his face, and she wanted to slap it. He knew damn well who John Torode was … probably. Actually, now she thought about it, there was probably a good chance he genuinely didn't.

'Well, there's a Wim Wenders season starting at the IFI next week. Why don't we go to something?'

'Sure. As long as it's not Friday.'

'Of course. You wouldn't want to miss karaoke night,' he said sarcastically.

'No. I wouldn't.'

Roly arrived home when they were lingering over coffee on the sofa and Ella was draining the dregs of the wine. He seemed to bring an air of energy and positivity into the room with him that was cheering to Ella.

'So, how was your evening?' she asked as he flopped into the seat beside her.

'Great!' A wide smile spread across his face. 'It's going really well.'

'Roly's working on some stuff with Phoenix,' she told Andrew smugly. She knew he'd be impressed by that, though he'd hate to admit it. He was a massive Walking Wounded fan. He used to have posters of them on the wall of his room in uni, and he could bore on about them for hours to anyone who'd listen, as if they were some esoteric band that he'd discovered.

'Phoenix? Really?' he said to Roly.

'Yeah, we're writing some songs together.'

'Wow!'

'And Roly's going to sing with them at the Aviva in September,' Ella said, relishing being able to wrong-foot him like this. He'd be shocked to think of someone like Roly getting the seal of approval from a band of Walking Wounded's stature.

'Well done!'

'Are you going?' Ella asked him.

'Yes, I've got tickets. Actually, I have a spare one now, if you want to come with me?'

He'd been going with Alice, she supposed. 'Thanks, but Roly will be getting me a ticket.'

'And a backstage pass,' Roly put in.

Andrew looked green. She could tell he was torn between admitting what a fanboy he was in the hope that Roly would get him backstage too, and acting cool and above it all.

'I wasn't that sure about their last album,' he said. 'I mean, I enjoyed it, but I didn't think it was their best. I feel they've gone very commercial in the last couple of years.'

Of course he'd go for the ungracious option. 'Yeah,' she said, 'and naturally a rock band would want to avoid being commercial at all costs.'

'You know what I mean.'

'Yes. I do.' She knew all too well. He meant that if Roly was involved, it could only be because Walking Wounded's stock was down. It was a ridiculous thing to say anyway – they were one of the biggest bands in the world, not some little indie group that only Andrew and a few of his friends knew about. Of course they were commercial. He was just jealous.

'I could get you a backstage pass too, if you like?' Roly said to Andrew. 'If you two want to go together.'

Ella was pleased he'd been the bigger man by offering – it was generous of him when Andrew was being such a knob. But she was annoyed too because it was more than Andrew deserved.

'Do you mind if I watch *Masterchef*?' Roly nodded to the TV. 'Did you tape it?' he asked Ella.

'Yeah, I did. And it's fine.'

'I want to see it before I see who went out on social media.'

'Let's all watch it!' Ella said brightly, trying not to laugh. She could practically feel Andrew grinding his teeth.

She'd thought it would be a suitable punishment for Andrew, but she was sorry she'd suggested it as he yawned and snarked his way through the show, making it obvious he was bored and found it ridiculous. She should have waited until he'd gone and watched it with Roly. It would have been fun, just the two of them; they'd have had a laugh.

She only had herself to blame. Still, at least this evening hadn't been a total loss. It had made one thing very clear: she didn't want to get back with Andrew.

20

Throughout the summer the Oh Boy! rumour mill gathered momentum, and talk of a reunion built to a crescendo of frenzied speculation as the band dropped ever more overt hints that it was happening. Their social media posts became less coy and cryptic as the weeks passed. Roly watched with increasing annoyance as they posted recent photos of themselves together, or nostalgic throwbacks to their glory days, arms wrapped around each other as they stood on stage, taking their bows at the end of a performance. And he wasn't in a single one of them. It was as if they'd completely obliterated him from their history.

Some of the fans, god bless them, continued to lobby for him, relentlessly asking 'where's Roly?' under every picture. When Zach posted a photo of the four of them with the caption 'All the Boys back together again', several people had commented 'not *all* the boys'. They'd even started a 'WewantRoly' hashtag. He was touched by their loyalty and love, especially knowing he'd done fuck all to earn it.

The tension and hysteria mounted to an almost

unbearable peak. And then, at the beginning of July, it happened: the reunion was officially announced. It started with Zack, Alex, Liam and Charlie all posting the same photo on Instagram and Twitter – the four of them waving goodbye to the crowd at their farewell concert, with the caption 'The Boys are back'.

Roly was glad. He'd been on tenterhooks for so long, waiting for the other shoe to fall, it was a relief when it finally happened. But it was the relief of the hypochondriac who finally gets diagnosed with a serious illness, or the paranoiac who discovers his colleagues really *have* been conspiring against him. It meant no more worrying and wondering, no more fighting an invisible enemy that might be nothing more than a figment of your imagination. This was real; it was happening. Now that he knew what he was dealing with, he could begin to tackle it.

'How are you feeling about it?' Ella asked him later over dinner. The announcement of the reunion had been on the news this morning, and it was all over social media.

'What do you mean?'

'Do you still want to try to get back with the band?'

'Of course.' He looked at her aghast. He couldn't believe she had to ask. 'I mean, that's the whole point of all this, remember?'

'I know, I know,' she said quickly, appeasingly. 'I just thought you might have changed your mind.'

She thought he *should* change his mind. That was what she really wanted to say. 'Well, I haven't. Why would I?' It pissed him off. She was supposed to be on his side, one hundred per cent.

'I don't know.' She looked down at her plate, twirling spaghetti onto her fork with unwarranted concentration. 'I just thought, you know, since you've been working with Phoenix, doing your own thing—'

'So now I have credibility because of being associated with a proper band, and I should do something better.'

'That's not what I mean.'

'I think it's exactly what you mean.'

'You just seem so happy the last few weeks – happier than you ever were when you were in Oh Boy!'

'Seriously? You don't think I was *happy* being in the biggest pop group in the world?'

She put her fork down and turned to face him squarely. 'No, I don't.'

'Yeah, you're right. It was a miserable existence – travelling all around the world, winning awards, playing giant stadiums. It was shit being at the top of my game, and the money really sucked. I'm much better off working in a crappy cafe and doing music in my spare time like some hobbyist.'

'Yeah, I think you are. You never seemed that happy back then, when you used to call me.'

'That's because I only called you when I was down – when I was feeling lonely or a bit homesick and there was no one else around.'

'Right. I see,' she said tightly.

He sighed. 'I didn't mean it like that. I just meant, obviously I wasn't messaging you when I was at a party or on stage or being taken out to some fancy restaurant. You weren't there, so you only saw one side of it.'

'I get that,' she said softly. 'I do. But that was still a whole side of it.'

Maybe she was right. There had been a lot of those nights. He remembered how he'd felt those times he'd called her – anxious, lonely, paranoid, homesick. He'd been lost, in need of grounding, craving the reassurance of her voice on the phone. But it was only because the highs had been so high, wasn't it? For every action there was an equal and opposite reaction. The crash was the price you paid for the elation of being on stage, the high of knowing you'd played a blinder, the adrenaline surging through your body when you stood at the centre of all that light and sound and joyful energy, thousands of fans all screaming for you – there had to be a comedown from that. The crash was worth it … wasn't it?

'And the music you're doing now,' Ella was saying, 'it's so different—'

'Different to the Oh Boy! crap, you mean?'

'No!' She was vehement. But that was exactly what she'd meant and they both knew it.

'I don't mean to criticise—'

'Don't, then.'

'I thought you'd want to keep doing your new stuff, that's all. It's so good. And you seem to be really enjoying it.'

'I am. But I want to be back in Oh Boy! more.'

'If you're sure that's what you really want.' She shrugged.

'I am.'

'Okay. So, what do you need to do to make that happen?'

No one in his life seemed to be behind the idea. He knew they were just looking out for him, but it still annoyed him.

'I don't like how they treated you,' his mother said worriedly. 'They weren't good friends to you when you were struggling.'

His nan was more forthright, as always. 'Why would

you want to get back with that shower of shites who abandoned you when you were in trouble?'

'I don't blame them. They had no choice but to cut me loose. I was dragging them all down.'

'But you weren't happy, Roly.'

They all said the same thing. He tried to tell them that was the drugs and the booze. It would be different this time. He'd appreciate it, enjoy it; he wouldn't throw it all away. But they didn't get it. He'd just have to show them. He'd get back with Oh Boy!, and he'd be on top again, and then they'd see; they'd understand.

For the rest of the week he waited for a call from one of the band, approaching him about the reunion, offering him a second chance. None came. It was everywhere now. Social media had gone crazy, and the former band members were being interviewed on the radio and TV – all of them except him. All the news channels doing the story included little snippets giving a quick background to the group – a brief history of their meteoric rise to fame, their record-breaking album sales, chart-topping singles and sell-out tours. There were invariably unflattering mentions of him – his drink and drug problems, failed solo career and recent money troubles.

He watched Zack being interviewed about the reunion in a piece on the evening news.

'It's not so much a reunion as a reboot,' he said in a clip. 'We're acknowledging the fact that we've all grown up and moved on, and so have our fans. That's why our new album will be called Oh Man!'

'And will Roly be joining you for the reunion tour?' the interviewer asked.

Zack gave a coy smile. 'Roly hasn't shown any interest.'

Yeah, Roly thought, mainly because I wasn't asked.

'It looks like it'll be just the four of us, the line-up as it was when we broke up. It's been a long time since Roly's been part of Oh Boy! He's moved on; he's doing his own thing.'

Yeah, what would you know about that? Twat!

'If he was up for it, would you be open to him joining the reunion?'

Zack shrugged. 'Never say never.' He gave a sly smile to camera. Roly knew he was just saying that to tease the fans, keep them on the hook. 'But, honestly, I don't think Roly's interested in being a member of the group again.'

Well, how do you know if you don't ask? Fucker!

Clearly, if he wanted this to happen, he was going to have to make the first move.

He called Liam first. 'So, this reunion…'

'Yeah, sorry about that, man. I've been meaning to call you.'

'I mean, it's a shock, hearing that on the news.' They didn't know Charlie had given him a heads-up and they didn't need to. They clearly didn't give a fuck if he heard it first on the TV.

'I take it my name didn't come up, then?'

'We just … didn't think you'd be interested,' Liam mumbled.

He took a deep breath, bracing himself. He'd just have to ask; try not to sound too desperate. 'Well, I am. So, how would you guys feel about making it a real reunion, the original line-up back together again.' He tried to sound bouncy and cheerful, like he wasn't that bothered either way. He kind of hated himself right now. 'I mean, I'm sure the fans would love it.'

Liam sighed. 'You know if it was just up to me…'

'Yeah, yeah.'

'But Zack…'

Oh sure, blame it on Zack, you spineless dick. At least Zack would have the balls to speak for himself.

'You should talk to him, though – and the rest of the lads. It'd be a laugh if you were with us.'

'I will. I'll talk to Zack and the others.' There was an awkward silence. 'Look, I know you guys had to cut me loose. I was a liability, I get that. But I've changed. I'm clean and sober now.'

'I know. Congratulations!'

'And I've been working on some new songs…'

'Oh, really?' A wary tone crept into Liam's voice.

Roly laughed, pretending not to be offended. 'These are actually good. Not like that shit on my first solo album.'

'I thought it was unfair that album got such a battering. There was some good stuff on it. The production really let it down.'

'Thanks.'

'But maybe don't lead with the song-writing when you're talking to Zack. You know what he's like.'

'Yeah.' He did. He knew exactly what Zack was like.

21

Meanwhile, Roly had to deal with the fallout of the news about the Oh Boy! comeback at work. A couple of days after the announcement, he arrived at the cafe to find a sign on the door saying it was closed for the morning. Through the glass he saw Ray inside with two men, one of whom was busy setting up a large professional camera on a tripod.

'What's all this? We're closed?'

The two strangers looked at him curiously as he stepped inside.

'Ah, Roly!' Ray rushed over to him. He put an arm around his shoulders and led him into the back room, shutting the door behind them. 'I contacted the local paper and they said they'd do a piece. You don't mind, do you?'

'A piece?'

'About you working here.'

'Oh!'

'I would have asked you first, but it all happened much faster than I expected. I didn't think they'd get it set up so soon.'

Roly nodded, frantically trying to take this in. Did he mind? Fuck, yes!

'It'd be really good for business,' Ray was saying. 'Great publicity for the cafe, especially now with Oh Boy! in the news again.'

'So … it's just the local paper?'

'Yeah. You know, the one we get here in the cafe.'

'Right.' Roly nodded, relaxing a little. It was just a free paper distributed to businesses in the area. They had a rack of it in the cafe for customers to take if they wanted, and people did pick it up sometimes. It wasn't exactly the *Irish Times*. He doubted many people would even see it.

'So you'll do it?' Ray grinned.

He couldn't really say no, could he? Ray was a good boss, and he'd been really encouraging and supportive of Roly's business aspirations. It wasn't his fault Roly didn't actually have any. Besides, he'd already set this up now, and he was clearly excited about it. He'd be gutted if he had to call it off. Ray was a decent bloke, and he worked really hard to make his little cafe a success – he deserved some recognition.

'Yeah, sure,' Roly nodded. 'No problem.'

'Great!' Ray clapped him on the shoulder. 'Thanks, Roly.'

They went back into the cafe, where the photographer was moving around, playing with a light meter. It was a very familiar process to Roly. He'd done countless photo shoots in his life, but it had been a long time, and it gave him a strange queasy feeling as he let the photographer order him around. He spent the next couple of hours posing in various positions – demonstrating his barista skills making coffee, pretending to serve the journalist who sat at a table posing as a customer, standing outside the cafe, Ray's arm around his shoulders as he beamed with pride.

When the photographer had finished, they sat down with the journalist for a brief interview. Roly cringed as Ray talked him up, praising his punctuality and conscientiousness, his popularity with the customers, his newly acquired barista skills and his willingness to learn.

'He's a great little worker, and I've never regretted taking him on,' Ray said, beaming proudly at his protégé. 'I think he's got a great future ahead of him in business. He really – and you can quote me on this – punches above his weight.'

'It's not that bad,' Ella said the following week when she'd finished reading the article in the paper. Roly had brought it home from the cafe. To his horror, and Ray's delight, the picture of them both standing in front of the cafe had made the cover. Ray had immediately taped it to the window facing out onto the street, alongside the article. The cafe had got a nice write-up, and Roly was happy for Ray's sake. But from his point of view, it was mortifying.

'It makes me sound like such a loser.'

'No it doesn't.'

Roly took the paper from her. '"While his old band mates prepare for a comeback tour, Roly's embarking on a new career as a barista in a small Dublin cafe",' he read out. 'You don't think that makes me sound like a loser?'

'I know it's crap the way they put it, but—'

'And it's not my "new career". It's just a job.'

'There's no shame in it, even if it was your career. And Ray says really nice things about you. Apparently you're very reliable, always on time, and not afraid of hard work.'

'Jesus! I sound like such a dork.'

'Anyway, don't worry too much about it. It's just a little free paper. Who's going to see it?'

'Yeah. That's what I'm counting on.'

But unfortunately, the article got picked up by other papers and media outlets, and was soon plastered all over the internet. It had the desired effect. In the following days there was a steady trickle of young women coming to the cafe to gawp at Roly.

'I told you it'd bring in business,' Ray said, rubbing his hands.

When people started tweeting and posting photos of the cafe on Instagram, the trickle turned into a constant stream of twenty-somethings lingering over their chai lattes as they took surreptitious photos of Roly to post on social media or asked him to pose for selfies with them.

Ray was happy at first with the boost in business, even when Roly was too busy taking selfies to make coffee, and Ray had to do it himself. But by the end of the week, there was a queue down the street of young women waiting to get in to see their idol, and Ray realised Roly's fans were crowding out the regular customers, who were getting fed up and taking their business elsewhere. Furthermore, the coffees they spun out while they chatted up Roly didn't make up for the loss of the cafe's regular lunchtime crowd, who weren't going to spend half their lunch break queuing when there were plenty of other places in the area they could go.

'I'm a victim of my own success, Roly,' Ray said to him ruefully as they cleaned up at the end of the week. He'd already removed the article from the window and moved the stack of free papers to the store room. But it was too late – the cat was already out of the bag and couldn't be stuffed back inside. The publicity machine had taken on a life of its own, and was gathering momentum daily with no help from Ray.

'Roly, can you come here, please?' It was the end of the shift the following Friday, and Ray beckoned him into the little room at the back as Roly was turning the sign on the door to 'Closed'.

Roly looked around in confusion. They hadn't even started clearing up yet. They always waited until the coffee machine was cleaned, the counter wiped down and the dishwasher loaded before they had tea and their 'debrief' in the back room.

'Don't worry about cleaning up,' Ray said.

Roly followed him into the back room and they sat down at the little table. In another break from their usual routine, Ray didn't make tea, and there was no plate of leftover cakes.

'You've been doing a really good job here, Roly,' Ray said as soon as they were seated.

'Thanks.' Roly wondered was he going to get a raise.

'But I'm afraid I'm going to have to let you go.'

'Oh!' Roly was stunned. 'But you just said—'

'It's not a problem with your work,' Ray said quickly. 'You know I'm very happy with you on that front. I wish I could keep you on.'

'So…'

'Unfortunately, it's become too disruptive having you here. All these women who come in to see you—'

'Um … I thought that was the idea? It's brought a lot of new customers to the cafe.'

'It has, it has. But that's the problem. They're not spending much, and they're hogging tables, lingering over a single coffee for hours just so they can ogle you. They're putting off my regular customers. It's not good for business.'

'But – you said it would be great for business.'

'I know.' Ray nodded. 'But you live and learn, Roly. You'll find that yourself as you go on in business. It's all trial and error. But we gave it a shot, right?'

'Um ... yeah.'

'You can't expect to win them all. The important thing is to learn from your mistakes and move on. That's my last bit of advice to you – if you want to succeed in business, don't spend too much time working on the wrong thing, focusing on the wrong idea. Fail fast, cut your losses and pivot quickly to another strategy. Fail fast – remember that.'

'Right. Thanks.' Failing fast sounded like something he'd be good at. 'Well, that's that, I guess.' Was it even legal, he wondered, for Ray to fire him for cluttering the cafe up with customers. Not that he wanted to fight him on it, but it didn't seem right.

'But don't worry,' Ray smiled, brightening. 'I'm pivoting as we speak, and I think I've got the perfect solution!' He got up from the table and went into the walk-in store cupboard. 'You'll be glad to hear I've already found your replacement.' His muffled voice came from the depths of the cupboard. 'I think he's the perfect man for the job.'

'Wow, that was quick.' Roly turned to see Ray struggling through the door with a long, oblong piece of cardboard.

'Ta da!' With a flourish he stood it on the floor and turned it around to face Roly. 'Roly Punch, meet ... Roly Punch!'

Roly couldn't believe his eyes as he eyeballed a life-size cardboard cut-out of himself.

'Oh my god!'

'I found it online. It's amazing, isn't it?' Ray grinned, delighted with himself.

'It's … incredible!'

'See, this way we have the best of both worlds. We'll still be the cafe that has Roly Punch, and people can come in and take selfies with him if they want to.'

'But … he won't be able to work the coffee machine. Or, you know … take orders and stuff.'

'Ah, no. I'll have to get someone to replace you as a waiter, of course. But they'll be able to serve customers at the same time as your fans take selfies with this fella. I can put you off in a corner where you won't get in anyone's way, maybe even set up a booth and charge people to take photos with you.' Ray rubbed his hands gleefully. 'It's a great idea, isn't it?'

'It's brilliant, Ray. Genius.' Roly couldn't take his eyes off the cut-out figure. It was surreal.

'He doesn't have quite your personality, of course.'

'Well, I'd hope not.'

'But he'll always be here – a sort of monument to you, as it were.'

'Like my very own Barack Obama Plaza.'

'Exactly!'

It wasn't Roly's proudest moment, being replaced by a piece of cardboard, but as he walked home, he found he was pretty cheerful on the whole about being let go. It would free up more time for him to work on getting in shape. Now that the Oh Boy! reunion was underway, he was on a deadline and he needed to step up his fitness training. Then a horrible thought occurred to him. Did this mean he had to go back to signing on? And how the hell could he explain this to Geraldine?

STOP DRAGGIN' MY HEART AROUND

It was the week before Christmas, and Ella was busy studying for exams amid a flurry of shopping, parties and get-togethers when Roly called. It was over a year since she'd last seen him. They still messaged and spoke on the phone sometimes, but increasingly rarely, so she was surprised when he said he was in Dublin and wanted to meet up. But she didn't hesitate, despite the fact that she had so much to do and so many people with more of a claim on her time.

Luckily it was the party season, so she didn't have to worry about having nothing to wear. She'd bought a sparkly silver mini dress last week that she loved, and as she got ready to go out, she felt all the excitement and anticipation of a big date. Except that it wasn't a date, of course, she told herself, pausing as she brushed her hair to give herself a stern look in the mirror. It was just Roly – two old friends catching up. That's what she'd told Andrew – that she was meeting up with an old friend from school – and it was the truth.

He suggested the place – a dark, trendy bar on the

quays that she'd never been to before. Even though she was the one who still lived in Dublin, he was more up to date on the cool new places.

He was already there when she arrived. She peered through the gloom and found him sitting at a table near the back. He was wearing a hideous red suit and sporting a scruffy old-man beard. His hair looked like it hadn't been washed in weeks. Why did beautiful people do that – as if ugly clothes and grungy hair were some kind of camouflage? He still looked lovely to her. But she noticed his eyes were glassy as he stood to greet her, and his breath smelled of whiskey as he kissed her cheek.

'This is nice,' she said, looking around. The bar was ostentatiously quirky, with plush red sofas and heavy crimson curtains giving it a bordello air.

'What'll you have?' Roly slid a thick, hardcover cocktail menu across the table.

Ella flipped through the pages. Each cocktail had a page dedicated to it, with long, whimsical blurbs and flowery descriptions of the ingredients. She plumped for a Death in the Afternoon, which apparently had been invented by Ernest Hemingway. Roly ordered something called a Corpse Reviver #2, which seemed appropriate.

'So, how've you been?' she asked as their drinks were delivered by an impossibly glamorous waitress.

'Brilliant, yeah. Our new single is top of the charts ten weeks running so far. The album went straight in at number one in the UK and US.'

'That's … great. Congratulations! But I meant *you*. How are *you* doing?'

'Well, great, obviously.'

'What have you been up to?'

'You mean apart from touring all over the world, playing sell-out concerts, and generally living the dream?'

Ella smiled. She liked his confidence. Even when it spilled over into arrogance, it could be kind of adorable when she was in the mood. Tonight she just found it tiresome. 'Apart from that, yeah.'

'Oh, you know – the usual. Counting my socks, taking the bins out… You?'

'Yeah, same.' She took a long sip of her drink. 'But mostly studying at the moment. I have exams coming up.'

'Oh, that's a drag. Poor you.'

She shrugged. 'It's fine. I'm doing what I want to do.'

He nodded abstractedly, then drained his drink and called the waitress over to order another. 'You?' he asked, pointing at Ella's glass.

'No thanks, I'm fine.' She wasn't even halfway down it yet.

'Drink up, brainiac! Do they teach you nothing in that college of yours?'

Before she could reply, he excused himself to go to the loo. When he returned, Ella sat in dismayed silence, unable to get a word in as he rambled on loquaciously, boasting about Oh Boy!'s next album, which apparently was going to be 'huge', the size of the arenas they'd played, the ridiculous spoiled brat riders they got away with, the producers they'd worked with, the famous people he'd met, the countries he'd been to, even the size and luxuriousness of the hotel rooms he'd stayed in. She waited for him to take a break and ask her something – anything – about what she'd been up to, but it never came.

Still, it served her right. She'd blown off drinks with her study group to come here tonight. This was what you got when you ditched your friends in favour of a 'better offer'.

'So, I'm really loving Trinity!' she said eventually, breaking into a long rant about Oh Boy!'s tour manager.

'Oh, right.' He nodded. 'Great.'

'Yeah, it is.' She felt like she was wading through mud.

'It's just putting real life off a bit longer, though, isn't it? Delaying the inevitable.'

Ella frowned, bristling. 'No. It's really not. It *is* real life, Roly. It's *my* real life.'

'But it's just more school.' He took a long slug of his drink.

'No, it's so different. I feel like my life is really starting, you know?'

'Seriously?' He gave her a pitying little smile, and she wanted to punch him.

'Yes, seriously.' She wished she could convey to him how exciting it all was to her — new people, new ideas, independence; the feeling of life opening up and broadening out, the world becoming so much more expansive than she'd ever imagined it was, and somehow all available, hers for the taking.

'That's how I felt when I started with the band,' he said, steering the conversation back to himself. 'Like everything before was just kids' stuff, and this was the real deal – seeing the world, earning real money. It's like … living life, instead of just reading about it in books.'

'Well, I'm not just reading about going to college in books – I'm actually doing it.'

'Sure, sure. I guess it's all relative, right? I mean, having drinks in the student bar is probably exciting for you if you've never—'

'Never what?' she snapped, finally losing her patience. 'Snorted cocaine off some groupie's boobs?'

Roly laughed. 'Well…'

Ella rolled her eyes, huffing in exasperation.

'Sorry, sorry. And I never did that either, by the way.'

'I'm glad to hear it, considering most of your groupies are underage.'

'Hey, that's not true. I mean, they may have been in the beginning, but they grow up too, like the rest of us.'

'Sorry.' She sighed. 'Let's not fight.'

'Deal.'

'Are you still seeing Pippa?' He'd told her about his girlfriend on the phone the last time they spoke, but she'd have known anyway. She'd seen the photos of them together online and on the covers of magazines. Pippa was a 'face' and appeared in celebrity reality shows, but Ella wasn't sure what had originally made her famous.

'Yeah, we're moving in together.'

'Where?'

'London. She's got this great house in Notting Hill.'

'Well, I've met someone,' she said, since he clearly wasn't going to ask.

'Oh? Who's that, then?'

'His name's Andrew.'

'And you're shagging him? Little Ella has lost her cherry?'

'Oh, fuck off, Roly.'

'No, it sounds romantic – shagging in the dorm, trying not to get caught by … whoever polices those places. Or are you allowed shag in college now?'

'We don't live in college, as it happens.'

'So you've moved in together already? That was quick work.'

'Was it?' He had no idea whether it was or not since he hadn't bothered to ask when they'd met or how long they'd been going out. 'Anyway, we were living together before we started going out – that's how we met. We're in the same house share. And he was in my philosophy tutorial…'

'Philosophy!' Roly gave a hoot of laughter. 'You're studying Philosophy? Seriously?'

'I was in first year – Philosophy, Politics, Economics and Sociology.' She'd already told him this. 'But on the degree we're doing, you gradually specialise in one or two of those. I'm not continuing with Philosophy.'

'Good call,' Roly said. 'I don't imagine there's a big demand for philosophers these days. What about Andrew? Is that what he wants to be when he grows up – a philosopher?'

'He's going for a single honours degree in Philosophy, yes.'

'Well, that sounds useful. I mean, how do you get a job out of that? Is there a philosophy circuit you can go on? Appearing in your flowing robes before a packed audience to tell them the meaning of life?'

'There are whole careers where you never have to go on stage at all, you know. And there are lots of things you can do with a Philosophy degree.' Unfortunately, right now, Ella could only think of one.

'For instance?'

'You can become an academic – lecture and write books. That's what Andrew plans to do.'

'You mean teach Philosophy to the next generation of students? So it's like one of those vicious circles.'

'A virtuous circle hopefully.'

'God!' Roly closed his eyes and threw his head back, pretending to snore. 'He sounds fascinating.'

In truth, Ella did sometimes find the world of pure academia that Andrew dreamed of stultifying. It was why she'd dropped philosophy to focus on modules that had more obvious practical applications, and was going for a joint honours degree in Economics and Sociology. She still planned to pursue an academic career, but she wanted to keep her options open. She wished she could talk about it with Roly, even have a sneaky little laugh at Andrew's expense without feeling she was betraying him. Much as she loved him, he could be pompous and hard work at times, and she wished he could lighten up a bit more. It would be cathartic to take the piss a little bit. But Roly was being so dismissive and obnoxious, it gave her no choice but to be on the defensive.

'Well, you know what they say. Those who can do, those who can't … But I guess no one actually *does* philosophy, do they? Unless you're like … Jesus or someone. Or was he more of a priest?'

'Preacher? Prophet?'

'Motivational speaker? There's big money in that. Maybe Andrew isn't so daft after all. Or he could be the leader of a cult. They always have loads of money, don't they – and sex. Until they blow up all their followers, of course.'

'Not such a great career path, then.'

'Not long term, no.' He signalled to a waitress to bring them another round of cocktails.

'Is there any food?' Ella asked desperately. 'I could really do with some soakage.'

'Food?' Roly raised his eyebrows, seeming surprised. 'Yeah, of course. You should have said.'

'Well, I just assumed…' She shrugged, annoyed that he was making her feel so basic because she needed to eat. 'I mean, aren't you hungry?'

'Yeah, I could do with a bite, now that I think about it.' When the waitress returned with their drinks, he asked her to bring them menus, then disappeared to the loo again.

To Ella's relief, the menus appeared quickly, and her mouth watered as she studied hers. She was starving.

'What do you fancy?' Roly asked when he came back,

seeming more wired than ever, his leg jiggling under the table, as if he couldn't sit still.

'There's a Middle Eastern mezze that sounds really good. Want to share?'

'Sure.' He glanced down at his menu, then closed it. 'Have you ever been to the Middle East?' He knew damn well she hadn't, and continued on without even waiting for her answer. 'We were in Dubai last year. It's amazing! You should go if you ever get the chance. Anyway, we had this incredible mezze – really authentic, you know, not like the stuff you get here…'

And he was off again. In between increasingly frequent visits to the loo, he boasted about the places he'd been, the food he'd eaten in Hong Kong, Sydney or Osaka, the night markets in Bangkok, the Las Vegas strip lit up to daylight at three am … Ella decided not to tell him about the trip to Greece she and Andrew had planned for the summer. She was so excited about it – the little three-star hotel they'd booked in Athens, the holiday apartment in Crete, the archaeological sites they'd visit, the cheap local wine they'd drink at little tavernas … But she knew Roly would make it sound small and pathetic, and she didn't want him spoiling it. So she kept it to herself.

Roly barely touched the food when it arrived. Ella didn't know if it was because whatever he was doing in the toilets had suppressed his appetite or if it was just that he couldn't stop talking for long enough. She ate silently, concentrating on the mezze, which was delicious, throwing in the occasional 'sounds amazing' or 'congratulations', which seemed to be all that was required of her. She polished off most of the platter by herself.

She felt sad and weary when they stepped out into the street. Roly's lips were cold when he leaned in to kiss her cheek. 'See you,' he said. But somehow she knew that he wouldn't, that this was the last time. Their strange on/off friendship had finally run its course. She huddled into her coat, wrapping her arms around herself as they walked away in opposite directions. At the corner she turned to wave goodbye, but Roly was already gone.

22

On the first Friday in August, Ella's phone rang as she lay snuggled in bed waiting for her alarm to go off.

'Good morning, honey! Happy birthday!' She smiled at the sound of her mother's voice.

'Thanks, Mum.' She sat up in bed, rubbing her eyes and yawned into the phone.

'Sorry, did I wake you up? I wanted to get you before you left for work.'

'No, I was already awake, and I was about to get up anyway.' She leaned over and switched off the alarm on her nightstand. 'What time is it there? And where is there?'

'It's two in the afternoon. We're in Hanoi – just got here yesterday.'

'Oh, lovely. Are you having a great time?'

'Oh, Ella, it's amazing! We're having so much fun.'

'I'm glad.' Ella smiled and settled herself against the headboard. It was great to hear her mother sounding so happy. She was always upbeat, but the enthusiasm in her voice now was on another level.

'We're spending a couple of days here and then we're

joining a group trip on Monday. What about you? Any plans for today?'

'Not really. Just the usual – work, home.'

'You're going to work on your birthday? You should have taken the day off, done something fun.'

'Well, I've had my birthday off for the last ten years, so this will be kind of a novelty. And work is quite fun at the moment.'

'I hope you're doing something to celebrate later, though. Maybe with your lovely new housemate?'

'Yeah, we'll do dinner together.' It was probably true. They ate together most nights, so in all likelihood tonight would be no different – unless Roly had something else on. She didn't want her mother to feel bad about her not doing anything special, but she hadn't actually told Roly it was her birthday. She'd wanted to, but she couldn't find a way to casually work it into the conversation, and if she just told him out of the blue, it might look like she was angling for a present.

'And Hazel's away this weekend, but we're going out to celebrate next week.'

'Have you opened your presents yet?'

'No. I've been very good and saved them for today.' Ella glanced across at the wardrobe where she'd stashed the birthday gifts and cards her mother and Nora had given her before they'd left. She'd buried them right at the back so they'd be out of sight and she wouldn't be tempted to open them before the day.

'Well, there's something else in the post for you. I hope it arrives in time. But at least you have something to open today either way.'

'Thanks, Mum. Tell Nora thanks and give her my love.'

'She's right here. I'll just put you on to her.'

'Hi, Ella. Happy birthday!'

Nora was buzzing about their travels, babbling away about how beautiful Hanoi was and the gorgeous lunch they'd just had by the lake. It was lovely to hear them both so happy. After they'd chatted for a while, Ella had to get up and get ready for work, while her mother and Nora were catching a bus to Halong Bay.

When she hung up, Ella went to the wardrobe and took out the gift-wrapped parcels. She settled herself against the headboard and opened the cards first, then unwrapped her presents. She opened her mother's first. A note on top said 'I bought this for you before I left as I knew I'd miss your birthday, so it may need an iron. Hope it still fits!' Beneath the layers of pink tissue paper, Ella found a floral-print Hobbs dress that she'd admired on her last shopping trip with her mother. She'd tried it on, and loved how it looked and felt, but had decided she couldn't justify spending money on it when she had no occasion to wear it.

Tears stung her eyes as she read the little card her mother had put inside that said simply 'Dress up! Go out! Have fun!' Ella swatted at her eyes with the back of her hand, then slowly unwrapped Nora's present, stretching out the moment. She smiled as she unwrapped a pretty pair of chunky wedge sandals from Camper in pale pink that would go perfectly with the dress and also looked comfortable. Nora knew she didn't do heels. It was a pity she didn't have anywhere to go tonight, but she could dress up next week when she went out with Hazel. She couldn't wait to try the dress on again, but there was no time now. She'd dawdled long enough.

As she got out of bed, she heard Roly going out for his run. She contemplated taking her birthday cards down to the kitchen and leaving them casually lying around for him to see, but decided against it. Instead she lined them up on her chest of drawers before heading for the bathroom.

When she'd showered, she ate a solitary breakfast scrolling through her Facebook and Instagram feed. At least her online friends knew it was her birthday, and she scrolled through the messages posted on her wall as she shovelled corn flakes into her mouth. She was going to miss her mother and Nora today. They always made a fuss of her birthdays. Maybe she should have taken the day off and done something nice and self-indulgent just for herself. But it was too late to change her mind now.

'Morning, Ella!' Kerry greeted her brightly as she walked into the office. 'Happy Birthday!'

'Oh! Thanks.' Ella frowned, confused. How did Kerry know? But as she pushed through the inner door and saw her desk decorated with balloons and a big birthday banner, she got her answer. How could Kerry *not* know? Jake and Dylan appeared as she sat down, both grinning and looking very pleased with themselves.

'Happy Birthday!' they chorused.

'Thanks.' Ella gulped, touched. 'This is … a surprise.'

'I'm sure you have plans later,' Jake said, perching on the edge of her desk. 'But you can stay for a quick drink after work?'

'Oh yes please, that would be lovely.' She wished she could tell them she didn't have any plans later, and she could drink with them for as long as they liked, but it would sound too pathetic. At least she'd have a bit of a celebration. It was more than she'd expected for today, and she was glad she hadn't taken the day off to mope around on her own, 'treating herself'.

At eleven, Kerry came in with a cake and candles.

Everyone gathered around her desk and sang 'Happy Birthday', and Jake presented her with a card signed by all of them. Then they cut the cake – chocolate fudge, her favourite – and handed around slices. At lunchtime, they ordered pizza in her honour, and everyone played Pictionary in the break room, which was hilarious because neither Jake nor Dylan could draw, but they were so uncannily in sync they could practically read each other's minds and won with the most indecipherable sketches. Ella partnered with Kerry and did abysmally, but it was good fun. At five, they all congregated in the meeting room and drank champagne. It had turned out to be a really nice birthday after all, Ella thought as she made her way home, slightly squiffy. She'd had a lovely day, and she was content now to spend a quiet night in. She'd try on her new dress, and maybe have a long, relaxing bath.

'Happy Birthday!' Roly greeted her as soon as she walked into the kitchen.

'Oh! Thanks. How did you know?'

'Facebook told me – since you didn't bother to. That arrived for you this morning.' He nodded to a large padded envelope on the table. She already knew it would be from her mother, even before she saw her handwriting or the Thai stamps. She threw off her jacket, then tore open the envelope. Inside there were several smaller packages gift-wrapped in colourful paper, along with a couple of postcards with some snippets of travel news. The presents were wrapped in a strangely textured paper, which Nora informed her in her postcard was made from elephant dung.

'Ew!' Roly said, reading over her shoulder. She opened the parcels one after another. There was a pair of silver earrings, a green silk shawl, vividly coloured scented soaps in the shape of lotus flowers, a carved wooden elephant and a little embroidered bag.

'Nice haul,' Roly said.

'I also got a new dress and shoes that my mum and Nora left before they went away.'

'Well, put them on because I'm taking you out.'

'You are?' Her heart skipped.

'Unless you have plans?'

'No, no plans. I'd love to go out.'

'Great! I booked that new Mexican place on Camden Street for eight.'

'Oh, brilliant! I've been wanting to try that, but it's not exactly diet-friendly.'

'Well, all bets are off for your birthday, so now's our chance.'

'Absolutely!'

'Better get your skids on,' he said, glancing at his watch.

She was later than usual because of the drinks party at work.

'Thank you.' She gave him a quick kiss on the cheek, then headed for the bathroom. This was shaping up to be the best birthday ever.

Ella's new dress not only fitted, but was a little looser than it had been when she'd tried it on in the shop. She felt a little shiver of excitement as she did a twirl in front of the mirror. She'd done proper make-up, which was a rarity for her, and she was wearing her new shoes and silver jewellery. She felt great – not like someone else exactly, but a much more glamorous version of herself.

'Wow, you look gorgeous,' Roly said when she joined

him downstairs, the admiration in his eyes giving her a warm glow. 'That's a great dress.'

'Thanks. You look really good too.' He'd changed into a crisp blue shirt and black jeans. He looked mouth-wateringly good.

It was a warm summer's evening, and the restaurant was a short walk from Roly's house. They had a table on a little garden terrace at the back.

'This is beautiful,' Ella said, looking around as they were seated. 'I love it already!' Fairy lights were entwined with climbing flowers on the trellises and coloured lanterns twinkled in the trees. Candles in boldly coloured glass jars bathed the wooden tables in a warm glow.

'Yeah, it's cool.' Roly picked up the drinks list. 'What are you going to have?'

'Well, what I'd really love is a Corpse Reviver #2, but they don't seem to have that,' she said teasingly.

'Oh god,' Roly groaned. 'Don't remind me of that night. I was such a tool.'

'You *were* kind of a tool. But you've more than made up for it since.' She looked at the drinks menu again. 'I'll have a margarita,' she said decisively, licking her lips. 'When in Mexico…'

'I'll have the same,' Roly said. 'Virgin, obviously.'

A friendly waitress took their drinks order, then left them to study the menus.

'God, I want the whole left-hand side,' Ella said. 'I always prefer the starters in Mexican to the mains.'

'Me too. Will we just get a bunch of stuff and share?'

'Perfect! A man after my own heart.'

The waitress returned with their cocktails in thick blue

glasses. Ella took a sip of her margarita. It was sharp, strong and utterly delicious.

'We'll have the left-hand side of the menu, please,' Roly jokingly told the waitress when she returned. They ordered quesadillas, pork pibil tacos, chilli sizzlers, chicken tinga taquitos, and a plate of nachos to share.

'So, have you had a nice birthday so far?'

'Yes, I've had such a nice day. I got lovely presents. There were balloons and a card in work, and we had cake and champagne. And now this.' She raised her glass to him in salute.

'Why didn't you tell me?'

She shrugged. 'I thought it would sound like I was angling for a present. I mean, it's not easy to work casually into a conversation – "by the way, it's my birthday on Friday".'

'You told the people in work.'

She shook her head. 'They had it on my CV.'

'Ah! I should have asked for your CV before I let you move in.'

'You should. I could have been anyone.'

'Luckily you turned out to be you.' His smile flooded her with warmth. Was he flirting with her?

'Taking your tenant out for her birthday will do nothing for your evil landlord image, by the way. You'll probably be drummed out of the business.'

'Ah well, I didn't have my heart set on being an evil landlord anyway.'

They had another couple of margaritas, and when the food came, they both moved on to beer – non-alcoholic for Roly.

'I think we may have over-ordered,' Ella laughed as the waitress struggled to squeeze all the dishes onto the table.

'Just a little.'

The food was all delicious, however, and Ella didn't regret one mouthful as they grazed their way through it. 'God, I love Mexican. Have you ever been to Mexico?'

Roly nodded. 'We were there on tour, but I never really saw it. It was the same with a lot of places. I've been all around the world and seen the insides of a lot of five-star hotels and concert venues.'

'Better than not having been around the world at all, I guess.'

'Yeah. I'm not playing poor little five-star prisoner here. We got taken to some amazing places. And the view out the window was always pretty great.'

'Still, I get that it must have been frustrating.' She didn't want him to think she was criticising.

He nodded. 'So near and yet so far. It sounds weird, I know, but I kind of felt I was missing out when Jack and some of my friends went travelling – I was envious.'

'So you never got to woo those French girls with your awesome linguistic skills?'

'Nope. I've been to Paris several times, but I've still never even gone up the Eiffel Tower. How about you?'

'I've never been to Mexico. But I have gone up the Eiffel Tower.'

'You're going to tell me it's shit, aren't you – that I didn't miss anything?'

She shook her head, smiling. 'No. It's great. Sorry!'

'It's fine. I hate when people tell you things you've missed out on are actually crap, like they're throwing you a bone because they feel sorry for you.'

Ella nodded. 'It's so arrogant too, as if their opinion is the last word. I'd rather make up my own mind, thanks. Although I'm pretty sure everyone agrees about the Mona Lisa. Now, that *is* shit.'

He grinned. 'I've heard. Too small, right?'

'Yeah. I mean, make an effort, Leonardo!'

'People have walls to cover.'

She laughed. 'It's not that it's shit, in fairness – just disappointing. Although maybe it's not anymore, now that the word is out and everyone's expecting it to be small?'

'I'd probably be impressed because it was way bigger than I imagined.'

Ella loaded up the last nacho with sour cream, guacamole and salsa. 'I'll be lucky if this dress still fits me tomorrow. At least I've got to wear it once.'

'You look gorgeous.' There was something in the way his eyes lingered that made Ella's breath catch and she was unable to look away.

'So do you,' she said, her heart beating faster. Suddenly she felt hot and jittery, and very aware of the sensual curve of his mouth, the dark hairs on his tanned forearms where they rested on the table, his beautiful hands with their long, elegant fingers, the glimpse of his tongue when he laughed. God, he was hot! She found herself imagining sucking on his plump bottom lip, touching her tongue to his, feeling his hot breath in her mouth. It had been such a long time…

Gah! It's Roly, she told herself. She'd just had too much tequila. But then, as if he'd been thinking the same thing, his eyes dropped to her mouth. And he hadn't had any tequila at all.

On the walk home, Roly took Ella's hand. She liked the feel of his strong, warm fingers wrapped around hers. She didn't know if he was doing it because she was a bit unsteady on her feet or just because he wanted to. But the way his thumb stroked idly over hers seemed intentional, like an unspoken agreement. She felt warm and woozy, and stumbled as they went in the door. Roly caught her.

'I'm a bit tipsy.'

He grinned. 'I can tell.' He held her arm as they walked up the hall into the living room.

'Thanks for my birthday dinner,' she said, unwrapping her shawl and dropping it on the sofa.

'You're welcome. Hang on,' he held up a finger. 'I have a present for you.' He strode out of the room, but instead of waiting, Ella followed him upstairs to his bedroom.

'I thought dinner was my present,' she said, standing in the doorway.

'That was only part of it.' He took a gift bag and a card from the nightstand and held them out to her. 'I meant to bring it to the restaurant, but I forgot.'

'Thanks.' Ella took them from him, then walked past him to sit down on his bed. She opened the card and read 'To Ella, my beautiful brainiac friend and the best tenant I've ever had.' God, she must be drunk, she thought, as tears sprang to her eyes. Inside the bag a little velvet pouch contained a silver charm bracelet with a birthday card dangling charm.

'It's not very imaginative, I'm afraid,' he said, sitting beside her. 'But I didn't have a lot of time,' he added accusingly.

'Oh, it's gorgeous! I love it,' Ella said as she put it on, turning her wrist this way and that to admire it. She leaned over to give him a kiss. She was aiming for his cheek, but landed on his lips, and instead of giving him a quick peck, she didn't pull away. She just stayed where she was, his lips warm against hers as she breathed in the deliciously warm, woody scent of his aftershave. He smelled amazing. After a moment he wrapped his arms around her and kissed her back – slowly, softly. She shuffled closer, pressing herself into him.

'Ella?' he pulled away, looking at her questioningly. He seemed as surprised by this development as she was.

'Sorry.' She snuggled into him, her eyes drooping closed. 'I'm drunk.' She nuzzled against his neck, loving the warmth of his skin and the sandpapery rasp of his stubble.

'I'm not. So I have no excuse.'

She sighed and lay back on the bed, kicking her sandals off onto the floor. 'Well, it's still my birthday for another…' she glanced at the clock 'fifteen minutes. Spend the rest of my birthday with me.' She shifted to one side of the bed and patted the empty space beside her.

To her surprise, he didn't hesitate. 'It's your birthday,' he said, smiling. 'You call the shots.' He kicked off his shoes, then lay down beside her.

'This is like old times,' he said as she turned to face him.

'Old times?'

'That night in my room at the Westbury, remember?'

'Oh yeah. How could I forget? My illicit night with pop idol Roly Punch.'

'That's the one.' He was smiling at her indulgently, and all she could think about was kissing him again.

'I love my present. Thank you again.'

His eyes dropped to the bracelet at her wrist as she fingered it lightly.

'You're welcome.'

'And the lovely dinner.'

'My pleasure. So, what would you like to do for the rest of your birthday?'

'This.' She nudged closer and pressed her lips to his. He didn't pull away, and he only hesitated a moment before he cupped the back of her neck and kissed her back.

His lips were soft and warm and chilli-flavoured, and he was an amazing kisser. His body felt so good against hers as he pulled her closer – hard and strong and warm. She moaned softly as he tugged at her lower lip, and she pulled him closer, burying her fingers in his hair. His mouth opened against hers, and she shivered as his tongue slid inside. They were both breathing heavily now, lost in the moment. Roly groaned deep in his throat as he grabbed her leg and hitched it over his hip, pushing against her so that Ella could feel his erection. But when she slid her hand down towards it, he stopped her and held himself away from her as he pressed soft, butterfly kisses to her eyes, her cheeks, the corners of her mouth.

'Ella?'

She opened her eyes. His looked heavy and drugged, which was exactly how she felt – like a fat bee, drowsy from gorging on nectar.

'Mmm?'

'We should stop.' His face was so close to hers on the pillow, she could still feel his breath on her mouth.

'Oh. Okay. Should we, though?'

'You're a bit pissed.' He stroked her face lightly with one finger.

'Not really.'

'And you need your sleep.'

'I'm wide awake.'

'And,' he turned and looked at the clock, 'it's not your birthday anymore.' It was ten minutes after midnight.

'Oh.' She sighed. 'Don't you want to, though?' She leaned in, seeking his mouth again.

'I just don't think it's a good idea.' He gave her a frustratingly chaste kiss on the forehead, like she was a sleepy child.

'Don't go, though,' she said as her eyes drooped closed. Suddenly she did feel sleepy. 'Let's just stay here like this. We don't have to get undressed or anything.'

'It's my bed.' She could hear the smile in his voice. 'I'm not going anywhere.'

She sighed, nestling closer to him. 'Me either.'

23

'Good morning.'

Ella opened her eyes to see Roly still on the bed beside her. They were both fully dressed, lying on top of the duvet. Light flooded in through the gap in the curtains, and memories of last night came crowding back into her head – mainly memories of kissing. It had been amazing, but it was probably a good thing that Roly had called a halt and they hadn't gone any further. There'd be morning-after regrets and then things would be awkward as fuck between them. She'd probably end up having to move out.

'Morning,' she said.

'How do you feel?'

She tested her head, shaking it a little. 'Good,' she said. 'No hangover. It probably helps that I ate my own body weight in Mexican food.'

'You did have plenty of soakage.'

'Maybe we should go for a run to make up for it,' she said without enthusiasm.

'I'd rather stay here and do this.' He put an arm

around her and pulled her closer, then leaned in and kissed her. She couldn't suppress a gasp of surprise.

'I mean, if you still want to?' he asked, pulling back. 'Last night you said—'

'That this was what I wanted to do for the rest of my birthday. But you stopped. You said it wasn't a good idea.'

'Just because you were a bit pissed. I didn't want you to do something you might regret.' His eyes glittered as they dropped to her mouth. 'But you're not drunk now.'

'Neither are you.'

'I never was.

'Oh. Yeah...' She wondered briefly if that made all his sexual encounters super-charged, never being able to pass it off as a drunken mistake. Every decision he made was clear-headed and intentional. There was no fuzziness for him, no blurring of the edges. Which meant that last night, stone-cold sober he'd wanted to kiss her...

'So if you still want to do this...' He edged closer.

'Do you?' She couldn't hide her surprise. Somehow she'd assumed he'd think better of it in the light of day – that they both would, and they'd laugh it off as heat-of-the-moment stupidity and agree never to mention it again.

'Of course. I wasn't drunk last night, remember. But if you've changed your mind—'

'No!' It came out so emphatically, she laughed. 'I still want to.' It seemed only fair to meet him halfway, to be as honest and vulnerable as he was.

'Me too,' he said, moving in to kiss her again. 'Really badly.'

He was an amazing kisser, and fireworks burst inside her as his tongue slid into her mouth. She thought how strange it should be to be kissing Roly Punch after all these years, all the time she'd known him. If her younger self could have seen this image – the two of them tangled together on his bed, her hand raking through his hair, their mouths locked together in a fierce kiss – she wouldn't have believed it. But in this moment it didn't feel strange. It just felt deeply, gloriously right.

His hands roamed over her body, sending sparks of electricity racing along her veins wherever they touched. When he tugged down the top of her dress, she arched into him as his hand cupped her breast, stroking the nipple through the lace of her bra. But as he slid a hand up her bare leg, pushing her dress up with it, she panicked. Because this was Roly – Roly Punch who slept with women like Pippa, women with flat stomachs and skinny thighs. No, not just women *like* Pippa, *actual* Pippa – an underwear model, as he never ceased to remind her.

'Maybe we should wait, though,' she said, stilling his hand and pulling away.

He sighed, moving his hand to her waist. 'Wait for what?' He frowned down at her.

'I dunno. Just until we're a bit more, um … ready.'

'If you don't want to do this, fine,' he said, tracing her lip with his thumb. 'But if you mean until we're thinner or more buff or whatever… Let's not wait until everything's perfect – until we're both perfect. Because who knows when that might be? And I really want to do this now.'

'Me too.'

'You sure?'

She nodded vigorously. 'Yes. God, yes!'

He grinned. 'Good. Now, where were we?'

Then his mouth was on her again, hot and urgent, parting her lips with his, their tongues tangling together. Everything seemed to melt inside her, and she relaxed into it, not caring how soft and flabby her stomach might feel or how thick her thighs were. She didn't have the headspace to worry about any of it when he was distracting her with his mouth and hands, driving everything out of her mind except him.

'I'm a bit out of practice,' she murmured as he nuzzled her neck. 'Just to warn you.'

'It'll all come back to you. It's like falling off a bike.'

'Ouch!' She giggled. 'That's not encouraging.'

He frowned, smiling crookedly. 'Log! I meant falling off a log! I can't think straight when you're being all hot like this. I'm mixing up my metaphors.'

'Similes.'

'Whatever. It's like riding a bike.' She shivered as his teeth tugged gently on her earlobe. 'Or falling off a log.'

'Why is that even a saying?' she asked as his hand slid up her leg. This time she didn't stop him. 'I mean, who falls off a log?'

'Me. I fell off a log once.' The skirt of her dress was bunched up around her waist now, and he bent to press kisses to her stomach.

'You did?'

'Yeah, on a school trip to Clara Lara Funpark. You know that log that you walk on across the pond? I lost my balance and fell in. I got soaked. It was freezing.' He tapped her hip. 'Sit up,' he murmured.

When she did, he tugged at her dress and she helped him pull it off over her head.

'That sounds really uncomfortable.' She lay back against the pillows.

'Yeah, I had to spend the rest of the day shivering in my wet clothes. It *was* easy, though. I'll give it that.'

'Didn't you bring a change?'

'I'd already got them soaked on the water slide.' As he spoke, his fingers trailed lightly over her skin, brushing down her arm and across her breasts, her nipples stiffening in response.

'Roly?' She shivered as he sucked on one nipple through her bra. Christ, that was delicious!

He lifted his head, and she wished she hadn't said anything. 'Ella?'

'Are we really going to do this? In the broad light of day?'

He nodded slowly, a grin spreading across his face, as he slid a hand between her legs. 'No better time.' He slipped a finger inside her knickers and stroked her slowly, his eyes glittering as he looked down at her, watching her face.

'Stone-cold sober?' She gasped as he pressed against her most sensitive spot, her voice coming out as a strangulated moan.

He pulled back and gave her a stern look. 'Do you want to talk or kiss?' His fingers were still teasing her sensitive flesh, making it difficult to formulate a response.

'Kiss,' she gasped.

'Shut up, then.' He leaned in and kissed her again, and Ella forgot all her questions and doubts as his tongue slid into her mouth.

Ella had worried that sex would take too much out of her, but instead it seemed to give her more energy, and she felt invigorated in a way that she hadn't in a long time.

'Bella Ella,' Roly murmured, stroking damp tendrils of hair away from her face as they collapsed on the bed beside each other. 'Am I breaking some kind of landlord code of ethics by sleeping with my tenant?'

'Landlords don't have any ethics, remember? They're evil bastards.'

'Oh yeah. That's okay, then.'

'But maybe I'm just seducing you so you'll let me off paying my rent. I bet you never thought of that.'

'Ooh, kinky! Wanna role-play that?' He sat up on one elbow.

'Okay. You start.

'Um … okay.' He rubbed his hair and shook his head a few times as if getting into character. 'Hello,' he said in a weird deep voice. 'I've come to collect the rent.'

'Uh … you shouldn't really start off in bed with me. Go out of the room and come back in.'

'Oh, right, yeah.' He leapt out of bed and went out, appearing again seconds later in the doorway.

'Hello, Ella,' he said again in his gruff voice. 'I'm here to collect the rent.'

'Oh, Mr Punch!' she gasped in a high, breathy tone. 'You've caught me unawares.' She scrabbled under the duvet, pulling it up to her chin. 'But … why are you naked?' She giggled. 'Did you drive over here like that?'

He frowned, trying to look severe and suppress his laughter. 'Of course not. As you well know, I live upstairs. And … I'm a nudist!'

'Oh yes, I forgot!'

'Yes, I'm ready for action at all times. So … pay up, little lady and I'll be out of your hair.'

'Oh no! I'm afraid I'm a little short.'

'Don't give me that!' He crossed the room and pulled back the duvet. 'I'd say you're five foot six if you're an inch.'

'Five foot five, actually.'

'Well that's no excuse. I want my money.'

'Please don't throw me out! I have nowhere else to go.'

'Well, I wouldn't want to put a pretty little thing like you out on the street.' He sat down on the bed. 'If you haven't got the money, maybe we could come to some arrangement.'

She gasped. 'You mean…' She put the back of her hand to her forehead in a dramatic gesture of despair.

He put a hand around her neck, then slowly slid it down to cup her breast, his thumb flicking across her nipple. 'If you don't have the money, you'll have to pay me some other way.'

'You don't mean … sex?' She widened her eyes innocently.

'Yes. I'll have my wicked way with you. And a landlord's ways are wickeder than most.'

'I've heard,' Ella said, swallowing a laugh.

'I don't do this for all my tenants, you know.'

'I should hope not. You'd go out of business fast!'

'But I like you, so I'll make an exception.' His hands were stroking her breasts, driving her wild. 'So what do you say? Sex or the street?'

Ella had always found sex talk cringey and a total turn-off. But someone making her laugh was a whole other story.

'Oh go on, then,' she said, flinging her arms wide. 'Ravish me!'

They were both shrieking with laughter as Roly flipped her onto her back and straddled her.

'Well, that beats a run any day,' Ella said later. They were lying close together, facing each other.

'Do you think we've worked off the Mexican yet?'

'I dunno. Does sex really work as exercise?'

'We'll have to Google it.'

'This is weird, isn't it – us, like this?'

'I dunno. I think I've wanted to do that since that night at the Westbury.'

'What?' She raised her eyebrows. 'No you haven't.'

'Maybe I did, on some level. You know, subconsciously.'

'You wanted to shag me subconsciously?'

'Yeah. I feel like it was always out there, hanging over us.'

'Like homework?'

'Like … unfinished business, you know?'

'Right. So now that's done and we can move on?'

'No, that's not what I mean.'

'So why did you never act on it?'

He frowned. 'I guess I always felt like if something happened with you it'd be … serious. Like that'd be it. Permanent. There'd be no going back.'

'No escape.'

'Yeah.'

'Like prison.'

He laughed. 'No.'

'Trapped with no way out.' She widened her eyes dramatically.

'No, I just meant we'd have ended up with a house and kids and everything, and I wasn't ready for all that.'

'You weren't the only one!'

'It was like if I'd been with you, that'd be it. My life would be over.'

'Gosh! Thanks very much.'

'Not my whole life, obviously. But that part of it. I wouldn't have been able to shag around anymore, because then I'd lose you.'

There were so many questions running through Ella's head, she struggled to take it all in. 'I can't believe you even thought about me in that way at all. Before last night.'

'Seriously?'

'All that time we were friends… I mean, we hardly even saw each other.'

'Come on! I mean, you were a girl. I was a horny teenager. You honestly think I never thought about getting naked with you?'

'No. This is a total revelation to me.'

'Didn't you ever think about me … like that?'

'Maybe sometimes … subconsciously.' She smiled teasingly.

'You didn't fancy me, even a little bit?'

'Of course I fancied you. Everyone fancied you.'

He smiled smugly.

'But I never thought anything would happen between us.'

'Why not?'

She didn't want to say he'd been out of her league because that would only make him more smug. Besides, she didn't believe that anymore. 'We were just … so different,' she said instead.

'Yeah, but you know what they say – opposites attract.'

She took his hand, playing with his fingers. 'So, do you still feel the same way?' she asked. 'Is it like your life's over? Do we have to get married now, buy a house and have some kids?'

'Well, maybe not right away.' A slow smile spread across his face. 'I mean, I have some stuff to do today. But how are you fixed for next week?'

'I'm pretty free next week.'

'And in the meantime,' he said, pulling her in for a kiss, 'I think we should keep doing lots of this.'

24

They spent almost all of Saturday in bed, only venturing out for food when they got hungry – which was often. Sex seemed to give Ella an enormous appetite, and she couldn't remember when she'd enjoyed food more. When they finally dragged themselves out of bed that evening, they were too impatient to cook, and instead went for an early dinner at a local bistro.

'Sex would have to burn off a serious amount of calories to justify this,' she said as an enormous burger was placed in front of her with a silver bucket of golden, crisp fries with mouth-wateringly frayed edges. All the sex was going to play havoc with her diet, but she found it impossible to care.

'It's still your birthday weekend,' Roly said, grinning. 'So we're off the hook until Monday. We'll have one last big blowout at Nan's tomorrow.' They were regulars at Sunday dinner now with Christine and Loretta.

'They don't know it's my birthday, do they?' Ella asked, the thought suddenly occurring to her.

'I may have mentioned it,' he said with a smug grin.

'Oh, you shouldn't have,' she gasped, mortified.

'Don't worry. You didn't tell them, so no one's going to think you're angling for a present.'

It was obvious as soon as they walked through the door at Christine's the next day that it was a celebration. The table was decorated with balloons and flowers, and before dinner they had prosecco in the tiny terrace garden, all squeezed around the little wrought-iron table. There were cards and gifts – a Molton Brown bath set from Loretta, a beautiful hand-painted silk scarf from Christine that had been made by an artist friend of hers.

'Oh, it's gorgeous,' she said, clutching the scarf to her chest. 'Thank you so much. Thank you, both.' She turned to Loretta, who smiled and pulled her into a hug.

'Happy birthday, pet.'

Ella wiped tears from her eyes. She was so touched. A few weeks ago, she hadn't even known these people, and now they'd welcomed her into their family and were treating her as one of their own.

Roly took her hand and squeezed it, and she returned the pressure, feeling giddy with prosecco, love and happiness. She noticed Loretta follow the motion of their hands, a knowing smile playing around her lips.

'Are you two…' She nodded at their joined hands.

Ella didn't say anything, unsure how Roly felt about his family knowing about them.

'Yep,' he said easily, clasping her hand tighter as he turned to smile at her. 'We're … what did you crazy kids call it in your day? Going steady?'

'Hey, I'm not that old,' Loretta protested, beaming at them both.

'Well, this is great!' Christine lifted the bottle and

topped up all their glasses with the rest of the prosecco. 'I must say, I'm relieved.'

'Relieved?' Roly frowned.

'I was telling Mum before you came,' Loretta said. 'I saw a thing on Facebook about you being seen with Pippa at some nightclub. It said you looked loved up and it was sort of hinting that maybe you were getting back together.'

'We were not loved up! Ella was there too that night. We're definitely not getting back together. But it's good to know what you really thought of my girlfriend,' he said to Christine huffily.

'Oh, she wasn't a bad sort really,' Christine allowed.

'She was just a little bit spoilt and selfish, but she'd have grown out of that,' Loretta said kindly.

She hasn't grown out of it yet, Ella thought. She'd want to get on that fast.

'She was a nice girl, really, when you got to know her.'

'We just like this one better,' Christine said, raising her glass to Ella. 'A lot better.'

They ate a glorious seafood stew fragrant with orange and cardamom, that Ella thought was one of the best things she'd ever tasted.

'It's lovely to see you two so happy, coupled up,' Loretta said, smiling fondly at Ella and Roly.

'Speaking of coupling up, will we be meeting your new boyfriend soon?' Christine asked. 'Isn't he supposed to be coming over next week?'

A shadow flickered across Loretta's face. 'He was, but he had some awful hassle with his papers. Now they've confiscated his passport, and he has to bribe them to get it back. The officials there are so corrupt.'

Ella had an uneasy feeling. She willed Christine or

Roly to ask the questions that were spinning around in her head, but to her frustration, neither of them did.

'And now someone's skimmed his bank card, so all his accounts are frozen and he has no way to access his money until he gets that sorted out.'

'Sounds like a nightmare!' Roly said.

'He does seem to have an awful lot of bad luck,' Christine said, her tone hard and devoid of sympathy. Ella was relieved that she sounded cynical. 'It's one disaster after another. Maybe you're as well off without him.'

'Poor Mike,' Loretta said. 'He's had an awful time of it, but it's hardly his fault.'

'He's never asked you for money, has he?' Christine asked sharply.

Loretta blushed. 'No, of course not.' She frowned. 'It's not that he's skint – you know he's always sending me expensive presents.'

'That's true,' Christine said.

'It's just a temporary setback; it could happen to anyone. Anyway, as soon as he gets it all sorted out, he'll come straight here.'

'I can't wait to meet him,' Roly said, smiling at her.

Dessert was birthday cake made by Loretta – triple layers of red velvet sponge, covered in white icing. But it was unlike any birthday cake Ella had ever had before. On top Loretta had created a whole scene – there was a tiny Ella running on a track towards a finish line that read 'Happy Birthday, Ella', while along the route little figures of Roly, Christine and Loretta cheered her on, their arms in the air. At the finishing post, another Ella stood in cap and gown, a rolled-up scroll in her hand, and a pile of books stacked up beside her. They all sang 'Happy Birthday' to her, but when she blew out the candles, her life in that moment felt so perfect, she couldn't think of anything to wish for.

'What do you think about this boyfriend of your mum's?' she asked hesitantly as they walked home later.

'He seems all right. He's very handsome, isn't he – for an older dude?'

Roly had always placed too much importance on looks. 'You don't think there might be something dodgy about him?' She was tentative. She knew how protective he was of his mum, and she didn't want to upset him. She just wanted to give him a nudge, plant a seed of doubt in his mind.

He groaned. 'You sound like my nan,' he said, rolling his eyes. 'She treats Mum like she's a complete idiot when it comes to men.'

'It's just because she's worried about her.'

'I know, but she should give her credit for having a bit of cop.'

'She's just trying to look out for her. She doesn't want her to get hurt.'

'Mum's tougher than she looks. She can look out for herself. Okay, granted she does have form for getting involved with complete tossers. I guess I'm living proof of that. But that was a long time ago. Sometimes Nan treats her like she's still a clueless teenager.'

Ella decided she'd better let it go, at least for now. 'I'm not criticising your mum,' she said, touching his arm. 'Lots of really smart people get taken in by catfishers.'

'Catfishers? Is that what you think is happening?'

'I don't know. I think it's possible.'

'You watch too much internet,' Roly scoffed and they walked on in silence. 'So, what exactly do you think this bloke is up to anyway?' he asked a while later. He sounded scathing, but there was a hint of uncertainty in his tone.

'It sounds like a romance scam to me. These people woo women online, convince them they're in love and they want to be together. Then they have a sick child who needs an operation, or they're being held hostage by corrupt officials in some foreign country and they have to bribe them to get out, or their bank account has been hacked and they can't access their money.' She glanced at Roly, but she couldn't tell what he was thinking. 'Then the requests for money start rolling in – medical bills, bribes for corrupt officials, loans for plane fares…'

'But you heard Mum. He hasn't asked her for any money.'

'Not yet maybe. Besides, would she admit it to your nan if he had?'

Roly frowned. 'No, probably not.' He was silent for a while. 'But what's in it for this bloke anyway? Mum's not rich. And besides, he's obviously got plenty money himself. He really does send her all these expensive presents. She wasn't just saying that to get Nan off her back. I've seen them – Gucci scarves, Marc Jacobs bags…'

'They could be knock-offs.'

'It's still an awful lot of trouble to go to for, what, maybe a few grand at the most? Not exactly a criminal mastermind, this suspect of yours, is he?'

'It's worth it if they do it to enough people.'

'It sounds like awfully hard work. Wouldn't it be easier to, like, rob a bank or something?'

'Ah, bank robbery isn't as easy as it looks in the movies.'

'Rats! That was going to be my next career move.'

'Thinking outside the box! I like it. Ray would be so proud.' She was glad they were back on joking terms.

'Look, I get what you're saying,' he said when they got to the door. 'But I really think this bloke is on the level.'

Ella didn't think he was a 'bloke' at all, but she didn't want to push it and risk putting Roly on the defensive. Besides, maybe he was right. For Loretta's sake, she hoped so.

'This might have been the best birthday weekend I've ever had,' she said to Roly as they lay in bed later. 'Definitely the most surprising.' They were knotted around each other, the window open to the humid evening air. The sheet was kicked off, twisted around their ankles.

'Do you want me to go back to my own bed?' she asked. She was so comfortable, she really didn't want to move.

'No.' He wrapped an arm around her and pulled her closer. 'Stay.' He dropped a kiss on her shoulder.

'But I have to get up early for work in the morning.'

He shrugged. 'That's okay. I like having you in my bed. When you're here, I can just … fall asleep.'

It wasn't how Ella had expected that sentence to end. 'Huh!' she huffed. 'So I'm a soporific presence?'

'A relaxing presence.'

'Boring, in other words. Sleep-inducing. Thanks very much.'

Roly grinned. 'You're not boring. You're very exciting.'

'Not exciting enough to stay awake for. I bet Pippa didn't make you feel like that?'

'God, no!' he said, way too emphatically for her liking. 'No way. I kept one eye open at all times with Pippa.'

'So it's just me who puts you to sleep?'

He laughed. 'Don't be so grumpy. It's a nice thing.'

She arched an eyebrow sceptically. 'Well, it's not very

flattering – here I am, naked in your bed, and you're telling me I send you to sleep.'

'That's not what I'm saying. It's more that it's okay to fall asleep when you're here. I can just … let go, and I know when I wake up everything will still be the same.' He sighed, a frown of concentration furrowing his brow as he searched for the words. 'It's like … have you ever had that thing on a plane where you feel like you have to really concentrate to make it stay in the air? So you can't fall asleep because if you do—'

'It'll plummet out of the sky when you're not paying attention and you'll die in a ball of fire.' Ella nodded. 'Everyone knows that.'

'Well, it's like that. When you're here, I can go to sleep because I know you'll keep the plane up.'

'What if *I* fall asleep?'

He smiled. 'You'd still keep the plane up.'

'How?'

'With the power of your mind.'

'Even when I'm asleep?'

'With your subconscious mind.'

His eyes were drooping closed, and she leaned forward and kissed him. 'You might want to work on your pillow-talk. I doubt many girls would be impressed by that as a compliment.'

'What about you?'

'I like it.' She turned away, smiling into the pillow.

'That's okay, then. Because you're the only girl I'm interested in impressing.'

25

Ella spent the next week in a haze of love. All she thought about was Roly – as she walked to work, as she went through her day at Citizens on autopilot, as she walked home again. Whatever else she was doing, she was also thinking of Roly. She couldn't quite believe this was happening – that they could just be in love with each other; that they could fall into a relationship so easily with no hiding, no games, no unrequited pining on one side and indifference on the other. She was constantly taken aback by how open and honest Roly was about his feelings, how easily he said he loved her and talked about the future as if taking it for granted that they'd be together – next week, next month, next year… At first she kept waiting for him to pull away, but he never did. Instead every day they got closer; he became more loving and affectionate. It was a revelation to her that it could be like this, and it made her realise how insecure she'd been in her relationship with Andrew.

And the sex was glorious. She was astonished that something so extraordinary could just be a part of everyday life, something she could take for granted and look forward to at the end of a working day. Coming home to Roly, cooking with Roly, eating together, kissing and kissing and kissing. He occupied her every waking moment.

'I should probably stop charging you rent now,' he said one night as they lay tangled together in bed.

'Now that we're having sex?'

'Yeah.' He brushed a lock of hair behind her ear.

'I didn't just sleep with you to get off the rent, you know.'

He laughed.

'Anyway, if you don't let me pay rent, I'll make you go back to signing on and you'll have to explain yourself to Geraldine.' Now that the Oh Boy! reunion had been announced, and Roly was writing with Phoenix, they'd decided it made sense for him to concentrate on his music.

'It just seems wrong, though, now that you're my girlfriend.'

She smiled. 'Am I your girlfriend?'

He frowned, looking pointedly down at their naked bodies entwined beneath the twisted sheet. 'Um … am I misreading the signals here?'

She giggled. 'Well, you never asked me – formally, I mean. Apparently that's what the kids do these days.'

'Really? Okay, then. Ella Quill, will you be my girlfriend?'

'Yes! I thought you'd never ask.' They sealed it with a kiss. 'So I have a boyfriend now,' she said wonderingly, playing with his fingers. She tried out the word, and it felt strange on her tongue. But what was most surprising about it wasn't that she had a boyfriend, but that her boyfriend was Roly Punch.

~

On Saturday, she went out to celebrate her birthday with Hazel at their favourite tapas restaurant.

'Happy Birthday!' Hazel raised her glass. 'It's so nice to be out with you like this, Ella.' Hazel gave her a heartfelt smile, and there were tears in both their eyes as they clinked their glasses.

'I know. It's amazing.' There had been times when Ella thought she'd never again have a normal night out like this with a friend.

'Well, shall we order?' Hazel picked up her menu. 'And then you can have your present.'

When they'd ordered way too much food, Hazel presented her with a gift bag with several individually wrapped presents inside. Ella opened the biggest one first – an A4 planner with a soft faux-leather cover that Ella had coveted for years. She'd never been able to justify the expense, especially when she'd had very little to fill its pages.

'Oh, I love it! Thank you so much.' She leaned across the table and gave her friend a one-armed hug. The other smaller parcels contained coloured pens, stickers and several rolls of washi tape. Hazel was as much of a stationery geek as Ella, and it was the perfect gift.

'The planner is undated, so you can start it now or save it for next year if you want.'

'You know I'm going to be getting stuck in as soon as I get home.'

Hazel smiled. 'I do know that, yes.'

'I can't wait. Look out, world!'

'There's something else. Kind of related to that,' Hazel said, nodding at the planner. 'Well … possibly anyway.'

They were interrupted by the arrival of the food,

falling silent as the waitress unloaded plate after plate onto the table, laughing as she tried to find room for the last dish of patatas bravas.

'So, you were saying…?' Ella speared a chilli and garlic prawn.

'Yes. I have news! I got funding for my research, so I'm going to be working on my book.'

'Oh, that's fantastic, Hazel! Congratulations!' Ella raised her glass in a toast. 'You totally deserve it.'

'Thanks.' Hazel took a sip of wine, looking really pleased. 'So, I get to hire a research assistant.' She looked at Ella meaningfully.

'Ooh, nice.'

'Would you like the job?'

'What, me?' Ella squeaked.

'Yes, you.'

'But … I've been out of academia for so long. Are you even allowed to ask me?'

'I can hire whoever I want. It's my money to spend as I see fit.'

'Gosh!' Ella was completely blind-sided, at a loss to know what to say.

'I hope I'm not offending you,' Hazel said, clutching her hand to her heart, 'offering you a job as my assistant.'

There was nothing but sincerity in her eyes and tone, and Ella felt a rush of affection for her friend. Hazel was one of the most genuinely good people she knew. She was so empathetic and careful of other people's feelings.

'God, no! Of course not. I'm just surprised.'

'We'd be more like colleagues, really. It'd be fun, working together.'

'You won't make me get you coffee and take out your dry cleaning?'

'No.' Hazel laughed. 'Though I have to warn you,

there'll be a lot of grunt work. But I'd make sure to give you some interesting stuff too. It's in your field, and it might be a nice way of easing yourself back into academia. What do you think?'

'Gosh, I don't know. I mean, thanks for asking me. But … it'd mean quitting my job, wouldn't it? Or would it be part time?'

'No, it's full time, I'm afraid – or at least, too full time for you to have another job. But, to be honest, I thought quitting your job would be a plus.'

'What's the money like?'

Hazel looked disappointed at the question, though she hid it quickly.

'I have to eat,' Ella said with an apologetic shrug.

'Of course. It's not great, I'll admit – it would mean taking a bit of a cut from what you're on now. But it's a great opportunity. And you don't want to work for Tweedledum and Tweedledee forever, do you?'

Ella was sorry she'd let Hazel in on that joke. It felt disloyal now. 'I could do a lot worse. They're really good to work for, and the pay is great.'

'But you still want to get back to doing your doctorate, don't you? I mean, that's still the goal, yes?'

Ella thought. 'I guess so.'

'So what's stopping you?'

'I'm not sure I'm ready yet. I'm really enjoying having some money for a change. It's so nice not freaking out about it all the time, being able to do stuff like this.' She waved a hand over the table. 'Plus I can pay my debts off a lot faster, working at Citizens.'

Hazel nodded. 'Well, I wanted to offer it to you first, but there's absolutely no pressure.' She held her hands up, showing Ella her open palms.

'Can I take some time to think about it?'

'Of course. I don't need to hire someone until October and I have a couple of other candidates in mind if you don't take it.'

'Thanks for the offer, though. I really appreciate it.'

Hazel waved her hand dismissively. 'Honestly, it's a completely selfish move on my part. I know you'd do a terrific job and wouldn't need me holding your hand. And I'd love for us to be working together. But I totally get the money thing too – I know I can't compete with the Tweedles on that score.'

'It's not just that, though. I really like working at Citizens. I'd miss it.'

'Seriously? I'm not having a go,' Hazel added quickly to Ella's look of frustration. 'I'm genuinely interested. Think about it. What would you miss apart from the money?'

'I'd miss Jake and Dylan, and Kerry ... everyone really. And the whole buzz of the place.' Ella smiled. 'I'd miss Friday night drinks, and karaoke—'

'Karaoke?' Hazel reared back in mock-horror. 'Okay, who are you and what have you done with my friend?'

'I know.' Ella laughed. 'I do a mean "Don't Go Breaking My Heart" duet.'

'Well, I see your karaoke and raise you sherry with the dean.'

'Ooh, now you're really upping the stakes.'

'I know. No contest, right?' Hazel said sarcastically.

'I really like my life now,' Ella said thoughtfully, spearing the last cube of potato. 'Maybe I'm a bit afraid to disturb anything.'

'Tell me more.' Hazel smiled, resting her elbow on the table, her chin in her hand, like she was settling in for a story.

'Well, I'm really enjoying work. And I love living with

Roly.' She couldn't help the smile that spread across her face.

'Oh my God,' Hazel gasped, widening her eyes dramatically. 'You're *in love* with Roly!'

'What makes you say that?'

'Um … the fact that you just told me?'

'I said I love living with him. He has a lovely house,' Ella said teasingly.

'Okay, maybe you didn't say it in so many words. But you should see your face when you mention him, you're all moony.'

'I'm thinking about his nice house,' Ella said, giggling.

'You're thinking about his nice body.' Hazel wiggled her eyebrows suggestively.

Ella shrugged. 'Fair cop. He does have a good body. And great hair.'

'What's so great about living with him, then?'

'I dunno. I love just hanging out with him … cooking together … the daft conversations we have, the way we riff off each other. We make each other laugh.'

'Sleeping with him?' Hazel raised her eyebrows. 'Has something happened?'

Ella smiled smugly in reply. 'Yeah, sleeping with him is actually pretty great – probably even better than cooking with him, if you must know.'

'That's great, Ella. I'm so pleased for you. You look really happy.' She drained her glass and leaned back in her chair. 'Anyway, I think you've answered my question.'

Ella raised her eyebrows questioningly.

'About the job. I'm taking it that's a no.'

'Oh. But I haven't had a chance to mull it over.'

'Well, take your time. But I don't think you need it.'

Ella concentrated hard, trying to imagine herself back in academia — getting stuck into some proper research work. She could smell the wood of the desks in the lecture halls, hear the background hum of muted voices in the library, taste the crisp autumn air she always associated with that world. But she couldn't conjure up any excitement about it. Once her heart would have raced at the thought of being part of it all again. Now the prospect left her feeling flat and empty.

'Just one more thing, though, and then I'll shut up about it,' Hazel said. 'About the money – don't get too used to it so that it stops you going after what you really want. It'll never be the perfect time to go back to being a student. If that's what you want, you'll have to compromise on money at some point.'

'Andrew said the same thing.'

'Oh gosh! I forgot – what about Andrew? Weren't you seeing him again?'

Ella shrugged. 'Not really. I mean, we'd met up a couple of times, and the idea was there, but we hadn't actually started anything.' She was so relieved now that they hadn't taken it any further. Nonetheless, Ella knew she'd given him the impression she was interested in getting back together, and she'd have to officially tell him that wouldn't be happening.

'I'll see him at the Walking Wounded concert next week. Roly's singing with them and got him a backstage pass. I'll talk to him then.'

'Am I allowed to say I'm glad?' Hazel said. 'I never thought he was right for you.'

'Really?' Ella was surprised. 'You never said anything at the time.'

'Well, you don't, do you? You might have ended up with him. And it wasn't that I disliked him particularly. I just didn't think you were your best self with him.'

'That's strange. I always thought the opposite.'

Hazel shook her head. 'When he was around, you seemed … constrained. Like you were always checking yourself; worrying about his reaction to whatever you did or said.'

'Wow.' Ella realised she'd always felt Andrew brought out the best in her because she'd tried to live up to his ideals. Now she saw it in a different light.

'It wasn't a big thing,' Hazel said, seeming anxious that she'd made Ella sad. 'I just preferred the Ella you were when it was just us. You seemed … freer, more yourself.'

'I think that's how I am with Roly.' She could just be herself with him – her truest, most authentic self.

'Can I get you ladies the dessert menu?' the waitress asked as she cleared away the plates.

'What do you think?' Hazel asked Ella. 'Are you too full, or do you have room for birthday churros?'

Ella grinned. 'There's always room for birthday churros.'

26

THE DAY before the Walking Wounded concert, Ella arranged to meet Andrew for coffee at a cafe close to Trinity. She got into town early, so she decided to go for a stroll around the college to pass the time. It was a warm, sunny evening, but she gave a little shiver as she passed under the front arch and through the darkened passageway into the sunlit cobbled courtyard.

Students milled about in front of the buildings or stretched out on the grass, sunning themselves. The college was at its romantic best on days like this, and she strolled around taking it all in, trying to imagine herself back here. In the distance she heard the soft whack of cricket balls, growing louder as she made her way to the cricket ground. Students sprawled on the steps of the Pavilion Bar, drinking, chatting and watching the match. The atmosphere was pleasantly familiar, yet she felt remote from it, as if she was looking at an old photograph or reading a page from her teenage diary.

She'd sat on those same steps, drinking cold white wine and flirting with Andrew to the soundtrack of the whack of cricket bats and the occasional light ripple of applause. She could almost see their shapes locked together on the grass, or walking hand in hand around the cobbled paths. She could see her and Hazel running to class together, late and out of breath; she could hear their giggles carrying in the air. But all she felt was nostalgia. She had no sense of what it would be like to be back here now.

She didn't feel any great pull to the place. It still had power to charm her, but there was none of the love and yearning it used to stir in her. She could admire it with the detached eye of a tourist, and like a tourist she could walk away without a qualm and move on to the next place. It wasn't a part of her anymore.

For old times' sake, she wished she could meet Andrew for a drink here instead, and they could bask in the evening sun sipping cold white wine, the sounds of the cricket match in the background mingling with the hum of laughter and chatter. But Andrew didn't drink now – just one more reminder that those days were gone.

She'd just sat down at the cafe across the road when Andrew came bustling in. She waved to him and pointed to the coffee in front of her to indicate that she'd already got one. He nodded and chatted to the pretty young woman behind the counter as she served him. They seemed to know each other. Or perhaps not. It was one of the things she'd always admired about Andrew, his ability to chat easily to strangers.

He crossed the cafe and put his mug down on the table, then leaned in to kiss her hello.

'So, I thought we should talk,' she said as soon as he sat down. She wasn't sure how to do this, so she decided to just launch straight in and get the awkwardness out of the way as quickly as possible.

'That sounds ominous,' Andrew said, smiling.

'Hmm.' Ella took a sip of her coffee. How did you break it off with someone when you hadn't really started anything in the first place? It seemed presumptuous. 'I just – I don't want there to be any misunderstandings, so I thought I should tell you—'

'You're dumping me?' At least it didn't seem to have come as a shock. Andrew didn't look very put out about it, which was a relief.

'Um … yeah. I mean, I know we haven't got back together, really.'

'But we were possibly heading that way.'

'Yeah. To be honest, I thought that was what I wanted. But it's not. It just doesn't work anymore, does it – you and me?'

Andrew nodded and took a sip of his coffee. It was impossible to tell what he was thinking. 'I guess the cracks were always there,' he said eventually.

That annoyed her because it wasn't true. She hated when people felt they had to rewrite the past to match the present. 'No they weren't. At least *I* never saw them. I thought we had a great relationship.'

He looked confused. 'If you think we're so great together—'

'I said *were* – past tense.' She sighed. 'I don't need to create some revisionist version of the past. I was happy. I was in love with you, and I didn't see any end to that. Maybe you did, but I was all in.'

'So … what happened?'

'Time.' She shrugged. 'That was then. This is now.'

He nodded. 'You can't go back.'

'And I wouldn't want to, even if I could. Things

change. People change. That's just life. We're not who we used to be.'

'I get it. You're not the same person who fell in love with me.'

She shook her head. 'I'm not the person you fell in love with either. Maybe I would be if I'd never been ill. But my life went in a different direction, and I like where I am now. I'm someone who works in business and sings karaoke, and watches *Celebrity Masterchef*. And I enjoy it.' She took a sip of coffee. 'It's not what I planned, but I'm happy where I've ended up.'

'And you're in love with someone else,' he said softly. 'You forgot to mention that.'

She smiled. 'Is it that obvious?'

He shrugged. 'Maybe just to me. Because you used to look at me like that.'

'Like what?' she asked, intrigued.

'The way you were looking at Roly the other night. The energy you had around him. It took me back.'

'Oh.' She stopped fidgeting with her mug and leaned back in her chair. 'Well, you're right,' she said, looking him in the eye. 'Roly and I are together now.'

'I'm glad,' he said, giving her a sweet smile. 'It's good to see you happy. You deserve it.' She felt bad for being so impatient and belligerent with him when he'd come over for dinner.

'Thank you. I'm sorry if I gave you the wrong idea. I didn't mean to mess you around.'

'I'll forgive you, on one condition.'

'Oh? What's that?'

He grinned. 'That I still get my backstage pass for tomorrow night.'

Ella smiled. 'Done.' She held out a hand to him. 'So, no hard feelings?'

He took her hand. 'No hard feelings.'

The following evening, Ella had dinner at an Italian restaurant near the Aviva stadium with Christine and Loretta, and then they went to the Walking Wounded concert together. Roly had been gone all day and for most of the preceding week, rehearsing and hanging out with the band.

It was the first night of Walking Wounded's European tour which would start and end in Dublin, and the atmosphere inside the stadium was electric. Ella was a big fan of the band, and they were on fire tonight. But she could hardly focus on them, just waiting for the moment when Roly would appear.

Then Rory Cassidy started playing the opening chords of a song that was familiar to everyone in the audience, but wasn't one of Walking Wounded's. Murmurs of surprise and curiosity rippled through the crowd as Phoenix stepped up to the microphone and began singing a slowed-down version of Oh Boy!'s first hit 'Cool Like You'. It took the audience a line or two to realise what it was, and a scattering of hesitant applause grew to an ear-splitting crescendo as they simultaneously recognised the song and Roly strode onto the stage.

The crowd went wild as he stepped into the spotlight and appeared on the giant screen so that everyone, no matter how far away, could see who it was. He waved to the crowd as he stepped up to the microphone beside Phoenix's, and Ella thought she might burst with pride as the audience cheered, whistled and clapped. This wasn't Roly's crowd, so she was taken aback by the reaction. There was so much love for Roly, so much goodwill directed towards him. She turned to Loretta and Christine who were jumping up and down, clapping and whooping joyously, and they grinned and hugged each other.

'Well, I guess this guy needs no introduction,' Phoenix said, laughing as he turned to Roly. 'Please welcome to the stage Mr Roly Punch!' he shouted, and the cheering got louder. Ella's eyes welled up. Roly looked so moved, blown away by his reception.

The band started playing again, and the crowd hushed as Roly and Phoenix leaned into the microphones and sang a mash-up of 'Cool Like You' and Walking Wounded's 'Love Made Easy'. The Oh Boy! song was a revelation, surprisingly haunting and beautiful, the slowed-down melody giving it a new gravitas as Roly and Phoenix's voices weaved around each other. It was a triumph, and Ella's eyes filled with tears as they finished, the applause seeming to go on forever.

'Roly's going to stick around for the next song,' Phoenix said, and then he introduced the new song they'd written together, 'Nightfall'.

The song was gorgeous. As they sang, Ella flicked her gaze between the stage and the close-ups of Roly on the giant screen. He looked so happy and just … right. Like he was where he was supposed to be, doing his thing. This was where he was meant to be, she thought. It was where he belonged. His talent was wasted in Oh Boy! But surely he wouldn't want to go back to them after tonight.

The rest of the concert went by in a blur. Afterwards she went backstage with Loretta and Christine, and found Roly. They all hugged him and told him how brilliant he'd been and how proud they were. Loretta and Christine left together then, but Ella stayed on with Roly. There were lots of people milling around, and Ella recognised Walking

Wounded's manager Will Sargent with Phoenix's beautiful wife Summer.

She found Andrew, and when the band were finished their technical debrief, Roly took them to the dressing room and introduced them all to the members of Walking Wounded – Phoenix and his sister Georgie, and the craggily handsome Cassidy brothers, Rory and Owen. Ella hovered for a while with Andrew, feeling responsible for him. But she quickly realised he didn't need her to babysit him, and she left him chatting to Phoenix.

Everyone was coming down from first-night nerves and on a high about how well the show had gone. They drank champagne and congratulated each other, going over the details of the concert again and again.

'I'm heading off,' Andrew said, finding Ella and Roly on his way to the door. 'Just wanted to say thanks again for this,' he said to Roly. 'Great concert!'

'Not too commercial for you?' Roly said with a sly grin.

Andrew laughed good-naturedly, rolling his eyes. 'Sorry. That was a wanky thing to say.'

Ella was pleased he had the grace to admit it.

'It was great to meet Phoenix. He's such an interesting guy. And I loved the song you did together – congratulations!'

'Thanks, man.'

'Bye, Ella.' He kissed her cheek. 'And good luck.'

'Do you want to go too?' Roly asked as they watched him leave.

'Really?' She looked at him in surprise. 'Don't you want to stay and party?'

'Nah, I'd really like to get home, actually.'

She noticed for the first time that he was kind of jittery. 'Oh, is it hard for you – being here?' She realised it would be the first time he'd been at a booze-fuelled backstage party since he'd left Oh Boy! It must be difficult for him being here now and not able to join in properly.

He nodded, giving her an odd look. 'It's hard for me all right,' he said with a smirk. 'I don't think I can stand much more of this, to be honest.'

She felt as if he was saying something she didn't quite understand.

'It's just all this – the high of being on stage and everything...'

She nodded understandingly.

'I'm all jacked up on adrenaline, I guess. And it's made me really...' He leaned down and whispered in her ear, 'horny'.

'Oh!' Just his hot breath in her ear gave her a funny feeling inside. 'Okay, then.' She put down her half-full glass of champagne. 'Let's get out of here.'

Roly woke the next morning to a changed world. The single of 'Nightfall' had been released at midnight and was already being played on the radio. Everyone was talking about Roly's surprise appearance at the Walking Wounded concert. He was trending on Twitter. Music critics mentioned his performance favourably in their reviews of the show, calling it a revelation – one even said it was the highlight of the night. Just like that, his star was in the ascendant again and everyone wanted a piece of him – including Oh Boy!

In the next few days, his phone rang constantly. Oh Boy! wanted him back. Zack and Liam called, claiming they'd always intended for him to be included in the reunion. Roly was buzzing. Ella was glad for him, but at the same time she felt like he was slipping away from her and it made her anxious, her new-found happiness suddenly feeling fragile.

Roly was achieving what he'd set out to do – he was getting his old life back. But, selfishly, Ella wondered what it would mean for them … for her. Would she be part of it, or would they go back to the way they'd been before – to late-night calls and messaging, and the odd brief catch-up whenever he was in town.

Even if he did still want to be with her, how long could they sustain it when he'd be off touring the world, moving around all the time? Their relationship would be long distance at best and, either way, she'd be back to occasional phone calls and sporadic meetings. Did she want that?

But there was another, greater threat that had been looming over her ever since they'd met up again, a guilty secret that was always there in the background, but weighed more heavily on her every day they were together. She should have told him when he'd offered her a room in his house, or when they'd slept together on her birthday, or any one of the days in between. But the longer it went on, the harder it was to say anything. She couldn't bring herself to risk sabotaging their happiness. Yet until he knew the truth, that happiness would always be a little tainted.

There was a very small part of her that would be relieved if Roly's new-found fame took him away from her and they simply drifted apart again – if he left her for a life that she couldn't be part of. It would be out of her hands, and Roly would never have to know how she'd betrayed him.

27

'Will Vince be there?' It was Friday night, and Roly and Ella were on their way to a party in Charlie's apartment.

Roly shrugged. 'I don't know. Probably.'

Ella nodded, looking out the window at the passing traffic, wishing she were going anywhere else. She felt jittery and on edge, and couldn't shake off a horrible sense of foreboding.

'You look great,' Roly said, smiling at her and taking her hand. 'Wow, your fingers are cold.' He closed his hand tighter around hers. 'Are you okay?'

'Yeah, I'm fine. Just … I don't know. Nervous, I guess.'

He frowned. She knew it wasn't like her. She wasn't particularly shy. She couldn't explain it to Roly, but the thought of being among that crowd again brought back bad memories and filled her with dread.

'No need to be nervous,' he said, his thumb stroking over her knuckles. 'There'll be loads of people you know there.'

That was the problem, but she couldn't say that to Roly.

. . .

Later she stood by the windows in Charlie's apartment looking out at the glittering lights of the Aviva Stadium, the scene of Roly's triumph. It was hard to believe it was only a week since she'd watched him on stage there. It had set in motion a chain of events that would change Roly's life – and probably hers too. Maybe it was already changing, she thought, sipping champagne from her crystal flute. After all, she was spending Friday night here instead of at karaoke with her work colleagues. She felt a pang at the thought of it, wishing she could be there singing duets with Dylan.

'Hi, Ella! Good to see you.' Charlie joined her at the window, breaking into her thoughts.

'Charlie.' She turned to him and smiled, and he kissed her cheek. She'd always liked Charlie. He'd been a better friend to Roly than any of the others. 'Nice place you've got here.'

'Yeah, thanks. So, you and Roly…'

'Yeah. We're together now.'

He nodded. 'He seems really happy.'

'Yeah.' She looked across the room at Roly, who was talking to Liam and a woman she didn't know. She smiled. 'We both are.' She turned back to Charlie. 'Were you surprised?'

'I was, to be honest. I mean, no offence. But I'd seen some stuff about him and Pippa getting back together.'

'It's fine.'

'But I'm glad. Pippa was never any good for him.'

Ella began to relax as the evening went on. Her stomach lurched when she saw Vince come in, but she managed to stay out of his way. It wasn't difficult – he seemed more interested in huddling over a table with his business partner Larry, doing lines of coke. Everyone was friendly and she chatted to some interesting people. To her surprise, she was quite enjoying herself. Maybe she'd been silly to be scared, and it was a good thing she'd come so she could lay her ghosts to rest. The last night she'd spent around these people hadn't been good, but that was a long time ago. They'd all grown up and moved on.

Across the room Roly detached himself from the group he was with and came towards her.

'Having a good time?' he asked when he reached her.

'Yeah.' She nodded. 'You?'

'Yeah, but I'm kind of ready to go home, if you are.'

'Why?' She laughed. 'Is it making you horny?'

'Well, well, well, look who the cat dragged in,' a voice said behind her. She spun around to see Vince glaring at her with cold, spite-filled eyes.

'Vince.' Roly acknowledged him as he joined them. 'You remember Ella?'

'Oh, I certainly do.' Vince crossed his arms and stared at her implacably. 'How could I forget our own little Mata Hari?'

'Huh? What are you talking about? Why would you call her that?'

'I must say I thought we'd seen the last of you,' he said, ignoring Roly and talking to Ella. 'You've got some neck showing your face here, after what you pulled.' His gaze darted between her and Roly. 'And Zack tells me you two are together now. What is it?' he asked Roly. 'Some kind of Stockholm syndrome?'

Roly frowned. 'I don't know what you're talking about.' He put his arm around Ella protectively.

'We were just leaving,' Ella said quickly. 'Nice seeing you again, Vince.'

'I can't say the same about you, sweetheart.'

'Come on, let's go,' she said to Roly, her heart beating wildly. Vince was talking as if he knew. But how could he? The only person who knew what she'd done was a man named Robert Casey and he wasn't at this party.

Roly shook her off. 'No, I want to know what he's shiting about. What are you trying to say, Vince? What's this Stockholm syndrome crap?'

'I'm just trying to figure out why you'd be with her after everything that happened.' He looked at Ella. 'You must be one amazing fuck.'

'Shut the fuck up, Vince!' Roly moved to grab him, but Ella held him back. 'How dare you talk to her like that?'

'Or is it that you're some kind of masochist?' he said to Roly. He turned a cold gaze on Ella. 'Well, I have my eye on you now, sweetheart. You fucked this up for him once, but I won't let you do it again.'

'What the fuck are you talking about, Vince?'

'Oh my god!' Realisation dawned in Vince's face. 'You don't know, do you?'

'Know what?'

I'm talking about how it all ended for you the last time. Why we had to cut you loose.'

'That has nothing to do with Ella!'

'Doesn't it?'

Oh Christ, he knew! Ella felt sick with fear. All she wanted was to get Roly out of here before Vince said any more. She didn't want Roly to hear it from him, not like this. She had to get him away so she could tell him herself. *Why* hadn't she told him when she had the chance? She prayed she hadn't left it too late.

'You're talking crap,' Roly said to Vince. 'We all know why I got kicked out of the band.'

'I do. Ella does, don't you, darling? But I'm not sure you do. Why don't you ask her?'

God, he was poisonous. He was relishing this. 'Come on, don't listen to him,' she said, taking Roly's arm. Her mouth was so dry she could barely get the words out. 'He's just high. He doesn't know what he's saying.'

But Roly shook her off. Vince had got under his skin as he always did. Roly looked unnerved.

'I got kicked out because I fucked up,' he said, but he didn't sound so sure anymore.

Vince shook his head. 'You'd been fucking up for a long time before that.'

'But then people found out. It went public.'

'Because someone sold you out.' Vince looked directly at Ella, his eyes flinty. When Roly turned to her, she felt she couldn't breathe.

'Don't be ridiculous,' Roly said, his voice jagged with fear.

'Who was it who was always nagging you to go into rehab?'

She could see the doubt blooming in Roly's eyes. She forced herself to hold his gaze.

'She would never.'

'Ask her!'

Roly shook his head, swallowing hard. His eyes were wide and panicked. She could feel him slipping away from her.

'Tell him.'

She glanced at Vince and she wanted to slap that smug smirk off his face. But she couldn't lie to Roly – not outright. She looked at him and nodded, unable to speak.

Vince gave her a triumphant smile. 'Well, I imagine you two have a lot to talk about. I'll leave you to it.'

'It was *you*?' Roly hissed as Vince walked away. 'You ratted me out to that journalist? You sold a story on me—'

'I didn't sell it—'

He fell silent, staring at her dumbfounded. '*Why*?' he asked finally. 'Why would you want to ruin my life?'

'I wanted to *save* your life.'

'Fuck off! Jesus, I can't believe this! You took away *everything*. I could have been the next Robbie Williams.'

'You could have been the next Kurt Cobain.'

'That's stupid. I would *never* have done that.'

'Not with a gun. That's the only difference.'

'God, I can't believe you made me think— All this time I thought you were my friend. You let me think that you— Shit!' His eyes glittered with tears and her heart twisted.

'I *am* your friend, Roly.' She tried to touch him, to reach him, but he jerked away from her hand as if she'd tried to hit him. 'I was scared for you. I couldn't stand to see you killing yourself and I couldn't think what else to do.' They'd been talking in hushed voices, but she was aware of eyes on them. 'I should have told you,' she said, dropping her voice to a whisper. 'I'm so sorry I didn't tell you.'

'*That's* what you're sorry for?'

'Can we just get out of here, talk about this somewhere else?' she pleaded.

'There's nothing to talk about. Just tell me one thing. How much?'

'What?'

'How much did you get for selling me out? I hope it was worth it.'

'I didn't get *money* for it.'

He huffed a bitter, scathing laugh. 'Well, that was dumb of you. It must have been worth … ooh, at least thirty pieces of silver.'

'I just wanted you to get help.'

'And you thought taking a wrecking ball to my life would help, did you?' His voice had risen and he was shouting at her now, his eyes wet with tears. He looked heartbroken, and she couldn't bear that she'd hurt him. 'Jesus, no wonder I didn't see your heels for dust after I came out of rehab.'

'I couldn't still be your friend and not tell you. So I thought it was easier to just … let you go. I only did it because I love you.'

He shook his head emphatically. 'You don't do that. You don't betray people you love. You don't lie to them, and trick them into—' He took a heaving breath that was almost a sob.

'I wanted to tell you, Roly.'

'Well, it's not like you haven't had plenty of opportunity. You seem to have done just fine keeping it to yourself the last few months.'

'Please can we go and talk about this at home.' There were tears pouring down her face now, splashing onto her collarbones.

'You can go wherever you want. Just get the fuck away from me!' With that he turned on his heel and stormed off in the direction of the kitchen, leaving her standing by the window with everyone staring. There was a moment's hushed silence before the murmur of voices started again.

Ella swiped her hands across her eyes, then made for the door. She kept her face averted as she passed Vince on her way to the exit, but she heard his whisper in her ear. 'Karma's a bitch'.

28

SHE HURRIED down the hall and ran down the stairs as if someone was chasing her, too impatient to wait for the lift. She summoned a taxi on her phone, relieved that she didn't have to wait long. When she got back to Roly's house, she raced to her bedroom, hauled her suitcase down from the top of the wardrobe and began opening drawers frantically, throwing clothes into it. She didn't waste time folding or sorting, just slung everything in randomly. She could sort it out later. Her hands were shaking too much to do it neatly anyway. She knew it was cowardly, but she was desperate to be gone before Roly got back.

Then she stopped. Her first instinct was to run and hide, not just for her own sake, but for his. He didn't want to see her again, and he shouldn't have to. This was his home, he shouldn't have to share it for another moment with someone he … hated. She winced even at the thought of the word. But she knew she was partly doing it because she couldn't face him, and that was cowardly. She should at least try to talk to him again. Maybe when he'd calmed down a little he'd listen, give her a chance to explain. She had to at least try. She owed him that much.

She upended the suitcase, emptying it onto the bed. Then she began packing again, more methodically this time, folding her clothes carefully. It would be hours before Roly came home, so she had plenty of time. He might not come back at all tonight.

When she'd finished, she sat on the bed, leaning back against the headboard and picked up her laptop. With shaking fingers, she typed Roly's name into the search engine. She knew what she was looking for and where to find it. But she had to take it slowly, ease herself into it. All the predictable hits came up – articles about Oh Boy!'s meteoric rise to fame, the salacious headlines when Roly left, stories about his problems with drugs and drink, scathing reviews of his debut solo album, spiteful blog posts and social media chat about his weight gain and financial difficulties. She scanned over the headlines, but none of the results were what she was looking for.

She clicked on the images tab, and was confronted with a kaleidoscope of photos of Roly – young and skinny, gurning at the camera and goofing off with the band; close-ups of his beautiful face, unlined and untroubled, and with an innocence she only recognised now at this distance of years. There were album covers and promotional posters, concert photos and paparazzi shots. But there was only one image she was looking for – an image she hadn't looked at in a very long time because she couldn't bear it. It was already there in her peripheral vision the moment she clicked the images tab. She didn't let her focus stray to it as she scanned the other pictures, but it was there all the time, in multiple frames – the most iconic photo of Roly in existence, the one that had changed everything.

She took a deep breath and forced herself to look at it head on. It was a kind of penance. She clicked to enlarge it, and her stomach clenched as it filled the screen, hitting her like a visceral thing. There was Roly, sitting on the floor of the bedroom in Marty's house – hunched over a mirror with four lines of white powder clearly visible on its surface, a rolled-up note in his hand. A half-empty bottle of vodka sat on the floor beside him.

He looked so lost and lonely – even though she knew the house had been filled with his friends, colleagues and hangers-on, a party raging in the next room. She could still hear the music pounding on the other side of the door, feel the bass vibrating in her chest along with the hammering of her heart. She felt once again the dread of that night, the horror as she was confronted with the reality of how far he'd fallen, the terror when she realised no one would help him. He was surrounded by people who were supposed to take care of him, but he was so alone.

An overwhelming sadness washed over her, and the image blurred as her eyes filled with tears. This photograph had been the catalyst for everything that had happened to him afterwards. It was the drop of rain that started the avalanche that would bury him. It was the beginning of the end — the beginning of his recovery too, she reminded herself, swiping away tears. It was his downfall and his salvation captured in one moment.

But all she saw was her hand in it – pushing him, catching him; she wasn't sure which. Maybe both. She still thought she'd done the right thing, the only thing she could have done. But that didn't stop her feeling guilty too. There was Roly – disgraced, exposed, shamed, poised on the edge of a precipice. He was about to lose everything. And it was all her fault.

HOW TO SAVE A LIFE

IT WAS A CHILLY OCTOBER NIGHT, but it was too warm inside Marty's Killiney house, and Ella was grateful for the cool sea breeze from the open terrace doors. People had spilled out onto the terrace to smoke, huddled together against the cold, while inside the press of bodies and the mixture of loud music and chatter made the atmosphere stifling and claustrophobic. Ella stood by the window sipping champagne, feeling sad and anxious, longing to leave and yet feeling she needed to stay.

Oh Boy!'s world tour had ended with a concert at Croke Park, and Ella had been in the audience. She'd gone on her own, more out of a sense of duty than anything. Afterwards, she'd gone backstage to say hello to Roly, and he'd dragged her off to this party in Marty's house. She hadn't wanted to come. She felt out of place with this crowd and it wasn't her kind of party. But there'd been something about him tonight, and she found herself unable to say no. He'd had a weird manic energy, and there was something desperate about his intensity that scared her. He wasn't the old, sweet Roly, but he wasn't the cocky asshole either. There was a blankness in his eyes, a lack of affect in his whole demeanour that chilled her – as if he'd been replaced by an android who looked and sounded like Roly, but had no blood or life force, nothing behind his cold, dead eyes. It was infinitely worse than the arrogant, swaggering git she'd met last Christmas, and she longed to have that Roly back. At least there'd been some life in him; there was a person there who you could rail against.

He'd called her a few times from the tour, and he'd said some things during those late-night conversations that worried her. He told her about drugs he'd tried, sounding blasé as if it was just part of being a grown-up, laughing off her concerns. Sometimes it did make her feel like she was just a gauche, naive student, while he was worldly and sophisticated. At other times she wondered if he confessed these things to her because he was scared and wanted an adult to intervene, to rescue him.

On the taxi ride over here, she'd tried to talk to him, but he was already high and glassy-eyed, and he'd blanked her, determinedly keeping the conversation light and frivolous. He'd told her about his girlfriend Pippa's antics on *Celebrity Cell Block*, which she was currently appearing in.

Once they got here, he'd quickly abandoned her. But though she longed for her bed, she hung on, afraid to look away. She'd never seen Roly so out of control, and she had a horrible feeling that something terrible would happen if she wasn't paying attention.

Earlier she'd tried to talk to the people around him, to get them to do something, but they'd all brushed her aside with varying degrees of dismissiveness. In a week's time they were leaving on the American leg of the tour, and who would watch Roly then?

Marty, Roly's party-loving accountant, had been patronising and avuncular. 'Don't worry, we'll take care of him,' he'd said when she mentioned her concerns.

She looked across at Roly, huddled with a group around a table, twitchy and loud, gesticulating manically as he held court. 'It doesn't look like it.'

'He's just letting off steam. You know Roly. He has a lot of nervous energy to burn off. He needs to be doing something. Once the tour gets underway and he has something to occupy him, he'll be fine.'

Ella wasn't convinced. But no one would take her seriously when she tried to tell them Roly needed help.

'Lighten up,' Zack said. 'He's just having fun. You remember fun, Ella?'

'I'm really worried about him. He needs to be in rehab.'

'Well, that's not going to happen anytime soon. We've got the American tour coming up. There's no way he can ditch that to go to fucking rehab!'

'I think his life is more important than some tour!'

'The tour *is* his life! This band is his life!'

'Well, it'll be a short one if he carries on the way he's going. I'm going to talk to Vince, tell him what's going on.'

Zack snorted. 'You think he doesn't know? Jesus! Who do you think keeps it all hush-hush? He's not going to let Roly fuck this up for all of us.'

Ella's eyes widened. She hated that Zack made her feel so naive.

On the off-chance that he was bluffing, she cornered Vince later and broached the subject. 'Roly's got a drug problem,' she said baldly. 'He's in a really bad way. You need to get him into rehab.'

Vince gave her a hard look, and she knew immediately that he was well aware that Roly was in trouble. With mounting panic, she realised he was not only doing nothing about it, but was actively facilitating it.

'I'd be careful who you say things like that to, sweetheart. And keep your fucking voice down!' he hissed.

'You don't give a damn about Roly, do you? Or any of them? They're just cash cows to you.'

'Look, we'll take care of it once this tour is over. It's only three months. He can hold it together that long.'

'I don't know if he can.' But Vince was already walking away. The conversation was over and she'd been dismissed.

Larry, Vince's business partner and the head of the record label, was almost the worst, because he understood the severity of the problem, but didn't seem to grasp the urgency. 'Look, I hear what you're saying,' he told her, 'and you're absolutely right.'

Ella had almost burst into tears of relief that someone saw the danger, that she wasn't going to have to handle this alone.

'Just wait until this tour is over, and we'll get him the help he needs,' he continued, and Ella's heart sank.

'But that could be too late.'

'That's a bit melodramatic, isn't it?'

'And in the meantime, what? You just let him carry on like this, so it doesn't threaten your golden goose?'

'Of course not. Don't worry, I'll keep an eye on him on the tour. We all will. None of us can afford to let him get out of control.'

'Afford! That's all you care about, isn't it? Money.'

'Come on, love. That's not true. We all care about Roly. I look after him like a father.'

Ella felt a chill creeping through her veins. 'Yes, you do. Just like his own father.'

'There you are then,' he said, smiling complacently.

'You've nothing to worry about. You know he's in safe hands with me.' He gave her a pat on the shoulder, while rage boiled inside her. He thought he'd reassured her — because he knew nothing about Roly and what kind of father he had. It just made her more frightened for him than ever.

Alex and Liam weren't much better. They were worried about Roly or angry with him, or both in equal measure. They knew he could ruin everything for them if it got out.

'Our fans are so young,' Liam explained to her. 'Some of them are just little kids. So we have to look squeaky clean, you know – be appropriate role models. If it got out that any of us were doing drugs, it'd be a disaster. Promoters won't want to know, sponsors will drop us.'

There were endorsements at stake, lucrative advertising deals. He knew it would be the end of everything, and he was scared of losing it all. But she didn't blame him like she did Vince. He was just a wide-eyed kid who didn't want his candy taken away.

Charlie was the only one prepared to stick his neck out. Lovely Charlie, Roly's best friend in the band. He'd looked reluctant at first, scared like the rest of them, but he agreed to help her try to talk to Roly.

'I know his family are worried about him. Do you know his mum?'

'No.' Ella knew his mother to see at school events, but she'd never met her.

'I know they've tried to get him to sort himself out – her and his nan. His nan's a bit of a force of nature.' He smiled. 'If Christine Punch can't get him into rehab, I don't fancy my chances.'

Ella deflated, thinking he was giving up.

'But we can only give it a go. Come on, and we'll see what we can do.'

'Oh, right now?' Ella was teary with relief. She could have kissed him.

They found Roly in one of the bedrooms with a couple of other people, all sitting on the floor around a low coffee table. They asked everyone else to leave so they could talk to him privately. It didn't go well. Roly didn't want to know. He wouldn't admit he had a problem. He'd blanked them completely at first. Then he'd become defensive, and finally aggressive.

'What is this, some kind of intervention?' he scoffed.

He became more and more vicious and scathing. He accused Charlie of wanting to get rid of him so there'd be less competition in the band. Charlie had dealt with it admirably, quietly stoic as he let Roly's insults roll off him. But Ella could see how hurt he was, how sad and scared for his friend.

Eventually other people drifted back into the room, Roly turned his back on them and they gave up.

'At least we tried, I suppose,' Charlie said as they returned to the party.

It was no consolation to Ella. They'd failed.

'Who the fuck brought that guy?' She heard Vince's hiss as they passed him on the way into the living room. Ella followed his gaze. He was glaring across the room at a gangly, red-headed man talking to Zack and Alex.

'Who's that?' she asked Charlie.

'Oh, bloody hell! It's Robert Casey. What the hell is he doing here?'

'Who is he?'

'He's a journalist from the *Record*.'

'A journalist?'

Vince appeared beside them. 'Where's Roly?' he snapped, his mouth a thin line.

'He's in one of the bedrooms,' Charlie jerked his head towards the door.

'Well, for fuck's sake make sure he stays there and don't let that dick anywhere near him.'

Charlie nodded.

'And watch what you say. He seems to have ingratiated himself with Zack, but he's not to be trusted.' Vince disappeared again, presumably to warn the rest of the band to be on their best behaviour.

There had been rumours about Roly's drug-taking before, of course. But they were always denied, brushed off, and with no evidence and no witnesses willing to dish the dirt, they remained just that. Occasional little snippets turned up in the press, unsubstantiated stories and bits of gossip that caused a brief stir and faded away again just as quickly.

The people around him would always be invested in hushing it up. They had too much to lose. But if the truth were to come out, Ella thought, they'd have no option but to do something. Roly would have to get help. She willed the journalist to somehow find his way into the bedroom where Roly was. She kept an eye on him the whole time as he moved around the room. It was why she was still here, hours after she would have gone home. Maybe if he stayed long enough for things to get messy, people would become careless, tongues would loosen, they'd forget to be discreet…

The party was winding down, but still she stayed, even though her nerves were frayed and she had a pounding headache. She watched Vince leave, and Marty had disappeared, probably gone to bed, but Robert Casey was still there. She saw him go out onto the terrace for a cigarette. When he came back in on his own, she seized her opportunity. Almost without thinking about it, she made a beeline for him across the room, as if her body was on autopilot. Feeling reckless and desperate, she approached him from the side and bumped into him, spilling her drink down his shirt.

'Oops, sorry!'

He turned to her with a smile. 'It's okay.'

She insisted on taking him to the bathroom, showing him where he could dry off. No one was watching as she led him quickly out of the living room and down the corridor to the guest bedroom. She swung the door open wide.

'Oh, Roly!'

He glanced up, but barely seemed to see her, his eyes glancing off her before he bent to his task again, cutting up lines of white powder.

'Sorry, wrong room,' she said to Robert, quickly pulling the door closed behind her. 'You do *not* want to go in there.' She put a finger to her nose, miming snorting, and rolled her eyes. 'The bathroom is over here.' She opened the door on the other side of the corridor and ushered him inside. 'I'll leave you to it. Sorry again.'

Afterwards, she told herself anything could have happened. It wasn't entirely down to her. It was his decision too, and he might have done nothing. She wasn't solely responsible for what happened next after she'd led him to the room where Roly was, once she'd closed the bathroom door behind her. She'd given him the opportunity, and it was up to him what he did with it. She'd just set it up and let the chips fall where they may. But, realistically, she knew they were only ever going to fall one way.

The next day, the whole world knew the story. The

fallout was swift and brutal. Sponsors dropped the band from lucrative advertising deals. Promoters threatened to pull out of the tour. Newspapers were damning and censorious. So they threw Roly under the bus. He went to rehab and Oh Boy! went to America without him.

29

SHE WAS SURPRISED to hear Roly come in less than an hour after her. He tossed his keys on the table by the door with a metallic clank, and came upstairs.

'What are you doing?' He stood in the doorway, frowning as he took in her bags on the bed.

'I'm leaving.' She looked away, unable to face the hurt in his eyes. 'Obviously I can't stay here any longer.' She sank onto the bed. 'You're home early.'

'Yeah. I wasn't really in the party mood anymore, strangely enough.' He raked a hand through his hair. 'So, you were planning to be gone before I got back?'

'No. I was waiting until you came home. I wanted to talk to you first – try to explain.'

He sighed, peeling away from the doorframe. 'Ella, I'm not kicking you out. You don't have to go.'

'I know you're not, but I can't stay here, not when you —' She choked on a sob. 'Not when you hate me,' she finished.

'I don't hate you. I hate what you did, and I hate that you lied to me about it ... or at least didn't tell me the truth. But I know you probably thought you were doing the right thing.' His voice sounded hollow, devoid of emotion. She almost wished he were shouting at her again.

'You think I did it for money.'

'No.' He dropped his eyes. 'I was … upset and I lashed out at you. I don't really think that.'

'But you don't forgive me, do you?'

He looked her in the eye then, and she could already see the answer. 'No. I mean … it's a lot.'

She nodded. 'Yeah. I know.'

He moved into the room and sat down on the bed beside her. 'I'm trying to get my head around it. I was talking to Charlie. He said you tried to talk to me that night, both of you.'

Ella nodded. 'But Charlie didn't know – about what I did. That was just me.' She didn't want him to think he'd been betrayed by all his friends, that there was no one he could trust. 'I was so scared for you. I was trying to make sure you'd get help.'

'I get that – I do. But how could you not have told me? All this time … when we were—' He broke off helplessly.

'I wanted to. I just couldn't find a way to tell you. And then we were so happy, and it was all so long ago, sometimes I thought … I don't know. I wondered did it even matter anymore.'

'Did it *matter*? It was *my life*. It *is* my life, still. Every day. And you think it's just water under the bridge? I don't believe you!' He took a shaky breath. 'And you're right – we were so happy. And now that's fucked up too.' His voice was thick with tears and he swiped at his eyes. 'You know what really kills me? Maybe I could have got past it if you'd been honest and told me from the start. But keeping it from me…' He shook his head.

'I know,' she whispered. 'I'm so sorry. I wish… I *wish* I

could go back, do things differently.' Tears streamed from her eyes. How had it come to this? Just yesterday they'd been so happy.

Roly was properly sobbing now, and she tentatively reached out and put an arm around his shoulders, expecting him to shrug her off. But instead he turned into her and allowed her to hold him. His breath was hot and damp on her neck, his tears soaking her top as she breathed in his scent, knowing it would be the last time. She held him tighter, as if she could absorb his pain, not wanting to let him go. For one crazy, desperate minute, she felt a grotesque spark of hope that they could get past this – that he'd forgive her and move on, that he could still love her.

Finally he pulled back, swiping at his eyes. 'You don't have to move out.' He sniffed. 'I'm not going to make you homeless.'

She smiled sadly. 'I think I do. It'd be awkward as fuck living here now – for both of us. Anyway, I won't be homeless.'

'Where will you go?'

'I can go back to my mum's for now. They'll be home in a couple of weeks anyway.'

'I guess you should go, then, if you're going.' He sounded angry again.

She nodded, but she didn't move, reluctant to leave him like this. 'Are you okay?'

He gave her an awful look – hard and hateful – and she flinched. 'No, I'm not okay. How the fuck do you imagine I'd be okay?'

'Sorry.' She got up and took her phone from her bag, but still hesitated, looking down at him. He seemed so sad and desolate.

'Don't worry, I'm not going to do anything stupid. I

won't let you screw up my life more than you already have.'

She swallowed hard and called a taxi with her phone app. 'Maybe you should call someone? Your mum maybe? Or Charlie – I'm sure he'd come over if you asked him to.'

'Christ, why are you still here? Please just go!'

'I just don't think you should be alone right now.'

'Yeah, you're right.' He sniffed, digging the heels of his hands into his eye sockets. He looked up at her. 'I'll call Pippa.'

She nodded, clenching her jaw, struggling not to react. He was being deliberately cruel, hitting out at her, and he had every right to. She deserved it. She just had to take it, let him rage at her as much as he wanted. What did it matter? It was over between them now anyway. If he needed to hate her to feel better, then so be it.

'Good idea,' she said softly, swallowing down tears as she picked up her suitcases.

'I'll take those.' He got up from the bed.

'It's okay, I can manage.'

Wordlessly he took them from her anyway and she followed him downstairs. He dropped her bags by the door.

'Thanks.' She fished the house keys out of her pocket and held them out to him. 'I'll have to come back for the rest of my stuff.'

'Keep those, then. You can let yourself in.'

'Okay.' Her mobile pinged. 'My cab's here.' She picked up her bags. 'Thanks, Roly – for everything.' She stood on tiptoe and pressed a kiss to his cold, taut cheek. There was so much more she wanted to say, but she knew he wouldn't want to hear it.

He nodded, swallowing hard. When she looked up at him through her lashes, his eyes were wet with tears.

Roly opened the door for her. The taxi was standing outside, its engine running. He stood in the doorway and she walked to the gate without looking back, praying he'd say something, have one last word for her. But he was silent as she left his house – and his life – for the last time. So many times she'd said goodbye to him and walked away, thinking she wouldn't see him again. This time she knew it really was the end. And he didn't even say goodbye.

30

ROLY HAD NEVER WANTED a drink so badly, or a hit of something. He wanted the taste of whiskey on his tongue, the soft burn as it slid down his throat. He craved the sweet, soporific release of opiates or the energising surge of coke through his veins. He had that old feeling of needing to destroy everything, starting with himself. The urge to go out and score was so strong, he couldn't sit still. He picked up the phone and called Tim, his sponsor. As he listened to the ring tone, he told himself that if Tim didn't answer, he'd go out to a bar and get a drink – just one. It was a throw of the dice, out of his hands. He wouldn't be responsible. He looked at his watch. It was almost midnight. Tim had a young baby. He was probably asleep by now. He'd just let it ring one more time…

'You okay, mate?' Tim's voice was thick with sleep.

'No.' Roly gulped, tears of relief and gratitude springing to his eyes. It never ceased to move him that a virtual stranger would do this for him; that he'd always be there at the end of the phone ready to save him over and over, however many times he needed saving. 'I need to talk. Is that okay?'

'Of course. Any time – you know that. You want me to come over?'

'No. It's late. We can just chat on the phone.' He sank to the floor, closing his eyes and leaning his head against the wall as he let Tim talk him down from the edge.

He felt better after they hung up – calmer, more rational, no longer craving the escape into drink or drugs. But he still wanted to see someone. He couldn't deal with being alone right now. He thumbed through his phone and dialled Pippa.

'That little bitch!'

Roly flinched. He'd just been lashing out when he'd told Ella he'd call Pippa. He'd wanted to hurt her. But then he thought why not? She may be shallow and brash, but she was forthright, which was something he particularly appreciated right now, and she had a good heart beneath it all.

'I can't believe she did that to you. Miss High and Mighty, acting like she was so much better than everyone else. Butter wouldn't melt.'

'She didn't think she was better than everyone else.' Damn it, why was he defending Ella? He should be joining in, bitching her up with Pippa. It would be cathartic. But no matter how he felt about her, it still got his back up when someone else had a go at her.

'Give me a break! Don't think I didn't see her looking down her nose at me.'

'She's not like that.'

'How can you still stick up for her, after what she did to

you? If it wasn't for her, you wouldn't be in the state you are now.'

'What do you mean "the state I'm in"?' He bristled.

'Come on, Roly. Don't make me spell it out. I know things are good now, but until a few months ago you were broke, depressed and overweight. No one would give you the time of day. Your career was down the toilet.'

'Wow, kick a guy when he's down, why don't you?'

'I'm just telling it like it is, babe. Oh Boy! moved on and you got left behind. Your solo album tanked. First you became a national laughing stock, and then everyone just completely forgot about you.'

Roly nodded. 'This is great. This is just the confidence boost I needed. Thanks.'

'And that's all down to her,' Pippa continued as if he hadn't spoken. 'I hate that she did this to you, and it's even worse that you're still sticking up for her. It's like you have that Stockport syndrome or something.'

Roly laughed. Maybe he'd done the right thing, calling Pippa after all. 'It's Stockholm syndrome.'

She shrugged. 'Whatever.'

'And Ella didn't exactly kidnap me.'

'No, but she hijacked your life.'

'She did it because she cared about me. She was worried. She thought she was doing the right thing.'

'Sure.' Pippa rolled her eyes. 'Classic Stockholm syndrome.'

'You might have done the same yourself if you'd been around.' They were still officially together at the time, but they'd both known it was over – his fault, of course.

'No way.' She reached out and put a hand on his leg. 'And if I had I'd have told you straight out.'

He could believe that at least.

'Of course I'd have supported you. But there was no need for anyone to stick their nose in like that. You had plenty people looking after you.'

'Yeah.' But he hadn't, had he? If that photograph hadn't emerged, he wouldn't have been kicked out of the band. He'd have gone on the American tour. No one would have called a halt.

'If it hadn't been for her, you'd have been in Oh Boy! right to the end,' Pippa said, echoing his thoughts. 'You could have had this amazing life. You wouldn't have to be trying to claw your way back like you are now.'

'Claw. Nice.'

'You'd still be famous and rich.'

'Not clean though, maybe.'

She shrugged. 'You could have done that without her. You'd have sorted yourself out eventually. You just think that because she's been gaslamping you.'

Roly laughed again, despite himself. 'Gaslamping!'

'What?' She punched his arm playfully. 'It's a thing. I've read loads of stuff about it. She gaslamped you into thinking you're an alcoholic—'

'No, I really am an alcoholic—'

'She made you think she was doing it for your own good.'

'Look, I may be pissed off about it, but she *did* do it for my own good.'

'See? That's gaslamping!'

He was glad he'd called Pippa. She was probably the only person who could have made him laugh right now.

'You need to be deprogrammed – you know, like people who've been in a cult.'

'I haven't been in a cult.'

'May as well have been. You missed out on the best years of your life, thanks to her. You'd have been a megastar. You wouldn't have ended up as some nobody, living on benefits and renting out your spare room like a fucking student!.'

'Well, it's really Marty I have to thank for that.'

'We might still be together…'

Roly jerked back in surprise. 'Really? So you were just with me for my fame and fortune?' He shouldn't be surprised – it was what he'd always suspected. But he was shocked even Pippa would be so upfront about it.

'No, silly. But if you hadn't gone off to rehab, we wouldn't have drifted apart like we did.'

'You wouldn't have shagged Adam Leader?'

She pouted. 'I was lonely. You'd abandoned me.'

'I didn't abandon you. I was fighting for my life, for fuck's sake. Not everything is about you.'

'You wouldn't have put on all that weight and got depressed.'

'I wouldn't have written songs with Phoenix or sang on stage with Walking Wounded.'

'You never know. You don't know what might have happened.'

'I'd probably never have seen Ella again.'

'Good riddance!'

He looked at her beautiful face. What would it be like, he wondered, being with Pippa again. He hadn't really thought about it when he put it in his goals. He'd just assumed that was what he wanted. Now all he wanted was Ella, and for things to be the way they were yesterday. He wished he could go back to not knowing.

He leaned in and kissed her tentatively. Her lips were soft and yielding and she kissed him back for a moment before pulling away. 'I don't think this is a good idea,' she said.

'I think it's a very good idea.' He grinned. 'It's a sure-fire way to make me forget my troubles.' He moved in for another kiss, but she held him away with a hand on his chest.

'I'm not going to be your consolation prize because you've had a bust-up with your girlfriend.'

'She's not my girlfriend.'

'And what about Adam?'

'Fuck Adam!'

'I do. That's the problem.'

'I thought you two had broken up.'

'We have. But he wants me back.'

'Jesus! You two would give me whiplash.'

'I think he's addicted to make-up sex.' She laughed. 'I'm a bit of a fan myself.'

'Do you want to get back with him?'

She shrugged. 'I don't know.'

'Well, I'm available for make-up sex right now.'

Her eyes dropped to his mouth, and she licked her lips.

He felt no desire – he was too numb for that – but he leaned in to kiss her again and this time she met him halfway. She ran her tongue along his bottom lip, and he shifted to get a better angle, pushing her back against the squashy sofa cushions. They both knew where this was going, but some instinct for self-preservation made him stop and pull back.

'Maybe you're right, this isn't such a good idea.' He sighed, rubbing a hand over his face. 'Do you want a drink?'

'No, thanks. I'd better get home.' She reached out and clasped his hand. 'Look you're lonely and sad, and I don't want to be your crutch just because you're feeling down.'

He nodded. 'I get it. Thanks for coming over, Pippa. It was good to see you. I really needed to see a friendly face.'

'Any time. I mean that.' She looked at him sadly, her head cocked to the side. 'I miss you, Roly. Call me when you're feeling better – if you still want to.'

31

Ella told herself her friendship with Roly wouldn't have lasted anyway. It was never meant to be forever, and it had already long outlived its use-by date. They'd had a good run, but it was always going to peter out eventually. For some reason they'd both dragged it out beyond its natural life span, and they'd managed to sustain it for far longer than either of them could have reasonably expected. But they'd just been delaying the inevitable. It had always bewildered her how Roly, of all people, was the one person from school she'd kept up with. Their friendship had never made sense. And as for anything else…

They'd both been kidding themselves. This was a good thing, she told herself, bringing their weird dalliance to a conclusion before they got in any deeper. It could never have worked long term. A cold blast of reality was just what they needed to bring them to their senses.

It was the same self-talk she'd given herself the first time, after the fallout from Marty's party. It was just as unconvincing now as it had been then, and, like then, she couldn't stop crying. She dragged herself through the days, just about managing to hold it together at work, then rushing home to spend the night crying her eyes out. Getting ready for work now involved a ritual of cold face-cloths and lots of camouflage work with concealers and highlighters to hide her ravaged face. She'd never spent so much time on make-up to so little effect, simply trying to achieve some semblance of normality.

It turned out she wasn't doing as good a job as she'd thought. On Friday morning, Jake came and perched on her desk.

'Are you okay, Ella?' His eyes were full of concern.

'Yes.' She gulped. 'I'm fine. Thanks.' *Heartbroken, but otherwise fine.*

'You don't seem yourself lately. We're a bit worried about you.'

'We?'

'Me and Dylan. Kerry. All of us. We've noticed you've been … well, you look like you've been crying a lot.'

She nodded, tears clogging her throat and welling in her eyes. Shit! She was going to lose it completely if he was kind.

'I don't want to pry, but if you ever need to talk…'

'Thanks,' she managed to choke out. She took a deep breath and swiped at her eyes. 'It's just … I've fallen out with Roly.'

'Oh no. I'm sorry to hear that.'

She nodded. 'I've moved out. But it's fine. I'll be fine.'

'You have somewhere to stay?'

'Yes. I'm back in my mum's house.'

'Okay.' He nodded. 'Good.' He waited a moment in silence, giving her space to talk, but when she said nothing more, he slid off the desk. 'Well, if there's anything we can do…'

'Thanks.'

. . .

As she watched Jake walk away, she looked around at the brightly lit office with its colourful pods and sofas, all the smiley, bubbly people with their bright smiles and enthusiasm, and wondered what the hell she was doing here. She didn't belong in this place. It was only ever meant to be a stop-gap, a temporary arrangement that, like her relationship with Roly, she had let go on too long.

Somewhere along the way, she'd lost sight of her goals and allowed herself to drift off course, tossed around by the tide until she was completely at sea, and about as far from her planned destination as she could possibly get. Maybe the split with Roly was the wake-up call she needed. She'd completely abandoned her dreams and ambitions. What had happened to getting her life back on track? All those wasted years when she'd been ill hadn't been her fault. But now every year, every day, every moment that she wasted was down to her, and she felt the weight of regret at the thought of losing one more second.

What was she doing here, dicking around with patent applications for someone else's inventions and funding proposals for someone else's business? She could only ever be on the side-lines in this world, cheering on the real players, watching someone else win. She should be chasing her own dreams.

She had to take charge of her life again and carve her own path, find her own way to where she wanted to be. She'd made some headway on paying off her debts, and Hazel was right, it was never going to be the ideal time to go back to college. She had to stop letting herself get side-tracked, and take steps to get back to the life she wanted – and there was no better time to start than right now. She grabbed her phone and called Hazel.

. . .

That afternoon, she found Jake and Dylan huddled together over a laptop in one of the pods, and asked if she could have a word with them in private.

'Yes, of course.' Dylan shot her a worried look, and Jake immediately snapped the laptop shut and picked it up as he stood. They brought her to the meeting room and shut the door. Ella smiled as she sat on the sofa opposite them, reminded of the day she'd come here for her interview.

'I'm glad you've decided to talk to us,' Dylan said. 'Jake told me you've broken up with Roly. I'm really sorry.'

'Oh! Well, I wouldn't say broken up. I mean, I *didn't* say broken up. We were just friends, really.'

'But you were … together?'

'For about five minutes. It hardly seems to count.'

'Right.' Jake nodded. 'Sorry. Anyway, the point is, you're upset. If you want to talk about it—'

'We're all ears.'

'Dylan's actually really good at this stuff.'

'Yeah, I'm a very good listener,' Dylan said. 'I've done years of therapy, so I've picked up quite a lot.'

'All our friends go to him for advice.'

'So if you want to talk through what happened with you and Roly—'

'You know you can always talk to us. Any time. Our door is always … non-existent.'

'Thanks.' Ella gulped, so touched she was afraid she was going to start crying again.

'You guys seemed great together,' Dylan said. 'I'm sure it isn't anything that can't be fixed.'

She shook her head. 'It can't. But it's not about Roly. I

mean, that is the reason I've been such a basket case. But it's not what I wanted to talk to you about.'

'Okay.' They both looked at her expectantly.

'I, um … I want to give my notice.'

'Oh.'

'Oh no!'

They looked stricken, and Ella immediately felt awful, like she'd kicked a puppy. For a moment they just stared at her in shocked silence, and she felt a wave of self-loathing as she looked at their earnest, open faces. She wished they'd be blasé about it, behave like the brash, callow idiots she'd first thought they were. But they wore their hearts on their sleeves, and it was plain to see they were upset.

'So, talk to us,' Jake said, rallying. 'What's the problem?'

'We thought you were happy here.'

'I am. I was.' Ella brushed her jeans, feeling as awkward as she had that first day. 'It's nothing to do with you, or this place.'

'You're saying it's not you, it's me?'

'Yeah. I guess. It's just … I'd always planned to have an academic career.'

'Right.' Dylan nodded. 'But you're so good at this.' His eyes were wide, pleading.

'Sometimes the best things in life are the things we didn't plan for ourselves,' Jake offered.

'Yes!' Dylan leaned forward eagerly. 'I was gutted when I had my knee injury and they told me I couldn't play rugby anymore. I thought I was going to have this brilliant career, playing for Ireland and everything. That was all I wanted to do with my life. But then I got injured, one thing led to another, and I ended up here. We started this company, and it's the best thing that's ever happened to me. I never thought I'd say that about being in business, and if you told my eighteen-year-old self that, he'd say you were crazy. But I *love* coming to work every day. I wake up feeling excited about coming in here, and I'm much happier than I'd have been playing rugby for a living.'

'Plus your career would nearly be over by now if you were playing rugby,' Jake chipped in.

'I'd have become a commentator, though – or gone into coaching. I could have been the hot rugby coach at a girls' school.'

'You still wouldn't be able to go out on the piss every weekend,' Jake said. 'You'd have to stay in shape.'

'Well … I'm pretty fit anyway.'

'Not match-fit, though.'

'Don't listen to him,' Dylan said to Ella. 'I'm very fit. If I get the call, I'm ready.'

She smiled. She was going to miss this. Miss them.

'So,' Jake said, in business mode again. 'Talk to us. What can we do to persuade you to stay?'

'More money? A promotion?'

Ella shook her head. 'I don't think you can. Sorry. Like I said, it's nothing to do with you. It's been really great working here, and I'm so grateful for the opportunity you've given me. But it's … time to move on.'

'Are you leaving us for someone else?' Jake asked.

'Well, yes. A friend of mine has offered me a research assistant post at Trinity.'

'Research assistant!' Dylan's eyes widened. 'I don't imagine that pays much, does it?'

'No, it doesn't. But it's in my field. It's what I've always wanted to do – what I'd planned to do before I got ill.'

Jake turned to Dylan. 'I suppose if you'd got over your knee injury and been offered the chance to play for Ireland, you'd have gone for it.'

'Honestly, I don't know.' Dylan directed his answer at

Ella, his blue eyes wide and sincere. 'I mean, yeah, if I'd been offered that when I was nineteen or twenty, I'd have bitten their hand off, no hesitation. But now, if I could go back and talk to my twenty-year-old self, I'd say don't do it. Honestly. Don't do it because there are better things coming, and your life is going to be so much more than you can imagine right now. Because the thing is, even if I could have gone back to it then, it still wouldn't be the same as if I hadn't had that injury in the first place. Do you see what I mean?'

'Yes, I do. I get it. I know I can't change the past. Those lost years will always be lost. But just because it'll be different doesn't mean it can't be as good — or better even.'

Dylan threw his head back against the sofa and sighed. 'Wow, this so isn't what I expected you to say when we came in here,' he said with a laugh. 'I thought I was going to be giving you advice on your love life.'

'Roly isn't my love life.'

'Relationships, then. Whatever. That's what I'm good at.'

'You're pretty good at the life coach stuff too,' Ella said wryly. She was surprised how insightful he could be.

'He's wise beyond his appearance,' Jake said.

'We really don't want to lose you.'

Ella felt a pang. Was that what was happening? Would she be lost?

'You're the best person we've ever had here,' Jake said. 'And that's including me and him.' He nodded to Dylan.

'Look,' Dylan said, 'you're upset about the Roly thing. Maybe now isn't the best time to be making big life decisions. Sometimes when one part of your life goes wrong, you make drastic changes in other areas that turn out to be a mistake.'

'Spoken like a man who bought a pair of leather trousers after his last break-up.'

Dylan laughed. 'Yeah, heartbreak can come out in ways you don't expect.'

'He's right, though,' Jake said. 'Why don't you go away and think about it for a while?'

'My friend needs an answer soon or she'll have to take on someone else. But don't worry, I won't leave you in the lurch. I'll work my month's notice.'

Jake gave a defeated sigh. 'Okay, well ... we'll talk to Kerry and she'll sort out the details. But if you change your mind at any point...'

'You'll be the first to know.'

Ella felt like she was walking around under a cloud for the rest of the day. She seemed to have cast a pall over everything, and there was a heavy, morose atmosphere around the building. She'd never seen Jake and Dylan so downbeat, their usual bounce and vigour gone. They looked troubled and dejected, their shoulders slumped and their expressions solemn.

In the afternoon, Kerry came to speak to her. She'd heard the news and said how sorry she was, but Ella couldn't help feeling there was a slightly accusatory look in her eyes too. She couldn't wait to get home that evening. She'd expected to feel more light-hearted and positive once she'd made her decision, but instead she felt leaden, weighed down with guilt for letting everyone down.

She told herself she had no reason to feel guilty. It was her life, and she didn't owe Jake and Dylan anything. They'd been good employers, and she'd been a good worker — it was a fair transaction on both sides, but that was all it was. She was expendable, and they'd replace her easily. No one could replace her in her own life. But no matter how hard she tried, she couldn't seem to convince herself.

It wasn't fair. She'd taken control and done something positive for herself. She should be feeling proud and purposeful. She was on her way to the life she wanted. So why did she feel so bloody sad? It was probably the break-up with Roly, casting a shadow over everything. She'd feel better once she started working in Trinity.

32

In the days after Ella left, Roly felt like he was living over a sink hole, as if the earth might split apart at any moment and swallow him up. He was wobbly and nervous all the time, as if aware that something bad was about to happen, a constant state of free-floating anxiety with no particular focus. He woke every morning with a feeling of dread, but couldn't put his finger on what was causing it. The world seemed to tilt dizzily on its axis and shake beneath his feet. He was cold and shivery, as if afflicted with some mysterious virus. Nothing seemed to make sense, nothing felt solid and reliable. He woke from nightmares shouting, desperately trying to escape some unidentifiable terror. He dreamed he was on a plane that could crash at any moment, only held up by the force of his anxiety.

His house felt empty now without Ella in it, his bed emptier still.

'Where's Ella?' his mum asked him when they went to his nan's for Sunday dinner.

'We're not together anymore.'

He felt her watching him carefully. 'You split up?'

He nodded. 'Yeah. She moved back to her mum's.'

'Oh no.' His mother flopped into the seat beside him.

'What happened?' his nan asked.

'We … we had a big row.' For some reason, he couldn't bring himself to tell them what Ella had done. Out of some sort of warped sense of loyalty, he wouldn't betray her – which was ironic. 'It just wasn't working.'

'I'm really sorry to hear that.' His mum put a hand over his on the table, giving him a sympathetic look. 'You seemed so good together.'

He hated the disappointment and sorrow in their faces. They loved Ella and they could see he was miserable. He felt he'd let them down and he wished he could tell them, justify himself, make them see that Ella was the one in the wrong and it was all her fault. But he couldn't bring himself to do it.

'Maybe you can patch things up between you,' his mum said, her eyes full of hope.

'No. I don't think so, Mum.'

His nan sighed. 'Well, that's a real shame. You were so happy.'

'Yeah, I was. We were.' And now he was so weighed down by sadness he could hardly breathe.

At least things were going well for him career-wise. Oh Boy! were in rehearsals for concerts, working on songs, and they'd be going into the studio soon to record a new album. He was grateful that he had work as a distraction and he threw himself into it with whatever energy he could muster.

It was strange being back with the lads, relearning their old dance routines, singing their old songs. But the weirdest thing about it was how normal it felt. Sometimes it seemed like only yesterday since they'd last performed together. Then he'd slide across the floor on his knees and feel every one of those intervening years.

They'd quickly fallen back into their old mix of camaraderie and rivalry. He didn't feel the old excitement he used to, but that would probably come back once they were touring and recording again. Bit by bit, he was reclaiming his old life. He decided it was time to start the Pippa offensive. He started stalking her on Instagram, posting flirty replies to her photos. If nothing else, it would piss Adam Leader off.

'None for me, thanks,' Pippa said as Loretta cut thick slices of lemon drizzle cake. Roly wasn't feeling a whole lot better, but he'd called Pippa anyway. He met her after his NA meeting, and took her for coffee at his mum's instead of going to a cafe. He didn't see enough of his mum or nan now that he was busy rehearsing with Oh Boy! But he was already regretting it. His mum would never say anything, never let it show, but he knew she'd never been that fond of Pippa. And Pippa … well, he was remembering she wasn't the most empathetic person on the planet.

'Just a small piece? I made it this morning, specially when I knew you were coming.'

'It's really good,' Roly said to her. 'You should try some. Mum's cakes are amazing.'

'I said no,' Pippa hissed under her breath to him, while his mum pretended not to hear. 'No means no.'

'Well, I know *you'll* have some,' Loretta said to Roly. 'It's his favourite,' she told Pippa.

'Thanks, Mum.' Roly held out his plate.

Pippa gave him an outraged glare. 'Roly,' she whispered to him.

He pretended not to notice her annoyance as he bit into the thick wedge of buttery, lemony sponge and sighed. It was divine.

'You're sure you won't have a slice?' Loretta asked Pippa. 'Just a little one?'

'You don't know what you're missing,' Roly said.

She ignored him. 'No thank you, Loretta. I don't eat cake.'

Roly tried to swallow down his anger, but he could feel his mum's disappointment. She'd done something nice, gone to the trouble of making a cake for them, and Pippa was throwing it back in her face.

'How've you been, Pippa? It's been a long time.'

'I'm great, thanks, Loretta. I'm launching a new collection next month, so I'm mad busy.'

'That's nice.'

They made stilted small talk for a while, and Roly had a second slice of cake more as a show of support for his mum than because he wanted one. It also didn't hurt that it pissed Pippa off.

'Will I see you on Sunday?' his mum asked him as they got up to go.

'At Nan's? Yeah, but I didn't think you'd be there. Isn't Mike coming for the weekend?'

A shadow passed across his mother's face, but she quickly replaced it with a smile. 'Oh no, he can't make it after all. He's having a dreadful time. He can't get his bank account sorted out without his passport. But the officials who have it won't give it back until he gives them money. So it's a vicious circle.'

Roly thought his nan was right to be cynical. Mike did seem to have implausibly bad luck. He remembered what

Ella had told him about romance scammers, and got a bad feeling. He wanted to ask his mum if she'd sent Mike any money, but he didn't want to embarrass her, especially in front of Pippa.

'Well, I'll see you at Nan's on Sunday, then.' He kissed her goodbye and left feeling worried and uneasy.

'Why couldn't you have just eaten the cake?' he hissed at Pippa once they were outside. 'It wouldn't have killed you. She was just trying to be kind.'

'Kind! The kind thing would be to respect my boundaries, and not keep on at me about it. I said no. Once should have been enough.'

'The kind thing for *you* to do would be to eat the fucking cake! For god's sake! It wouldn't kill you to loosen up, just for once.'

'Are you accusing me of being uptight?'

'Never!' He rolled his eyes. 'You're the most laid-back person I know.'

'Maybe it wouldn't kill me just the once, but if you give in every time, it might. I mean, look at you! It's no wonder you're in the shape you're in.'

'The shape I'm in!'

'You're a grown man. You should be able to say no to your mother at your age. It's pathetic!'

'You think it's pathetic to consider other people's feelings?'

'No, it's pathetic that you can't stand up for yourself – set your own boundaries and stick to them. There's such a thing as killing with kindness, you know.'

'There really isn't.'

'Well, there *is* such a thing as killing with sugar. Obesity can be lethal.'

'Right. That's what this is all about, is it? That I'm a bit chunky and you don't like it?'

'Roly, it's not about what I like. It's not good for you. You know that.' She put a hand on his arm, her tone placating now. 'I'm saying this because I care about you. You know that. I just want you to survive.'

'You want me to survive my mum's lemon drizzle cake?'

'Oh, you're impossible,' she huffed, stalking off down the path ahead of him.

Bitch, he thought, following her. Ella would have eaten the cake, whether she wanted it or not, regardless of whether it fit in with her diet – just because it was the nice thing to do.

When he caught up with Pippa, she had her phone out and was texting.

'Do you think my mum's boyfriend might be a bit dodgy?'

'How would I know? I've never met the guy.'

'Well, neither has she. They met on some dating site.'

'There's nothing strange about that.' She glanced at him distractedly. 'That's how everyone meets nowadays.'

'I know, but … he keeps saying he's going to come and then there's always some excuse why he can't. His daughter is sick and needs an operation or his accounts have been hacked… Ella thought he might be some kind of con artist.'

'It sounds like he just has shit luck.' She was barely paying attention to him as she continued texting. 'You shouldn't be so involved in your mother's love life anyway. It's creepy.'

'It's not creepy! I'm just worried about her, that's all.'

'For God's sake, she's a grown woman. Give her some credit. She's old enough to look after herself.' She finished texting and tossed her phone back into her bag.

He nodded. 'Yeah, you're right,' he said, even though she'd done nothing to allay his fears. 'I'm sure it's nothing.'

At the corner, she stopped and turned to him. 'Well, I'm going to get a cab, so I'll say goodbye here.'

'Oh. You don't want to come back to my place?'

'No. Look, Roly, the thing is I'm back with Adam now.'

'Oh! Right. You never said.'

'Well, I wasn't when we arranged to meet up.'

'You mean … this morning?'

She nodded. 'Yeah. It just happened.'

'*When*?'

'Just now.' She pointed to her bag. 'We were texting there, and … now we're back together.'

'Well, that was sudden!'

She shrugged. 'When you know, you know,' she said brightly. 'There's my ride,' she said as a cab turned into the street. 'Well, bye, Roly!' She gave him a peck on the cheek. 'Good luck with everything.'

She hopped into the cab before he'd even replied, waving at him as she drove off. Roly stood there, looking after her in bewilderment. Then he turned and went back to his mum's house. He needed a sit down and another slice of cake.

33

Ella was back where she belonged. Every morning she went to work in Trinity, leaving the bustling city streets behind her as she entered the sanctuary of the cobbled courtyard. Students called to each other as they weaved past on bicycles or hurried to lectures. The weather was mild, but autumn was just around the corner, the leaves on the trees turning yellow and crunching underfoot as she made her way across the campus to her tiny office. She sat at her own desk and had coffee with Hazel at eleven every morning. She ate lunch in the canteen or got a sandwich and picnicked on the lawn if it was sunny. She wandered down Grafton Street on her way home, window-shopping and people-watching. She went for drinks with Hazel and her colleagues. They had sherry with the Dean.

True to her word, Hazel had been conscientious about giving her interesting work and not just lumbering her with the drudgery. Every day she breathed in the rarefied air of college, absorbing the atmosphere of calm studiousness, and tried to feel the rightness of it. She was exactly where she was meant to be. This was the life she'd dreamed of for so long, and she was lucky to be here. So why was she always reaching for a feeling that wasn't there?

She told herself it was an adjustment. She'd got used to the dynamic environment of Citizens, and it would take a while to adapt to the more staid pace of academic life, the hierarchical structures, the formality and bureaucracy. Meanwhile, it was good to have meaningful work to focus on and take her mind off Roly.

When she finished work, she went home and spent the evening cleaning the house. Her mother and Nora were due back from their trip soon, and she kept herself busy getting the place in shape for their return, scrubbing every inch until her hands were red and raw. Then she would crash into bed exhausted, too tired to think, and fall into a blessed, oblivious sleep.

Loretta and Christine called and messaged her occasionally, inviting her to knitting club, asking if they'd see her at Pilates. She felt bad about ignoring their calls or fobbing them off with excuses, but she told herself it was for the best in the long run. She could only suppose that Roly hadn't told them why they'd split up. Once he did, they'd stop calling.

There was nothing from Roly. She wasn't surprised, but she couldn't help hoping he'd forgive her, even though she knew it was impossible. Hazel had gone with her to collect the rest of her stuff, but he hadn't been there. He'd just left a note asking her to drop the keys through the letterbox when she was done.

On the day her mother and Nora were coming home, she did a big supermarket shop, buying all the food she imagined they'd been missing while they were away. Then she went home and prepared a big dinner for the evening, cooking a warming autumnal casserole and a plum tart that Christine had given her the recipe for. That reminded her of Roly, and she burst into tears that wouldn't seem to stop. Eventually she decided to just give into them, and she lay on her bed sobbing for almost an hour.

When she got up, she splashed her face with icy water, and put on some make-up to hide the ravages of her crying jag. By the time her mother and Nora arrived home, she felt calm and in control again. She rushed into the hall, her heart skipping at the sight of the two of them, struggling through the door with more bags than they'd left with. A couple of colourful embroidered holdalls had been added to their luggage. They were both tanned, a little scruffy and dishevelled, and the most gorgeous sight Ella had ever seen.

'Welcome home!' she squealed as they hugged each other. 'It's so good to see you two.'

'It's so good to see you, darling.' Her mother squeezed her tight.

Then it was Nora's turn. 'We've missed you so much.'

'Are you tired? Hungry? I've made dinner.'

'It smells delicious.' Her mother sniffed the air. 'We're starving!'

'And we're not tired at all,' Nora said. 'We had a great sleep last night at Heathrow.'

'It was such a good idea to stay overnight at the airport – especially with all the delays last night. We'd have missed our connecting flight anyway if we'd had one.'

They were still buzzing about their travels, chattering all through dinner about the places they'd been, the things they'd seen and done. Ella was happier than she'd been in ages as she listened to their stories.

'So, tell us what's been happening with you since we've

been gone?' her mother said. 'It's great you got that job with Hazel. It was nice of her to think of you.'

'Though we're a bit disappointed you're not working for Tweedledum and Tweedledee anymore. We did love hearing about what went on at that place. They sounded fun.'

'They were.' Ella smiled fondly. She missed Citizens so much.

Her mother frowned. 'But you're happy working with Hazel? I mean, it's what you always wanted to do…'

'I guess.' She pushed her food around her plate. 'It's just … not as interesting as I'd expected, I suppose. And I don't feel…'

'What?'

She shrugged. 'Needed, I guess.' It sounded daft when she said it out loud – arrogant, even. It wasn't as if Jake and Dylan hadn't been doing perfectly well before she turned up, and no doubt they were managing just fine without her now. 'I felt like I really made a difference at Citizens, you know?'

'I'm sure you did.'

'They were lucky to have you,' Nora chipped in supportively.

Jake and Dylan had always made Ella feel like that. But she was being childish, expecting her employers to make her feel special – she was a grown-up, for fuck's sake. She'd done her job well and was paid for it accordingly. She shouldn't need Smarties and cupcakes to make her feel valued.

'I suppose it'll just take a bit of time to adjust,' her mother said. 'It's a different environment.'

'Yeah, I'm sure that's all it is.'

'And what about Roly? How's he? How come you're not living with him anymore?'

To her horror, Ella felt her eyes well up with tears. She'd kept the details vague while they were travelling. She'd merely told them that she had to move out of Roly's place, without going into the reason.

'We thought maybe you two…' Nora left the sentence hanging suggestively.

Ella swallowed hard and shook her head. 'It was nothing like that. We were just friends.'

Neither of them looked convinced, and she caught them exchanging a worried look.

'So what happened there?' her mum asked. 'Why did you move out?'

'Did he meet someone else?' Nora asked.

'No. I mean maybe. He might be getting back with his ex, but that's not why—' She gasped and a sob escaped as the tears she could no longer hold back spilled from her eyes. 'Oh god, I messed everything up.'

Her mother took one of her hands, and Nora clasped the other tight.

'Whatever it is, I'm sure it's not as bad as you think,' her mother said.

'It is.' She sniffed, wiping her eyes with the back of her hand. 'I did something – years ago – to Roly, and now he's found out and he'll never forgive me.'

'Whatever it is, it can't be all that bad.'

'It is, mum. It's really terrible. You don't know—'

'We know *you*,' Nora said. 'You wouldn't do anything to hurt someone, not deliberately.'

'Nora's right. What could you do that would be so dreadful?'

So, when she'd managed to stop her sobs, she told them. She'd never told anyone what had happened that night, what she'd done – not even her mum. Not even

Roly, she thought with a pang. It was a secret she'd buried deep inside herself.

'But you did it for his own good,' her mother said when she'd finished. 'You were worried about him – and rightly so, by the sound of it.'

'You were being a good friend,' Nora added. 'You did him a favour. Thanks to you, he got the help he needed.'

'Roly doesn't see it that way.'

'Well, I'm sure he will once he calms down. It must have been a shock when he found out. It's understandable if he's upset. But I'm sure he'll come round and realise that you were just trying to do what was best for him.'

'But it's the fact that I didn't tell him,' she wailed. 'That's the really unforgivable part. I should have told him when we met up again. Now it's like I tricked him into—' She stopped abruptly, realising she'd been about to say 'into loving me'. *Had* Roly loved her? It had felt like it. 'But he didn't have all the facts – about his own life.' Or about exactly what kind of person he'd fallen in love with.

'I agree you should have told him,' her mother said. 'But I know how hard that would have been and I totally understand why you didn't.' She put an arm around Ella and hugged her. 'Oh, darling, I hate seeing you so unhappy.'

'We seem to have come back in the nick of time,' Nora said.

Ruth smiled at her sister and nodded. 'You do seem to have made a bit of a mess of things while we've been away,' she said to Ella. 'But it's nothing that can't be fixed.'

'I don't see how.'

'Well, let's start with Tweedledum and Tweedledee. Do you think they'd give you your old job back?

34

'THANKS FOR MEETING ME.'

'No problem. It's good to see you, Ella.'

'It's really nice to see you too.' She meant it. They were a sight for sore eyes. She was once again seated on the other side of the coffee table from Jake and Dylan in their little office area. Outside the door she could hear the low hum of Citizens life going on.

'So, what can we do for you?' Jake asked.

This was it. She twisted her sweating hands in her lap and swallowed, her throat dry.

'I… I was wondering if I could have my old job back. If you'd have me, that is.'

'Ah!'

'Told you,' Dylan said, grinning at Jake. 'You owe me a tenner.'

'So the research job didn't work out?' Jake asked.

'No. I mean, it's fine. I haven't been fired or anything. I just … made a mistake. I'm sorry I left this place. I know it's a long shot. I'm sure you've replaced me by now. But I just thought I'd ask – in case.'

'Don't ask, don't get,' Jake said.

'Yes. Exactly.'

'Well, we'd love to have you back,' Jake said, 'but—'

'We did take on someone else,' Dylan finished for him.

'Right, okay.' She nodded.

'She's no you, but she's pretty good and we'd have no reason to let her go. So I'm afraid we can't give you your old job back.' Jake glanced at Dylan as he said it, and they exchanged a look she couldn't decipher.

'No, of course not. I wouldn't expect that.'

'Anyway, how've you been?' Dylan asked.

'I'm okay.' She gave him a shaky smile. 'I've screwed everything up, but I'll be fine. How are things going here?'

'Great!' Dylan beamed. 'We're all systems go, getting the new urban collection together.'

'It's been hectic,' Jake said.

'Are you still doing karaoke?' she asked wistfully.

'Of course. Never too busy for a bit of fun.'

'And how's my replacement working out at that?'

'Fantastic,' Dylan said. 'She does a mean Kiki.'

'Oh.' It was ridiculous how gutted she felt at that. 'Well, I'd better let you get on. Thanks for your time. It was nice to see you anyway.' She got up to go.

'You too. We told you don't be a stranger. And you've been a stranger.'

'Sorry.'

'Yes, don't let that happen again, young lady,' Dylan said. 'You should join us for karaoke on Friday.'

'And the door's that way,' Jake said, pointing to it.

As she turned to go, she heard them laughing and calling to her.

'Ella, don't go!'

'Come back!'

She turned around to find them beckoning her over.

'We were only kidding.'

'What? I don't—'

'Your replacement is crap at karaoke.'

'Oh.'

'Hasn't got a note in her head.'

'Sit down,' Dylan waved to the sofa opposite them and she lowered herself into it uncertainly, not sure what was going on.

'Sorry, we were just kidding around,' Jake said. 'Of course we want you back.'

'But you said … you can't just give my replacement the sack. You said she hasn't done anything wrong.'

'No, we can't give you your old job back,' Dylan said. 'That part is true.'

'There's another position we'd like to offer you.'

She looked at them in bewilderment.

'It's something new that's just opening up,' Jake told her.

'Oh?'

'Like I said, we're getting ready to launch the urban collection, so we're going to be expanding, and we'd love for you to be part of that. How would you feel about taking over as Head of Marketing?'

'Oh!' she gasped. 'Seriously?'

'Would you be up for it?' Dylan asked eagerly.

'It would mean a lot more work,' Jake said.

'And a salary increase, of course.'

Ella smiled. 'Well, I still think your interview technique needs a lot of work. But I'd love it.'

'So that's a yes?'

'Yes please! I accept.'

'Yes!' Dylan pumped a fist triumphantly. 'The gang's back together.' He and Jake high-fived each other, grinning, then turned to Ella, palms up.

'Seriously unprofessional.' She laughed as she high-fived them both. It felt good to be back.

If only she could fix her relationship with Roly so easily, she thought as she made her way back to work. But she didn't expect him to forgive her. There was a limit. She'd just have to accept that and move on. At least she'd be kept busy at Citizens. She'd have no time to mope about Roly. Now she just had to break it to Hazel.

'Oh thanks goodness!' Hazel's reaction to the news that she was leaving wasn't quite what Ella had been expecting. She was relieved her friend wasn't upset, but it wasn't very flattering.

'Not that there's any problem with the job you were doing,' Hazel hastened to add, reaching out across the table and putting a hand over Ella's. After work, they'd gone for a drink in a little wine bar off Grafton Street. 'You've been nothing but conscientious, and I can't think of anyone who'd do a better job.'

'Oh. Okay…' Ella frowned, confused.

'But your heart isn't in it. I can see that you're miserable, and I feel guilty that I pressured you into it and dragged you away from a job you really enjoyed.'

'Sorry. But you didn't pressure me into it – not at all. I really thought it was what I wanted. I guess I wasn't thinking very clearly at the time.'

Hazel nodded. 'You shouldn't make big life decisions when you're heartbroken.'

'That's what Dylan said.' Ella sighed. 'I guess I needed to feel I was in control of something in my life – that I could go after what I want and get it. So I changed the thing it was in my power to change. But what I really want…' She shrugged. 'There's nothing I can do about that.'

'Nothing from Roly?'

Ella shook her head. 'No, not a word. I don't expect there to be.' She took a sip of wine and put her glass down. 'Anyway, I hope I haven't made things too difficult for you.'

'Not at all.' Hazel shook her head emphatically. 'You know there are lots of people who'd love that job, and I already had someone else lined up if you didn't take it.'

'Good. I'm glad at least I'm not fucking up your life as well as my own.'

The following evening, Ella was in her bedroom, chilling out before dinner when there was a ring at the door. She heard voices and when she went to the top of the stairs, she was astonished to see Loretta standing in the hall.

'Ella, hi!' She looked up at her with a soft smile. 'I just came to drop off your cardigan – you left it at Mum's.' She lifted a plastic bag. 'And I wanted to have a word.'

'Sure,' Ella said, descending the stairs towards her with some trepidation. 'We can go in here.' She jerked her head towards the living room.

'Dinner will be about fifteen minutes,' her mother said, giving her a sympathetic look.

'Thanks for bringing this,' Ella said as Loretta handed her the bag. They sat side by side on the couch. 'There was no need.'

'I really wanted to see you,' Loretta said. 'We've missed you at Pilates.'

'Yeah, sorry about that. I've … been busy.'

'And Mum was expecting you at her knitting club last night.'

'Oh, was she? I assumed … I mean, now that Roly and I have split up, I didn't think…'

'It doesn't mean we can't still be friends, does it?' Loretta frowned enquiringly. Ella realised it wasn't a rhetorical question. 'It feels like you've been avoiding us. Which is fine,' she added quickly. 'But we didn't want you to feel you have to. We're very fond of you, Ella.'

Ella sighed. 'Roly hasn't told you why we broke up, has he?'

'No, he hasn't. But I know he's miserable about it.'

Ella swallowed hard, tears welling in her eyes. She hated to think of Roly being unhappy, especially knowing she was the cause of it. 'I know how he feels,' she whispered, looking down at her hands.

'Oh, love.' Loretta put an arm around her. 'I didn't mean to upset you. But surely it's nothing that can't be fixed. If you're both so miserable without each other—'

Ella shook her head, swiping at her eyes. 'It can't. It was my fault, and I think it *does* mean we can't be friends. It's not that I don't want to be. But when you know what I did—'

'There was no cheating, was there? Roly said—'

'No, nothing like that.' She took a deep breath, and looked Loretta in the eye. She had to face up to this squarely – no more lying or obfuscating. So she told her the whole story.

'That photograph…' Loretta breathed when she'd finished. 'It was you?' Her chin wobbled, and then she did the strangest thing. She threw her arms around Ella and hugged her so fiercely it took her breath away.

. . .

'Dinner's up,' Ruth said as they both emerged from the living room. 'Loretta, have you eaten? Would you like to stay for a bite?'

'Oh, thanks, but I won't impose.'

'You're not imposing. The more, the merrier. I'd love to have a proper chat.'

Loretta looked at Ella uncertainly as if asking her permission.

'Stay,' Ella said. 'If you'd like to.'

'In that case, thanks, Ruth. That would be lovely.'

'Great! Come and meet my sister, Nora.'

Loretta got on famously with her mother and aunt, and dinner was fun. Nora and Loretta compared horror stories about internet dating and laughed until tears were rolling down their faces, and Loretta loved hearing about Ruth and Nora's recent trip, listening raptly as they told her about their adventures.

'I'd love to travel,' she said wistfully. 'I mean travel properly like that – not just go on holidays. But I didn't have the money when I was younger and, anyway, I had Roly.'

Ella tried not to flinch at the mention of him, but she was aware of everyone darting her anxious looks, and an awkward silence fell, as if his name was taboo.

'Then when I could afford it,' Loretta continued, 'all my friends had settled down and I had no one to go with. I didn't fancy it on my own. It's hard when you're single at my age. My friends are great, but at the end of the day, they have their own families.'

'We're lucky to have each other,' Nora said, nodding at Ruth.

'You are.' Loretta smiled. 'Anyway, I've met this lovely man – a good one for a change,' she said in an aside to Nora, 'and we're planning a trip to India next year.'

'Oh, lovely! That's next on our list,' Ruth said. 'Nora's been, but a long time ago.'

'I've wanted to go back ever since,' Nora said.

'So tell us more about this man,' Ruth said, pouring more wine.

'His name's Mike. We met on a dating site, but we moved onto private messaging very quickly. It's funny, I feel like I've known him my whole life, and we've never even met. We've spent hours and hours messaging and talking on the phone, of course. But he's moving here next weekend, and that's the first time I'll see him.'

'Mike's finally coming, then?' Ella asked Loretta later as she saw her to the door.

'Yes. He still can't get access to his money, and the bank are no help. So I sent him some cash and paid for his flight, and we'll sort it out when he gets here.'

Ella felt a creeping dread.

'Don't tell Mum, if you see her,' Loretta added in a rush. 'It's just a loan. I know he'll pay me back straight away once everything's sorted out. But if Mum found out, she'd think I was being taken for a ride.'

Her cab arrived before Ella could say anything more. She hugged Ella goodbye and made her promise she'd come back to Pilates if she wanted to, and visit Christine.

'I know Mum will feel the same,' she said, and then she was gone.

'Loretta's lovely, isn't she?' her mother said as Ella helped her clear up. 'Would it be awkward for you if we inducted her into our gang?' Her mother and aunt loved finding new people to bring into their circle.

'No, not awkward for me at all.' She thought of what Loretta had said about all her friends being coupled up. 'I think Loretta would really like that. Besides, you're three grown women. I'm not going to police your friendships.'

It had been good to see the three of them getting on so well tonight and having fun. But what Loretta had said about Mike niggled at her, and she wished she hadn't promised not to say anything to Christine about the money she'd given him. She was more convinced than ever that Loretta's 'boyfriend' was a scammer. But she couldn't voice her concerns to Loretta in front of her mum and Nora – it would be too humiliating for her – and then she didn't get a chance before she left. Maybe it was just as well. She should have learned her lesson about interfering in other people's lives. And it was possible she was wrong and Mike was on the level. She hoped so. Either way, it was none of her business and she should stay out of it.

35

ROLY WAS SHOCKED when he walked into his nan's house to find Ella sitting at the kitchen table with her, drinking tea.

'Roly!' Christine looked up. 'I wasn't expecting you.'

He frowned at Ella. 'What are you doing here?'

'I was just leaving,' she said, getting up. She appeared flustered as she quickly pulled on her jacket and made for the door. 'Thanks for the tea and cake, Christine. It was lovely.'

'I'll see you on Thursday,' his nan said.

Ella swept past him and rushed out of the room. He heard the front door close. 'I'll be back in a sec,' he said to his nan, then hurried after Ella.

She was already halfway down the street when he got outside. 'Ella!'

She stopped and turned, and he jogged to catch up to her. 'What are you doing here?' he asked, narrowing his eyes at her.

'I was visiting Christine.'

'Obviously. But why are you visiting my nan?'

'What's it got to do with you? You don't own her, Roly. She's a person in her own right.'

'I know that!'

'Do you?'

'Of course!'

'Why are you questioning me about seeing her, then?'

'Because … it's weird. We're not together anymore.'

'She's entitled to have her own relationships, separate from you. We're friends.'

'Friends? You're *friends* with my nan?'

'Yes. Why is that so hard for you to understand?'

'Well, I mean … she's seventy.'

'And you don't think seventy-year-olds should have friends?'

'Yes, but … friends their own age.'

Ella rolled her eyes in exasperation. 'It's not as if we're shagging! What's the age difference got to do with it?'

'Nothing, just … I mean, what have you got in common with a seventy-year-old woman?'

'Plenty, if you must know! Not that it's any of your business. But we have similar interests and we're on the same wavelength about a lot of things. She's teaching me to knit, and we watch *Queer Eye* together. She's a really interesting woman and we like each other. Okay?'

He nodded. 'Okay. Sorry.' He couldn't believe she was making him feel like he was in the wrong.

'Well, bye,' she said, but she still stood there. She seemed hesitant, and opened her mouth to speak, but said nothing. She turned to go, then turned back to him immediately, her face set, as if she'd decided something. 'Actually, I'm glad I bumped into you. I wanted to talk to you.' She took a deep breath. 'I'm a bit worried about your mum.'

'*You're* worried about my mum?'

'Yeah. About this boyfriend of hers...'

'Not this again!' Roly shook his head. 'Where do you get off, interfering in my family?'

She blushed. 'Sorry. But I had to say something.'

'Yeah, because you know what's best for everyone, right? Look, Mum's fine. She's happy. Just leave her be. He's coming over next week, you know.'

'Yeah.' She nodded. 'Did you know she paid for the flight?'

His stomach plummeted. She could probably tell by his face that the answer was no, and he hated being wrong-footed by her, resented her knowing things about his family that he didn't.

'So what?' He shrugged. 'Look at all the stuff he's given her.'

'What's the price of a few gifts in the grand scheme of things?'

'The *grand scheme* of swindling my mum out of the price of a flight? Sounds like the work of a criminal mastermind, all right.'

'It wasn't just the flight. She sent him money too.'

'Well, if he's after my mum for her money, he's barking up the wrong tree.'

'She doesn't have to have much, just some. Whatever he can persuade her to part with.'

Roly flicked his eyes to the house. 'Have you said any of this to my nan?'

Ella shook her head. 'No. I promised your mum I wouldn't tell her she'd sent him money. She said Christine would just over-react.'

'And you didn't sneak off behind her back and tell Nan anyway? Well, that's something.' He saw her flinch at that.

'She said it's just a loan, and he'll pay her back as soon as he gets here.'

'There you go, then.'

'Do you have any photos of him?'

'Me? Why would I have photos of my mum's boyfriend?'

'I don't know.' She shrugged. 'I just thought she might have sent you one in a WhatsApp message or something.'

'Why do you want a picture of him anyway? Are you thinking of printing up a Wanted poster?'

She didn't laugh. 'If you had a photo of him, you could do a reverse image search – see if that picture has been used on different profiles. Do you know how to do that?'

'No, and I don't intend to find out.'

'There's no harm in checking, is there?'

'Well, I can't anyway because I don't have a photo. Have you said anything to my nan about this scammer theory?'

'No. I didn't think it was my place to.'

'Well, you got that right at least.' He sighed. He knew she was genuinely worried about his mum and she was trying to help. He shouldn't be so hard on her. It was just Ella being Ella.

'Look, I know you mean well. But Mum isn't as clueless as Nan makes her out to be. She knows this guy, she's spoken to him loads of times. She'd have a better idea if there's anything dodgy about him than you would.'

'Okay. Right.' Ella nodded, but he could tell she wasn't convinced. He didn't blame her. He wasn't even convincing himself. 'I hope you're right. Well, bye.'

She turned and walked away, and he went back into the house, cursing her. Damn her! Why did she have to go and plant that doubt into his mind? He tried to shake it off, to tell himself she was jumping to conclusions. But now that the idea was there in his head, he couldn't dislodge it.

'I can't believe you've been seeing Ella behind my back,' he said to his nan when he went back into the kitchen. He was still fuming and confused, and on edge now about what Ella had told him. It wasn't fair. His nan should be on *his* side. But then, he'd never told her what Ella had done.

'It's not behind your back,' she said. 'You just saw her.'

'You know what I mean. You never told me you were still seeing her.' He sat down beside her in the seat vacated by Ella.

'Oh, I wasn't aware I needed your permission.' She poured a mug of tea and handed it to him.

'She's my ex, Nan. It's weird for me seeing her here.' He took a sip of tea. 'The thing is, I never told you why we broke up.'

'No, you didn't. But Ella did.'

'What?' He hadn't expected that. 'So you know what she did?'

'I do, yes,' she said calmly, reaching for a biscuit.

'And you still want to be friends with her? She ruined my life, nan! She's the reason that photo got out, she's why I got kicked out of the band!'

'She's the reason you went to rehab,' she said quietly. 'Oh, Roly.' She put a hand over his. 'We were so worried about you – me and your mum. We didn't know what to do. We tried – remember? We tried to talk to you, tried to persuade you to get help. But you wouldn't listen. You were too far gone.' To his horror, her eyes welled up with tears. He'd hardly ever seen her cry. 'We were beside ourselves.'

He swallowed hard, tears pricking his own eyes at the thought of all the hurt he'd caused the people he loved most in the world, the pain he'd put them through.

'I'm sorry. I didn't mean—'

'I know you didn't, sweetheart.' She squeezed his hand

on the table. 'You weren't yourself. The boy we loved was … gone. It was like you'd vacated your body and there was just this empty shell walking around where you used to be. We were at our wits' end. We thought we'd never get you back.' She wiped her eyes and stood. 'So yeah, I know what Ella did,' she said in a firmer voice, 'and I'm bloody grateful to her. Because I'm not sure you'd be sitting here today if that photo hadn't got out.'

He looked up at her in shock, unable to speak. He didn't like feeling so in the wrong – not here, not with her. But confronted with all the heartache he'd caused her and his mum, he couldn't avoid his guilt.

'You think she ruined your life,' she said. 'I don't know if you'd even *have* a life anymore, if it weren't for her.'

It reminded him of what Pippa had said – that he didn't know what his life would have been like if Ella hadn't done what she did. But that cut two ways.

'But she lied to me about it!' he said, grasping for some moral high ground. 'She should have told me. That's what I really can't get past.'

To his relief, she nodded. 'She should. But we all make mistakes.' She gave him a pointed look. 'She was just a kid, Roly. You were both just kids, trying to do your best.'

36

'Roly, you shake that beautiful tush of yours, and grind up against Zack.'

They were rehearsing for the video of what was to be the first single off their new album, once again working with Boo Sanchez, choreographer to the stars. Roly liked Boo, but he'd always hated his ideas. He was talking them through the dance moves for the video.

'Zack, you're doing the same. Then you turn to each other at the same time. Big moment.' He held his hands up, palms open. 'You eyeball each other. Eyeball, eyeball, eyeball – three beats. Then key change, crescendo, crescendo crescendo – and you kiss.'

'We what?' Boo had really lost the plot this time. Liam and Alex sniggered.

'You kiss.'

'Me and Zack?'

'Yes. You cup the back of his head, pull him in and then you kiss. Fireworks, confetti, whatever. The end.'

'So … we kiss to the end of the song? That's, like … a whole minute almost.'

'I know, so romantic!' Boo clutched a hand to his heart. 'The fans will love it.'

'They'll go nuts for it,' Zack grinned. 'And it's what you've always wanted, isn't it?' he said to Roly.

Roly groaned. 'Yeah, right. I've always wanted to get with you, Zack.'

'Come on, we all know it's true. You wrote a whole book about it.' He smirked.

Back in the day some uber-fan had written a torrid fan fiction story about him and Zack falling in love and having sex all the time. It had blown up in their fandom, and Zack thought it was hilarious. It had been a running joke with him that Roly was the anonymous author, and sometimes when he was high he'd insisted on reading out long, lurid passages to everyone about them lusting after each other and sucking each other's knobs. To Roly's mortification, the novel had eventually been picked up by a publisher and became a huge bestseller.

'It's the only reason I came back,' Roly said now. 'To get inspiration for my next porno blockbuster.'

'I knew it!'

'Okay, let's take a break,' Boo said, clapping his hands. 'I'll see you back here in fifteen minutes, and I want you two ready for some serious lip action.'

'Seriously, though,' Roly said as Boo left the room, 'I don't think I want to do this.'

'I won't slip you the tongue, I promise.' Zack laughed. 'Unless you beg me to, of course. Come on, don't be such a wuss. It's just one little kiss.'

But it wasn't just one little kiss. If it was in the video, they'd have to perform the routine night after night, at every concert, including the kiss – the fans would expect it. They'd demand it. He could already hear them baying for it. It would be there every time the video was played, giving rise to endless prurient speculation and gossip about his love life, his sexual orientation … But it wasn't just that.

He didn't want to spend his time bickering with producers over songs he didn't really care about anyway and scrabbling for the limelight with Zack. He didn't want to keep singing the same songs he sang ten years ago. He wanted something new. He wanted to wake up feeling excited about what he was doing, like he'd been when he was writing with Phoenix.

'I don't just mean the kiss. I mean all of it. The video, this song. I hate this song.'

'You wrote it.'

'Co-wrote it. And I hate the arrangement. I hate the cheesy as fuck dance routine, I hate the whole video concept.'

Maybe Charlie was right and he'd been lucky to quit when he did. Being in Oh Boy! was all about compromise and sucking up. That was fine when they'd been a bunch of gormless teenagers, but now they were five grown-ass men with their own ideas, their own creativity, pulling in five different directions and none of them getting to go where they wanted.

'Look, we don't like it either,' Liam said to him.

'You don't?' He looked around at the four of them. 'None of you?'

'No.' They all shook their heads.

'Of course not.'

'You're not the only one who thinks Boo has his head up his arse, you know.'

Roly was astonished.

'You really think you're the only one with taste?' Zack asked. 'You think you're above all this now just because you sang one song with Walking Wounded?' He flopped onto a sofa and uncapped a bottle of water. 'Suck it up. It's just one video.'

'But it's not, is it?' Roly sat down beside him. 'It's one video, one single, then it's just one album, just one tour. And then it's interviews and chat shows, and concert after concert singing the same old stuff, doing these stupid dance routines.'

'Come on, it's not that bad. It's not exactly working down the mines.'

'Yeah, that's the only other option.' Roly laughed, rolling his eyes.

'All this because you don't want to snog me?' Zack pouted. 'I'm hurt.'

'It's not even about that. I don't mind kissing you for one video.'

'Course you don't. It's your dream come true. We all know that.'

'But I don't want to make it my career.'

'Beats working down the mines.' Zack grinned.

Roly laughed. 'And it's all the crap that'll come with it – all the rumours and gossip, and people writing stuff about our sex lives.'

'You could get another novel out of it. Pen a bestselling sequel to *Blue for a Boy*.'

Roly laughed, then shook his head. 'I don't think I can do this.'

'You mean…'

'I mean the whole reunion.'

'But the song—'

'You can have the song. I don't care. I'll even do the single with you if you want – if Vince will allow that. But I'm not going on the tour.'

'But you can't quit.' Charlie was wide-eyed, horrified.

'Ah, but that's the beauty of it. I can.'

. . .

'You can't pull out.' Vince's eyes were chilling, his jaw set.

'I can, though.' Vince was one intimidating dude, but Roly was determined not to be cowed by him. 'I haven't signed anything.'

Vince was almost trembling with rage now, his jaw clenched, his hands balled into fists on top of his desk. It had been his idea to keep Roly's involvement hush-hush for now. They were rehearsing behind closed doors, Roly under strict instructions not to let anyone see him coming and going to the studio or hanging out with the other guys. There had been rumours of course, but nothing had been announced yet. And Roly still didn't have a contract.

That had been Vince's idea too. He'd kept stringing him along, saying they'd wait and see how it was working out first, if he gelled with the band, if he could handle the pressure, if he could keep his nose clean – basically making him audition like some wannabe. Roly knew the idea had been to humiliate him. Vince was making him pay for screwing things up all those years ago. But now it had shot him in the foot.

'I don't have a contract. I can quit whenever I like.'

Vince eyeballed him, his mouth a hard line. Roly suppressed a shiver, and tried to enjoy the moment. He had the upper hand now, and Vince knew it.

Vince sighed and leaned back in his chair. 'Fine. Go ahead. Bale on everyone, like you always do. Leave your friends and colleagues in the lurch. I should have expected this. You always find a way to fuck up, don't you, Roly?'

Roly shrugged. 'Yeah, I guess I do.'

'Have you any idea the lengths everyone's gone to to accommodate you? The strings I've pulled? The work everyone else has put in just so you can prance around on stage for a few hours wiggling your arse? Which is twice the size it should be, by the way.'

'You're saying my bum looks big in this?' Roly just let it all wash over him. Vince was nothing but a thug, a playground bully, apoplectic because someone was standing up to him.

'You're such a loser, Roly.' He shook his head. 'Well, we gave you a chance and you blew it. Again. If you're going, go. We'll pick up the pieces, as usual. That's weeks of rehearsals down the drain. You've wasted everyone's time. Boo will have to rethink the video, all the dance routines…'

'I'll do the single, if you want, and the video. I'll even turn up at a couple of the shows if you like, and do a guest appearance. But that's it.'

Vince's face turned very red. Roly didn't care either way, but this was what Vince wanted, and he couldn't stand Roly having a hold over him.

'That's very big of you,' he said drily.

'Well, think about it. Let me know what you decide and my agent will be in touch about the contract.'

He turned and walked out of the room without looking back. Then he ran down the stairs and jogged half the way home, fired up on adrenaline.

37

ALL WEEK, Roly couldn't get what Ella had said out of his head – especially when he called his mum on Friday and she was all excited, planning the weekend with Mike. 'Tonight, I'm cooking dinner just for the two of us. His flight gets in around six. Tomorrow we'll go out – I've booked a table at Chapter One. But you must come for dinner on Sunday – Mum's coming too. I can't wait for you to meet him.'

'Great! I'm looking forward to it,' he said, even as he had a sick feeling of foreboding in the pit of his stomach.

'Oh, Roly, I'm so excited! I'm all jittery, and I can't settle to anything. I feel like a bloody teenager. I can't believe I'm going to meet him finally.'

'Are you picking him up from the airport?'

'No, he's getting a cab here. He'll be so relieved to finally get here after all he's been through the past few months.'

'I bet. Mum, could you send me a photo of him?'

'What do you want a photo for?' she asked, laughing.

'It's just … I want to make something for Sunday. It's a

surprise,' he said, hating himself for lying to her. But he still hoped Ella would be wrong, and he didn't want to make his mum feel like a fool for no reason.

'What are you up to? You're not going to get his face put on a cake or something, are you?' She sounded so happy and light-hearted, and it killed him.

'You'll have to wait and see.' If it turned out Mike was legit, that wasn't a bad idea.

'Okay, I'll send it to you now.'

Roly found instructions online for doing a reverse image search and uploaded the photo of Mike his mum had sent him. The results were everything he'd dreaded.

He tried calling his mum, but she wasn't answering her phone. He really started to worry an hour later when she still hadn't responded to his constant calls and messages. He checked his watch. It was almost seven. She'd probably know by now that Mike wasn't coming. He'd just have to go over there.

Almost without thinking about it, he called Ella. She sounded surprised to hear from him.

'So I did that image search thing on Mum's boyfriend,' he said.

'Oh?' Her tone was wary.

'Yeah. And you were right. It's a scammer. His photo came up on loads of social media profiles, different names…'

'Oh no! I'm so sorry, Roly. I really wanted to be wrong.'

'I know.'

'How's Loretta?'

'That's the thing. I haven't been able to reach her. You know he was supposed to be coming tonight?'

'Yes. She … told me.'

'Well, obviously that won't be happening. She's not answering her phone, so I'm going to head over there.'

'Good.'

'And I was wondering…' He cleared his throat. 'Um … would you come with me? I mean, if you're not doing anything. I know it's Friday night—'

'Of course,' she said without hesitation. 'If you want me to. I'll leave now.'

'Where are you?'

'I'm … in town. At the karaoke bar.'

'Look, I don't want to mess up your evening—'

'No, I'm leaving now,' she said firmly. He could hear that she was moving as she spoke. 'I'll jump in a cab and meet you there?'

'Okay. Thanks, Ella.' He hung up feeling a little calmer for speaking to her.

~

Ella saw Roly just turning into his mum's street as her cab pulled up and she jumped out.

'Thanks for coming,' he said. 'I really appreciate it.'

'It's no problem.'

'God, poor Mum!' he burst out, seeming on the verge of tears. 'She's going to be gutted.'

'I know.' She reached out tentatively and touched his arm.

He took a deep breath. 'Well, let's go.' He took his key from his pocket.

Ella's heart was hammering as he opened the door, scared of what they were going to find.

'Mum?' Roly called softly as they walked quietly down the hall.

Ella realised she was holding her breath. They found

Loretta in the dining room, slumped in a chair pulled out from the table. Ella's heart twisted in sympathy as she took in her tear-streaked face. The table was set for an intimate dinner for two, with flowers and candles, and a bottle of red wine sitting on a silver coaster. A small gift-wrapped parcel sat in front of one of the plates. Loretta was wearing a silver wrap dress and high heels, obviously dressed for a romantic evening *à deux*. It was heartbreaking.

'Mum.' Roly sank to his knees in front of her, and she looked up, her face a picture of dejection.

She turned to him as if in a daze. 'He should have been here by now,' she said forlornly. 'I checked the website and the flight he was meant to be on landed ages ago. He's not coming, is he?'

Roly shook his head slowly. 'No, he's not,' he said, his voice gentle.

Oh, Ella, pet.' She looked at Ella as if she'd only just noticed she was there. 'It's lovely to see you.' It broke Ella's heart that she made the effort to dredge up a smile for her. 'Have a seat.'

Ella sank onto one of the chairs.

'He's stopped texting. I've been ringing him all day, but he's not answering his phone. You don't suppose something's happened to him, do you?' Her voice was almost hopeful.

'No. He's just a con artist, Mum. He was never coming.'

She nodded. 'It wasn't real, was it? Any of it?' Her voice was hollow. 'He was just stringing me along to get money out of me.'

'Yeah. Sorry, Mum.'

'And I let him. God, I'm so pathetic! How could I have fallen for all that bullshit? We'd never even met and he was carrying on like he was madly in love with me – and I was stupid enough to believe it.' She drew a heaving, shaky breath. 'Oh, Roly, what's wrong with me?' she wailed.

'Nothing's wrong with you, Mum.' He rubbed her leg, looking up into her face. 'He's a dickhead, that's all.'

'But why do I never learn?' She sniffed. 'You must think I'm such a gullible old fool,' she said, looking across at Ella.

'No, of course not.'

'I should have known better than to think a man like him would be interested in me.'

'Don't be daft, Mum. Anyone would be lucky to have you.' He rubbed her arm soothingly. 'But there is no "man like him". He doesn't exist. It's just a scam.'

She nodded furiously, tears spilling from her eyes. 'And of course I was eejit enough to fall for it. I should have known when he asked me for money. How could I not have realised? Your nan is right about me, Roly. I don't have the sense I was born with when it comes to men.'

'Don't beat yourself up, Mum. Lots of people get taken in by these scammers.' He looked to Ella for back-up.

'These people are very clever, Loretta,' she said. 'They know what they're doing. I read an article just the other day about a high court judge in America who'd fallen for a scammer. She'd given him hundreds of thousands of dollars before she realised.'

Loretta heaved a deep breath, wiping her eyes with the back of her sleeve. 'Well, would you two like a cup of tea?' she asked, rousing herself.

'I'll make it.' Ella jumped up and went to the kitchen, glad of the excuse to leave Roly and Loretta alone for a bit. She wasn't good at looking after people. She wasn't naturally motherly. But she knew Loretta would do it for her in a heartbeat. She had to step up and be the grown-up for once.

The kitchen was hot, and there was a delicious smell wafting from the oven. She peeked inside – it looked like she'd arrived just in time to save Loretta's dinner from burning. She'd just flicked on the kettle when Loretta came in behind her.

'I turned that off,' Ella said, nodding to the oven. 'I hope that's okay? It looked like it was done.'

'I'd totally forgotten about it. Thanks, Ella. I'm not thinking straight, offering you tea. There's wine open, if you'd prefer?'

Ella looked to Roly, who'd followed his mum and was standing in the doorway. He gave her a nod.

'I think that'd be a good idea.'

'Well, I know I could do with some. And you two should stay for dinner. There's all this food. Have you eaten?' Loretta looked between them.

'No, we haven't, and I'm starving. It smells really good, Mum.'

'Why don't I go and leave you and Roly to it?' Ella said. 'You can have dinner together.'

'I'd love you to stay, Ella. I could do with the company. And I'm not in the mood for drinking alone.'

'Okay, if you're sure…' She looked doubtfully at Roly.

'Yes, stay,' he said, nodding.

'I only cooked for two, but I was allowing for Mike,' Loretta's voice caught on the name, 'to have a big appetite. Being a military man and all that,' she said, rolling her eyes. Ella was relieved she seemed to be cheering up, and seeing the funny side.

'I'm sure there'll be plenty,' Ella said.

'There's some garlic bread in the freezer,' Loretta said. 'We can bulk it out with that. And we've three courses. I was pushing the boat out.'

'I'll do the garlic bread,' Roly said, shooing them out of the kitchen. 'You two can get started on the wine.'

'He said it was because of being in the military that he couldn't do video chats,' Loretta told Ella when they were ensconced on the sofa with a couple of glasses of wine. 'Something about having to keep his location a secret.'

Ella nodded. 'That's why so many of these scammers pretend to be soldiers on a mission somewhere. It gives them lots of excuses for not being in touch. They say they have no phone reception, or the internet is dodgy, or they're not allowed make calls for security reasons.'

'You must think I'm such a chump, falling for it.'

'Not at all. They wouldn't be so successful if they weren't so plausible.' Ella toyed with her glass. 'Did you give him much money? You don't have to tell me if you don't want to,' she added hastily.

Loretta took a deep breath. 'About five thousand altogether. I sent him the money for the flight, and I paid some of his daughter's hospital bills. At least, that's what I thought I was paying for.'

'Well, you should go to the police,' Ella said.

Her eyebrows shot up. 'Because my boyfriend dumped me? Hardly a matter for the police, is it?'

'He's not your boyfriend,' Ella said softly. 'He was never your boyfriend.'

'Oh yeah. I keep forgetting that.'

'It's a crime, and it should be reported. You won't be the only one. They get cases like this all the time.'

'God, I'm such an idiot.' She shook her head.

'No, you're not. You trusted someone, you took him at his word. There's no shame in that. You didn't do anything wrong. He's the shitbag. He's the one who should be ashamed.' He's the one who should have his balls cut off, she thought to herself.

'I was an easy target, I suppose. I was just a bit lonely.'

'That's nothing to be ashamed of.' So why was it so hard to admit it, to say it out loud? Loneliness: it was like the last taboo.

'How did you know?' Loretta asked Roly as he came back into the room.

'That picture you sent me. I did a search for it online and it came up on lots of profiles under different names. But I found the real man who owns the photo on Facebook. Do you want to see?'

Loretta nodded, and Roly hunkered down in front of her and took out his phone. He turned it to face her and Ella, and showed them a Facebook page. The profile photo was Loretta's 'Mike'. The man's real name was Neil Miller. Loretta took the phone from Roly and Ella looked at it over her shoulder as she scrolled. There were other photos on his page, family pictures with a smiling wife, three teenage boys and a little girl.

So … he's married,' Loretta said, frowning. 'I should have known. He seemed too good to be true.'

Ella shook her head. 'That's not him at all. Mike doesn't exist, remember? This is just someone who's had their identity stolen.'

'Oh, the poor man,' Loretta said. 'Do you think he knows?'

Ella shrugged. 'Probably. His picture has been used so often, I reckon he's bound to have been made aware of it at some stage.'

'Do you think I should contact him and tell him? They look like such a nice family.' She smiled, fingering the screen of Ella's phone.

'I don't know. I guess see what the police say?'

Loretta nodded. 'Yeah. I'll do that.'

'This is really good, Mum,' Roly said later as they sat around the table, eating a complicated prawn and salmon roulade starter. They were all studiously ignoring the romantic setting. '*Mike* doesn't know what he's missing.'

Loretta took the gift-wrapped parcel from in front of her plate and slid it across the table to Roly. 'You might as well have this.'

He picked it up. 'Are you sure? You could return it?'

'No, I'd like you to have it. You're the most important man in my life.'

Roly smiled and opened the gift tentatively. Inside was a Cartier box containing a pair of gold cufflinks.

'Lucky I didn't get them engraved,' Loretta said as he lifted them out.

'They're lovely, Mum. Thanks. If you're sure you don't want to return them?'

'No, I want you to have them. I know cufflinks aren't really your thing—'

'I'll definitely wear these. I love them.'

Loretta gave a hollow, bitter laugh. 'Your money paid for them anyway,' she said. 'Not much of a present.'

Roly frowned. 'Don't think of it like that. Any money I gave you is yours. And these are a gift. So thank you.'

Loretta smiled, her eyes welling with tears. 'You're such a good kid, Roly. I don't know what I did to deserve you,' she said shakily.

'Don't you?' he asked softly. 'You did everything, Mum. You did everything for me.'

She shook her head. 'If it hadn't been for your nan…'

'Nan's great, but she's not you.'

'Sometimes I think you'd have been better off without

me. Maybe I should have just let you live with her. She was a better parent than I ever was.'

'I know she's sensible and all that, and she has her head screwed on. But being a kid wouldn't have been half as much fun with her as it was with you.'

'You wouldn't have got away with half as much, you mean.' Loretta laughed.

'Yeah, that too.'

Loretta's face softened, and she smiled. 'We did have a laugh, didn't we? Despite everything. Even when we were skint, we had fun.'

'Yeah, we did. We do.'

'And we will again. Screw Mike!' Loretta said loudly, raising her glass. 'And the horse he didn't ride in on.'

'Screw Mike!' Ella and Roly chorused, as they crashed their glasses together.

Loretta cheered up considerably after that, and Ella was impressed with how quickly she rallied. All her romantic disappointments had made her resilient, if nothing else. The dinner was delicious, and it quickly turned into a light-hearted affair. Roly offered to stay the night, but Loretta waved away his concerns, and told him there was no need.

'Don't worry about me. I can't say I won't do anything stupid,' she said with a laugh, 'because that ship has sailed. But I'm fine.'

'You're sure?' Roly asked.

'Yes, absolutely.' She did look a lot perkier already. 'I'm just a bit tired. But come to dinner on Sunday. You too, Ella, if you like.' She looked between the two of them curiously as if just realising how strange it was that they'd come together. Her eyes twinkled, and she looked like she was dying to ask questions, but restrained herself. 'And bring Ruth and Nora, if they're free. I'd love to see them again.'

'Thanks,' Ella said. She gave her a kiss on the cheek. 'I'll let you know.'

38

'Do you think she'll be okay?' Ella asked as they walked away.

'Yeah.' He dug his hands into his pockets. 'She'll bounce back. She always does.'

'You were so good with her. You really cheered her up.'

'I just wish … I wish she didn't keep having to pick herself up again. God, I could kill those bastards! It's not fair. I've seen her getting knocked back so many times, and it … it just kills me, you know?'

'I know. It's awful. She's so lovely.'

'Thanks for coming with me. It was better with you there.' He took her hand. 'It's always better with you there.'

Ella wasn't sure what to make of it, but it was nice. She stopped at the corner. 'Well, I guess I should get a cab. Are you walking?'

'Yeah.' It was almost eleven, but it was still bright. 'Come home with me? I want to talk.'

Ella's heart picked up a beat. He'd already said all the worst things. Talking could only be good. 'Okay.'

He smiled and they walked on, hand in hand in silence.

'How are rehearsals going with Oh Boy!?' she asked.

'Oh yeah. I quit.'

'What?' she gasped. 'You quit? Why?'

He shrugged. 'Been there, done that. I decided it's not what I want anymore.'

'Oh.'

'I think the memories are better than the reality. I'd rather remember the good stuff and leave it in the past, where it belongs.'

Ella nodded. 'I know what you mean. I went back to work in Trinity.'

'You did? You left Citizens?'

'For all of five minutes. I'm back there now. I missed it too much.' She could hardly concentrate on the conversation, too aware of Roly's hand wrapped around hers. 'Was Vince mad when you quit?'

'Vince was apoplectic. I wish you'd been there. If spontaneous combustion was a real thing, he'd have done it.'

Ella laughed. She was glad they were back to their old ways, talking nonsense to each other. But at the same time, she felt they were skirting around what they really needed to talk about. Too soon, they got to Roly's house.

'Come in?' he asked, jerking his head towards the gate.

'Okay,' she nodded. She felt a pang as she followed him inside. She'd loved living here with him. She'd loved coming home with him after a night out, when his house was her home too.

'Do you want tea, coffee? I don't have any wine since you moved out.'

'No thanks. I'm fine.'

She yawned as they sat down together on the couch.

'Sorry, are you tired? Do you want to leave this to another night?'

'No.' She shook her head vehemently. She'd never get to sleep now anyway, wondering what 'this' was.

Roly ran a hand through his hair, and she suddenly noticed how weary he looked. 'It's been kind of a long day.'

'Yeah, and stressful. If you'd rather I go—'

'No.' His eyes were wide, almost panicked as he raised them to her. 'Stay. Please.'

'Okay.'

'So, I just wanted to say sorry for being such a shit to you when I found out, you know… about what you did.'

'It's fine. I deserved it.'

'No. You didn't. I was so angry—'

'Understandably.'

'But I think maybe part of me was glad to have someone else to blame. It was a relief.'

'How so?' She frowned.

'Because the worst thing about what happened was knowing I'd done it to myself. It's like, what ruined your life wasn't your fault. There was nothing you could have done differently that would have changed it. But me – I threw it all away. It was all my own choices.'

'You don't choose to be an addict. It's an illness too.'

'But you only get it by making stupid choices in the first place. So it was a relief to have someone else to blame. I was angry at myself, and I took it out on you.'

'If you want to beat yourself up for messing up your life, then you should give yourself credit for turning it around too. They were also choices you made, going to rehab—'

He gave a derisory laugh.

'Okay, so you didn't want to go in the first place. But you stayed. You stuck with it. Maybe other people forced your hand and helped you get sober. But you *stayed* sober.

You did that yourself. You got fit, you wrote amazing songs, you got your career back on track. *You* did all that.'

He gave a small smile. 'With a little help from my friends.'

'We all need a bit of help now and then. But if you want to take responsibility for your life choices, take it for the good stuff too. Own it. You should be proud of yourself, Roly.' She took a deep breath. 'And by the way, my life isn't ruined,' she said quietly.

His eyes glistened. 'Neither is mine. And that's thanks to you.'

Her eyes welled up with tears and she shook her head, her throat too clogged to speak. Because there was so much tenderness and love in his eyes, and he hadn't said it yet, but she felt it was out there, hovering just out of reach – forgiveness.

'I've been thinking about something Pippa said recently.'

Oh great, she was going to get the Wisdom of Pippa. Way to ruin the moment, Roly.

'She said I'd never know what my life might have been like if you hadn't done what you did that night. I'll never know what might have happened if that photo hadn't gone public. And she's right – I won't.'

'I'm so sorry—' she began, but he held up a hand to stop her.

'But I do know what happened when you did,' he continued. 'I know that I'm sober and solvent, and doing creative work that I love and that I'm really fucking proud of.' He took a shaky breath. 'And I know that my best friend is a woman who loves me no matter what and doesn't care if I'm a big pop star or working in a crummy cafe or even living on benefits. A woman who'll do what she thinks is best for me, even if it means losing something she wants.'

He reached out and took her hand. 'I have a life that I love and a best friend who's always been there for me, even though there were times when we didn't see each other for ages, and you probably thought I'd forgotten about you. And maybe I had on some level. But subconsciously I always knew you were out there somewhere, keeping the plane up. Deep down I always knew you'd be there, waiting for me. Like a home I could always go back to. You're my home, Ella.'

She choked a sob, tears spilling down her face.

'You're the only thing I lost from back then that I miss, the only bit of my old life that I want back.' He smiled wearily. 'And I've hardly slept since you left, so will you please move back in with me? And will you please stay here tonight, and come to bed with me? I need my brainiac friend to keep the plane up so I can sleep, because I'm fucking wrecked!'

She was too choked up to speak, so she just nodded, smiling through her tears.

'I love you so much, Ella.'

'I love you too,' she sobbed when she'd caught her breath.

He pulled her into his arms and they kissed and kissed as they clung to each other – long, slow, languorous kisses that seemed to go on forever.

'Just one thing, though,' she said when they finally broke apart. 'There's something I feel I should tell you. That thing about keeping the plane up? You kind of make me feel the opposite.'

'What, that the plane is going to crash?' His eyes were wide with alarm.

She laughed, shaking her head. 'No. That I can just let

go and everything will be okay. It'll stay in the air whether I'm paying attention or not, and I don't need to concentrate at all. So I can just relax and enjoy the ride.'

He grinned and pulled her into his arms. 'Wow, we're not compatible at all, are we?'

'Not even a little bit.'

'So, what do you say? Give it a go anyway?'

'Why not?'

'I can't think of a single reason.'

I FOUND

'Hi!'

Ella looked up from her book. Roly Punch. He was sitting right in front of her desk on a chair turned around backwards. On top of it, his chin rested on his folded arms. She wondered how long he'd been there. He grinned at her.

'Hi,' she said, puzzled. Why was he talking to her? They never talked.

She looked around the classroom. Everyone was in their usual groups. His gaggle of friends were huddled by the door, talking among themselves. Why had Roly suddenly decided to pay attention to her? He was the most popular boy in their year. Was it just that he was a completist and she was the only person in the class he hadn't won over yet with his charm and charisma? He needed to be friends with everyone, so he had to squeeze her in before time ran out? She hoped he wasn't taking pity on her because her best friend Julie wasn't in today. She and Julie may be the class swots, but it wasn't as if they were social outcasts. There were other people she could spend break with if she chose to. She'd just wanted to get on with her book.

'So, Ella. I thought we should talk.'

'Why?'

He shrugged. 'We never talk.' He cocked his head to the side. 'Why do you think that is?'

'Because we're not friends?'

'Well, we can fix that right now. We've got' – he checked his watch – 'fifteen minutes until the bell goes.'

'Isn't it a bit late for making friends? School's over in two months.'

'So?'

'So then we never see each other again.'

'Just like that? After all we've been through together?'

She laughed. 'Not much point now, is there?'

'It's never too late.'

She hesitated a moment. 'Okay, then.' She closed her book. 'What do you want to talk about?'

'Hmm. Let's see.' He tapped the top of his chair. 'We could discuss the themes of class and patriarchy in *Wuthering Heights*. Or the effects of the famine on Irish society from 1850 to … a date of your choosing.'

'Is this just a ploy to pick my brain for the exams?'

Roly laughed. 'No, it's honestly not. I'm only doing the Leaving to keep my mum happy.'

'Really? You'd have dropped out before it?'

'Yeah. I don't see the point. I mean, I'm not going to college, so why do I need to know all this random stuff?'

Roly had famously aced an audition earlier in the year to be in one of those manufactured boy bands put together by a music mogul, and they were already taking off. He was going straight from school into a ready-made music career.

'Still, your mum's right. An education is never a loss. You'll always have something to fall back on.'

'Yeah, I can talk about my aunt's pen in fluent French. *Où est la plume de ma tante*,' he said in an exaggerated French accent. '*Voici la plume de ma tante*! That'll get me far.'

She shrugged. 'You never know. It could come in handy.'

'Not really, I don't have an aunt.'

She laughed. 'Well, for chatting up girls in Paris, then.'

'I still don't have an aunt.'

'The girls in Paris don't know that.'

He laughed. 'Want a Rolo?' He produced a crumpled half tube from his pocket and offered it to her.

'Thanks.'

'Sorry, they're a bit melty.'

She licked chocolate off her fingers as she popped one in her mouth. It was warm from his pocket.

'No *soeur* or *frère* either,' he said, chewing his sweet. 'Only child.' He jerked a thumb at himself.

How had she not known that about Roly? But she supposed there was a lot she didn't know about him.

'How about you?'

'Same. No brothers or sisters. I do have an aunt, though.'

'Show-off! She's the other woman who comes to concerts and stuff sometimes with your mum?'

'Yeah. My Aunt Nora.'

'I thought maybe she was your mum's … partner. You know, that you had one of those "Ella has two mums" set-ups.'

She shook her head. 'No. Just one mum and one aunt.'

'Well, I've got one mum and one nan. So I guess we're even.' He picked up the book on her desk and turned it over. '*Middlemarch*. Any good?'

'Yeah. I like it.'

'That Dorothea was a bit up herself, though wasn't she?'

'You've read it?' She was amazed. It wasn't one of their set texts, and Roly never showed much enthusiasm in English class. She couldn't see him reading Victorian novels in his spare time.

'No. I saw the TV series. My mum loves all those costume dramas. I mean, I was on my PlayStation, but I was in the same room, so I got the gist.'

'Dorothea meant well. She was just a bit naive. And she married the wrong person.'

He nodded. 'Classic schoolboy error.'

'Yeah, schoolboys are notorious for rushing into bad marriages!' She laughed.

'She definitely didn't deserve that bloke she married, though. What was his name again?'

'Casaubon.'

'Yeah. What a tool! He kind of reminds me of my mum's boyfriend, actually.'

'Oh? Is he … an academic or something?'

'Nah, just that he's a knob and she can't see it.'

The electronic bell sounded for the next class and everyone started shuffling back to their seats.

'So, what do you say, Ella? Friends?' Roly held out his hand.

'Why not?' She shook his hand and he grinned at her like he'd just won a prize.

'I'll see you around.'

'Yeah. See you.'

She watched as Roly walked away. Nothing had changed. It wasn't as if she thought they were going to be best friends now. She wouldn't suddenly become one of his inner circle. Everything would go on just the same as before until school ended and they all went their separate ways.

But something had shifted inside her. It was as if a veil had been lifted and she'd caught a glimpse of the world as it really was, and it was different to how she'd thought. It burst inside her like an epiphany, a little explosion of relief and joy: nothing was set in stone.

Roly looked back and smiled at her as their eyes met. Then he turned away again, but the sunshiny feeling remained. She felt as if anything could happen.

A NOTE FROM THE AUTHOR

Thank you so much for reading *The Reboot*. I hope you enjoyed it!

If you'd like to hear more about me and my books, and keep up to date with my writing news, you can sign up for my mailing list at :

www.subscribepage.com/clodaghmurphy

I will never spam you, and you can unsubscribe at any time.

You can also visit my website or find me on social media. I'd love to chat!

www.clodaghmurphy.com
Facebook.com/clodaghmurphyauthor
Twitter.com/ClodaghMMurphy
Instagram.com/clodaghmurphybooks

ACKNOWLEDGMENTS

Thanks to Sarah Painter, Hannah Ellis, Trish Murphy and Emer Kochanski for reading early drafts of this book and providing invaluable feedback and encouragement.

Thank you to Nicola Cornick for thoughtful edits, and Stuart Bache for the wonderful cover.

Much of this book was written during the strange times of lockdowns and Covid restrictions, so I'm especially grateful to my writing buddies Sarah Painter and Hannah Ellis for keeping me sane with all the Zoom chats. This job wouldn't be half as much fun without you, and I can't wait until we can meet up again in real life!

Thanks to all the lovely book bloggers who have supported my books over the years, and especially to Rachel Gilbey and everyone who took part in the blog tour for my last book.

Most of all, thanks to you for reading.

ALSO BY CLODAGH MURPHY

The Disengagement Ring

Girl in a Spin

Frisky Business

Scenes of a Sexual Nature (novella)

Some Girls Do

For Love or Money

CPSIA information can be obtained
at www.ICGtesting.com
Printed in the USA
LVHW101951111121
702895LV00012B/103

9 781916 265684